Outstanding praise for Robin Reardon and
A SECRET EDGE!

"A sweet novel, but it's laced with enough humor and teen angst and situations with no clear, easy answers, that it doesn't cloy. In fact, much of it rings true enough to snap you right back to your high-school years like a giant rubber band. The teasing, the daydreaming in class, the lockers, the milling about at the mall or the library . . . it's all here. There is tenderness, and admirably written joyful discoveries of falling in love (and lust) and its fragility, as well as the pain of loss. Lessons are learned in this page-turner where things sometimes take an unexpected turn."—*Edge* magazine

"Robin Reardon's *A Secret Edge* is a fun, compelling story about one young man's coming-of-age, but it's also a book of interesting ideas, touching on (but not limited to) cross-cultural relationships, family dynamics, friendship, honesty, Hindu philosophy, and the morality of violence vs. non-violence in a complicated world. It's well worth your time, and Reardon is an author to watch."—Bart Yates, author of *The Brothers Bishop*

"Fans of works like *The Front Runner* should log off Out-Sports.com long enough to try this addicting and refreshingly non-tragic tale about an athletic adolescent's coming of age."—*Next* magazine

"Dealing frankly with the challenges of being an out gay teen, Robin's tale of a cross-cultural romance between two young athletes is as sexy as it is surprising. Jason and Raj are two characters that stand out in young adult fiction for being so wonderfully nuanced and emotionally real. In the end, *A Secret Edge* is a refreshing spin on the coming out story as well as a memorable new love story for the new millennium."—Brian Sloan, author of *A Tale of Two Summers*

"This year's must-read coming-of-age story."—*H/X* magazine

"A sweet tale of first love with an abundance of heart, guts and faith."—Brian Francis, author of *Fruit*

"Engaging . . . This is the kind of novel I would have loved to read as a teen. I hope that many gay teens find *A Secret Edge* and beg the author for more books as well."—AfterElton.com

"Charming."—*We The People*

Books by Robin Reardon

A SECRET EDGE

THINKING STRAIGHT

Published by Kensington Publishing Corporation

Thinking Straight

Robin Reardon

KENSINGTON BOOKS
http://www.kensingtonbooks.com

KENSINGTON BOOKS are published by

Kensington Publishing Corp.
850 Third Avenue
New York, NY 10022

ISBN-13: 978-0-7582-1928-2
ISBN-10: 0-7582-1928-8

First Kensington Trade Paperback Printing: May 2008
10 9 8 7 6 5 4 3 2 1

Printed in the United States of America

For my mother, who taught me to hate injustice and stupidity, and who urged me constantly to use the mind God gave me.

Jesus said to him, "You shall love the Lord your God with all your heart, and with all your soul, and with all your mind."
—The Gospel According to Matthew, 22:37

Taylor Adams's Favorite Scriptural Reference

If a man says, "I love God," and hates his brother, he is a liar; for he who doesn't love his brother whom he has seen, how can he love God whom he has not seen? This commandment we have from him: he who loves God should also love his brother.

—John's First Letter, 4:20

Chapter 1

*He strictly warned him, and immediately sent him
out, and said to him, "See you say nothing to anybody, but go show yourself to the priest, and offer
for your cleansing the things which Moses commanded, for a testimony to them."*

—Mark 1:43

It's the end of the second day. Almost. And there's only . . .
counting, counting . . . only forty more to go.

Only forty?

That's going to seem as long to me as it must have to Noah.
And for me it'll be only forty if I'm lucky. If I behave.

I wish I knew the best approach to take. Should I play along
and let them think I've drunk the Kool-Aid, or are they smarter
than I am? They've done this before. I haven't. Would it be a
better plan to do my damnedest—oops, not supposed to use
words like that!—to get expelled, or whatever the term is?

Maybe I should look that section up again. Where the
hell—more demerits—is that booklet? I mean, Booklet? Ha.
It's not like it'll get lost in my other stuff. I mean, there ain't
no "other stuff." I can't have any of it here. My cell phone, my
iPod, even a wire-bound notebook is forbidden. No keeping
of journals here. I remember that one. But what about getting
expelled?

Here's the stupid thing. Let's see. . . . Temperance. Cleanliness. Program Rules. . . . Ah—Violation Consequences. According to this—and I'm not making these capital letters up—my
punishments can go up on a scale from Public Apologies for
what I'd done wrong, to some number of SafeZone days when I

can't talk, to having to Write a Three Thousand Word Paper About My Offences, to Expulsion, to Isolation from the Group.

Isolation is worse than Expulsion? Is that what they think? Don't they know I'm used to isolation?

Expulsion. I could do that.

But then what? Dad said it would be military school for me if I don't finish here. I didn't even know they still had places like that, but Dr. Strickland had all the info Dad could want.

Back to the forty days, then. And all because I was honest.

That part really kills me, you know? I mean, if I hadn't told them they'd never have known. But they kept bugging me, and I had to keep lying. Jesus hates lies.

It was, "Taylor, why don't you want to go to your own junior prom?"

And then when I did, it was, "Taylor, why don't you ever ask that nice girl Rhonda out any more?"

Then when I told them Rhonda was nice but she wasn't my type after all, it was, "Taylor, the Russells are bringing Angela when they come over for dinner tonight. Why don't the two of you plan to go for a walk afterward?"

Then, when they'd about given up, "Taylor, isn't there *any-one* you're interested in?"

Yeah. There is. His name is Will.

So I told them. I'd tried so hard not to, 'cause I knew they'd freak. And I was still working my way through the Bible concordance, looking for all the references to homosexuality, and men lying with men, stuff like that, so none of it would surprise me. So I could arm myself.

The Bible is one thing I'm allowed to have in here, so I can continue my research. But I can't take notes. And just reading some of those sexual references makes me think of Will.

My Will. Brown hair with spiky, bleached ends. And that impish grin, sliding up slowly from the left side of his mouth and making me wonder what he's thinking. Leather thong around his neck, another on his wrist. Silver chain draped between front and back left pockets of his scuffed black jeans. Golden hairs on his forearms, catching sunlight. Sweet, smooth skin on the undersides of his arms. Sweeter, softer skin on his lips.

The first time I ever saw him I knew he was special. His family had moved from out-of-state just last summer, and I saw him at church first, the week before school started—my junior year. He was sitting on the other side of the center aisle, a little ahead of me, between his two younger sisters, keeping them from talking and whatever else girls do when they don't care about causing a scene. Or when they actually want to attract everyone's attention. They looked maybe eleven and ten, something like that, and he . . . well, he looked older than me, and so, so gorgeous.

I'd figured out at the end of sophomore year that I was gay. It hit me like a ton of bricks when my friend Jim and I decided to celebrate the end of school by skinny-dipping in his folks' pool really late one night. I had stayed over, which I'd done a few times, sleeping in the other twin bed in his room. When the alarm went off a couple of hours after midnight, it was hard to get up, but he flicked on a small bedside light and swung his legs over the bed. He had nothing on. This was hardly the first time I'd seen him, but something about it being the dead of night, and the way the shadows were falling on his crotch, and maybe the fact that he'd been asleep—let's just say I woke up pretty quick then.

We wrapped towels around our middles and tiptoed through the house, trying not to giggle and wanting to at the same time, bumping into each other with an elbow, a forearm, a shoulder. I remember being keenly aware of the terrycloth rubbing against my dick, which was getting harder by the nanosecond.

It deflated in the cold water, but then Jim and I started horsing around. And touching. And holding each other under the water. That sort of thing. Once I grabbed his dick by accident, and he laughed and pulled away. I think now that it was a nervous laugh, but not one that really meant anything. The next time I grabbed him there, it was no accident. And he didn't laugh.

"Hey!" He tried to keep his voice a loud whisper, but he was upset. "What the fuck do you think you're doing? You some kind of faggot or something?"

Think fast, Taylor. . . . "What're you, crazy? It's dark, in case you hadn't noticed. You think I want to touch your freakin' dick?"

It sure threw some, uh, cold water on the festivities for the night. Needless to say, I was not invited back for another overnight. And maybe needless to say—but I'll say it anyway—what I'd felt, reaching out underwater for my friend's penis, hoping against hope he'd reach for mine, praying against everything I'd ever been taught that we might even go on from there, stayed with me through the rest of that summer. It might not be too much to say I thought of it all the time. It was, to quote Mr. Dickens, the best of times and the worst of times. (Get it? *Dick*ens? LOL!) A time I never want to live through again, and a time I wouldn't give up for anything. Well, maybe for some things. . . .

But as for my supposed friendship with Jim? Well, some friendship that turned out to be. He dropped me like I'd come down with leprosy. After that night, every time I saw him I felt like I'd put my shirt on over a sign that said UNCLEAN. Like I'd stuffed tissues into the little bell I was supposed to be ringing. You know the one? In the Bible, the bells warned the Godly when a leper was approaching. That's what he made me feel like.

If I'm fair, though, I might have to admit that it would have been tough after that. I mean, just being friends. Imagining things from his side, it might be like he suddenly found out a person he thought he knew really well actually came from outer space. Or that I was a girl, and not a boy like him at all. Because, really, even though I'm not a girl, in one very important way I'm not a boy like him. And I wanted him the way a girl would. And since he's not gay, that might have felt too weird to deal with.

I wish we could have gotten over that, though. I wish I hadn't lost a friend by just being myself.

Anyway, back to that day in church. After noticing how gorgeous Will was, sitting in that pew between his two stupid sisters, what I noticed was how well he handled them. He never seemed to lose patience. Sometimes he held one sister's hand in each of his, and sometimes he joined their hands and held them in both of his, and sometimes he wrapped an arm around each of their necks and kind of hugged them. Eventually it dawned on me that what the girls wanted wasn't everyone's attention. They wanted his.

And amazingly he also seemed to be paying attention to the service. Which was something I was trying to do, except he was so distracting. But it's important to me, you know? I mean, church. God. Jesus. Sure, I swear more than I should. Sure, I do things I shouldn't. But I love God. And I know God loves me. And seeing Will, gorgeous, a loving brother, taking God seriously—it stuck with me.

Once school started he turned up in my World History class, and I found out that he wasn't older than me after all and that his last name was Martin. History isn't one of my favorite subjects, but I do okay. But Will? He knew so much. He hardly ever volunteered, but one time the teacher called on him for something really obscure no one else knew, and he knew it. After that, kids started turning to him kind of facetiously whenever the teacher asked them something they didn't know. He always kept his eyes to the front and wouldn't say anything unless the teacher called his name, but when she did he always knew.

And then one day the question was if anyone knew something very interesting about the personal life of Richard the Lionheart of England. She called on me. I didn't have a clue. So I turned in my seat and looked at Will. And he was looking at me. Not at the front of the room. At me.

"Taylor, are you admitting defeat?" the teacher asked, a kind of tongue-in-cheek sound to her voice. Eyes still on Will's face, I nodded. She said, "Very well. Will, do you know this one as well?"

Still looking at me. He was still looking right at me. "He was gay."

This brought a hoot of laughter from a few of the guys in the class. Ted, a bit of a bully who'd terrorized me in elementary school, shouted, "How do you know that, Mr. Genius? You one, too?" And he laughed louder.

In a way, this scared me. I mean, all a guy has to do is point out that some historical figure was gay, and all of a sudden the kid is, too? Would it be easy for bullies to pick me out as gay? But then I considered Ted. Socially, he was a total moron, with about as much sensitivity as a sloth, and about as smart. And he was probably looking for something—anything—to throw at Will, because Will was so obviously more interesting, and more appealing, and more intelligent than Ted. Plus, he was new. So any stone would have done, but "gay" was the one that came to his hand, and he threw it.

Will turned to look at Ted and waited patiently until the laughter subsided, waited through the teacher saying, "That's enough, class." He kept looking right at Ted until the room was quiet enough to hear him say, "Would you dare make fun of King Richard? He'd have carved you up with one hand tied behind his back and fed you to his dogs."

Will turned back to the front and said nothing else, but what hung in the air unsaid was, "Don't fuck with me. Gay or straight, don't fuck with me."

The teacher did what she could to smooth things over, and actually the perspective she gave on being gay so long ago was pretty cool. She went into a lot of less memorable stuff, like how Richard married to bring more land to England's empire. But what I focused on was more personal.

She said, "Will is correct about King Richard, also known as *Coeur de Lion*, although the word Will used would not have been one the people of that time would have recognized. We're talking about twelfth-century England. The word *homosexual* wasn't even a word until the late nineteenth century, and the word *gay* came after that.

"You see, few people in the Middle Ages had the luxury of marrying for love, and most—even royalty—married out of sheer necessity. Richard himself married for his kingdom's gain. But Richard spent almost no time with his queen, Berengaria of Navarre, and they had no children. Although he was rumored to have at least one illegitimate son, he was known to have multiple liaisons with men. Most of his time was spent fighting in the Crusades or leading battles over land in what is now France. He was the archetype of the medieval warrior king—noble and

fierce—and he was known as the Lionheart because of his leg-
endary courage."

Take that, Ted, I was thinking. But as usual, he made a bad
joke out of it. "Maybe he spent all that time fighting in battles
'cause he liked hanging out with the guys!"

Ted Tanner. Boy genius. More like AOB. Or, for anyone who
doesn't know IM lingo, Abuse Of Bandwidth. But I'm not supposed to be using that in here. In my incarceration. Another
demerit, then.

After that I sometimes heard kids talk about Will and specu-
late, but no one—not even Ted—had the guts to say anything
to him directly about it, and all of a sudden lots of girls were interested in him. Then the talk of him being gay dropped, 'cause
he started spending time with these girls. So I figured he hadn't
really noticed me the way I'd hoped. But I also decided he was
a terrific guy; he'd drawn the fire that day in class and had carved
Ted up with one proverbial hand tied behind him.

Then one day in early November, right before a big exam in
World History, I was on my way out of study hall when suddenly
Will was walking next to me.

"Big test coming up. You ready for it?"

It seemed like more than a casual question, so I looked at his
face. There was definitely something more there. I said, "Not
sure. You?"

"Might help to study with someone. Might help both of us."
He waited.

"I suppose it might. Got something in mind?"

He came over to my house after dinner that night, and we
went up to my room after I'd introduced him to my parents.
They were all for studying, and they had no reason to think Will
and I were all for anything other than studying.

We did study, actually. A little. Eventually. I'd never really made
out with a girl before. Will, it seemed, had probably made out
with lots of people. That night, for the first time, I made out
with a boy. And unlike my old friend Jim, Will liked my hand on
him.

And man, I wanted my hand on him. But I wasn't gonna do

anything right away, even if I'd had a real clue what to do. For one thing, I thought Will was a pretty special guy, and if he wasn't gay, then I didn't want to blow things the way I had with Jim. So I just walked into the room and started toward my desk. He came in behind me. And he shut the door.

I heard the click and turned, and he was just standing there with his hand still on the knob, looking at me, his head tilted a little like he was asking a question he already knew the answer to. I set down the notebook I'd just picked up, and I guess that was enough of a sign for him. He stepped right over to me, stopping when there was about an inch between us, and put his hands on my shoulders.

My arms went around him so fast, and so without any thought, that it was like some puppet master had yanked on them. It was everything I could do not to wrap my legs around him as well. There was this invisible cord pulling us together. Pulling on our mouths. Pulling on our hearts. Pulling on our . . . well, let's just say we had matching lumps in our pants.

His hands came up to my face, his tongue went into my mouth, and when he started rubbing his lumpy pants crotch against mine, my knees went out from under me. He followed me to the floor, laughing softly, and then he was in my mouth again.

In romantic scenes you see, like in the movies, they often show the lovers taking each others' clothes off, like that's supposed to be making things more fun. But—hell, I didn't want *fun*. And neither did Will. We took the short route and each unfastened our own jeans as quickly as we could. I don't know if it comes from being a teenager, or being gay, or being a gay teenager, but I didn't have time for a sexual tease. I just wanted sex. And, in particular, sex with Will.

Somehow he managed to reach for the box of tissues on my desk, and we needed them almost immediately. I came in his hand, and he came in mine.

I wish I could describe, better than I can, how I felt after that. All I can say is, there was some voice in the back of my head trying to tell me how evil I was, how much I was hurting my immortal soul and Will's. It was trying to sneak in there with Bible

verses about homosexuals not being able to enter the Kingdom
of God. Or about how the law was made because of immoral
people, like homosexuals and others who behave in ways con-
trary to nature. Or verses that put men lying with men in the
same category as having sex with animals, or committing adul-
tery, or sacrificing your children. But I could barely hear that
voice, try as it might to break through, because of the one that
was screaming, "*Yes!* Oh God oh God oh God. Yes!"

I think if the verses had been right, and some bolt of lightning had come down at that moment and killed both of us, the
hell we'd have been sent to wouldn't have been worse than living a life in which what we had just felt was wrong.

We lay there breathless for a few minutes, and my eyes were
still closed when I felt Will sit up. At first I was sad; I didn't want
this to be over. When I opened my eyes he was only half sitting,
leaning on an elbow, smiling at me.

He said, "You were a virgin, weren't you?"

I could have lied, I suppose. I mean, on the one hand, that
term can imply virtue, and strictly speaking it means that a girl
is still intact, if you know what I mean. On the other, when
you're called a virgin, it can make you feel ignorant and maybe
even undesirable; and girl or not, nobody had just been inside
me. But there was nothing of any of that in Will's voice. Just affection. So I grinned and nodded. And he kissed me. Softly this
time. So, so sweet. And then more intensely. And then . . . Oh
thanks be to God, it wasn't over.

I could probably have stayed there for hours with him, just
lying on the floor, taking turns massaging each other into ecstasies. But that night we limited ourselves to two ecstasies each.

Afterward, sitting up and leaning against the bed, and holding hands, I asked, "When did you first notice me?"

He leaned his head back, closed his eyes, and grinned. "You
kept staring at me in church one day last summer."

I'm sure I blushed. "How did you know? You were closer to
the front."

"I knew." The tone of his voice made it seem like it was something that was meant to be. Like fate.

Whether he intended that or not, I didn't question him. I changed the subject to something related. "I loved it that day you put Ted Tanner in his place."

"Ted? What did I do to Ted?"

"He laughed when you said Richard the Lionheart was gay. And you—"

"Ah, yes. Ted. WAI." He turned his head and looked at me.

I knew this was a kind of test: did I know IM lingo as well as he did? I knew enough to respond to that. I said, "Yeah. What An Idiot. That's for sure. PONA." This was my test. Did he know this one? It means Person Of No Account.

Will laughed. "No account at all."

Yes! This was going to be an amazing year. "How come you know so much about history?"

"It's always been really interesting to me. I like seeing how little people have changed. You can go back one year, fifty, seven hundred—and people have the same reasons why they do things. It's true the ways they go about getting what they want can change, and maybe society at one point in history makes us believe something is important that another society doesn't even believe in, but people are predictable. It's what's underneath that's interesting. The why. What drives us."

He sat up a little. "You know what I'd really love to do? After college? Maybe after grad school, too. I want to write. I'm going to write historical fiction, about us. About guys like us, anyway. One book might be what it was like for Richard to be gay in twelfth-century England. Another could be about a gay man's life in ancient Egypt. Or during the French Revolution. Wouldn't that be cool?"

His face was almost shining, and I felt like he'd given me some special gift, telling me that. I got up and planted my knees on either side of his thighs. "That would be totally cool." And I kissed him. And he kneaded my ass.

The feeling I had was like I'd been given another gift, too. Only this one was from God. Because only from God could there come a feeling as wonderful as this.

We spent some time, maybe half an hour, reviewing material for the test. But it was a history test, after all, and Will hardly needed to work. So really it was more like he was helping me study. But even though his perspective on things was more interesting than any I'd thought of, my mind was on other things. I couldn't help asking him about the girls he'd been seeing.

He shrugged. "It's just study sessions. And I don't mean like the one you and I are having. I don't ask them out on dates, though. I won't lie. I just don't feel the need to give anyone a direct response to personal questions unless I feel like it." He kissed me. "With you, I feel like it."

"Why?" It was out before I knew it.

"Why what?"

"Why me?" I'd been wondering this ever since study hall, ever since he'd asked about getting together with me for anything.

He cocked his head at me, a question in his eyes. "Why would you ask that? Don't you know how sexy you are?" I just blinked. Well, I guess I must have shaken my head, too, because then he said, "You don't worry about those other idiots." He pushed me down onto the floor on my back, his hands propped on either side of my head. He kissed me again. "It's just who you are, Ty. You're your own person. It's a kind of self-confidence."

The funny thing was, that's exactly what had attracted me to him. Other than the fact that he's gorgeous. Self-confidence in someone is seductive, you know? Makes you want to be with that person. Makes you want that person to call you a special name. Like Ty. No one had ever called me that before. I decided not to call attention to it, just to cherish it.

What I said instead was, "But I've never thought of myself as self-confident. That's you, not me." And it's true. If I seem not to care about whether I'm in a clique, or a group, it's because I don't want anyone to figure out what I really want. I don't want to make the same mistake I made with Jim. It's isolation more than self-confidence. But maybe the two have some things in common.

Will gave me another kiss, and I thought, I could get used to this. Then he said, "Truth is, self-confident people are attracted to self-confident people. We feel comfortable with each other. We understand each other." He pulled away, but he was smiling.

I sat up again and said, "But wouldn't it make more sense for someone who's self-confident and someone who needs that in someone else to pair up?"

He shook his head. "That happens, sure. But usually it's not really self-confidence. It's more likely to be arrogance. And that person actually wants to be with someone who's less confident, so they have the upper hand. They may not take unfair advantage, but they know they've got it." He reached out a hand and lifted my chin just for a second. "And if there's one thing you are not, Taylor Adams, it's arrogant."

"And are you?"

"Can't be, if I'm attracted to you."

I looked at him out of the corners of my eyes. "I think you might be, just a little."

That's the first time I remember him flashing that lopsided grin at me. That grin that makes me smile back, that pulls pleasantly on my dick. "Well, maybe just a little."

I have to stop this. He's not here now, is he, Ty? You're trapped in this place, and he's out there. Christ!

I have to stop thinking about Will kissing me, touching me, even just grinning at me, or I'll have to report it in my MI.

Ha! Like I'm going to report anything important. Morality Inventory? How can anyone take an inventory of morality? It ought to be Immorality Inventory. That's what they want to hear about.

It's in this Booklet someplace. I'm supposed to be memorizing this stuff, but . . . here it is. I'm to write up any struggles, thoughts, or temptations that have to do with sex, drugs, violence, or disobedience. Step One clients must complete four MIs per week unless otherwise instructed.

That's me. Step One. In the Program under four weeks. It goes all the way up to Step Three—in the Program eight or more weeks. Eight weeks! And I'm praying to get out in six. Hell, just to survive for six!

Demerit.

If only they'd freakin' let me talk to someone! I feel like I'm going insane. They call this SafeZone, but it feels downright dangerous to me. My roommate, Charles, Step Two, has been here five weeks now. He can talk. I can talk after tomorrow, but not until then. I hate how sanctimonious Charles is. Seems. I'm not sure anyone is what they seem to be in here.

He was called to the office on Sunday, the day my folks brought me here, just after the program director, Dr. Strickland, read me the riot act. Strickland sat under that all-too-realistic crucifix on the wall behind his desk and kept looking at me over the tops of his eyeglasses, I guess to make sure I was listening. Or maybe to see if there was a devil whispering into my ear.

"We're not going to talk about the reasons your parents have brought you here, Taylor."

I tried to look into his piggy eyes so he'd think I was following him, but that crucifix kept screaming at me: Look! Look at me! You think *you're* suffering?

My dad was listening, though. He boomed, "What do you mean, we won't talk about that? It has to be addressed!" He sat forward on his chair, the last strings of hair still attached to the front of his scalp flopping around. He swiped at them distractedly with one hand.

I'll give Strickland this: he spoke only to me. He didn't try to calm Dad down, didn't get defensive, didn't even turn toward my folks. Looking at me still, he said, "You'll meet other residents whose sins are the same as yours, and others whose sins are different. The important thing is not what the sin is. The important thing is that it is sin. Your entry into this Program represents a clean slate for you. It's a chance to start over, to be born new into the Church, into God's ways. When you leave this office, your roommate, Charles, will give you an orientation and then take you to the chapel, and Reverend Bartle will pray with you and cleanse you. You'll stay there with him until your sins are forgiven. Only then will you be ready for the Program here at Straight to God."

Dad sat back with a thud, arms crossed over his chest. He'd

probably been hoping they'd give me thirty-nine lashes or something. You remember the thirty-nine lashes? The Old Testament says that you aren't supposed to actually kill anyone with a whip, just hurt them really bad. They figured that for the average guy, forty should be the max. But the Jewish lawmakers wanted to be really sure they never overstepped the limits; after all, forty-one might kill somebody, right? Where forty wouldn't? Sticklers. Anyway, to make sure they never went beyond merely getting the guy to wish he were dead, they always counted to thirty-nine and stopped. And I figured that would be my fate here. They'd only make me wish they'd go ahead and put me out of my misery, but they wouldn't actually do it.

Strickland went over the Program Rules. All of them. My folks were following along in the Booklet (not to be confused with the Book, you understand), or at least my mom was, and we read through everything in painful detail. He told me that as soon as Reverend Bartle was done with me (not his words), I would be in SafeZone, which would mean I wasn't allowed to speak. With anyone. For anything. For Three Fucking Days.

And then he reached into the file cabinet behind his desk and pulled out, of all things, a digital camera. I was clueless and just sat there, arms crossed on my chest, a look on my face that basically said, "Do your worst, all of you. And fuck off while you're at it." My nothing brown hair was falling in that stupid curl just a little left of center on my forehead, my eyes were clouded with repressed fury, and the crooked part of my nose—from when I fell out of a tree when I was ten, and the spot Will likes to lick—offset the curl. I know this because I've seen the photo. But more on that later.

I couldn't wait for my folks to get out of there. But when they finally stood up to leave, I panicked. I felt like I couldn't get enough air, and I wanted to scream. Mom hugged me and I leaned over so I could rest my head on her shoulder, wondering when she had gotten shorter, and I inhaled the smell of her perfume. When she let go, Dad just nodded at me and took her arm. She looked back at me as she went through the door, her sweet face so sad, and I had to hang onto the back of my chair to keep from running after them.

They were leaving me in this prison!

Strickland picked up his phone and spoke to someone about sending Charles in to get me. Then he said, "Do you have any questions, Taylor?"

I tried not to shake as I sat down again. There was one thing I was dying to ask: How many other kids here are in for the same thing as me? How many other queers do you have?

I took a deep breath and asked the only thing I could think of that he was likely to answer. "What's SafeZone supposed to do for me?"

He could almost have closed his eyes and taken a nap, his response seemed that memorized. "SafeZone provides residents with an opportunity to maintain an internal focus while remaining physically present in an environment designed for their enlightenment." He stopped there. I waited for him to go on, 'cause that didn't really tell me anything, but he gave me this half-smile that didn't affect any other part of his face, like he was done. Like I was expected to know what the hell that canned statement meant. Then he said, "Other questions?"

I shook my head. MWBRL. I mean, More Will Be Revealed Later. Isn't that what the Bible says? Though I had my doubts about getting an answer to the SafeZone question.

We sat there in silence, him pretending to read something on his desk, me trying not to stare at the crucifix and clenching my hands so hard my knuckles were white, until someone knocked on the frame of the open office door.

"Ah, Charles. Come in. I want you to meet Taylor Adams, your new roommate. Taylor, this is Charles Courtney. Charles will show you around the facility, where the meeting rooms are, the dining hall, bathrooms, laundry room, library—everything. And then he'll take you to the chapel, as I mentioned earlier. Are you ready?"

Was I ready? I was ready, but not for what he meant. I was ready to run screaming from the place. Bad enough I'd be trapped here for six weeks minimum, but to have to deal with Charles Courtney was adding insult to injury. He was maybe seventeen, a year older than me, tall, so clean-cut he looked artificial. Light brown hair at what was certainly the perfect length for this place, thin nose, pale brown eyes, and no lips. Oh, and his nose sat a little high in the air. Kind of an Aryan android.

He smiled, or did something he meant to pass as a smile, and his thin lips got even thinner. "Taylor. Welcome." He held his hand out and I had little choice but to stand and shake it. Then he turned to Strickland. "Sir, if Taylor is ready, we'll leave you now."

"Taylor, I'll see you in a few days—when you're out of Safe-Zone—for our first talk. God bless you."

Yeah. Gesundheit to you, too.

The first place Charles showed me was the laundry room, following a map of the place that he gave me.

"This will be your first work assignment," he told me. "They'll show you what to do. It's the first one because it's pretty straightforward work and there won't be any need for you to speak. You'll be here for a week."

He looked like he expected me to say something, but I was practicing. Practicing not speaking. Wouldn't do to fail at Safe-Zone, would it?

Dining hall was next. "If you're lucky, Reverend Bartle will release you in time for you to get something to eat. You might need to get here as quickly as you can or you'll miss dinner. I'll keep an eye out for you." To which I was dying to respond, *Don't do me any favors.*

We went through the meeting rooms, starting with a really huge space that had nothing in it. "After dinner we'll come to this room for Fellowship, for around half an hour, and then we'll have an evening Prayer Meeting. We don't always have one on Sundays, but this week we do."

Fellowship? Well, I couldn't participate in that; how can you have Fellowship with people you don't even know if you can't talk? Now, Fellowship with Will—*that* I could do with very little talking. But Charles didn't give me time to dwell on any images.

The meeting rooms, where Charles said our evening Prayer Meetings would take place, all had names from the Old Testament. He stood proudly in front of the one named Isaiah.

"This one is ours. We meet here after Fellowship."

Then he led the way past Ezekiel, Obadiah, Esther, Daniel, Ruth, and Malachi (I kind of liked that one) to the boys' wing, pointing down the hall toward the girls' rooms as we passed it. "We're not to go into the girls' wing under any circumstances."

No worries.

Before going to the chapel, Charles took me to the bathroom. There were no urinals, just stalls with doors only halfway up so you could see the back of anyone standing in there, and probably the face of anyone sitting down.

"I don't need to piss," I told Charles, which was true, but mostly I didn't want him standing there watching the back of my head while I took a leak.

"Maybe not now," he said, a warning in his tone, "but you won't get another chance for a while."

I shrugged and went into a stall, unzipped, and let go of the little there was. What I was really feeling was like I needed to take a shit. My intestines were churning, and when that happens I usually get diarrhea. But I was damned if I would do that with him standing there.

I left the booth and headed toward the door, but Charles stopped me. "We always wash our hands here, Taylor."

I looked at him like he had three heads, but he just gestured toward the sinks. I thought of flipping him the finger but decided it wasn't worth it. There would be more important things to lock horns over.

The chapel was pretty spartan. White paint everywhere, and not much in the way of amenities. No cushions in sight. And there was this humongous cross that *had* to have been designed for a bigger space hanging in the middle of the room, suspended from the ceiling. Reverend Bartle was kneeling in front of the altar, head bowed over folded hands, and he didn't look up when we came in. I expected Charles to say something, but he just stood at the back, hands folded in front of him (hiding an erection, Charles?), waiting. Finally Reverend Bartle stood up slowly and turned toward us.

"Ah, boys. Come forward, please."

I'd met Reverend Bartle once before, when my folks had driven me up to see the place. It had been a grueling forty-minute trip, with me sulking in the backseat, terrified and frantically searching my brain for ways to convince my parents that this was a bad idea. When I met him, Reverend Bartle had seemed—well, fatherly, I guess, in a religious kind of way. Maybe patronizing is closer. Tall, with white hair and sharp eyes. They were probably blue, but they seemed almost metallic.

Things had happened pretty quickly once my dad decided it was going to be Straight to God for me. And here I'd been looking forward to the best summer of my life, spending as much time as possible with Will. We'd been a kind of secret item all through the school year. Sometimes it was super hard not to sit with him when we were in the same class, not to hold hands every chance we got, not to go out on real dates. Hell, I even wished we could have gone to junior prom together. Wouldn't that have turned some heads? But we didn't need dates. We just needed to be together.

So summer was going to be a special time for us as a couple. Until I was practically forced to confess my "sin." To tell my folks I'm gay.

It was their own fault, actually. Pestering me about girls. I'd taken stupid Rhonda to the prom when they made it obvious they weren't going to stop poking at me until I did, but that wasn't enough for them. It was kind of like, now that I'd taken her out, all of a sudden they noticed I didn't take any other girls out. So when they failed with Rhonda, they tried with Angela. The night she and her folks came over to dinner, my mom arranged things so we sat next to each other. That was bad enough, but then—true to their threat—they practically shoved us out the front door for our walk, while the four parents sat around drinking coffee and no doubt talking about how sweet it would be if these two kids "got together." The Russells, Angela's whole family, went to our church, too. So it would be that much more wonderful. YR. Sorry: Yeah Right.

So I went with Angela—who was actually a pretty nice girl—out for our forced march. It would have been awkward even if I'd been interested in her, because both of us knew our folks had set this up, and there were expectations. To her credit, and although it took about two minutes, she was the one who broke the ice.

"Feels pretty weird, getting shoved out the door like that, doesn't it." Not a question.

"Weird? How about retarded?"

She laughed. It was a pretty laugh, and I got a little worried. Was she interested in me and just trying to put me at ease so I'd feel like I could make a move? I risked looking at her.

She stopped walking. "You hate this, don't you." Also not a question. "I'm not happy about it, either. I mean, I like you, Taylor. You seem like a nice guy. And maybe that's why I'm going to trust you with something. Is that okay?"

"Trust me?"

"With a secret. Because I think you deserve to know. Especially if you ever thought that we, you know, might come to something. So . . . is it okay?"

I shrugged. "I guess so." I could floor her with a secret of my own, but I wasn't sure she deserved to know mine. She turned and started walking again, and I fell into step.

"I have a boyfriend. Well, I can't really call him that. Not in front of anyone. My parents don't want me to see him. That's why they want us—you and me—to get together. They think I'll forget about him."

Wow. We have something in common, Angela and I, besides meddling parents. "Why not?"

"He's not saved. And he doesn't want to be. His parents are freethinkers."

It was my turn to stop dead in my tracks. "Atheists?" The idea that there were people who didn't believe in God had always been a startling one to me. Sure, I knew they were out there, but I didn't talk to them. I'd heard only terrible things about them.

"No, they're not atheists, exactly. They would say they're god-centered, but they wouldn't capitalize *god* in writing. They believe in rational approach. To everything." She kind of giggled. "Danny says—that's my boyfriend—he says that when you don't have to make sense, you can say anything at all!"

"What does that mean, not making sense?"

"Think about it, Taylor. How many times have you been told something that made no sense at all, but the church insists you take it on faith?"

I got the concept, all right—like, why would God make me gay and then tell me it's a sin to be gay? But the freethinkers were confusing me. "I don't get it. They have no religion, but they sort of believe in God, but they don't believe in faith?"

"No, no, they have faith. It's just much more—I don't know, more free-form. So they don't have a scripture they follow. And they don't go to any church."

"Wait. How can you have faith and not have a religion?"

"Well, Taylor, they aren't the same thing. A religion is just a specific way of applying faith."

This didn't synch up with anything I'd ever heard before. I started shaking my head, sure she was just repeating pat phrases she'd heard from this Danny character.

Angela must have decided we'd gotten too far off the track she wanted to be on. "Anyway, what I'm saying is, I can't be interested in you. And since you're a nice boy, it seemed unfair to lead you on, in case . . . you know."

"Okay. Thanks." And I moved forward again.

For the next minute or so of our walk, I was going round and round in my head about whether I could tell her about me. In the end, I approached it a little sideways.

"So, Danny's parents. What would they say about homosexuality?"

"Oh that. Such a fuss. There are so many things in the Bible that we ignore, and everybody seems to make their own decisions about what things those ought to be. Danny's folks would just say, Who cares? As long as people aren't hurting each other—and it doesn't hurt you if someone else is gay, does it?— then leave the gays alone." I guess I was quiet too long, and she said, "That upsets you, doesn't it? I'm sorry. That must sound like sacrilege to you. I just get so into these discussions with Danny. His parents have always encouraged him to question everything—"

"No, that's not it." But that's as far as I got before I froze.

"What is it, then?" She stopped walking. Again. I stopped and turned toward her. "Oh my God, you're gay! Taylor, are you gay?"

Well, that got me moving again. "Will you be quiet? Is there anyone on the street who didn't just hear you say that?"

"Taylor, I was practically whispering. You barely heard me. I'm right, aren't I? This is so cool! I don't think I know anybody who's gay. Except you, of course."

"Oh yes you do."

"Who? Tell me!"

"No way. I'd never tell that about anyone else. Especially given how everyone in church feels about it." Which reminded me I hadn't extracted any promises. "So, you wouldn't, like, tell anyone, would you?"

"Oh, Taylor, of course not. You'd be crucified. And besides, you have my secret, too."

She took my hand. It was a weird moment. But she held it most of the way back to the house, and it felt a lot less weird by then and a lot more like friendship.

So it's kind of ironic that it was Angela who outed me to my folks. Not directly; she didn't do anything wrong. But after the Russells left that night, there was all this pressure from my folks to tell them how much I liked her.

"She's great. A real sweet girl. We had a nice walk."

Mom asked, "So do you think you'll see her again? Will you ask her out on a date?"

I felt like there was a bat in the room. You know how they fly? Sort of all over the place, and it's impossible to know how to duck to avoid them. All I could say was, "Maybe sometime."

"Sometime?" Dad bellowed. "*Sometime?* Taylor, there's nothing wrong with the girl, is there? She's pretty, she's smart, she's Christian," by which he meant *our* kind of Christian, "she's polite, her parents are fine people—what more could you want in a girl?"

"Nothing, I guess." I headed for the stairs, hoping to make it up to my room and bring this inquisition to an end. But no. Dad was right behind me, with Mom behind him; he had more to say, and he wasn't letting me avoid it.

"Do you have any idea how rude that is? How inconsiderate? To make a girl think you like her and then leave her hanging like that?"

I wheeled, nearly ducking to avoid that bat in the air. "Look, I'm not the one who suggested this little get-together, so she doesn't have any reason to think I'm interested in her that way. If anyone has led her on, it's you." I stood there, my back to the stairs and relative safety, my folks in front of me and looking about as sad and confused as I'd ever seen them. Into the silence, I said, "So I want both of you to stop pestering me about asking girls out. I have to do what's right for me."

Almost whining, my mom asked, "Taylor, isn't there *anyone* you're interested in?"

I took a breath. Then another. I clenched my hands into fists, balling up the fabric of my pants. I released the fabric. Gathered it again. I ground my teeth.

"Yeah. There is."

Mom stepped forward, and maybe the look on my face was what made her afraid, but she was afraid. I contemplated telling her I was in love with a girl whose parents were freethinkers. That might actually be better than the truth, as far as they were concerned.

Mom said, "Who is she?"

I opened my mouth and closed it a few times, thinking it was really too bad Angela and I hadn't been smart enough to set up a conspiracy. I would pretend to my folks that we were going out, and she could pretend to hers. But there's that thing about lying. I bet even freethinkers believe that's wrong. Time for the truth. So I said, "It's not a she, Mom. I'm gay."

They both stepped back, and then Dad lunged for me. He grabbed my arm before I could duck and dragged me into the living room, practically throwing me onto the sofa. I stood back up as he turned to start pacing around the room. Out of the corner of my eye—I didn't dare not watch Dad—I saw Mom kind of sink into a wing chair.

Dad wheeled on me, and I nearly fell back onto the sofa. "I don't ever want to hear you say that again! Do you hear me?

You're talking Satan. You're talking Hell. You're talking about your immortal soul. And I won't have you disgracing this family!"

Maybe if he hadn't said that last bit, about the family, I would have just let him rant and rave. But it was too much for me. "Oh, we can't have that, can we? Family disgrace. You know, God made me who I am. It's between me and God."

Dad's voice got quiet. Hard. "I'll tell you what's between you and God. Satan is between you and God right now. So don't pretend you know what you're talking about, because right now you're just Satan's mouthpiece."

"I do so know what I'm talking about!" My voice was nowhere near as calm as his. But I had more to lose. "I've spent a lot of time this year thinking about this, praying about this, and reading the Bible about this. I know where Satan is. And he's not standing between me and God."

Dad marched around the living room, kicking aside a small table that got in his way. He's got a bit of a temper, so despite the comical look of the wispy hair strings on top of his head when he moves around, it's a bad idea to get him riled.

Too late to avoid that, though.

"You've done it already, haven't you? You've been active. You've committed sodomy."

My mind went two different places when he said that. One was to Will. Not that I pictured the act, but that I didn't want my parents to do that. If I said yes now, they'd want to know who was with me. I didn't want to give Will to them. Plus I didn't want them to say I couldn't see him again.

The other place was the word itself. Sodomy. If you read the Bible carefully, the people of Sodom committed all kinds of sin. It wasn't just a matter of men having sex with men. They were greedy, and they proved frequently that they were without mercy. And Abram's nephew, Lot, lived there; why? And when two angels—who were always men, of course—came as guests to Lot's house and some local guys wanted to have sex with them, do you know what Lot did? He offered instead his two virgin daughters! Talk about abomination. But my point is, sodomy means just one

thing today, but the original meaning was more than that. So
had I committed sodomy? Not biblically. Not in *all* its aspects.

So for at least two very different reasons, I said, "No. You're
wrong."

He stopped and stared at me, looking triumphant. "Then you
really don't know anything about it." He walked over to where
Mom was still sitting in the chair and put his hand on her
shoulder, I guess to set up something like a wall of interven-
tion. Solidarity against me. "Then I know what to do. We'll all
go, the three of us, and talk with Reverend Douglas. He'll know
what steps to take. In the meantime, young man, you should
consider yourself grounded. We can't take any chances."

And as if that settled it, he nodded in my general direction
and said to Mom, "I'm going to read the last section of the
paper." And he plunked himself down into his recliner.

I stood there feeling like the spaceship I'd arrived on had
taken off toward home without me. Mom got up kind of suddenly and disappeared, and I skulked off to my bedroom, fighting the urge to call Will, terrified that if either of them found
out I was talking to him they'd figure out who he was to me.

So Dad made the decision of what was gonna happen next,
like he was the only one who needed to be consulted, and Mom
disappeared. Which left me—where? Sometimes the weirdest
part of a confrontation is what happens right afterward. It's like
no one's on the same terms they were on with anyone before it
happened, and there's all this psychological dancing that goes
on as everyone tries to find out what the new boundaries are. I
was feeling a powerful need to set some new boundaries, starting with my mom.

Practically tiptoeing so my dad wouldn't know I was anywhere
near, I moved through the house toward the laundry room. I figured that's where Mom would be; it's where she goes when
she's upset.

And sure enough, the door was shut, and I could hear her
quietly crying in there. I knocked once and opened it, and she
was standing in front of the ironing board ripping an old pair
of my pajamas into rags. Therapeutic, I suppose. She dropped

all of it when she saw me and wrapped herself around me, crying harder, calling my name between sobs.

"It's okay, Mom. Really. I'm fine."

"Oh, Taylor!" was all she said for a while, until she let me go so she could blow her nose. Then, "Your father is so upset. I don't know what he'll do. Why does it have to be like this? Why do you . . ." She kind of fizzled out and blew her nose again.

"Mom, I don't know what else I can tell you. This is who I am. It's not something I chose, just like being who you are isn't something you chose."

"But Taylor, it's a sin!"

"We're all sinners, Mom."

"But you're choosing to sin!"

"No. You aren't listening. I didn't choose this, any more than I chose brown hair or what day I was born on. I can't change my birthday, and I can't change the color of my hair—not really, and I can't change this."

"But . . . you're our only child." She raised her arms into the air and let them flop down again, helpless.

"And that means what, exactly? That you don't get another chance to do it right?"

I must have shouted. I probably sounded like Dad. She sort of squeaked, "It means we won't have grandchildren."

I let out a tired breath. "Mom, I don't know why I'm gay. I don't know if God made me like this to test me, or to test you and Dad, or if there's some other reason, but it's who God made me. Do you think I haven't prayed about this? Do you think I haven't asked God why?"

She perked up a little. "Have you talked to Reverend Douglas already? Why didn't you tell your father? What did the reverend say?"

Well, no, I told her, I hadn't talked to Reverend Douglas.

He'd been our pastor for my whole life, and even before my dad dragged us in to see him, I already knew where he stood on this issue so near and dear to my heart.

Mom and I talked a little longer, but just so we could both calm down some. We didn't really get anywhere.

The meeting with Reverend Douglas went about like you'd expect. He came out of his office all smiles and sweetness and light.

"What a pleasure! I'm delighted to see all of you." He turned to me. "Taylor, your father tells me you're feeling troubled. Why don't you and I go into my office and talk about it?"

I could give him about seventeen reasons why not. But at least we were leaving my folks out here. I followed him in and sat in the chair across from his desk. I guess this is my year for sitting across desks from sanctimonious homophobes.

"So, Taylor, what seems to be the trouble?"

"Actually, I'm not having any trouble. It's my dad who has a problem."

"What problem is that?"

"He thinks I'm confused."

"You're not?"

"No. I'm gay. I'm not confused."

Just a slight twinge. But then, I was watching for it, so maybe I imagined it. "There's not much difference between the two at this stage. Your father tells me you haven't yet engaged in fornication, so we're catching things early. Confusion can be cleared more easily if sin has not yet occurred." When I didn't reply to his last volley, he said, "Is what your father told me correct? You haven't yet fornicated?"

I ground my teeth. He could mean almost anything. "I'm not sure I know what you're asking me. What do you mean by fornicated?"

"Fornication, strictly speaking, is sex outside of marriage. For our purposes, it indicates sexual intercourse that has not been blessed by God."

"If I had fornicated with a girl, would that be okay?"

"Of course not, as you know very well. You're no stranger to God's laws. But because you're saying that you're homosexual, the most likely fornication would have been with another boy, or a man. Has that happened?"

I took a breath and tried to think while I let it out. He was being very patient, which meant I wasn't likely to get out of this quickly. And I didn't. I won't go into all the back and forth with scriptural references, and me clenching my hands into fists to stop myself from trying to argue with him, because arguing would mean making this take even longer. It's enough to say that he got more out of me than my dad had managed.

"There's a program that's designed for teenagers with problems. It's called Straight to God. Have you heard of it?"

Oh God. Oh God. Please stop him. Please let the heavens open and—well, the guy doesn't have to die or anything, but can't you stop him from saying any more?

"They're associated with our church only loosely, but they hold similar views when it comes to the importance of right behavior and how to reinforce it in troubled youth. The program can be especially helpful for boys like you, who are already trying their best to abide by God's laws in every other respect. I'm going to recommend that you spend some time there this summer, Taylor."

Trying to keep my voice calm, I asked, "So what do you expect them to do? Pray part of who I am out of me?"

"The confusion I mentioned earlier is causing you to think you're something you're not. Homosexuality is an abomination in the eyes of the Lord, and there's no way he would have made you that way. Satan is responsible for this, but you are responsible for casting him out. Straight to God will help you do that."

"Wait. So you're telling me God let Satan plant something in me that God didn't want there? I thought God was all-powerful. Is Satan stronger? Is that what you're saying?" I knew this would get me nowhere, but I couldn't stop myself.

"Taylor, God gave man free will. Something in your heart became weakened, perhaps by the godless influences around us all the time, and Satan took advantage of that. He tempted you, and through your free will you accepted what he offered. Because this can happen only when you're weak, you need the power of specialists to help you. Straight to God is where you will find them. It's where you will find the path back from sin."

He handed me a pamphlet, and I took it with a shaky hand.

My head felt like it was going to explode. Christ! Am I really this helpless? Is there really nothing I can do? My only hope was that my folks wouldn't agree. And that's where my next prayer went, since the heavens-opening idea had been rejected.

During dinner that night I said absolutely nothing. I didn't trust myself. But afterward Dad dragged me into the living room. To talk about what he was going to do to me. Or, what Straight to God was going to do.

"Your mother and I have decided to take Reverend Douglas's recommendation, Taylor. This Saturday, we will all drive up to look at the place and enroll you, and a week after that you'll start the program."

I'd had enough of helplessness. I exploded. "You've got to be kidding! You're out of your mind! I won't go. You can't make me. And you can't make me straight, you know."

"You will go. And I don't have to make you straight, because you aren't crooked. What you need is God's help so you can understand that you're confused."

Confused was one thing I was not. "That's bullshit!"

"Taylor!"

"I mean it, Dad. That's crap. I know exactly who I am."

"You don't know anything. You're still a child." I opened my mouth to yell again, but he took a step toward me. "Don't you talk back to me or this will be worse. How do you think you'd enjoy attending a military academy?" I stepped back, dumb-struck. WTF? "So you have a choice to make, young man. Six weeks, minimum, depending on how well you do, at Straight to God. Or it's military school in the fall." He started to turn away from me like that was the end, but then he turned back and added, "And in either case, young man, you're to consider yourself grounded until further notice."

I felt nearly hysterical. Ridiculously, what flashed through my head was a series of images of King Richard on a crusade, sent to the Holy Land to fight the infidels and, while he was at it, to purge the devil that made him want men, and all the time he was surrounded by men. Made that idiot Ted Tanner's com-ment a little less idiotic. I came so close to pointing out to my father that he'd be sending me to a place where all feminine wiles would be missing and I'd have lots of boys to choose from, but something stopped me—probably the fear that he'd be so furious he'd send me there anyway, out of spite. And if I couldn't be with Will all summer, then I sure as hell wasn't gonna let him be out of reach all next year on top of that.

I needed to kick something. Desperately. Maybe I was grounded, but that didn't mean I couldn't go into the backyard. So I headed for this big old maple tree that grows near the house, the one I'd broken my nose falling out of. I can see it from my bedroom window, and I'd always felt like it knew everything that was going on. So I knew it would understand. I kicked it till my feet hurt.

When I got up to my room, things looked different on my desk. Like someone had been here, searching. But—for what? Gay porn?

Then it hit me. If I was grounded, I couldn't use my cell phone. I dived for where I'd left it. Gone.

I pounded on anything that wouldn't make too much noise. I screamed into my pillow. Eventually I calmed down and sank onto the floor, right where Will and I had sat that first night we kissed. Touched. Loved. Fighting tears, I relived my interview with Reverend Douglas, trying to come up with arguments that countered his insistence that this wasn't real. That *I* wasn't real. I kept hearing Angela's words, quoting her freethinking boyfriend: if you don't have to make sense, you can say anything you want. The problem was twofold. Angela was quoting people who didn't even capitalize the word *God*. And what Reverend Douglas had said made a certain amount of sense. He almost had me wondering if maybe I *had* allowed Satan in.

But then I thought of Will. And Will was no Satan, and this love was from God. It *had* to be. Reverend Douglas was wrong. After all, he wasn't infallible. God *did* make me who I am, and he made Will who he is. Just thinking of Will, though, made me cry.

The worst thing in the short term was that I was, like, totally grounded. Which meant I could spend my time reading only the things they approved of. No phone calls, no computer time, no visits from friends—my folks would be suspicious of everyone male, maybe because I hadn't told them about Will specifically—so I was losing my mind trying to figure out how to let Will know what was happening to me. I cried myself to sleep that night, and just before I fell asleep it came to me.

That Sunday, in church, I slipped a note for Will to one of his sisters. I watched as he read it, and when he looked over at me from way too far away, the look on his face nearly made me burst into tears on the spot.

And now I was here for real. My sentence had begun. The reverend was waiting.

Charles moved forward, and I followed. Wasn't much else I could do. Reverend Bartle looked right at me, but he said, "Thank you, Charles. You can leave your charge with me now." He held an arm toward me, and I tried to avoid his open hand as I moved forward. I didn't want him to touch me. But he grabbed my neck, squeezed it until it almost hurt, and then stroked the back of my head once.

"Come, Taylor. Come and shed your sin."

Christ.

He made me kneel beside where he'd been earlier, and then he knelt as well. I didn't look at him, and I don't think he looked at me. Nothing happened for maybe five minutes. I wasn't sure what I was supposed to do, so I figured I was supposed to pray.

I prayed, all right. Jesus, I begged, get me through this. Don't let them turn me into a Charles. Don't let me forget Will. Don't let me forget who I am.

Please.

Finally Reverend Bartle spoke. "Tell me about it, Taylor. Tell me why you're here."

I looked at him, but he was facing forward, eyes closed. What the hell did he want me to say? I'm here because it was either this for the summer or military school in the fall. I'm here because my parents can't handle that I'm gay. I'm here because they think God can make me "normal" again. Like I'd ever been anyone other than who I am. Like God would create abomination in the first place.

All I said was, "I don't know."

Maybe thirty seconds of silence passed, in which I assumed I was supposed to be growing more and more anxious. I wanted to make him wrong about that, but I failed.

Then he said, "I think you do know. I think you're very well aware of how ungodly your feelings and actions have become, how you've allowed your baser needs to overrule your true spirit." He paused again, but I didn't say anything. So he said, "Tell me about them."

"About what?"

"Tell me about how you've given in to your ungodly feelings to satisfy your baser needs. Tell me what you've done." His voice was calm, no impatience in it.

Okay, I could have gone one of two ways here. I could have just told him about some of the things Will and I have done, the ways we've come to know each other, the way he makes me feel when he's holding me, teasing my hair, kissing my neck. I could have described those "baser" needs, how the energy would move through me like lightning bolts seeking the ground of Will's body, and how it felt afterward like heaven and hell had met and clashed and canceled each other out so that we floated in a sea of total calm. I could have said that I love Will so much that it seems like a window into the love God offers, as though I could follow this path to the source of all Love.

I could have. But I didn't. I took the other road. I took rebellion. It may have been a mistake. Guess I'll never know. But at least I didn't give Will to him.

"I haven't done anything ungodly."

"You and I both know that's not true, Taylor. We're in God's house. Don't dishonor it by lying. Do you love God, Taylor?"

"Yes." That was true; I do love God. I even love Jesus. He wasn't the one who called my love for Will a sin.

"Then tell the truth."

"I did. It is the truth."

His voice grew so loud so suddenly, I jumped. "For their

women changed the natural function into that which is against nature. Likewise also the men, leaving the natural function of the woman, burned in their lust toward one another, men doing what is inappropriate with men, and receiving in themselves the due penalty of their error."

Then, quietly, "Do you recognize that text, Taylor?"

"It's from Romans."

"That's right. Do you know what it's saying?"

"It's talking about lust. Not love. And it's not Jesus speaking."

I should have known better. I should never have tried to fight back, to counter his approach. Should never have revealed my own thinking. He went into this rant, quoting chapter and verse from all over the Bible, stopping in between to paint these horrid pictures of all kinds of sex as evil. Especially sex between men. It was like he knew everything I'd ever felt for Will, every tingle, every touch, every longing. Like he knew how it felt when Will's fingers caressed the inside of my thigh. Like he knew what went through my mind when I wanted to be with Will and couldn't. And he made it sound like everything that had ever been between us, between Will and me, made Satan laugh. Made Jesus cry.

I didn't argue with him. For one thing, he wasn't giving me time to say anything. For another, pretty soon I was in tears anyway and couldn't exactly debate the issue.

He kept me in there for almost three hours. It was torture. And it got worse when he dragged my parents into it, using scripture to show how much pain I was putting them through. Especially my mother. I can't remember everything, but I think I managed not to actually say that what Will and I have is sinful. But I can't be sure that I didn't say yes or something else that sounded like a confession to Reverend Bartle. All I do know is that I was sobbing like a baby, lying on the floor in fetal position, holding onto my ribs, and feeling like my chest was going to burst open.

I guess he must have thought I'd confessed my sins, or maybe he figured I'd die if he kept at me any longer. That's what I thought.

He pulled me up from where I lay sobbing and walked me out of the chapel, an arm around my shoulders. As we walked he said, "The pain you're feeling is the tearing out of sin. The ripping out of evil. It's good pain, Taylor."

I tried to shake my head, but since every part of me was shaking I'm not sure he noticed.

"I'll walk you to your room now. I'm afraid you've missed dinner, but it's my guess you don't feel much like eating."

By the time we stopped at the doorway to the room I would share with Charles, I'd stopped crying, but I was in some kind of emotional haze. Reverend Bartle let go of me and flipped on the light. I kind of slumped against the door frame and watched from some far-off place as he picked something up from the desk on the left. It looked like a yellow piece of paper, but when he peeled off a rectangle about two inches by three, I saw it was from a sheet of labels. He pressed the piece in his hand against the left side of my chest and held it there.

"You're in SafeZone now, Taylor. This yellow warning will let the other residents and staff know that you can't speak to them, so you need to wear one of these until you're out of SafeZone or else you might violate this part of your residency. That would have serious consequences." Now the hand dropped. "Your staff leader, Mrs. Harnett, will let you know when you can stop wearing these. Then you may speak again."

He set the sheet back down on the desk and looked around the room.

"Is this your luggage beside the bed over there? Just nod or shake your head."

I nodded. It was mine. Full of clothing that Mom had had to buy especially for this incarceration, complete with name tags that read T. ADAMS. Not much of my own stuff met the standards of this place.

"And here's the map Charles left for you." He leaned over to the other side of the desk and picked it up. "Did he show you what room your Prayer Meeting would be in this evening?"

Nod.

"Good. Now, you might want to take a few minutes to collect yourself before you go there."

A few minutes? How about a few days? How about a few years?

"God loves you, Taylor. God wants you to learn how to love him. We'll show you how."

Before I knew what was happening he moved forward and took me into his arms. We stood there like that, him totally wrapped around me, my arms hanging limp. And he just held me.

I don't know why, and I don't even know if I had a choice, but I reached around and hugged him back. I wanted to cry again. This was the man who had torn me apart, and yet his embrace felt so tender, so loving. I wished he could hold me forever.

He pushed me away rather abruptly, cleared his throat, said, "Don't close the door," and left me there.

Limp, wrung out, I sat on the side of the bed where my luggage was for some amount of time that isn't clear to me now. Finally I decided I may as well unpack. Everything on the left side of the room seemed to be mine, so I opened my bags, took things out, and stuffed them into drawers. Then I found the bathroom and took a long time, mind empty as I sat there. Then I remembered I wasn't supposed to be in a bathroom for more than five minutes for "elimination" or fifteen for "cleansing and grooming." I'd already exceeded both.

But who would know? Nevertheless, I got up, washed my hands and face, and went back to my room.

Standing in the middle of the room, not seeing anything, I wondered how in hell I was going to just show up at an in-progress Prayer Meeting, wearing my warning label, eyes puffy and face blotchy from crying, and sit there silently in a room full of strangers I would be living with for weeks.

I couldn't do it. Plus I felt completely drained. So I stripped, threw my clothes in a corner, found my pajama bottoms and put them on, and crawled into bed. Didn't even turn the light out.

I must have been in some other universe, some other dimension. At any rate I was deeply asleep, face to the wall, so that when Charles called my name, I heard it being repeated, louder and louder, before I realized I had to respond to it.

I turned over and half sat up.

"Taylor, this is not what you were supposed to do. You were supposed to go to Prayer Meeting. Believe me, your absence was noticed." Something about his voice, some edge, seemed like an overreaction to this misdeed of mine. Like he took it personally somehow. SOHF. Oops. Should I give up counting demerits yet? Translation: Sense Of Humor Failure.

A number of retorts came to mind, and I think I even opened my mouth.

"Don't speak!"

Oh yeah.

"Are you wearing pajama pants?"

Nod.

Charles moved over to my bureau and started pawing through things. He found what he was looking for—my pajama top—and brought it over to me.

He held it out. "Here. You have to wear the full set. You know that. It's in the Booklet."

I tried to glare at him, but I doubt it came across quite as fierce as I wanted. I snatched the top from him and put it on while he watched.

Before I could throw myself back onto the bed and dive under the sheets, he said, "Pray with me."

"What?"

His hand shot into the air so quickly that I thought he was going to strike me, but he just held it up, palm out, and gave me this hard stare—reminding me, by not speaking, not to speak.

Then he said, "Pray with me. You missed Prayer Meeting. But you need God now more than you ever have before, and praying is the best way to acknowledge his presence. It's how we open our hearts so he can heal us."

I just stared at him, but he wasn't backing down. I heaved a shaky sigh and got out of bed.

Charles went to the desks and pulled first my chair out and then his. He knelt in front of his, elbows on the wooden seat, and looked at me. I sighed again and went to my own chair. He closed his eyes, so I figured it was safe to close mine. Maybe I could fall asleep again.

But no. He prayed aloud.

"Almighty Father, thank you for bringing Taylor to us. Thank you for loving him enough to bring him here, and thank you for giving me the chance to show him the power your love has. To show him the miracles it can bring. To reaffirm in my own heart the steps I have taken toward you.

"Open Taylor's heart the way you have opened mine. Let him see the light so he will know the right path to take. Let all of us here be examples for him, to support his faith and give meaning to his longing. He longs for you, Father. Help him to understand that, to use this time fully and well, to cross the bridge we are all on, to reach the other side in joy and rapture and fulfillment. Amen."

He didn't get up right away, so I didn't either. I guessed that he was giving me time to speak silently and say my own prayer. So I did.

God, I know you love me. And you know I love you. I don't know why you've brought me here, unless it's some kind of test. Can I live with these people and still be the person you made me? Can I believe, despite everything I'll go through here, that you don't make mistakes? Is this like what happened to Job? Do I have to prove that my love for you is more important than anything they can do to me here?

I waited. If this was a Job test, I knew better than to expect any kind of sign. But I focused my mind hard on loving God. And I felt a warm glow. More tender than Reverend Bartle's hug. Deeper even than the sweet peace of being with Will. I smiled.

And then I stood and went back to bed, leaving Charles there worshiping at the altar of his desk chair. God and I had an understanding. And the gift he'd given me was that since I wasn't allowed to speak, I didn't even have to tell Charles about it. He couldn't even ask. It was between me and God.

Charles had thanked God for me, and he was right to do that. He just didn't understand the reason. I was going to show him another path.

Chapter 2

But about midnight Paul and Silas were praying and singing hymns to God, and the prisoners were listening to them.

—Acts 16:25

I woke up to this piercing ringing noise, sitting bolt upright before I knew where I was. Charles sat up in his own bed, hair whorled in a couple of places where his head had been on the pillow but the hair was too short to be really messed up. He got out of bed before I did, rubbed his face and exhaled, and then knelt on the floor.

Was this part of what my daily routine was supposed to be? I couldn't remember seeing it written anyplace. Maybe it was just Charles. I got up and went to find my bathroom kit and a towel, knowing that if I did something wrong he'd tell me.

Without even looking up, Charles said, "Don't go to the bathroom without me." And then he knelt there another couple of minutes while I leaned on my desk, getting irritated. Did I really have to obey him like this? I was afraid I did.

Finally he stood and grabbed his own kit and towel. "You probably don't want to wear a yellow tag on your pajamas or on your shoulder. If I'm with you I'll be able to explain to anyone that you can't speak."

I shrugged; fine. I followed him to the shower room, adjacent to the toilet room, with an archway between. It was full of stalls like the ones in the toilet room, but longer, with a little space near the door that stayed dry enough to hang your clothes.

The space was evidently designed for some compromise between privacy and revelation. I couldn't gawk at the other naked guys, but I didn't have quite enough privacy to—well, to enjoy myself in here.

The towels were huge—I think they called them bath sheets—and we were expected to wrap them under our arms tightly before we stepped out of the shower stalls.

Back in the room, before I could do so much as look for underwear, Charles closed the door and said, "Let me show you how we dress."

Was he kidding me with this? But he selected some clothing for himself and threw it on the bed, and I did the same, and then he pulled at something on the wall between our beds that I hadn't noticed before. A thin curtain was suspended from a track in the ceiling, and Charles pulled it across.

"Only when we're both dressed does the curtain go back again. If you finish first, you can start making your bed."

Wow. Did they really think the sight of Charles's naked body would drive me over the edge of self-control? Or maybe the sight of mine . . . SorG? I mean, Straight or Gay?

Suddenly I really wanted to know. Why was Charles here? I knew the Program included kids who'd been caught on drugs and some kids who were violent or drank a lot. What had been Charles's sin?

I dressed quickly, in my new clothes, which were not my style—khakis, leather belt, knit polo shirt. I was making my bed when Charles said, "I'm about to pull the curtain back. If it's too soon, clear your throat." I was silent.

When the curtain was pressed once again against the wall, I glanced at Charles's bed. Not made yet. Good; I was ahead of him. I finished quickly and went to my desk. There was a pad of paper there, and a pen. It was for me to use if I had to say something I couldn't communicate with hand gestures. Well, all right, it was supposed to be for emergencies, but that's a relative term. I wrote, "Why are you in here?"

When he turned away from his bed and saw me holding it up to him, he froze. I will always remember the expression on his face after he read it, because it was the only honest one I ever expected to see there. It had fear in it, and admission. It told me all I needed to know.

Gotcha.

He said, "You're supposed to do that only in emergencies." He wouldn't look at me. If he had, he'd have seen that I knew. Instead he looked at my shoulder, saw it was missing something, and pointed to the page of yellow labels on my desk. I shrugged and slapped one onto my shirt.

Without speaking he jerked his head in a follow-me kind of way, and he led the way to breakfast. He herded me silently through the line, pointing at trays and silverware and napkins, and I followed him to an empty table for four. What else was I going to do?

We'd been there just long enough for Charles to say a quiet grace that I guess was supposed to apply to both of us when two girls sat down in the other two chairs. They saw my yellow sticker—looked for it, or so it seemed to me—and asked Charles how he was. The smile that appeared suddenly on his face was a lie.

"Happy and grateful," he replied. "Jessica Rifkin, Marie Downs, this is Taylor Adams. Today's his first full day with us, and as you can see he's in SafeZone. He's my new roommate." To me he said, "Jessica and Marie are roommates, too."

I tried to look at them without looking at them; didn't want to draw attention to myself too soon in this place. Marie was one of those girls who, for sure, will be in one sorority or another at college. You know the type? Dark hair pulled back on one side with a plastic tortoiseshell barrette; white blouse with one of those collars that has round edges that meet in the middle when you button it all the way up, which of course she did. Something prissy about her. Just missed being pretty. Jessica seemed more normal, at least in my terms, though she was definitely plain-looking. Longish light brown hair, no particular style to it. She's the one who got the conversation going, while Marie watched Charles closely.

"You were so quiet in Prayer Meeting last night," Jessica said, and I couldn't quite tell whether her glance at him was more concerned or inquisitive. Did she know something interesting about Charles? What was special about last night's meeting, other than the fact that I didn't show up?

Charles didn't look at her. "I just had a lot to talk with God about." He reached for the jar of maple syrup, watching the stream of it intently as it cascaded down the stack of pancakes on his plate. Then he held it out to me, his glance questioning.

I had pancakes, too, so I reached for it. He must have been watching my face closely, 'cause when my mouth opened to thank him he withdrew his arm a little. Instantly I understood the warning. I nodded and held out my hand for the syrup.

But Jessica wasn't done with him. "We're supposed to be sharing our communication with God. In Prayer Meeting. Do you need some coaching, brother? Are there secrets that need to see the light?"

I glanced at her sharply, feeling—to my total surprise—defensive for Charles. At least he'd treated me decently so far. But I couldn't speak. So all I could do was notice that the smile plastered on Charles's face seemed to hurt him. But his voice, hard but clothed in something soft, cut her off at the proverbial knees.

"Why, sister, I'm touched at your concern. Thank you. But no, nothing God and I were talking about at the meeting was secret. Nothing you don't know."

I looked at her, thinking, Take that, sister Jessica. Then I sat back, a rather stunning idea occurring.

Whoa. Could this be deliberate on their part? Are they playing "good cop, bad cop" with me? Is this just a ploy to get me on Charles's side somehow? So I looked at him again, assessing.

No. Don't think so. He looked genuinely uncomfortable, and uncomfortable knowing that was how he looked. No one could fake that. Don't be so suspicious, I told myself. Silently, of course. So I went back to my original suspicions. They were bad enough: lying, brainwashing, mind control, hypocrisy.

At least Jessica showed a true color, even if it was an ugly shade of passive-aggressive. But her voice, as well as her words when she asked Charles if he needed "coaching," had sounded spooky. Haunted. Haunting, that's for sure.

Their conversation changed rather abruptly, which I was sure was okay with Charles, when Marie said, "I've been trying to reach out to Leland, but he hasn't been very responsive. Any hints you can give me, Charles?"

For just a second, Charles stopped chewing. Maybe it wasn't so okay after all. But he didn't look up from his plate, and he sounded calm enough when he said, "Leland may need a little more time. He might not be ready to see that what you did was in his best interests."

"You've been talking with him, then?"

Charles's head snapped up. I wasn't sure if it was anger or fear in his eyes, but all he said was, "Sister, you know that Leland is in SafeZone again." Then his voice got really pointed. "If anyone is speaking to him now, especially about what happened, it would be irresponsible. We must all help him to preserve his current parameters. Perhaps now is not the best time for you to be reaching out to him."

Jessica looked like she had an opinion about this, but before she could get it out, there was a woman smiling down at me. She wasn't very tall, but something about the way she had her hair pulled back made her seem—I don't know, stern or something. And there was this streak of white, almost two inches wide, that swept up from her forehead adding to the effect. The rest of her hair was pretty dark, though there were a few shots of white in it. She might have been pretty, but it was hard to tell with that hairstyle, and with the way her face seemed pulled tight.

Charles practically jumped to his feet, so I figured I had to stand as well.

The woman said, "Taylor, I know you're in SafeZone, so let me just introduce myself to you. I'm Mrs. Harnett, and I'm the staff leader for your group. I'm sorry I couldn't be here yesterday to meet you, but I had to be elsewhere."

I nearly said, "That's okay," but Charles was boring a hole into the side of my head, so I remembered in time and just nodded.

"As your staff leader, I'm here to help you in any way I can. Please stop by my office before you report to your first assignment. Charles will show you where it is. God bless you, Taylor."

And she left. It was only at that point that I noticed that Marie and Jessica had not stood when Charles and I had. I made a mental note to review the rules about how "men" and "women" were expected to act with one another, if only so I would know what was going on.

I kind of wanted the interrupted conversation to continue; it had been making Charles uncomfortable in one way or another, and I'd been thinking that might be a useful thing to know how to do. But evidently Charles wanted to talk about other things.

"Have you both got companions for Friday's barbeque dinner?" He pushed a forkful of pancake into his mouth.

"Marie hasn't. But I'm sure she will." Jessica's smile was as big as Mrs. Harnett's, but it didn't look warm. "What about you, Charles?"

He nodded, and when he had swallowed he said, "Danielle has agreed to go with me."

I swear Marie's tongue nearly poked through her cheek as she took over from Jessica. "That will be nice. The two of you must be getting to know each other quite well. Hasn't she accompanied you a number of times now?"

He didn't look at her. "If you recall, sister, Andrea went with me to the lake for our Fourth of July picnic." He stabbed the last bit of pancake and ate it with the last piece of bacon on his plate, and then he looked at my empty plate. "You must have been hungry, Taylor. Why don't you finish your juice, and then we'll go to Mrs. Harnett's office."

I was dying—dying!—to ask Charles what was behind the questions those girls had been asking. What was the link between Charles and Leland, if any? What had Marie done to the guy? And who was this Danielle person? Marie had made it sound as though seeing too much of her would be, like, frowned upon. And she'd done that mostly by making it sound like the opposite.

Christ, I hoped everyone wasn't going to be like this. Would anyone actually say what they meant around here? Would *anything* be real?

It wouldn't be Mrs. Harnett, from what I could tell. She thanked Charles for his escort service, dismissed him, shut her office door, and steered me to a chair with an iron grip on my shoulder.

She walked around her desk and didn't speak until she was settled in her chair, from which she gave me her full attention.

"Welcome to Straight to God, Taylor. We're pleased to have you here. I trust you've studied your Booklet? Just nod if it's true." I nodded. "Good, good. So you're familiar with the Program Rules. They may seem strict, but let me assure you that if they were any less strict they wouldn't be nearly as helpful to you. Can you understand that, Taylor?"

She smiled and waited. I came so close to shrugging, but the last thing I wanted was another session in the chapel with Reverend Bartle. Not even for another one of his hugs. On the other hand, I didn't want to lie. Can a nod be a lie if the answer is no? Actually, though, I did understand. Maybe not in the way she meant—I understood that I wanted out of this place, and anything that would help that was okay by me—but I nodded, saying inside my head, You bet, lady.

"Then please remember that at times when the rules may seem a little harsh. Do you understand what your MI is?"

I nodded, saying in my head, Yeah, but I don't think you do. After all, the thing was so incorrectly named.

"Good. Then I'm sure you also know that you will write four of them a week, at least for now. You will submit them to me." She reached into a desk drawer and handed me four large envelopes. "Start today. While you're in SafeZone, you'll be required to spend two hours of quiet time alone in your room from four to six o'clock. With the door open, remember. This would be an ideal time to write your first MI. Then seal it in one of these envelopes and put it in the basket mounted on the wall beside my office door on your way to dinner this evening. I'll expect the next one tomorrow night, and then one on Thursday and one on Saturday. Always in the basket sometime before dinner." She was scribbling as she spoke. "Any questions about that schedule?"

I shook my head. At least this response was honest, and she didn't ask me what I thought about it.

"I will read each one no later than the morning after I receive it. On Thursday, please stop by my office at ten o'clock in the morning, and we'll review the first two. Most residents need some guidance in order to get the most benefit out of this exercise. Next Monday we'll meet at ten again to make sure you're on the right path. Starting the week after that, we'll meet each Tuesday at eleven o'clock; that will be our time together, to talk about anything we need to discuss." More scribbling, and then she handed me the paper, which had MI due dates and meeting times on it. I pocketed it. "Clear?"

Nod.

"Good. Now, if I think we need to meet at other times, I'll let you know, either by finding you, as I did this morning, or by leaving you a note in your mailbox in the front office. And if you need to speak with me in between our scheduled sessions, you may leave a note in my mailbox. Now, do you have any questions that you need answered right away? If so, you may write them down." She was still holding the pen.

I had questions, all right. Like why would they give a gay transgressor—that would be me—a gay roommate? But I just shook my head.

She smiled hugely. "Taylor, everyone here loves you and wants your life to be a glory to God. Sometimes residents find this hard to believe in the beginning, but in time I'm sure you'll come to feel that love coming from everyone, and you'll love them as well. And that's where the glory starts." Another few smiling seconds and then she pushed her chair back. I stood as well.

"Do you know where your first assignment is?" I nodded. "Good." It seemed to me she said "Good" an awful lot. "Then just take this slip of paper and give it to the laundry supervisor. He'll know you've been with me and you won't be marked down." She handed me a small bit of paper with something scrawled on it, probably her signature. One final "God bless you, Taylor," and I was free. Of her, anyway. And on my way to the next room in this prison.

I walked into the laundry room with my little piece of paper clearly visible and waited to be noticed. The place was warm, and there was a loud thrumming noise from huge industrial fans set high in the walls sucking air out. I stood there a minute, and then this black guy with a bald head—maybe twenty years old— saw me. He was talking with a repairman, and he held up his hand, like he wanted me to just wait here. Fine. I looked around the room.

The door from the hall opened onto a kind of upper level, with an office off to one side, and five steps down was the rest of the laundry room. Washing machines—all white—were all on one side of the lower section, and the white dryers on the other, and there were all these white wire carts that must be how the wet stuff gets to the dryers. I'd been in a public laundry a couple of times, and they had baskets like these, but usually they were all scattered around, like people just left them someplace when they were done with them. But not here. Any carts that weren't in use or waiting patiently next to a machine were pushed to- gether like grocery carts at the front of the store. Very neat, very orderly.

The dryer area had lots of long, white tables, and some kids were using them to hold things they were folding. Boys were doing sheets and towels toward the back, and at the front tables girls were folding clothes. Lots and lots of clothes.

I felt like I needed to giggle. Not wanted to; needed to. And I almost did. With all the white, including the white linoleum floor, the place seemed positively antiseptic. The kids all looked like so many little robots, all dressed in similar clothes, all with similar haircuts, all moving in this regular, automated motion. No one looked up, and no one talked. Some of them had yel- low stickers on their shoulders. Like me. Antiseptic white every- where, like a sterile toilet seat, with the occasional yellow spot of piss.

"You must be Taylor."

The voice startled me, and maybe saved me from giggling,

which probably would not have been a good idea. I turned toward the guy, the black guy who'd seen me come in, and opened my mouth, and he held up a hand. I nodded.

He took the paper from my hand. "I'm Sean. Come with me and I'll show you the ropes." He jerked his head sideways and led the way down to the lower level, while I, following behind, watched his ass. I couldn't help it. The guy was gorgeously built, muscles showing through his clothes as he moved.

He showed me the ropes, all right. Not that he needed to. I was put to work folding towels, which were—can you guess?—all white. Sean told me that after lunch I'd be learning how to run the washers. In my head I told him, Can't wait.

So I stood there on the white floor in front of the white table folding white towels, looking down at my work like all the other kids, except when I cheated and looked around. Not that it did me much good; what was there to see? Pretty soon, after spending some time contemplating how weird it was that a black kid with an Irish name was supervisor over this blindingly white environment, I began to zone out from boredom. I kept my mind occupied by humming one of the tunes Will and I like—the usual stuff about being in love, with a few references to, um, the physically enjoyable aspects, without getting too terribly explicit. But it also talks about touching souls. I could barely hear myself, though; the place was humming itself, what with all the machinery. I was thinking, just before the bell rang for lunch, that if I could do mindless stuff like this and keep my own thoughts, I might just make it through without incident.

At lunchtime, the quiet and coolness outside the laundry room were a bit of a shock.

Charles was watching for me, standing just outside the dining hall entrance. Was this normal behavior, I wondered? Not that there was much I could do about it. I couldn't complain even if I wanted to. But to tell the truth, I was actually kind of glad to see him. Since I couldn't talk to anyone, I couldn't make any connection with the other kids in the laundry room. And there were so many of us with yellow stickers that anyone who wasn't in SafeZone probably didn't talk out of—I dunno, maybe courtesy? Or maybe they'd been told not to talk at all so they wouldn't accidentally speak to one of us? Anyway, it was a relief to be with someone who had even the vaguest idea of who I was.

This time Charles took no chances about having trouble-makers sit with us. He steered us to a table with two guys already seated, and after he said grace for us, he introduced me to Hank and Sheldon. Sheldon had a yellow tag like mine, and when Charles introduced us and we nodded obligingly, he said that Sheldon was Hank's new roommate. So we were a matched set, though Hank seemed almost as humorless as Charles, so no one who could talk made any cracks about bookends.

Lunch conversation went from how great it had been to have Kelley—whoever she was—open up at Prayer Meeting last night about her sexual escapades with any boy or man she could get and how Jesus had led her to safety, to anticipation of the dinner on Friday. Hank, it seemed, had not convinced any girl to "ac-company" him, as they kept phrasing it, so I was thinking that he wouldn't be going. And, for that matter, that I wouldn't. But at some point Charles turned to Sheldon and me and explained that although Danielle would accompany him, everyone would go. He talked about it being a great time for Fellowshipping. Made me wonder why anyone would care about having a "com-panion." I mean, if you wanted to go someplace with a date, wouldn't you want a little quality time alone together? It made no sense to me. But I was new here. And, I reminded myself, Charles was gay—he had to be. So how much quality time would he want with a date named Danielle, anyway?

Sean pulled me aside as soon as I got back to the laundry room, and we went into the office just inside the entrance. He closed the door.

"Taylor, I need to coach you about something. This morning at the folding table, you were humming. Is that correct? Nod if it is."

Good thing he said to nod; I was about to say, Sure, so what? And then, How the hell did you know that, anyway?

"And the song you were humming had FI lyrics. Do you re-member what that is? From the Booklet?"

I had to think about that one. I wasn't quite sure what the FIs were all about, anyway. Former Images—what did that mean? I must have looked puzzled, 'cause Sean opened a drawer and pulled out a Bible. He flipped through to find the spot he wanted and read.

"Ephesians, chapter four, verse twenty: 'But you did not learn Christ that way; if indeed you heard him, and were taught in him, even as truth is in Jesus: that you put away, as concerning your former way of life, the old man, that grows corrupt after the lusts of deceit; and that you be renewed in the spirit of your mind, and put on the new man, who in the likeness of God has been created in righteousness and holiness of truth.'"

He set the Book down. "We all need to remember to leave our old selves behind. I'm sure you felt those songs were great in your former life, but they have no place here. They have no place in your new life, and they don't suit the new you. In fact they make it harder for you to come into your new life. They help trap you in the old one, the one you have to leave behind. So it's bad for you, and it's bad for others, too, to hear those songs. Do you understand?"

I should have nodded, I suppose. He'd made it clear enough what he'd meant. But instead I had to be a wise ass. I went over to the desk, found a pen and pad, and wrote, "I hear what you say."

Sean's teeth ground together. "Don't make this harder for both of us, Taylor. If you resist, it means I'll have to report you, and I don't want to do that. I hate doing that, do you understand?" He actually looked like he meant it. "Now, please, nod to let me know you'll stop. Please."

He looked almost desperate. I nodded. But then I wrote again. "How the—could they hear me in there?"

Sean obviously didn't know how to answer that one, so I scratched it out and wrote, "Who told you?"

Sean's eyes closed just for a second. "I can't tell you that. Now, come on. Let's go to the washers so I can show you how to use them."

So I had three hours before my "quiet time" to think about what had just happened. Someone who recognized that tune had ratted on me to Sean, who seemed like he didn't want to be the disciplinarian. Someone who must have been close enough to me to hear what I almost couldn't hear, myself, and close long enough to figure out what I was humming. I tried hard to conjure up the faces of the two guys who had been nearest me, but all I could remember was that one of them was short and had really black hair.

At break, around two thirty, we went in single file through a door in the back of the room that led out to an enclosed yard. There was a green roof over part of the yard, fiberglass I think, the kind with white swirly strings. Some of the kids who weren't wearing yellow tags talked to each other, but I was looking for Shorty. I mean, the short guy with the black hair. I felt like I wanted to punch his lights out, but when I saw him, I realized how pathetic that would have been. First, I wasn't sure it was him who'd ratted. Second, he was a pipsqueak. So instead I decided to find out more about him. I needed to believe that not everyone in this place was a rat, which meant that it would be really helpful to me if I knew which ones were which.

Slowly I made my way over to where he was kind of huddled into a corner, watching everyone else. I stood near him, which wasn't hard, since no one else did—not a good sign for him; it could mean everyone knows he's a rat and hates him. Then I started humming. Very quietly I began the tune from the "Battle Hymn of the Republic," which has at least seventeen different sets of alternative lyrics, ranging from silly to scatological. I watched Shorty out of the corner of my eye for any signs at all. If he hadn't ratted, he'd look puzzled. If he had, he'd look either guilty or defensive or both.

At first I wasn't sure he could even hear me, 'cause I couldn't catch a sign that anything had registered at all. So I started humming a little louder, in my head hearing lines like "We've wandered down the halls writing cuss words on the walls," and "Shot 'em up to heaven with an AK47."

Suddenly his hand flew up to cover his mouth, and this confused me enough that I looked right at him. He was laughing. Laughing! Like he was thinking in his head some of the raunchier lyrics and couldn't stop himself singing along silently. Well, this didn't seem like the reaction of someone who had just ratted on me for humming, so I grinned at him. He dropped his hand and grinned back.

Even though he didn't have a yellow sticker I couldn't talk to him because of mine, so I wandered away again before anyone wondered what was going on. I lost sight of him after that, until he wandered out toward the other end of the yard.

This little encounter brightened my whole afternoon. For the first half-hour I hummed for all I was worth, going over the "Battle Hymn" again and again, loudly enough that I was sure to be heard over the other noise in the room, until Sean finally came over to me, looking like he was trying not to grin.

He said, "Okay Taylor, that's enough. You're driving everyone around you crazy, you know." He squeezed my shoulder and said, really quietly, "You've made your point. Quit while you're ahead."

So I had to stop humming. Which meant I had to find some other way to occupy my mind, because otherwise I knew I was gonna be looking around trying to figure out who'd ratted on me. I looked around anyway, trying to identify something that would lead to other thoughts. And that happened in a way I really didn't want it to.

What came to me was thinking about Mom. It was the laundry room itself that did it, actually. Like I said, the laundry room at home is where she usually goes when something awful has happened, like when Dad got arrested a few years ago for getting into a fight at this beer joint he goes to some Friday nights. He hadn't started it; one of his buddies had. But when he tried to break it up, the thing escalated, and . . . well, he never was one to walk away from an injustice, as he saw it, or from a friend in need, as he probably would have seen it. So he got involved, and a whole bunch of them were hauled into jail for the night. Nothing came of it, but Mom spent quite a while in the laundry room that evening.

What hurt was that she'd freaked as much as Dad when I'd told them I was gay.

It had nearly made me crazy seeing Dad go over to Mom and put his hand on her shoulder, like he was making it them against me. 'Cause I don't believe she saw it like that. And I don't think she sees it like that now. I don't know if it has anything to do with being gay, but I've always felt closer to her than to Dad. Well, I suppose some of the reasons I might not feel close to him are obvious. The gruff approach to everything, the temper, the heavy-handed attitude toward anything that smacks of gay or veers in any way from the literal Word of God. I mean, I believe in God. And I read the Bible. It's just that . . . well, here comes Angela's voice again. If you don't have to make sense . . . And sometimes taking scripture literally just doesn't make sense. But to Dad, that makes no difference.

Mom's attitude toward everything is gentler. More reasonable. More . . . human, I guess. Sure, she's devout, she believes. She's saved. Maybe the difference is in the way they see God. Dad's God is this big, powerful guy who throws down justice in the form of punishment when he's disobeyed. The God Mom prays to is a loving God, a God who understands and forgives despite being just as strict about the rules. I like Mom's God better. And I've always liked being with her more than with Dad, probably for the same reasons.

Interesting. Dad's God acts like him, and Mom's acts like her. And here I'd thought God was supposed to have created us in his image, not the other way around. B,WDIK? For that matter, what does *anyone* know?

I was feeling pretty sorry for myself by four, when Sean called all the kids with yellow stickers—about eight of us—together toward the front of the room. The way he spoke you could just hear the capital letters. "It's Contemplation time for everyone in SafeZone. For many of you, this is your first Contemplation. If you have questions, please refer to your Booklet. It's a good time to write your MI and a good time to pray or read your Bible. And remember to leave the door to your room open at all times. Dinner is at six. See you all tomorrow."

So we all experienced for the second time that day the change from the warm, noisy room to the relative cool and near silence of the rest of the building. It felt like some kind of rite of passage, though what kind I couldn't have said. It was part relief, part emptiness.

My room felt kind of like that, too. I knew I was supposed to leave the door open, but I shut it part way anyway, just to see if anyone would notice. I had to leave an MI at Mrs. Harnett's office before dinner tonight, so I sat down at my desk to get that over with. What to write? "Struggles, thoughts, or temptations that have to do with sex, drugs, violence, or disobedience . . ."

Well, I could say that I'd been reprimanded about humming a song—no words, but even so—that had FI lyrics in it. That was true enough. But what were they going to do with this stuff after I wrote it? If Mrs. Harnett asked me whether I understood why that was wrong, what would I say?

"Well, idiot, you can't say anything, because you can't speak."

The sound of my own voice was kind of creepy. I hadn't heard more than a word of it in—well, for some time. I looked up at the half-open door to see if there was anyone out there who might have heard me talking to myself, but it didn't seem like it.

Anyway, I was wrong, because by the time we would sit down for another cozy little chat, Mrs. Harnett and I, it would be Thursday morning at ten and I'd be out of SafeZone. That is, unless I did something horrendous between now and then.

She'd said we'd review the MIs together. Something about my getting benefit from them, wasn't it? Ha. Benefit. And she'd called me a Resident. I felt more like an Inmate.

I allowed myself a loud sigh—no words in that—and started to write. I figured it would be a little unbelievable if I didn't write anything, and I'd get hell anyway. So I wrote about the bad words that had come into my head at various times since I'd been dumped off here. And I wrote that I'd been caught humming that tune. I also said that I'd tried to make up for it by switching to the "Battle Hymn" after Sean had yelled at me. And maybe it was a lie of omission, but I didn't put down that I'd been imagining the alternate lyrics.

Then I put down that I'd accidentally spoken aloud to myself in my room during Contemplation.

I was about to write something about how I understood why all these things were wrong and that I would repent, change my ways, but I decided to let her say that. It should make her feel like she was having some effect on me. Besides, there was enough untruth in the thing already. And I'd always prided myself in the past on telling the truth as much as possible.

But pride is a sin, no? I'd have written that down, but then I'd have had to say why I wasn't proud anymore, and that would've meant confessing that I had lied in my MI, and—man, what a freakin' complicated thing this is! And then I remembered one reason I'd always tried to stick to the truth. I wouldn't have to remember what I'd lied about, or what I'd said when I'd lied.

Thanks to my concentration on this ethical dilemma, I was barely aware of someone passing in the hall. Only after I couldn't hear footsteps anymore did my brain register that they had slowed a little as they passed my partly open door. And when I realized this, it made me angry. It seemed like they were spying on me. Some anonymous "they."

More on impulse than anything else I wrote: "I hate that writing this thing makes me want to lie. Lying is wrong. But I didn't mean to hum something forbidden. I just wanted to pass the time and I liked the melody. So I hated being reprimanded for it, and I wanted to lie by omission and not put it in. I don't blame Sean, or whoever turned me in, because they couldn't understand. And I couldn't help them understand, because I couldn't talk to them. So SafeZone makes things worse because I can't explain myself, and this 'exercise' (Mrs. Harnett's word) makes me want to lie about it."

I was kind of hoping this would confuse her. At least it would give her something relatively harmless to sink her teeth into, and maybe she wouldn't bug me for more.

So then I was done, the half-truth/half-lies sealed in the manila envelope Mrs. Harnett had given me, and I still had over an hour until dinner. I could read the Bible, I could pray, I could contemplate my sins. Or I could just sit here and feel alone.

I decided to contemplate my sins. Specific sins. Which was to say, times with Will. I'd made a pact with myself that I'd spend at least half an hour every day, even if it wasn't all thirty minutes together, thinking about him. And not just in passing. I hadn't really done that today, so maybe this would be a good time. Of course, there are certain dangers involved in thinking about Will. At least, in this place they're dangers. I glanced at the half-open door. Then I went and stood in it.

From the doorway, there were certain spots in the room I couldn't see. One spot, of course, was behind the door, but that was on Charles's side of the room. The other place that I couldn't really see, not very well at least, was the near corner to the left of the door. The room was just big enough that I had to step into it before I could see into that corner. Plus my desk was in the way.

I took the folded blanket from the foot of my bed and set it on the floor almost in the corner. I grabbed a handful of tissues from the box on my desk. Then I put my desk chair right into the corner, and I knelt on the blanket with my elbows on the seat of the chair. It was the position Charles had assumed when he was going to pray last night, and I'd done it, too. So I knelt there, facing the corner like some naughty kid doing time-out, thinking of Will.

Will.

I closed my eyes. I must have looked very penitent with my brow going into knots as I imagined running my fingers down the side of his naked body, seeing the wicked grin on his face that turned slowly into something else, his mouth and eyes half-open as my hand explored other parts of him. With my other hand, the one not touching Will, I undid my belt—only not just in my imagination. I stopped and listened carefully, then undid the button. Oh so slowly I pushed the zipper down, tooth by anxious tooth, until I was touching both of us—me and Will, at least in my mind—one hand for each.

My ears strained for anything like a quiet footfall, a voice in the distance, the creak of a door. Nothing. I bent my head. And I pulled.

Fortunately I'd gotten very good at keeping quiet doing this at home. It's true my breathing was a little—well, raspy. But other than that, the only thing I heard was in my mind, when Will came, that rich "ah" sound he makes at the very end. And a little grunt of my own. I gritted my teeth and clamped my lips shut so I would be as silent as possible.

I got the tissues into position just in time.

That had hardly taken half an hour, so I had the luxury of kneeling there for a while longer, eyes still closed, picturing Will's sleepy eyes, his smile languid with satisfaction and affection. For me.

Elbows on the chair seat again, head bent against my hands, I resumed a prayerful attitude. "Please, Will," I begged in a whisper, "don't forget me. Don't give up on me. I'll be with you again." I swear I felt something on my lips. Like he had kissed me.

Kissing Will. I thought of the first time we'd kissed. Now, don't get me wrong; I wouldn't give up my first kiss with Will— or what happened afterward—for anything. But once we got back to school, we had to act like nothing had happened. Straight couples have this whole scene they can get to know each other in. Dates, dances, mixers, parties—it goes on and on. They get to have their first kisses in as romantic a situation as they want, and then they get to talk about it. Not us.

My friend Nina Stern came running to me every time she had a new boyfriend, or any time she thought maybe she was going to. But do you think for one minute I could go running to her with stories about Will? And all over school you could tell when some new couple was forming. The kids who went to my church were a little more reserved about it, but even with them you could tell. Between the googly eyes and sitting as close together as possible in the cafeteria, the hetero couples were all over the place. So sweet. So cute. So infuriating.

I didn't begrudge them their happiness. Well, maybe just a little, because after all, weren't they begrudging me mine?

Will was brave. He smiled at me, at least, whenever he saw me. But you didn't catch us holding hands as we walked down the hallway. Hell, you didn't even see us walk down the hallway together.

All that next day in school, after that first kiss, I could barely pay attention to what was going on in my classes. I kept wondering what gay couples do to arrange their next nondate. Should I call Will? Would he call me? If he didn't call me in a few days, was that a bad sign, or was he just being cautious? We'd exchanged cell phone numbers before he left my bedroom the night before, so calling was an option. But would it be a reality?

The test in World History, of course, was the hardest part of a difficult day, because Will was *right there*. I could almost feel his tongue in my mouth.

The teacher asked Will to collect all the papers at the end, and as he was coming down my row I looked up at his face. He was smiling at me. Something welled up in my chest, and I couldn't trust myself not to do something really stupid, so I closed my eyes until he was past. After that, the challenge was to catch my breath and adjust my jeans.

I was on the bus on the way home when my cell rang. Will's number! "Hello?" My hand was shaking, and it wasn't just the bouncing from the bus's lousy suspension.

"Hey! Where are you?"

"On the bus."

"Why?"

"What?"

Silence. I checked my signal; still okay. Then, "Didn't you get my note?"

My silence now. Note? "What note?"

"You goof. I dropped it onto your desk when I picked up your paper in History. I was gonna try and sneak it to you after class, but then I got that opportunity."

"I didn't see it. What did it say?"

"I asked if you wanted to go and watch the football team practice. More homoerotic subtexts out on the field than in *Ben Hur* and *Lord of the Rings* put together. I'm here at school, waiting for you."

"Oh . . ."

He laughed. "Look, never mind. Next time. Call me after dinner. Say, nine-ish?"

I tore into my messenger bag for any sign of the note, irritating the hell out of the guy next to me in that cramped space. Finally, toward the bottom of the bag, I saw it.

Meet me by the bulletin board EOD and come watch boys being boys. CUL.
—W

Green ink. CUL. See you Later.

Repacking my bag, I forced myself to stay calm. It wasn't like I'd missed another make-out session, after all. We would have been no freer to make moony eyes or hold hands on the bleachers than inside the school. But I would have been with Will. God, but I was pissed.

I called him that night, and we talked. And talked. We went over the test, and it seemed I hadn't done too badly after all. And then we talked about us.

I told him how upsetting it was that we couldn't be ourselves. That we had to hide who we really are, what we really are to each other, from everyone.

"Well," he said, "not everyone."

"Yeah? Like who? Who can we be honest with?"

His voice took on a funny edge. Like he was teasing me or something. "What about your friend Nina?"

"What about her?"

"I can't believe you haven't told her you're gay."

"Will, I haven't told anyone I'm gay." With a shock, I realized that was true; I'd never said the words out loud before. "And why would I tell her?"

"Isn't she a good friend?"

"Yeah, so . . ."

"She knows I am."

"What?"

"Calm down. I didn't say anything about you, silly. I'd never out someone else. But she doesn't go to our church. And she's cool. She's got no problem with my being gay."

Well, no, she didn't go to our church. She's Jewish. "How did you . . . When did you . . . I didn't even know you knew her!"

"We live next door to each other."

Holy crap. Will lives right next door to Nina? It wasn't like I'd been to her house a lot. We didn't want her kid brother to start thinking we were an item and making a pest of himself. But still . . .

I took a shaky breath. "Okay. I'll think about it."

"Ty? I just want you to know I loved being with you last night. I hope you're still feeling good about it, too."

"I loved being with you, too. And I still feel frigging wonderful."

"So, we could do it again sometime?"

"Sure. Wanna come over now?"

I loved the sound of his laugh. "I wish. Tell you what. Can you hold the phone in one hand?"

It took me a nanosecond to figure out what he was headed for. "Let me lock my door."

Phone sex. I'd never had phone sex. Hell, I'd never had any sex, really, before last night. This guy was opening my world. And I have to say that although I preferred his hand on me, when his "ah" sounded right in my ear it was still great.

Before we hung up, I asked, "What's with the green ink?"

"My signature color. It helps me to remember to take chances. To keep going forward, like a green light. To try new things and open myself to new ideas. And always to do it my way. You like?"

"I love. Yeah."

"Good night, Ty."

"'Night."

It had felt like he'd kissed me that night, too.

Once or twice as I knelt there—after my ministrations, that is—I heard someone walking by in the hall. When I finally got up, there was no sign of anyone, and of course I couldn't know if anyone looked in on me. But if they had, all they'd have seen was my back bent over the chair.

The wastebasket next to my desk seemed the best place for the used tissues, so I dropped them in. Blanket back on the bed, chair back at the desk, I sat down and opened my Bible.

But the words just blurred in front of me, running together, no meaning to them. I sat there staring at nothing for a minute before I realized I had to take a leak. Was I allowed to do that during Contemplation? I couldn't remember seeing any rules about that, so I left the Bible on my desk and went down the hall.

I couldn't have been gone more than three or four minutes tops, but when I got back to the room, there was Charles. He stood there, his face a weird combination of anger, pain, and something that looked like betrayal. He was holding my wastebasket.

Shit.

I stopped in the doorway and waited for him to say something. When he didn't, I acted like I didn't know already what he'd found. I shrugged like I was asking, "What's your problem?"

Anger won. "Don't pretend with me," he said, nearly snarling. "You know very well what I found in here." He held the wastebasket at arm's length in my direction and shook it.

Jesus. He must have held the tissues to his face and smelled them; how else would he know what was on them? And he obviously knew what was on them. I shrugged again. This time it said, "Whatever." I walked toward my desk while he rotated in place to follow me, the basket still held out. I picked up a pad and pen and scrawled, "Enjoy yourself?"

Even as I held it up to him I knew it was a stupid thing to do. I should have apologized, cried even, anything to make him feel I understood the need for contrition. He looked as though he wanted to throw the wastebasket, but instead he walked back to where it had stood before he snooped into it and set it firmly down onto the floor.

He said, "I see you've already sealed your MI. Did you include this—this episode—in it?"

I just stared at him. No answer. No head motions.

"You must open it again. You must confess this infraction."

His eyes and mine entered into this battle of wills. Then I reached for the pen again and I wrote, "This is *my* Contemplation time. You're supposed to leave me alone. So leave me alone. Go away."

This was true enough, and Charles knew it. He shouldn't even have been in the room. Come to think of it, why had he come here, anyway? Sure, it was his room, too, but the resident in SafeZone has two hours of solitary Contemplation in his or her room that are not supposed to be interrupted except by someone in Leadership. (See? I'm getting the hang of this.) Strictly speaking, Charles was just another resident.

His eyes shot darts at me before he turned on his heel and left. From over his shoulder I could barely hear the words, "Don't forget to bring your Bible to Prayer Meeting tonight."

That's it, Charles. Stay on message, whatever you do. However angry you are.

I went back to my Bible, looking up in the concordance section things like *spy* (Galatians 2:4: "This was because of the false brothers secretly brought in, who stole in to spy out our liberty which we have in Christ Jesus, that they might bring us into bondage") and *observe* (Isaiah 42:20: "You see many things, but don't observe"), and *betray* (Proverbs 11:13: "One who brings gossip betrays a confidence, but one who is of a trustworthy spirit is one who keeps a secret").

This was amusing but not terribly instructive. I've had to admit in the past, and again now, that using the concordance at times like this may lead me to something really true and painful, something that stabs directly at a sin and sears into me like a hot poker, but mostly it's just a way for me—or anyone, really—to find what I want to find, to prove my own point. It takes things out of context and lets me apply my own interpretation.

So I gave that up and, feeling a little sinful and self-indulgent, I turned to the Song of Songs and imagined myself with Will again. No tissues this time; it was just love.

Chapter 3

Yes, a sword will pierce through your own soul, that the thoughts of many hearts will be revealed.

—Luke 2:35

At around five minutes of six, I left the room and headed toward Mrs. Harnett's office. The basket was there, as were several other MIs from other residents. I added mine and went to the dining hall.

Again—and I almost could have predicted this—Charles stood there at the entrance, watching for me. It was as though he was saying, "This isn't over. You can't get rid of me that easily."

Fine. Whatever.

Dinner was silent. Charles led us to a table where two guys in SafeZone were already seated. I wanted to ask them, my tongue in my cheek, "Where are your escorts? You see I've brought mine."

No trouble finding my way to Fellowship tonight, since Charles wasn't letting me out of his sight. Fellowship was in the huge open room that Charles had shown me yesterday. No furniture. No chairs. Everyone just milled around, talking, and the din was unbelievable. After listening to a few conversations as Charles dragged me around from clutch to clutch of intensely chattering residents, it dawned on me why it was so loud. And it wasn't an acoustical phenomenon due to architecture. It was that everyone was talking loudly. What I noticed was that the more inane, forced, and desperate the conversation, the louder it was.

So there was one guy who was going on at fever pitch about this verse he'd discovered new meaning in, and I was so overwhelmed by his enthusiasm that I missed what the verse actually was. But I got that he considered the revelation to have been one of life-altering proportions for him. One girl wanted everyone to know that another resident had chastised her for some miniscule infraction of behavior, or attitude, or something, and how humbled she was, and how much she had learned as a result of the other girl's courage and insight.

I began to wonder what I would find to say in this crowd once I was out of SafeZone. Then I realized that maybe I wouldn't have to say anything, that everyone else would be so focused on getting their own story out that I wouldn't have to "Fellowship" in an active way. Just listen. Passive. A pair of understanding, compassionate ears. Probably I'd be able to carry that off indefinitely. At one point I nearly started to giggle, most inappropriately, as some guy was describing something unutterably wonderful and enlightening that he'd just realized this morning, when I speculated that if I wore a yellow sticker on my shoulder and stuck to corners of the Fellowship room where I wasn't known, I could get away with doing precious little at all. I stowed the idea away for future consideration. Of course, they might take my sheet of yellow labels away from me.

Something magical happened after we'd been in there half an hour. There was no bell. I didn't hear anyone call for attention. Nothing. But everyone stopped talking almost at once and said goodbye to the people they'd been yammering at, and they left. Charles, who hadn't let me get more than a couple of feet from him the whole time, led me out the door and on to Isaiah. I wasn't sure—in fact, I didn't have a clue—who would be in our group, other than Charles and me, and probably Jessica and Marie, given what they'd said at breakfast.

As it turned out, our group included about twenty kids, including Shorty. I looked right at him as he was heading for a chair across the room from me, wondering if he'd smile or

what. But he looked right through me, as if he hadn't been re-
duced to giggles at break this afternoon by my effrontery and
his own unexpressed irreverence. Jessica and Marie were there
as well, of course. And from where Charles and I stood—dead
center at the very front—I had to turn and look around to see
that there were three other kids in SafeZone, including Sheldon, who was by a chair about as far away from the front of the
room as he could get. I figured Hank must be here as well, but
he wasn't next to Sheldon. I looked around and finally saw
Hank in the row behind me and off to the side. So it would
seem there was no rule about hanging with your new roomie,
despite Charles's irritating tenacity.

Mrs. Harnett had told me she was our group leader, but even
so, it surprised me somehow to see her there, sitting in a larger
chair than ours (enthroned, perhaps?). At least our chairs
weren't in neat little rows. They were in a kind of semicircle,
facing the throne.

I started to sit, but Charles's hand shot out and caught my
arm. "We wait for the ladies to sit." Jeez. Guess I'd forgotten
that part of the Booklet. I looked around. There were three
girls standing off to one side of the seating area, chatting. Most
of the other "ladies" were seated, including Mrs. Harnett, but
all the guys were standing. A couple of them were talking, but
most of the guys were at some kind of casual attention in front
of their chairs, hands clasped over their crotches, waiting.

Finally Mrs. Harnett stood and clapped her hands once. The
talking petered out pretty quickly, and when all the girls were
sitting, Mrs. Harnett resumed her throne. And then all the guys
sat at once. It was eerie.

Charles leaned toward me. "Mrs. Harnett might stand again
when she talks, but we don't have to. Watch me for a cue when
we need to stand again."

Sure enough, Mrs. Harnett stood. I wasn't feeling particularly well-disposed toward Charles, but I thanked him silently
anyway.

"Brothers and sisters in Christ Jesus," our fearless leader
began, "we will bow our heads in a prayer of thanksgiving."

So we did, and—silly me—I thought it would be a moment of silent prayer. But no.

"Almighty God, Jesus our Savior, we are humble before you. We are grateful for everything you have done for us, everything you have given us. And we know that if you gave us only pleasure, only joy, we would not learn what we need to learn to be worthy of your grace. So we thank you for the challenges, for the difficulties, for the pain, for the sorrow. And we thank you for your patience, your forbearance, your limitless presence in our lives. We thank you for helping us to be worthy of the ultimate joy that exists only in you."

She sort of had me. I could identify with everything she'd said. And I was ready for the "amen." But she wasn't.

"Merciful Father, open the hearts of everyone in this room. We are sinners, every one of us. Help us to see that, and help us to put behind us the things that tempt us into sin. Some are tempted by things that alter our consciousness, by drugs and drink that pull us into evil and make us do Satan's bidding. For some it's Inappropriate Love [my capitals this time], whether for a boy or a girl, a man or a woman, that takes us away from your intended life for us and into a pit devoted only to earthly pleasure. For some it's the exhilaration of disobedience, of stealing, of flaunting the authority of those you have put in charge over us. There seems to be no end of ways we can find to sin. We are grateful that there is also no end to your forgiveness. And we understand that this forgiveness is granted only to those who truly repent. To those of us who confess our faults, our temptations, our misdeeds, and earnestly vow to take a new path. A path to holiness. A path to you.

"We pray that you forgive the sins we are about to confess, that your patience and love will hold us up as we strive to be worthy."

Long pause.

"Amen."

Inappropriate Love, indeed. From inside my head I yelled, My love for Will is not inappropriate! All right, she hadn't been very specific, but I knew damn well what she meant.

I couldn't quite tell whether this sort of all-inclusive prayer was something she spouted off at the start of every Prayer Meeting or whether she was improvising. It sounded practiced, but it also sounded spontaneous. I know this seems conflicting. It is. When I heard her again the next night, I learned that although the themes didn't vary much, the words did. I give the lady credit; she came up with something fresh—at least relatively fresh—every night I heard her pray.

Everyone raised their heads up again, although I noticed Charles didn't. He was still looking at the floor. Mrs. Harnett sat down again and said, "We have three new penitents in our group this week. Let's welcome them. Taylor Adams, please stand."

I wasn't prepared for this. Should have been, probably. I stood, penitent or not. In unison, everyone around me chanted, "Welcome, Taylor. We love you." I said my own tiny prayer of gratitude that I was in SafeZone and so could not be expected to reply to that. It would have gotten me into trouble. Maybe *that's* what SafeZone is all about?

"Sheldon Wainwright, please stand."

Sheldon, way in the back, shuffled to his feet and then stared fixedly down at them.

"Welcome, Sheldon. We love you."

"Monica Moon, please stand."

Monica Moon? With a name like that, no wonder she'd ended up in here. A girl about fifty pounds overweight, long dark hair kind of stringing around her face, heaved out of her chair and looked anything but penitent. I thought I remembered seeing her in the laundry room earlier, but I wasn't working near where the girls were. Maybe she couldn't speak, but her expression said plenty. I felt a certain kinship with her immediately. What had I looked like when I'd stood? I kind of hoped it was a lot like her—impenitent. Minus the extra weight.

"Welcome, Monica. We love you."

I expected another introduction, with three kids besides me wearing yellow stickers. But no one else was asked to stand. I looked around for the fourth kid, a guy, looking comatose. Or autistic. He was actually rocking back and forth in his chair, staring at the floor. At first I had no clue who he was, but then I remembered something Charles had said at breakfast, something about Leland being in SafeZone. "Again." Could this be the famous Leland? What had he done?

Mrs. Harnett smiled at everyone in the room, one at a time. It took nearly a minute. And she must have noticed that Charles was still looking at his hands, clasped in his lap. She said, "Brother Charles, you seem troubled. Tell us what's in your heart tonight."

Charles didn't start, he didn't snap to attention, he didn't budge. He must have expected this. In fact, I wondered if he'd deliberately planted himself at center front and then set about to look as distracted as possible so he'd be called on. At any rate, that's how things happened.

"I need forgiveness" was all he said at first.

"Tell us why."

At first Charles just took a couple of shaky breaths and fidgeted with his fingers, but our Fearless Leader waited with saintly patience until he went on.

"I have broken a Program Rule [my capitalization again; I'm getting good at this]." And he stopped again.

The Saint prodded. "Which rule, Charles?" Her voice was gentle but insistent.

"I interrupted the very first Contemplation of my new roommate Taylor." He took a breath before he could go on. As for me, it nearly stopped my breathing. He looked up at the throne. "His very first one! It was his time, his own time, for reflecting on how he came to be here, on what he needs to learn, for understanding what things will help him and what things will hold him back. I was overwhelmed by the temptation to check on him. I—I confess my own lack of faith."

Holy shit. (Demerit be damned.) Charles was confessing his violation of my privacy! Where would he go next? Is he going to talk about what he found when he committed this "interruption"? I was really holding my breath by now.

Mrs. Harnett was nodding. Then, "And what do you think led you to lose faith, Charles? What was preying on your mind?"

More finger fidgeting. "I think it means I'm still too attached to my own failure." He closed his eyes, and for a second I thought I saw something fall. A tear was the only thing I could think of, but his voice didn't sound like he was crying. "I haven't been successful in turning over to God what happened to Ray. I've held onto it."

No one else was breathing either, I swear. At least, that's how quiet it was in the room. Then Mrs. Harnett, obviously knowing the answer but wanting him to say it, asked, "And what happened to Ray?"

Honest to God, I saw him shudder. But he went on bravely. "He took his life. He overstepped the limits of Free Will. He lost ultimate faith."

Whoa! Was he telling me that the last guy to sleep in my bed, use my desk, had *killed* himself? The shock almost made me miss the Saint's next question.

"And how does this concern you?"

Eyes still closed, it was obvious now that he really was crying. His breath was catching oddly as he went on. "He was my roommate. And I took too much responsibility upon myself. And he's gone." The word *gone* was almost inaudible.

"Did *you* lose him, Charles?"

"No."

"Did you falter in your determination, in your own thinking or acting?"

"No."

"How have you sinned?"

"In my lack of faith."

"Go on."

He took a deep breath, a shaky one, but it seemed to help. He snuffled, and opened his eyes. "I did everything I could to help Ray remain steadfast. I loved him. I set a good example for him. But I wasn't enough. I tried so hard, like I was trying to do God's job. I took on myself the things that are God's to do. And when Ray was lost, I blamed myself."

"And who else?"

"What?"

"Who else do you blame?"

Charles blinked. "No one."

"Not Ray?"

"No! Ray was lost. He couldn't be blamed, not by me, not for anything."

"Not Leland?"

Several kids turned to look at the unfortunate fourth in our SafeZone club. So that was Leland.

"No. Not Leland. I can't blame Leland for his weaknesses. It's not my place to judge."

Weakness? There was some kind of weakness of Leland's that had to do with Ray? You know where my mind went; they must have been lovers. Or wanted to be. Whatever. And my breakfast companion Marie had done something that—according to what Charles had said this morning—was in Leland's best interests, whether Leland agreed that it was nor not. But what?

The Saint already knew what it was, of course; it was old news to her. So she went on pinning Charles to the floor. Wall. Cross. Whatever it was he was begging to be pinned to. She said, "Do you blame God?"

Silence. Now, this was interesting. Everyone seemed to think so, for now all eyes were back on Charles. There was a tense moment, and then Charles was out of his chair and on his knees. "Jesus, Savior, forgive me!"

Holy shit. I'm not repeating myself. I'm not repeating myself.

I had started listening to this little confession of Charles's thinking it was all about me. It wasn't about me at all. It was about my role, though. My role as the gay roommate of Charles Courtney.

And suddenly it was all about me again.

"Taylor, come forward, please." The voice from the throne.

In a trance, I moved toward her.

She handed me a pad and pen she had reached for after I'd stood up, and said, "What would you like to say to Charles?"

I wrote, "I'm not Jesus. Charles isn't talking to me," and Mrs. Harnett read it aloud.

"Does Jesus work through us, Taylor? Nod or shake your head."

Nod. Of course he does.

"Then what would you say to Charles?"

I looked at Charles, who had raised his wet face to look at me. I knew what he wanted to hear. Or see. But I had a question first. I wrote, "What happens if you fail with me, too?" Mrs. Harnett read this silently and gave me, I swear, a look of interested respect. Or maybe it was concern; how many suicides could there be in her group before she got into trouble? Kinda gives a new meaning to *Straight to God.* Anyway, she read it aloud for Charles.

Charles started to speak, had to stop, and started again. "I would pray for guidance. I would pray for the strength to lean on Jesus. I would ask God to show me what to do and what not to do. I would pray for the safekeeping of your soul and know that I can't provide that for you."

One side of my brain was thinking, What a drama queen. The other was thinking, I've misjudged him. He's really sincere. He really believed that prayer he prayed last night, the one thanking God for me. He meant it. He was goddamned fucking honest. And he desperately needs a second chance.

I was still staring at him when Mrs. Harnett asked me, "Is there something else you'd like to say to Charles?" She held the pad out to me and I took it.

I wrote, "If I were Jesus, I would forgive you."

She looked at it but didn't read it aloud. "Take it to him," she said.

I walked back to where Charles was still kneeling on the floor. He read it and started sobbing. He stood up and wrapped me in his arms and dropped tears all over my shoulder.

WTF? I mean, What The Fuck? (Which is worse—IM or what it means?) What am I supposed to do with this?

What *could* I do? I hugged him back. Everyone in the room stood up and started clapping. I heard, "Praise the Lord!" and "Thank you, Jesus!" and "Amen!" It was like being at a revival, or at least the way I'd always imagined a revival would be. And I have a little confession of my own to make. It felt great.

Hell, it felt fucking fantastic. Before I knew it, I was getting a little misty. Not sobbing like my new best friend Charles, but still . . . I don't remember who pulled away first; not sure it matters, anyway. But I do remember being on such a high that I had a hard time focusing on anything that was said, by anyone, for several minutes afterward. Everyone turned in their Bibles to the different places the Saint called out, and she asked some kids to read, but I couldn't tell you what the verses were. My own thoughts kept preempting the regular programming. They ran something like this:

1. Charles turned himself in.
2. Charles *didn't* turn *me* in.
3. The Saint didn't ask him if he'd seen anything worth interrupting, or even if he'd had a reason to suspect that he would.
4. Charles has a trustworthy spirit; Proverbs says so.
5. The Saint might just be okay.

When I started listening once again, a girl was standing, reading from her Bible. I had been able to focus just well enough to turn to the references the Saint had been calling out, so I was open to Hebrews. She was reading chapter 4, starting at verse 12, the one about the sword of God being sharp enough to divide soul and spirit, not to mention bones, joints, and other unmentioned body parts. The sword knows our thoughts, actions, attitudes—it knows what's in our hearts, and we can't hide anything from it. In fact, it leaves us cut open in a way that lets those we might have injured see into our hearts as well.

I was sort of familiar with this text, but I'd never really understood this bit. I mean, what's the difference between soul and spirit? How can the two be divided? And as for a sword being able to judge . . . It was some kind of metaphor, I'd figured that out. But it all seemed kind of jumbled.

The girl who'd been reading sat down again, and the Saint let several seconds go by before she said, "All of these verses we've just been listening to can help us to understand what Charles is going through. But I think these verses from Hebrews are the clearest. Who would like to offer their thoughts?"

Marie, the girl from breakfast, raised her hand. The Saint called on her, and Marie said, "God saw that Charles's faith was too focused on himself. On what he thought he could do on his own. So he had Charles break a Program Rule that affected Taylor. Then God's sword cut into Charles so that everyone could see what was wrong."

I hated what Marie said. In fact, I was getting to hate Marie. She'd tried like hell at breakfast to get at Charles, and she was at it again. It was like she needed to cut him down to her size.

The Saint smiled in a knowing kind of way and asked the group, "Could this have had such an effect on Charles if his heart had not been open?" No one said anything. I had to stand up for him. I raised my hand.

The Saint blinked at me. "Taylor, you're in SafeZone. You can't take an active role in the discussion this evening."

What the hell had I been doing before, then, during the "Charles Tells All" routine? I picked up the pad of paper, still at my feet from before, and held it aloft.

Such a sad smile she gave me. "I'm sorry, Taylor. We can't allow that. It was necessary to call on you earlier for Charles's sake. That was a decision I made. But it was an exception. Anyone else?"

I didn't know whether I was more confused or more hurt. Here I'd been thinking this was all about love and connection and good will, but I'm obviously not to be included in all that wonderfulness. I'm on the outside.

I decided what I felt was anger. I barely heard the Saint call the name Nate, but when everyone turned to look at him, I turned with them. I almost didn't; I mean, if I was ostracized, then I may as well just go sit at the back of the room, and I was thinking of doing just that. But before I could decide, Nate started to talk. And when I turned, I realized it was Shorty. From the laundry room.

"God's sword is part of God. And when we invite God into our lives, the sword comes, too. If we don't know that at the start, it isn't long before we figure it out. Because we get cut by it. And we don't always know where it's likely to cut, because we can't always see into our own hearts as clearly as God does. Some people shut themselves away from God when they get cut because they thought it was going to be all sweetness and light and it isn't."

"Do you think Charles will turn away?"

Nate shook his head. "No. Charles wants to be cut." Most of the kids giggled nervously. Perhaps Charles had a reputation for spiritual masochism? Nate looked around and smiled. "I guess that sounded funny. What I mean is, he wants God to cut away anything that isn't righteous. And the fact that Taylor forgave him will encourage him to keep his heart open."

Well. Shorty may like ribald lyrics, but he's also a mean hand at applying scripture. And maybe at understanding Charles. Charles wanted to be righteous, that's certain, and he was trying to be just that when he interrupted my Contemplation. But if I understood Shorty, Charles himself didn't know at the time that it was actually lack of faith that made him interrupt me. So in comes God with his sword to cut Charles open.

Was that me? Was I God's sword? I mean, I'd reminded him what the Program Rule was. I'd practically accused him of sniffing my cum-covered tissues, too.

And then I'd forgiven him.

Maybe Jesus really does work through us. I'd meant that nod earlier, but it was mostly pro forma, something I'd been told and hadn't really questioned. Now it seemed real.

Other people were talking but I wasn't listening. Again. I was still staring at Shorty. I'm not sure when he realized it, but finally he looked back at me. And winked. And then smiled. And then turned to look at whoever was speaking.

Okay, so what was that all about? It was almost like he was letting me know he didn't take any of this seriously. But I was taking it very seriously. And he must have meant what he'd said. It made so much sense. And it was so true.

Now I was really confused. I felt like I was on some kind of roller-coaster ride. One minute I'm isolated and can't communicate, the next I'm in the middle of a really moving little scene, then I'm isolated again. Then I'm really getting high on this idea that I'd been used by God to help Charles, mostly because of what Shorty said, and then Shorty winks at me and takes me down from that spiritual height again. Somewhere in the back of my mind I realized I was still thinking of him as Shorty, but I wasn't yet convinced he deserved any better.

Suddenly I needed to know how the other SafeZone kids were feeling. As soon as I could do it without sticking out like a sore thumb, I glanced at Monica Moon. She had this look on her face like, "I hate this. I don't want to be here. I don't want to know what any of these people think, and I refuse to listen to what they say. I hate everything. And maybe everyone."

Sheldon's expression, when I could look at him, was like, "Please get me through this. Help me survive."

Getting a chance to stare at Leland was more of a challenge. No one around him was saying anything, so the group didn't turn his way. It wasn't until the end of the session that I got my chance. And I didn't know what to make of it. He was still rocking in his chair, even though everyone else had stood up, but he wasn't staring into space. He was looking at Shorty. And somehow I knew that Shorty knew it. In fact, as I watched, on his way toward the door to leave, Shorty walked behind Leland. With the smallest gesture, he barely raised his hand and laid it, just for a second, on Leland's shoulder. Half of Leland's mouth twitched into a smile.

On the way back to our room, I was feeling pretty overwhelmed. I'd seen and felt so many conflicting things that I was falling back into that place where, like, nobody was real. Nobody was honest. I couldn't count on anybody to be what they seemed to be.

Except maybe Charles. Just outside our doorway, he stopped and turned to me. He extended his hand for me to shake, so I did, and he said, "Thank you."

Yup. Masochist. Righteous. But honest about it. All I could do was nod.

Christ! I wanted to talk to Will so badly! He has this wit, this quirky way of looking at things, that ties everything together. Here, the good and the bad, the serious and the funny, all seem to be sharply divided. It's like there's a time for this and a time for that, and don't mix them.

Will mixes them. Will can talk about serious stuff, but something about the way he brings lightness into it makes it go in that much deeper. He's all about connection, not separation. And, man, did I feel separated.

Back in the room I sat at my desk and leaned on my folded arms. Behind me I heard Charles say, "I'm going to the bathroom. You should come now so you won't be in there alone."

I lifted my head and stared at him, trying to project what I was thinking: "You're overdoing things again, Charles. You're not responsible for me, or for the kids who don't look for a yellow sticker before they talk to me."

He must have gotten it. He shrugged and left. And I leaned my head on my arms again.

I was beginning to get this SafeZone thing. On the one hand, it was a kind of protection. I wasn't expected to know what to say or not to say, or to understand yet what all the little unwritten rules were. Not talking had kept me from being embarrassed sometimes, but more important it'd kept me from saying some things I'd regret. Things I'd get into trouble for.

On the other hand, I was getting a good taste of what it would feel like to be ostracized. Isolated. Remember that? It was supposed to be the worst consequence for behavioral violations. And I'd thought I knew what it was. In a way, I do; being gay is its own form of isolation. But unless you do something really queer, or unless someone's shouting that word at you or beating you up for it, it's quiet. Unspoken. You can hide from it. Pretend it isn't happening, or that it isn't real, or convince yourself that you could decide to change it by changing yourself. You can pretend you're one of the "normal" people.

Not here. Gay or not, you wear this sticker and you're isolated. You can't communicate with anyone, you've got to just take what anyone gives you. It's like you're not really there, or not really important. You're someone whose opinions don't matter. Whose thoughts and feelings no one wants to know.

But then I thought, "If I got expelled from this place, how

could they ostracize me?" I considered my life outside this prison. Who would ostracize me? My parents? There are worse things than that.

But I knew that wasn't true. That would be terrible. I hadn't allowed myself to think about it so far, but if I let my thoughts go in that direction, I knew that underneath, I was homesick. My mom is one of the sweetest women alive. And since her God is like her, it's almost like I miss God as much as I miss her. And my dad—well, he's gruff, no doubt there; look how hard he's been on me. And like his God, he's a little narrow-minded about some things, but I could do a lot worse than him. Who else? I supposed Dr. Strickland could tell everyone in my church to ostracize me.

So I wouldn't go to church.

But what if he told my teachers and the kids at school why I was in the Program, and how evil I am? There are only a few kids who know I'm gay. Like Nina.

After Will had told me she knew about him, I'd figured I should tell her about me. YR. Easier said than done. I even went so far as to ask her to go out for sodas with me one Saturday afternoon, and she turned it into a whole mall thing, which was fine with me, but when we finally sat down in the food court, it was all wrong. I mean, it felt wrong to say it there, in that mecca of American standardization, which definitely does not include being gay. I tried to. I really did. But after the third or fourth time I looked around to see if anyone I knew was nearby, Nina said, "Taylor, what's with you? You're acting kinda weird today."

I just shook my head. "Nothing. I'm okay. Anything else you need before we split?"

It ate at me that I hadn't told her. I've known Nina since . . . jeez, since elementary school, I guess. She knew everything else about me by now. And yet this one thing, this really really really important thing, I was keeping from her. Didn't I trust her? She'd been cool with Will; why was I worried?

I finally realized that my problem was that although the words "I'm gay" had just come spilling out of me to Will, that had been easy, because he's never known me any other way. And that would have made it easy for Nina to accept him as gay, because since he was new here, she didn't have a history with him. So whatever he told her just went into the pile of data she was still collecting about him.

She'd already collected all the important stuff about me. So what would she do, what would she say, what would happen to our friendship, if all of a sudden the entire platform underneath all the other stuff she knew about me turned out to be— I don't know, maybe round instead of square? Maybe oak instead of plastic? Would it shift all the stuff that was sitting on that platform?

A few nights later I called her. I didn't plan it. I'd just gotten off the phone with Will, and we'd had phone sex again, and— God, but everything about him felt so fucking *right*—I knew I couldn't lie to Nina anymore. And I couldn't call her my best friend and have her think false things about me. Especially really important things.

"Hey, Taylor! D'you need help with math homework?"

I often did. It wasn't my best subject. "Sweet of you, kid. But no. I, uh . . . I need to get all serious on you." It sounded stupid, but if I didn't do something to let her know more was coming, I'd never get to that "more." We'd start chatting about our usual stuff, and I'd crap out like I'd done at the mall.

"Ooh, sounds heavy. Should I sit up?"

"Up to you. But don't stand up yet."

Silence. Then, "Are you okay, Taylor? Nothing's wrong, is it?"

"I wouldn't exactly say that, no. I, uh . . . Okay, that's the second time I've said 'I, uh.' I'll try and stop now. Do you want me to lead up gradually, or should I just spit it out?"

"You've known me how long?"

"Right. Okay, then. Here goes." Shallow breath. "I'm gay."

Laughter. Then, "Oh, Taylor, I'm sorry. I really am. It's just that . . . Did you really think I didn't know?"

Stunned. I felt stunned. "How could you know? My God, Nina, I didn't even know! Not until last summer, anyway."

"So you haven't been gushing to me about Will Martin? You haven't spent every spare minute at school scouring the horizon for any sign of him? And besides. What kind of heterosexual boy would you be if you could be 'just friends' with a vamp like me?"

She had me there. She was a vamp. Not that I minded. She was a lot of fun, and much more—maybe irreverent?—than my parents would have approved of, if they only knew. Which they didn't. They know her, but she's very careful about how she presents herself when it doesn't suit her to be outrageous. What boggled my mind about what Nina had just said wasn't the vamp comment.

"I've hardly mentioned Will to you! What do you mean, *gushing*?"

"Let's see. It's been, 'Will Martin is, like, some kind of history genius.' Or, 'Did you finish the English Lit assignment? Will Martin mentioned he wanted to be a writer. Historical fiction. Wouldn't that be cool?' Or how about at the mall, just the other day. You were all, 'Will Martin wears a leather thong like this on his neck. Do you think it would look good on me?' Do I need to go on?"

I could barely breathe. Had I really done that? After all that fury about how I couldn't?

"Nina, I—I don't know what to say."

"Just tell me your folks, and all the tight-ass people in your church, aren't giving you grief about it. You know, I often hear comments from Gentiles about how fierce the Jewish God is, but I don't think he can hold a candle to yours."

"My folks don't know. They don't have the kind of access to my innermost thoughts and feelings that you do. And besides, y'know, Will is one of those people in my church."

"Mmm. And how's his ass?"

"Nina!"

But she was laughing again. "Taylor, listen. Thanks for trusting me. What made you decide to tell me?"

Will said he'd never out anyone else. But I knew he'd told Nina. "Will. He's braver than I am. He said he'd told you."

"Ah, so you really do know a little something about his ass, then? I was only guessing that something was actually going on, other than you drooling. I'm glad, you know. It's about time you met someone you could fall for. And I like Will."

She must have liked the idea of Will and me together a lot, because a couple of weeks after this revelation—confession— whatever, she handed me an old *Die Hard* VHS cover she'd found in this used-everything store she loves, saying, "Can you think of a better place to hide condoms and lube in your room?"

And just after Christmas, the strangest thing happened. Will and I were at a Burger King that was, like, nowhere near our school or anyone we knew, in a booth way in the back, when it wasn't crowded. We were sharing a soda and holding hands across the table. And suddenly there was this girl from World History, Maureen West, standing there.

"Hey, guys! What are you two doing way out here?" I tried to snatch my hand back, but Will hung onto it. She saw that. "Oh, I'm sorry. Am I interrupting? I'll go away. . . ."

"No, please," Will said. "Have a seat. Are you here alone?"

"No, my mom is back there someplace. I'll sit with her when she's got everything she wants. She's so fussy, I'm surprised she'd even eat here. I just saw you and thought I'd come over and say hi. And, um, don't worry. I won't say I saw you. Some of the kids are pretty Stone Age, aren't they? See you!"

I reclaimed my hand and propped my head up with it, fingers rubbing. When I finally looked up, Will was grinning at me. I said, "That was a huge risk."

"Not really. I'm friends with Maureen. She might not have known you were gay, but she knew I was."

But Maureen had been right. Stone Age was about the right time frame for the outlook most of the kids I knew had on what I was. Partly that's because so many kids in my school also went to my church. If Strickland spread the word about me at school, it would be—hell. It would be hell.

So this ostracizing thing is about separation. Being in Safe-Zone is supposed to give me a taste of that. Make me want connection badly enough to take it on their terms. Again, that hard line between one thing and the other. All or nothing. Good or evil.

Oh, Will!

"Taylor, I'm back." I sat bolt upright to see Charles standing there, a worried look on his face. "Have you been talking this whole time?"

Talking? Was I talking? I shook my head and shrugged at the same time. I felt like crying, but I was damned if I'd do it in front of Charles the Drama Queen. I dropped my head back down again, breathing sharply in and out through my nose to keep the tears away.

"Pray with me."

I sat up again and saw that Charles had knelt at his chair like last night. He looked at me, his eyes kind of soft and pleading. I stood up, shaking my head hard, and grabbed my towel and bathroom kit. I left him kneeling there, alone.

In the shower, as long as I was quiet, I could hold my face in the streaming water and no one could see my tears. I wanted Will so badly! I wanted to hold him, to have him touch my face and smile his magical smile, and laugh gently and tell me that almost nothing is ever quite as bad as it seems. I wanted to hear his voice, to fill my hands with his hair and my mouth with his dick. I wanted all of him, no separation. I wanted his touch, his voice, his scent, his taste, and most of all I wanted his love. It was a real love. A love for me, Ty—his special name for me— the real me. Not a love for some kid named Taylor who had to be trained to leave this huge part of who he is in the gutter someplace. Not a love for the new penitent no one knows anything about even though they have to say "We love you, Taylor." That wasn't love.

They were trying to separate me from love, all of them, by offering this false substitute. And Charles was the worst, because he was honest. Because he really believed it.

Suddenly I welcomed the dishonesty of everyone else. It would help me remember how fake their love was. And if their love was fake, then any separation they forced on me must be fake, too.

I took a few deep, shuddering breaths and picked up the soap. May as well get clean while I'm in here. Plus it would keep me away from my room that much longer.

But when I got back there, Charles was gone. He'd left a note on my desk that said he'd gone to the library, and it also reminded me to keep the door open. I'd forgotten about the library. I sort of thought everyone was supposed to go to bed after the meeting, but there was over an hour left before lights-out. Charles must have sacrificed his own free time last night to come right back and stay with me.

Damn him, anyway, sacrificing for me. Who asked for that? Who the hell did he think he was?

So what was I going to do next? Did I want to go pitter-patter behind my role model, Charles Courtney, and follow him to the library? Did he expect that? Well, no, his note sounded like he kind of assumed I'd stay here. But I could go to the library if I wanted to.

Did I want to? What was in there? There were PCs with Internet access, but you had to get special permission to use them, and the Booklet is very clear that said access is extremely limited. And the filters on them are fierce.

I decided to leave exploration of the library until another time. Right now I just wanted to sleep. It felt like I'd lived through two or three days since Reverend Bartle had dragged me, limp and bleeding spiritually, to this room last night—Jesus, Mary, and Joseph, was that only last night?

I turned on Charles's desk light—partly to keep Ray's ghost away and partly so Charles could see when he got back. I turned out any others and got into my pajamas—the full set this time so Charles would have no reason to haul me out of bed—and crawled between the sheets. At least, I told myself, these were not the same sheets Ray would have slept on. But I hadn't been there more than a few minutes when I remembered the other thing Charles had made me do last night. I sighed aloud to no one in particular and climbed back out of bed again. I knelt at the bed, though, not my desk chair this time, and started my prayer.

Or I got ready to pray. But I felt like there had been so much talk of God this, God that, and Jesus the other that nobody up there needed to hear anything more from me today. And as for me? Anything more I needed to say? Beg? Whatever it was, it had to be silent.

Sweet Jesus, be with me in here. I know you love me for who I am. I know God doesn't make mistakes, and if I'm gay it's because that's what he wanted. What you wanted. And I think the challenge is to get everyone else to see that. This is *their* test, not mine. They need to learn that you love me for who I am, and they need to understand that if they're going to love me, they need to follow your example.

This can't have been your idea. You're all about connection and loving each other. This doesn't feel like love to me. I can't ask anything about anyone, can't get to know them. The only way I learn about anyone is by watching them react to this place, and I can't tell who's pretending so they won't get into trouble. But they aren't here by choice any more than I am.

Maybe there are some of them who hate it here and would talk to me about it if I could ask, if I could let them know I wouldn't rat on them. Maybe we have some things in common. I'm sure some of them are gay like me. Help them to trust me, and help me to trust them, so we can connect. So we can help each other.

God, I have so many other things to say to you. So many things to ask. But that about does it for tonight, I guess. Amen.

Once I got over the creepy feeling of being in dead Ray's bed, sleep surprised me by coming quickly. I didn't even hear Charles come in or get ready for bed or anything. For all I know, he masturbated before he fell asleep.

Chapter 4

Whoever is born of God doesn't commit sin, be-
cause his seed remains in him; and he can't sin, be-
cause he is born of God. In this the children of God
are revealed, and the children of the devil. Whoever
doesn't do righteousness is not of God, neither is he
who doesn't love his brother.

—John 3:9

Tuesday began with the same piercing shriek as Monday. ADIH. Demerit. Another Day In Hell. Would I ever get used to that noise? Charles, as usual, was looking out for me.

"Remember not to talk, Taylor. Do you need any reminding about how we start our day?"

Start our day? Where was this guy from? I shook my head.

He finished his morning prayer, grabbed his bathroom kit, and stood there waiting. For me, I supposed. But I'd showered last night. So I shook my head and pointed to the floor like I was going to stay here.

"You need to shower, Taylor."

I tried several hand gestures (nothing obscene, though it was tempting) to let him know I didn't need to, and finally I had to resort to my pad and pen.

He glanced at my scrawled message and shook his head. "The Booklet is very clear on this. We shower every morning. It's in the section on Cleanliness."

Now, I remembered the Cleanliness section. And yeah, it said something about a daily shower, but did it say in the morning necessarily? I glared at Charles and picked my Booklet up from my desk. And sure enough, it said "All residents are to shower each morning before breakfast."

I scrawled again. "But I showered last night!!!"

"The Booklet says we shower in the morning. It doesn't say we can't shower at night, but it does say we shower in the morning." And he stood there, patience incarnate, waiting.

This was not a good start to the day. Already Charles had the upper hand. And I couldn't even argue with him because I couldn't speak. Man, I came close. But then what? Was it worth getting into trouble so soon just to avoid taking a shower? Of course, lots more than that was at stake, really, in this battle of wills between me and Mr. Sanctimonious, but nevertheless I followed him, looking as surly as possible as he led the way to the bathroom.

To make matters worse, he had to remind me to put a yellow sticker on my shirt before we went to breakfast. Again.

In the dining hall I wanted to veer away from Charles and sit elsewhere, but during my protested shower I'd come to the conclusion that I needed to keep a low profile until I'd figured a few more things out. And certainly until I could speak, which wouldn't be until Thursday. So I trotted along with him and sat at a table where two girls were seated. Not Jessica and Marie, this time. One of them was Monica Moon, and after Charles's obligatory grace I found out that the other was her roommate, Dawn Voorhees. Odd name, I remember thinking. I had yet to meet the famous Danielle who was Charles's nondate for the Friday night barbeque. I'd almost forgotten about her, but sitting with girls over breakfast reminded me. That, and the fact that Dawn brought it up.

"Do you have a companion for Friday yet, Charles?"

Awfully forward of her, I remember thinking. It hadn't occurred to me to think that of Jessica; don't know why not. But there was something pointed, or forceful, about Dawn.

"Yes, actually. Danielle has agreed to go with me. And you?"

"Nope."

Nope? It was the most casual response I'd heard anyone give anyone else since I got here. And there was a note of pride buried someplace inside it. I found myself liking Dawn immensely. I looked at her. She winked.

Shit! This was cool. Maybe she was actually a real person. I looked at Charles to get his reaction, and he looked distinctly uncomfortable. Kind of like he really wanted to say something but didn't know how to follow *Nope* with any of his usual lingo. Like she didn't know how out of place her response had been, and he didn't know how to get her to see it.

Now, one of the rules that all residents are supposed to follow is not to jeopardize the silence of someone in SafeZone. So far the only people who'd spoken to me had done so like they were walking on eggshells, or by reminding me that I shouldn't respond. So Dawn surprised me again.

"How are you doin' so far, Taylor? I'll bet you've been able to form a lot of impressions in safety, since no one can ask you that and expect an answer!" She laughed, a deep-throated, honest laugh. "You started Monday?"

I nodded, delighted that she hadn't reminded me to limit my response to one head motion or another.

"Monica, too, like you heard last night. Say, that was some scene you two played out for us." Her glance took Charles in, too, and despite the offhand nature of her words, her expression made it seem she'd been favorably impressed. She turned back to me. "You two should make great roommates, once you're able to talk. I'll bet you're going to give Charles a run for his money!" She chuckled.

Note to self: get Dawn alone after tomorrow and ask what she meant.

Dawn next launched into a story about someone she was working with in the library, but since I didn't know anyone else she was talking about, I just watched her. I loved the way her whole, big, round face was called into action when she wanted to emphasize something, which was most of the time; otherwise there would have been little about it to notice. And when she laughed her blue eyes squinted tight shut. Even her hair seemed to make some kind of statement. It was very light blonde, and it might have been pretty if she'd let it grow. But she didn't. It was very short, almost hacked. Like she'd decided pretty wasn't her style and she was forbidding her hair to dilute her true image. I was a little surprised they didn't make her wear a wig here. They had rules about Appropriate Appearance for girls and boys, and hacked hair on anyone was against the rules. Maybe they had her on orders to pray every night that her hair would grow quickly into a sweet bob, or something.

Monica looked pretty much the same as she had last night. Except her hair looked clean. Man, if I'd had Dawn for a roommate, I'd be a lot more cheerful. At least, I think so; was Dawn like this all the time, or did she turn into some kind of terror when she was alone with a silent impenitent?

At any rate, I was sorry when breakfast ended and all of us had to move on to our work assignments for the day. On the other hand, I'd get to see Sean again. What a bod. And Shorty, aka Nate, would be in the laundry room, too; he intrigued me, and I really wanted to know what was between him and Leland. Then I remembered I couldn't talk to anyone, and I nearly said "Shit" aloud. Double whammy if I had; speaking and profanity all at once.

Sean looked just as good as yesterday, and he even smiled when he saw me. I hadn't known Nate was right behind me, but I saw him as he passed Sean; evidently Nate didn't need instructions like I did. I glanced at him, hoping for some sign of recognition or acknowledgment, but he didn't even look in my direction. It hurt, so it made me angry. Fuck you, too, I hurled at him silently. Just one more turnabout for Shorty; consistency did not seem to be his strong suit. I turned back to Sean.

That morning I learned how to clean lint out of the dryers. Big whoop. Sean did his best to make it seem like it was some kind of honor; evidently they didn't trust just anybody with this task, which was a lot more than just emptying the lint catchers. I had to turn the machines off, unplug them, open up the fronts of the machines and dig in with this special plastic doohickus. So I spent most of my time on the floor, leaning into the innards of the machines, and I didn't get much chance to look for familiar faces. Even so, I did manage to locate Monica (easy target, I admit), and I even saw Sheldon folding towels—white ones, of course—at one of those white tables. He seemed pretty morose even from a distance.

My back was ready for a break when we all filed into that courtyard with the green fiberglass cloister. Feeling a little more independent today, I walked alone out onto the grassy area, into the sunshine, put my hands on the backs of my hips, and leaned back. Man, but crouching into those dryers was tough after a while. I decided to be really bold, and I got down on the grass and lay on my sore back, eyes closed, soaking in the sun.

Gradually I grew aware of the conversation a couple of guys were having not too far away. One of them sounded like Shorty, but I was damned if I was gonna look. So I just listened. They were going on about some controversy regarding the English interpretation of some wording in the Bible.

"It makes a huge difference!" the guy who wasn't Shorty said.

Shorty's voice, calm and patient, replied, "It makes none at all. So what if it should have been *rope* instead of *camel*?"

"Look, it makes some sense to talk about how hard it would be to get a rope through the eye of a needle. At least that would be possible, even if you had to strip the rope down to fibers. To say it's a camel that can't go through is stupid!"

"It amounts to the same thing." I could almost see Shorty shrug.

"Prove it. Make sense out of it."

"Fact is, whether it's a rope or a camel, to get it through the eye of a needle you're going to have to tear it to shreds. And letting go of worldly goods tears most people to shreds. And the more you have, the harder it is. The more like the camel it seems. Don't you know that when the stock market crashes, lots of people lose lots of money, and many of them throw themselves out of windows? Maybe for a less wealthy person, it's more like a rope. I say that for people too tied to their wealth, it may as well be a camel."

All was quiet for a stretch, and I thought, "A moment of silence for Shorty's spiritual intuition." Then the other guy spoke again.

"Well, you know, there are other areas where people disagree on the interpretation. You're saying none of that matters?"

"You'd have to identify them. Then we can talk."

"Aaaaahhh . . ." The guy made this noise of disgust, and it sounded like he got up and left. Then there was nothing. I barely squinted one eye open, just enough to see that it was Shorty. He got up and walked in the other direction from the guy who had been arguing with him, ignoring me, sauntering aimlessly further out into the yard. So I closed my eyes again. I wondered if this was what Shorty did. What he was known for here—interpreting scripture, applying it, arguing about it. His insights from Prayer Meeting last night were still with me. But that didn't mean I wasn't still angry with him. And anyway, did no one here talk about anything else? Just Bibles and barbeque?

When break ended, as I scrambled to my feet I noticed Shorty, hands in his pockets, shuffling back from the far end of the yard, where there was a small stretch of chain-link fence that gave a fractured view of the outside world. Wishing yourself out of this prison, Shorty? See any seagulls? His eyes were on the ground, and if he knew I was there he still didn't let on.

Praise the Lord, I didn't have to do any more dryer cleaning. Sean had me portioning out laundry detergent and fabric softener into little containers. Only so much was supposed to be used for any one load, you see, and evidently no one who was actually doing laundry could be trusted to measure it out. It was so boring I almost wished myself back at the dryers with my doohickus. I killed time by humming every hymn I could remember. Quietly.

I'd hoped to avoid Charles for lunch, but there he was, waiting for me. For some reason he led us to a table way over to the side of the dining hall. No one else sat with us, and we just chewed and stared. He didn't talk to me at all. What a prick. But—did I really want him to talk to me? What I wanted was Dawn talking to me. Even Shorty would have been interesting, even if kind of overfocused on the Holy Writ. He had ideas I'd never thought of, that's for sure.

I helped Sheldon, my SafeZone comrade, fold sheets after lunch. Two mutes, nodding and jerking our heads to indicate who should do what with which corner. We got into a kind of rhythm, though, and it was so in synch for a while that it was almost fun. Hypnotic. But then Sheldon accidentally dropped a corner, reached too quickly for it, and his whole end landed on the floor. I distinctly heard him say "Sh—!" before he clamped a hand over his mouth to stop the last two letters from sneaking out. He looked at me over the fingers that still gripped his offending mouth, absolute panic in his eyes. Before I could stop myself, I was on the floor.

I laughed and laughed, and then Sheldon started, and the two of us were rolling on the floor giving off these wordless howls, parts of the sheet under us. Sean came running over shouting, "Don't speak! Don't talk! Get up!" We were helpless, though, and suddenly Shorty was there. I'd say he was standing over us, but—well, he's so short. His quiet voice cut through the fading giggles.

"You have wasted soap, softener, water, electricity, and time. Not only your time, but the time of everyone who stopped working to watch you." He turned on his heel and walked away.

I was on my feet in a split second. "Hey!" It wasn't what I wanted to say, but I was ready to say a lot more.

Sean was on me, his hands on my shoulders. "Quiet! Don't say anything else!"

Shorty never even turned around.

I didn't get to go out into the yard at break that afternoon. Instead I was hauled into the laundry office with Sean. He sat there across the desk from me, head in his hands. Finally he spoke.

"Taylor, I hate this. But I've had to report that you spoke. Everyone heard it."

I shrugged. Then I grabbed a pad and pen and wrote, "I'm putting it in my MI today, anyway."

Sean read this and nodded. "Okay, that's good. But they may make you apologize to the group anyway, on Thursday, or they may extend your SafeZone another day."

"What?" It was out before I could stop it.

Sean's head snapped up and he glared at me. I grabbed the pad again and wrote, "No!" But then I scratched it out. I mean, if they put another day on, it was that much more time before

I'd have to pretend, before I'd have to respond to people who said inane, insipid, dishonest things to me. I threw the pad onto the desk, flipped the pen onto it, and shrugged again. "So fucking what?" is what I wanted Sean to hear.

"You need to stay in here until someone comes to get you. I'm sorry, Taylor."

I picked up the pad again and scrawled, "What's with Nate? Who is that guy?"

Sean read it quickly and his hand snapped over the page, tore it off, and then crumpled it. For a minute I thought he might be about to eat it. But he opened it out again and folded it until it was small and flat enough to fit into his front pants pocket, which is where he put it.

"Look, if you're so hot on writing, then take this time and get started on your MI. I'm going out onto the floor." And he left.

What's eating him? I thought. Why is he angry with me? And what did this have to do with Shorty?

There was something really creepy going on in this place, I decided. I felt like I'd landed in the middle of this horror flick, maybe one where some of the people were real people and some were aliens, or had been real people but had been taken over by some supernatural force. It was almost like I could go up to some of them and rip their face off and there'd be this hideous creature underneath.

And the worst part was that I wasn't sure whose faces were real. I couldn't tell which ones had hideous creatures inside them. I wasn't even sure what planet I was on anymore.

Okay, I decided, this was hell. I'd found my way into a little corner of hell. So, who were the devils, and who were just sinners who'd ended up here like me? That was the torture. I might never know.

A sudden bang startled me before I realized it was me. My hand hurt where I'd brought a fist down onto the desk. Quickly I looked out onto the floor to see if anyone had noticed. No one had turned toward the office, so I guessed I was okay.

But—holy shit! This was totally weird.

I stared out at all those kids, desperate for some sign about how to tell the real ones from the fakes. Knowing some of them were devils inside, I looked for red. Anything red. Red . . . red . . . red . . . Jesus Fucking Christ, nothing out there was red! It had been forbidden; it must have. Otherwise *some*body would have had *some*thing red on! But not even a hair scrunchie on one of the girls was red. Not one blouse, not one belt, nothing. Which meant that by its very absence it was present. It was pervasive.

I stood up, breathing hard, hanging on to the edge of the desk to keep from shouting, "Is nobody out there human?"

Down, Taylor. Down, boy. Down. Sit down.

I sat.

Now, calm. Deep breaths. Close your eyes.

But I couldn't close my eyes. I felt like I had to know if one of them got too close. If one of them did something really freaky out there, I had to know. What I would have done is anybody's guess, but I had to know.

Get a hold of yourself! Chill! Knock it off!

I managed to close my eyes, just for a few seconds. But I couldn't bring myself to turn my back to all of them out there.

I was still standing there when some kid I'd never seen before showed up. He looked for Sean, waved at him, and came into the office.

"You Taylor Adams? Nod or shake."

Nod.

"I'm Jeffrey. I'm to bring you to Mrs. Harnett." He turned to leave but waited at the door for me to go out first. I looked down toward Sean, who had suddenly stopped being a potential devil and had started to look like a lifeboat. I shot a pleading look at him: did I have to go? He just looked at me sadly and turned away.

Mrs. Harnett wanted to see me. It had to be about my speaking. And Sean had said he'd had to report me. All I could do was stand firm and brazen it out. I was ready to run, though.

She didn't give me that warm smile this time. "Shut the door please, Taylor."

Jesus, save me. If she kills my body, protect my soul.

She didn't invite me to sit, so I stood.

"I understand you violated SafeZone this afternoon. Do you understand how significant a transgression that was?"

Did I? Not yet, maybe; that would depend on what happened as a result. But I nodded.

"Sean tells me you plan to write about it in your MI for today. Is that correct?"

Nod.

"When I read your MI, which I'll do later tonight, I'll determine what the consequences will be. I'll let you know tomorrow morning. Come to my office after breakfast. For now, you should assume this will mean full punishment, which would mean an extra day of SafeZone. This is to help with your resolution, Taylor. To help you feel the effects as deeply as possible in order to bring about a truer repentance. Do you know what repentance is, Taylor?"

Shrug. I was feeling a little less panicky, and I was getting irritated. What had I done that was so terrible?

She answered for me. "It means to change your path. It means you will not repeat the transgression you are repenting."

Okay, this was getting to me. It wasn't like I'd committed some heinous sin. I hadn't even sworn, for God's sake. If anyone was at fault, it was Nate for tempting me. I lunged toward her desk to grab a pad of paper. Her hand shot out and held it down.

"Taylor, I'm afraid that you've been abusing the rule about writing during SafeZone. It's intended to be done only in emergencies, and I understand you've been doing a lot of it even though you've had no emergencies. Now I'm going to ask Jeffrey to walk you back to your room, where you will begin your Contemplation time early. By all means, write; but write your confessions, your repentance. Write to God and convince him you understand what he wants from you."

Repent what? I wanted to ask. What did I do wrong?

So I sat at my desk to write my second MI, furious, resentful, wanting to hit something. It was a little after two o'clock and I was stuck in here until six. On the one hand, I wanted to get this thing over with, write the fucking MI, and seal it in its tidy little envelope. On the other hand, if I wrote anything right now, it would just get me into more trouble than I was already in. So I hit something.

I went over to my bed and picked up my pillow. I grasped it with one hand and hit it with the other. Over and over again. I wanted to shout. Hell, I needed to scream! So the pillow changed from a punching bag to a muffling device, and I screamed into it. I screamed until I was hoarse.

I can't say it helped, but at least it tired me out. I fell onto the bed, curled into a ball, hugged the pillow tight, and willed myself not to start blubbering. And then I heard myself say, "Jesus, help me."

"Taylor!"

Someone was calling my name. Where are they? Who is it?

"Taylor, wake up. You're supposed to be contemplating, not sleeping."

It was Jeffrey. I looked at my watch: nearly four o'clock. At least sleep had gotten me through a couple of hours. I nodded to Jeffrey and got off the bed, running a hand through my hair. He gave me a look like he had his doubts, but he left.

Was I calmer now? Was I still going to see devils everywhere? Did I hate Nate or Mrs. Harnett more?

But hate wasn't something I wanted. Hate just ends up turning back onto you, hurting you. Maybe even hurting your soul. So I dragged myself over to my desk and sat with a pen in my hand, staring at the paper that would become my second MI.

How had she known? How had she known that I was writing things? Are other people, people like Charles and Sean, under some kind of orders to save the papers and give them to Mrs. Harnett? Is that why Sean had kept my question about Nate? But he'd torn it off and crumpled it. Was he trying to help me by hiding it?

Okay, now I was starting to feel weird again. I walked around the room, searching corners for hidden cameras. Under the desk? On the back of the bureau? I looked all over. They'd have to have been those little Minicams or I'd have found them. But then, a camera would have caught Sean putting that paper into his pocket. No cameras, then. So, how? It must be that Charles had been turning over the papers. And Sean, too, except maybe for the one he'd crumpled.

I sat there tapping the pen on the pad, trying to think whether I'd ever seen any pages I'd written on after I'd written on them. I looked in my desk drawers. Then I checked Charles's. I looked under mattresses and in wastebaskets—which was futile, since they got magically emptied every day. Must be the job of some lucky resident to do that. So—was that how they got turned in? Someone went through the trash?

Note to self: see if you can volunteer for trash duty once you're out of SafeZone.

If I ever get out of SafeZone.

But I had to know whether Charles had done that to me. It would be just like him to think it was for my own good. But had he done it deliberately, or had he thrown the papers into the trash? And had he ever done trash duty? If so, he'd have known what would happen to them.

Wait! He'd found my wet tissues yesterday. Did that mean he really was going through my trash? And what had he done with them? Had he turned those in, too? Was he, after all, not the honorable man of the proverbs, as he'd led me to believe at Prayer Meeting last night? Or had he flushed them down the toilet to keep anyone from knowing because he'd felt guilty interrupting my Contemplation? Maybe someday I'd be able to ask him; until then, I wasn't going to figure this one out on my own unless Harnett confronted me with it.

I was beginning to feel decidedly penned-in. And it wasn't like I hadn't been feeling that way already; it was just getting worse. A lot worse.

Okay, so writing was no guarantee of privacy. At least I knew that much. But my thoughts, as far as I could tell, were still my own.

Will. I thought about Will. I sat in my chair and leaned back, eyes closed, and thought about Will. You know how a lot of people ask, What would Jesus do? Well, here's what I asked: What would Will do? What would Will say?

What would Will say about what had happened today? I pictured his face, his lopsided grin, the twinkle in his eyes as he raised one teasing eyebrow and dropped it a few times. And I heard him laugh. He opened that sweet mouth wide, and he laughed, and I heard it. All through the room.

I knew what he was laughing at. It was all these people taking themselves so fucking seriously, thinking they had some corner on Soul, on Good, on God. I smiled.

And then I felt his arms resting on my shoulders and his forehead leaning against mine. And here's what Will had to say: "Ty, my boy, here's what you tell them. Say it quietly, and sincerely, and like it's the most important thing anyone ever uttered. Tell them, 'Jesus loves you. But I'm his favorite.' "

And he was gone. But behind my closed eyelids, his grin hung, like the Cheshire cat's. It disappeared slowly, and as it did, the layers of what he'd just said started to peel back, revealing the nasty things underneath.

"Jesus loves you." Okay, that's obvious. We hear it all the time. And when you hear it, it sets you up, gets you into that holy mood, that soulful head. Yes, Jesus loves me, you think when you hear it. Jesus loves me.

Then you hear, "But I'm his favorite."

Wham! It slams you right back down to earth. It's like, "Daddy loves me best!" coming from the mouth of the younger brother who makes your life miserable, who's always getting you into trouble and lying because he can get away with it, because Mom and Dad will believe him and not you.

It's like, "Can Jesus *have* favorites?"

But most of all, it's like, "But I thought *I* was his favorite!"

I heard the sound of my own laughter before I knew I was laughing. It was different from when I laughed with Sheldon in the laundry room. That had been silly, a kind of release, slapstick. This was real. It put this whole fucking place in its place, you know? Everything. And I laughed. I saw Mrs. Harnett's stern face alternating with her fake smile; I saw Sean panicking and scrabbling at things he didn't want to deal with, afraid for his life. I saw Shorty standing there trying to make me feel like

I'd done something wrong when I hadn't, just so he could be seen as doing something that was supposed to be righteous. They were all so pathetic!

There was a knock at the open door. It was Jeffrey. He looked scared and determined at the same time.

"Um, you're making noise."

At first I was going to pick up the pad and write this: "But I wasn't speaking, even though you must have been spying." And then I realized that would be taking this thing too seriously. So I just smiled at him. It was a beatific smile, not a so-what smile. It had all the fake love in it that I could muster.

"You need to stop."

I wanted to write, "Are you going to report me?" But instead I just lowered my head like some kind of humble martyr. When I looked up again he was still standing there, embarrassed, uncomfortable, not knowing what my response was, really, and probably knowing he'd have to report something. I knew he wanted me to nod and let him know I'd understood and had agreed to behave myself, but I just smiled gently. Finally he left, and I sat down to do my second MI for real.

1. Yesterday I masturbated. During Contemplation. It was after I'd sealed my MI, so I'm putting it into today's instead.

2. Today I shouted at Nate. Sheldon and I had been folding sheets, and we'd been doing it for so long that we got into a flow. But then one of us [I opted against having this fall on Sheldon] dropped a corner and the whole thing fell apart and landed on the floor, and it was funny. We laughed so hard we fell on the floor, too. Sean came over, and then Nate, and Nate told us how much waste we'd caused. This may sound like I'm criticizing Nate, but he shouldn't have done that. He didn't understand how the sheet had fallen or that it was already on the floor by accident. He judged us, and I don't think he should have. Sean already knew what had happened, and if he felt it was a reportable incident, he would report it. We didn't need Nate telling

us how sinful we were. And that made me angry, and so as he was walking away all I did was shout "Hey" at him. That's all. So I admit I spoke, and I know I shouldn't have. But I don't think it's fair that Nate was allowed to make me so angry when he knows I'm in SafeZone. [If Nate wanted to take this place so seriously, then he could be held to its rules, too. Besides, I was kind of hoping that if I could spread the blame around a little, maybe I could avoid getting another day of SafeZone piled onto my sentence, which I really didn't want despite the advantage I'd considered in Sean's office.]

3. I've been abusing the emergency writing rule. It's supposed to be when something really important needs to be communicated by someone in SafeZone. But I have to say that at the times I did it, the times I wrote something, it felt pretty important to me. Now I see that it wasn't. [I didn't put why; I didn't put that I'd been taking everything seriously and that now I was going to stop doing that.]

I probably could have dug up some more stuff, but these were the highlights of the last twenty-four hours or so. And they were big enough: masturbation, talking in SafeZone, abuse of rules. Nothing had been said about my having to put in here why these things were wrong, or how I promised on somebody's grave never to do it again, so I didn't go there. I just signed my name and put the thing into its envelope. I didn't even read it over first.

Chapter 5

*The words of the wicked are about lying in wait for
blood, but the speech of the upright rescues them.*
—Proverbs 12:6

So, here it is, the end of the second day. And only forty more
to go. And here I am contemplating Expulsion like it's some
kind of option. Which it isn't. I'm here for the duration, but
not a second longer. I'm gonna have to just toe the line. And
think of Will.

Charles comes to get me for dinner. He doesn't speak, he
doesn't check the wastebasket, he just stands there. I nearly forget to bring my MI, but he picks it up and hands it to me, and
we take a detour past Harnett's office so I can drop it off.

This time we sit at a table with two guys, neither of them with
yellow stickers. I don't remember seeing them before. They're not
in our prayer group. Charles says, "Rick Caruso, John McAndrews,
meet Taylor Adams. Taylor is my roommate, and as you can see
he's still in SafeZone."

Rick nods and smiles and goes back to his dinner. John, who
seems like he's a few years older than me, looks right at me.
He's smiling, but his eyes are so intense it's like they're in someone else's face, or coming from some other world. In a voice
that sounds unusually deep and rich, he says, "So this is the
brave young man who shouted at brother Nate today."

Well, now, this is weird. How the hell does he know that? And
what does he mean by calling me brave when everyone else has

been falling over each other to chastise me? Damn, but I want out of SafeZone. I try to let my eyes speak for me, to ask those questions.

John laughs. At first I think he's laughing at me, but the way he looks at me makes me smile, too. "Are you puzzled?"

Nod.

John chuckles. "I won't criticize Nate. He means well, I'm sure. But sometimes I think he takes an awful lot onto himself. And tell me this: if he hadn't spoken to you the way he did, would you have said anything at all?"

Negative shake.

He just smiles, like he knows he doesn't need to add, "He tempted you." Instead, he says, "Taylor, Rick here and I have decided not to ask companions to this Friday's barbeque dinner. Now, I know Charles will be with Danielle, so I'm wondering if you'd be willing to come with us. What do you think?"

I'm thinking two things. One is whether Charles had already set up this little meeting with John before he brought me here. The other is that I'd been waiting until I could speak so I could ask Dawn to go with me; I'm sure I'm not supposed to ask a boy. But this is my first week, and it might not do to stick my neck out. Maybe it would be better if I go with these guys, with John, who at least seems to understand what happened to me today. So I nod.

"Great! You'll be out of SafeZone by then and we can talk. I'm looking forward to that." His smile lingers on me for a few seconds before he turns it to Charles. "And you, brother, I heard about what happened in your Prayer Meeting last night. My heart went out to you."

"Thank you, brother." Charles looks like he wants to smile.

John is watching his face. "As we all know, I can't speak for God. But I feel sure that if he hasn't rewarded you yet, he will. He knows the courage it took, and it's obvious how much you love his Word." We all eat in silence for a few minutes, and then John says, "Charles, you look troubled. Are you still holding onto last night's pain?"

Charles shakes his head. "No. I'll be all right, really."

Chewing thoughtfully, John watches him, and I can almost see thoughts flash behind his eyes. "You know I wouldn't push you, brother. But when I see you so unhappy I can't help but want to change that. And you do seem to be holding on to something that hurts you. Why do that, when we're right here to help? When you can release that burden to Jesus through us?"

I steal a glance at Charles. Is he in pain? He's been awfully quiet since last night, it's true. And he hasn't said a word to me about my little exchange in the laundry room this afternoon. Hey, maybe that's it; he's holding back from saying anything so he won't tempt me to—

"It's tonight." Charles's voice is sharp, like he was trying to keep it inside but it got out through some tiny crack, and coming out through that narrow space makes it pointed. "It's Leland. He's going to read his Public Apology tonight." He looks like there's more to say, but he clamps down on the words, gets them safely back inside again. He pushes the overcooked green beans around on his plate without eating anything.

"Charles." John waits. Charles takes some time before he finally looks up. John says, "Let it go, brother. Stop playing tug-of-war with Jesus. He will take this burden from you, but you must allow it. If it would help, you know we can talk about it. Why don't we see how things go tonight."

Charles nods and attempts to wipe his eyes surreptitiously, and Rick starts telling this supposedly inspirational story about something that had happened to him "on the outside." It doesn't have anything to do with anyone else I know, and I can't make much sense out of it, but John keeps laughing like Rick is quite the comic. It would have been intolerably boring except that John's laugh is so nice to listen to.

As for me, I'm still focused on what Charles said about Leland: he's going to read his Public Apology tonight. What did Leland have to apologize for? It was Ray who'd killed himself. Am I right about them being lovers, and are people trying to lay this on Leland? I'm getting angry already. And even though I realize I'm not doing a very good job at not taking this stuff seriously, it's hard not to get angry.

During Fellowship, after dinner, I manage to move away from Charles pretty early on. I edge around the room, sticking close to the walls, watching, and catching snatches of conversation. It's about like last night, really: kids talking loudly about their epiphanies and chastened hearts.

I see Monica Moon huddled in a corner. She looks at least as glum as ever. Maybe it will cheer us both up, or at least give us someone to be glum with together, if I go over there. I nod at her. She looks at me with something that's almost a glare, and as soon as I lean against the wall a couple of feet from her, she leaves.

I stare after her, not quite sure what to make of that.

"What are you doing all alone here in the corner, Taylor?"

It's Marie Downs, smiling for all she's worth, looking like she expects an answer. I point to my yellow sticker. She laughs.

"Oh yes. I know. Monica's not very friendly, is she?" Marie's eyes look toward where Monica disappeared into the crowd.

What's she getting at? She knows I can't answer, so I don't.

"I heard you yelled at Nate Devlin in the laundry room today."

Christ! Is there anyone who hasn't heard about that? Then I think, Devlin? His last name is Devlin? It has a Satanic note to it.

"Were you sticking up for Sheldon?"

I just blink at her. Sheldon had nothing to do with it. It was between me and Nate.

"You don't want to answer? You can just nod, you know."

I almost nod, to say I do know that, but I don't want her to think I'm answering her other question. I retreat into SafeZone. I point at my sticker, turn, and walk away from her. As far as I'm concerned, what she's doing is trying to tempt me to speak. I'm thinking about this, walking along the wall again, when I remember what she said yesterday. That she'd been trying to—how had she put it?—reach out to Leland. And Charles had basically told her to leave him alone. She'd done something, something that Leland might not think was for his own good, if I remember Charles's words right. Well, she's not doing anything to me. I won't give her a chance.

I catch sight of Monica again. Not in a corner this time; she's with Dawn, shadowing her like a dancer. Then suddenly everyone starts to disperse, just like yesterday. Man, this place is creepy.

I find my own way to Isaiah for our group, not waiting for Charles, and I take a seat near the back this time. No more front-and-center for me, thank you. And Charles, bless him (sarcasm alert), appears beside me. Perhaps he wants to hide tonight, too, given how scared he seems to be about Leland's True Confession, or whatever it's supposed to be.

"Up," Charles says to me. "Stand up, remember?"

Oh yeah. So we go through the same ritual as last night, waiting for the girls and Mrs. Harnett to sit first, hearing Mrs. Harnett pray again just as sincerely, just as practiced, and just as spontaneous as before. Same message: we're all sinners for our own reasons, and my love for Will is wrong. She doesn't move me as much tonight, even before the bit about Inappropriate Love.

She smiles at everyone again, even me. And then she bows her head for just a moment. No one else does, so I don't either. Then she looks around the room.

"We have a very important mission this evening. We have a brother in trouble, and we must help him. He's had some time to consider his relationship with God, to understand his trouble, and to prepare his confession. Open your Bibles, please, to James, chapter five, verse thirteen."

Most everyone in this little group knows the Bible so well that they don't need to be reminded where in the New Testament the book of James can be found. I know where a lot of the books are, but James is tiny, and I can't remember anything from it. So I watch Charles, who of course knows the exact page number it's on in his Bible, and I'm able to figure out that it's right after Hebrews.

I expect Harnett to ask someone to read, like she did last night, but she reads the verses herself. The Prayer of Faith. It talks about people who are in trouble or sick or have sinned, and how we must all turn to each other for help. How we must confess our sins to each other and pray for each other to be healed. How these are the prayers of the righteous and are powerful.

She closes her Bible. Then she says, "Brother Leland, please come to the front."

Nothing happens, except that everyone looks toward where Leland is rocking back and forth in his chair. Slowly, Harnett walks over to him and holds her hand out. When he doesn't take it, she puts it on his shoulder. He curls forward a little and then stands, wobbly but on his feet, paper clutched in one hand. Harnett walks him to the front, one hand on his shoulder and one on his elbow. She strips the yellow sticker off his shirt and then sits in an empty chair where she can watch.

Leland, who would be tall except that he's hunched over and miserable, doesn't look up. He does manage to raise the paper so he can read, clutching each side, and it rattles with the shaking of his hands. He's thin, so the shaking makes it look like he's cold, but I can tell it's fear. He stands there, eyes tight shut for a moment, and then he starts to read. His voice shakes, but you can tell he's doing his best. He reads slowly, each word hanging in the air as he releases it, like each one takes a special effort.

"I have sinned. I allowed myself to feel Inappropriate Love for a brother, and I encouraged him to feel it for me. We were discovered, and we were reported. He is gone now"—and his face crumples a little here before he forces himself to go on— "to be judged by God. To you, my brothers and sisters, I make my confession. I beg forgiveness."

He lowers his arms slowly and looks for all the world like he's about to follow Ray into the Great Beyond. I scour every inch of him that he presents—anguished face, clenched hands, trembling legs—for a sign that he doesn't really believe what he's just said. That's not sinning! I want to shout at him. That's not evil! Jaw clenched, hands in viselike grip on the seat of my chair, I manage somehow not to say anything, not to jump up and run to Leland, not to condemn everyone here for making him feel like it was his fault that Ray is gone. But the silence is killing me.

This silence is shattered by the voice of sister Marie, who's on her feet, quoting scripture at the top of her voice: "First Corinthians, chapter six, verse nine: 'Or don't you know that the unrighteous will not inherit the Kingdom of God? Don't be deceived. Neither the sexually immoral, nor idolaters, nor adulterers, nor male prostitutes, nor homosexuals, nor thieves, nor the covetous, nor drunkards, nor slanderers, nor extortioners, will inherit the Kingdom of God.'" She points not just her finger but her whole arm at Leland, who stands cowering. She must have memorized that just so she could do this tonight! Everything in me wants to lunge at her, knock her over, and trample on her. And I actually start to get up, but Charles grabs my upper arm with both his hands and holds on.

Then another voice chimes in; Brother Nate stands. "Sister," he says, looking at Leland, "the chapter continues: 'Such were some of you, but you were washed. But you were sanctified. But you were justified in the name of the Lord Jesus, and in the Spirit of our God.'" When he's done he turns toward Marie. Turns *on* Marie, would be closer to it, like he's preaching to her, condemning her. It's eerily like last night; there'd been a textual confrontation between these two then as well, and Nate had come to Charles's rescue. Tonight, it's to Leland's.

Before anything else can happen, Mrs. Harnett rises and goes to where Leland stands quivering. She touches his shoulder. "You may return to your chair, child."

She nods first at Marie and then at Nate, and they sit down again. She spreads her arms to the room as if to embrace us all.

"Children of God," she says, her tones large and round, "do you see what sin can do? Even among those who want so much to love God and each other? Even here, there is sin. For sister Marie is pushed toward hatred of sin that borders on hatred of the sinner, and brother Nate becomes angry with sister Marie for her fervor.

"Romans, chapter twelve, verse nineteen: 'Don't seek revenge yourselves, beloved, but give place to God's wrath. For it is written, *Vengeance belongs to me; I will repay, says the Lord.*

"Romans, chapter fourteen, verse ten: 'But you, why do you

judge your brother? Or you again, why do you despise your brother? For we will all stand before the judgment seat of Christ.'

"Children of God, reject sin but not the confessed sinner. Do not allow sin to cause discord among us. Brother Leland?" And here she turns toward him. He seems startled, as though he'd been sure the worst was over and yet now he's faced with more.

"Brother Leland, do you repent?"

Warily, it seems to me, he nods.

"Speak it! Say it aloud so that we may all know your heart."

Leland begins to speak but nearly chokes. He tries again and manages, "I repent."

Mrs. Harnett looks like she'd just won the lottery. "Halleluiah! Children, rejoice with me!" And all around me there are shouts of "Halleluiah!" and "Praise the Lord!" just like last night. Only this time it's for a reason I can't accept.

I do *not* repent, I say deep inside me. I do not repent. I *so* do not repent.

And then the most awful thing happens. Marie, tears running down her face, goes over to Leland and practically lifts him out of his chair. She takes his hands in hers and shouts, "I forgive you, brother! I forgive you!"

For his part, Leland is crying, too. But it doesn't seem to me there's any joy in it. I could swear he doesn't want the forgiveness of sister Marie, or of anyone else, except possibly Ray himself. Which he can never have. So he cries, all right. He cries. And I feel so bad for him. If it had been me, I would have pushed her clear across the room, but he stands there and does his best to pretend it's a good thing. Pretend all is forgiven. Pretend he doesn't know that she hates him as much as a dog turd she's stepped on in her new Sunday shoes. I watch like I can't turn my gaze away from a train wreck.

I feel kind of like crying, too, some for Leland and some for me. I mean, how am I going to fake this crap? My mind is sending up a prayer that's part thanks, because I can't speak and so don't have to celebrate the way everyone else does, and part a plea to help me figure out how the fuck I'm going to get through six weeks of shit like this when I want to run screaming from the room after only two days.

I look right at Mrs. Harnett, the founder of this feast. She's looking right at me. So I think of Will. And in my head, I tell the Saint on the throne there, "Jesus loves you. But I'm his favorite."

I guess my expression is calm enough; she smiles as though satisfied with what she sees and turns to look around the room at other kids. So I turn my attention back to Nate, who's confused me by coming to Leland's rescue, only to see that *he* is looking at *me*. Christ, is everyone in this room looking at me? He smiles, too, but it doesn't look like the same kind of smile as the one the Saint had given me. It's like I've passed some kind of secret test. And it confuses me even more.

Meanwhile, the room is gradually calming down. The thing between Marie and Leland has turned into a mini hugfest, but kids are backing off now and returning to their seats.

It dawns on me suddenly that Charles is very quiet, that he didn't shout when most everyone else did, and he didn't go over for the group hug. I look at his profile, and he must sense it, because he turns to me. And I get yet another smile, from him this time. Such a sad smile, so much pain in it.

I don't go to the library after Prayer Meeting. I'd thought I might, but instead I turn in early. Despite my nap that afternoon, I feel drained and exhausted. Charles sits at his desk for a while, and I hear him get onto the floor just before I fall asleep, no doubt praying at his chair again.

Halfway through the night or so, I wake up. At first I'm sure I'll fall asleep again, but my mind starts making lists. Lists of impressions I'm getting about the other inmates here. I start with my roommate, snoring quietly in the other bed.

Charles. Pious, even self-righteous. Wants to do everything right. Wants to love people, but seems to have as hard a time as St. Paul in his first letter to the Corinthians (the famous text starting in chapter thirteen that talks about how useless and empty he is if he's without love). Tries hard; a little too hard.

Seems desperate to leave his past behind—including his gay past—and to convince others to do the same. Desperate: an important word in understanding Charles. He needs to give up desperation before he can let Jesus take any burdens off him. But if you're desperate because you're afraid, how do you let go of desperation when that increases the fear? Faith, that's how. Faith. And Charles is desperate for it.

Nate. Inscrutable Nate Devlin. Interpreter of scripture. Rescuer of those in pain, of those under assault. Especially if they're under assault from Marie Downs. Condemner of those in disobedience. Irritating. Arrogant, and self-righteous in his own way, though it's different from Charles's way. Gay? Don't think so. Then why's he here? Drugs? Disobedience? That would make sense; he comes down so hard on others who are disobedient, including me. Mysterious. Intriguing. Gives off mixed signals. I've no clue what others, except maybe John McAndrews, think about him. And what does Sean think? Why was it so important that no one see I'd asked that about Nate? "What's with Nate? Who is that guy?" That's all the paper had said. But Sean wanted no one to see it. Why?

Sean. Gorgeous body. Pretty sure he's gay. Sweet nature, doesn't want to rat on people, doesn't want anyone to get into trouble. I need to know what gives between him and Nate. There's something, I'm sure of it. He seems to frighten easily; probably doesn't have enough backbone to be relied upon in a crunch. Remember that.

Marie. The word *bitch* comes to mind immediately. I'd guess she's one of those people who look for ways to cut others down. Probably makes her feel more righteous, more holy. I don't believe for a second that she embraced Leland tonight out of any sense of sisterly love, or any other kind for that matter. Putting on a show for Harnett, more like. Likes being the center of attention. Avoid at all costs.

Jessica. Friends with Marie, or just taking the opposite approach from me? Does she feel safer if she always knows what Marie is up to? So there won't be any sneak attacks on her? And something about the way she poked at Charles at breakfast

Monday didn't ring true. Almost like she was playacting. Hard to know what to make of her. Avoid whenever possible.

Dawn. Now, there's someone I'd like to talk with. Refreshing. But I don't think she disobeys the rules—despite that hair. One reason it looks unruly might be just that it's growing out. She reacted positively to Charles's Monday night confession scene. Coming from some of these other characters, I might have doubted what was said about it. But I think Dawn was sincere. Make friends with Dawn.

Leland. Shattered. That's the first word that comes to mind with him. Then tragic. I think I have a pretty good idea what happened with this Ray thing, and even though I didn't see Leland react to the suicide, I have enough imagination to get there anyway. I wonder if there's any way to reach out to him. Not the way Marie meant, I'm sure! More like one gay brother to another. I'm convinced he said he repented tonight just to escape the spotlight, just to be left alone sooner. I wonder if anyone has *him* on suicide watch.

Somewhere in there my mind drifts off, coming up with bizarre ways to watch someone who might be likely to do himself in. And then I have this dream.

I'm in some room, without windows, but it's brightly lit. Too brightly, really. Other guys are in the room with me, and there's some kind of difference between one group and another. It comes to me that I'm in prison, and there are other prisoners like me, and there are guards—fewer guards than prisoners— who aren't armed, but no one makes any attempts at escape. The feeling of hopelessness, of despair, is enough to keep us prisoners contained.

I have a kitten. I've had it since before I was in prison, and it's with me now. It's very attached to me, and I love it very much. But I'm worried for it. How can I protect it in here? Many people in this place will want to hurt it. And it's inquisitive. It likes exploring and doesn't want to be held all the time, so it's difficult for me to protect it. I hold it as much as possible, and often it asks to be picked up, but also it wants to explore. It wanders off, and I'm frantic with worry, and then it's at my side, reaching a soft paw up for me to hold it.

I'm in a smaller room now, with only a couple of other prisoners. I'm sitting on a wooden chair, and my kitten is exploring the room. A man sitting on another chair, between me and the door, is reading a newspaper. One ankle rests on the opposite knee. He has a different feeling about him, different from me and the other prisoners. He's some kind of warden. Not just a guard, but someone with real power. He's flaunting his power.

As I watch the kitten, worried about it, the man begins to talk. He tells me that he can do things for me, take care of me, see that nothing bad happens to me. Or to that little cat. But I'll have to pay the price. Whatever the warden says, I have to do. And if I don't, the kitten will pay.

I imagine myself agreeing to one demand, and then to another, and then balking at the next, and I know the man will hurt the kitten, torture the kitten. The man keeps talking about how pleasant he can make my life, and the kitten's, or how miserable. I know the pleasant part is really a lie.

I feel the kitten's paw on my leg. It's asking to be held.

The man sets his paper down and looks at me, a smirk on his face. And then he looks down toward my lap, and so do I. The kitten is there. Dead. I've snapped its neck.

Suddenly I'm sitting upright in a bed, breathing hard. It's my bed. Or rather, not mine, but the one I've been assigned in this prison. And even though I know where I am, even though I know that was a dream, even though I'm in SafeZone, and even though I might wake Charles up, I ask, "Where's my kitten?"

Chapter 6

But he who is greatest among you will be your ser-
vant. Whoever exalts himself will be humbled, and
whoever humbles himself will be exalted.
                                        —Matthew 23:11

Charles says absolutely nothing in the morning until we've showered and dressed, I've put my yellow sticker on, and we're preparing to head out for breakfast. Only I have to stop by Harnett's office first to hear my sentencing. I'm just contemplating how I'm going to let Charles know that without writing when he says, "Listen, Taylor, would you be okay on your own at breakfast today?"

His voice sounds odd. Strained, kind of. I wait for him to say more, to tell me why, but when he doesn't I just nod.

"Thanks. I just don't feel like dealing with all those people this morning. Not after last night." He starts to turn toward the door but stops. "Do you understand?"

I do, I guess. I nod again.

"If anyone insists on knowing where I am and they ask you, you can write that I went to the chapel." He turns, then says over his shoulder, "Don't forget your sticker." And he's gone.

I reach up and slap my shoulder, expecting to feel nothing but cloth. But the sticker is there already. Weird. I pocket a pen and a sheet of paper, just in case I have to explain Charles's whereabouts, and head out on my own errand.

The door to Harnett's office is open, so I just knock on the frame. She looks up.

"Ah, Taylor. Come in. Sit down."

I sit, and watch her finish some writing she's doing. She starts speaking again before she puts the pen down.

"I've read the MI you left last night. We'll still talk tomorrow at ten, as arranged, so I won't go over it in detail right now. But I want you to know that although I understand you feel as though Nate pushed you into speaking, I know two important things that render that a little irrelevant. One is that Nate has voluntarily returned to us twice since his first summer here, so I understand him pretty well. And I do not believe that he would step over that line in the way you imagine. He is extremely well aware of the protocol here, and he makes every effort to stay within it. This does not mean he makes no mistakes, and I will speak to him about how he approached you to find out where his heart was. But that is not your problem.

"The other thing is that you've been with us only a couple of days. And even if you've been exerting your best efforts to maintain the integrity of your SafeZone, it's important for you to understand that sometimes our best efforts fall short. Yours fell short, and there are consequences. If there were not, your motivation—especially as a new resident—could falter.

"So I've decided what your punishment should be. During your Contemplation time this afternoon, you will write an Apology to your brothers and sisters. It doesn't need to be long, but it must be long enough to communicate these points: one, that you understand what you did wrong; two, that you blame no one but yourself; and three, that you apologize to all the other residents, especially the ones in SafeZone, who may have heard you break protocol yesterday."

She sits back, and I think she's done. Certainly that's bad enough. But then she adds, "And tonight, during Prayer Meeting, you will emerge from SafeZone by reading it aloud."

Stunned. I think *stunned* is the best word for how I feel.

"Any questions?"

Yeah; are you fucking kidding me with this?

She must see that question on my face. "Taylor, this may seem harsh. But remember what I told you Monday about these rules? They are here to help you. A diligent sheepdog keeps his sheep from straying too near the cliff edge. Our job here is to teach you how to herd your own thoughts, your own actions, for the sake of your immortal soul."

So now they want my thoughts, too? And I've just finished telling myself that my thoughts are my own. That Harnett might find out what I write, but not what I think.

Alone, I make my way to the dining hall for breakfast, kind of on autopilot. I don't care whether I'm even going to know anyone else at whatever table I end up at. I'm Safe, so I don't have to explain anything. My mind is racing, jumping, frantic to come up with something that will make it possible for me to keep the attitude I know Will would have and at the same time avoid outright insubordination. Like, how can I stand up in front of the whole prayer group, tell them everything the Saint just laid out, not lie, be true to myself and to Will, not get expelled, not have to go to military school, where I won't see Will in class every day—hell, where I won't see him for months!

I can't do it. God, it would take someone with the maneuvering skills of Machiavelli or Houdini to do it! If only my last name ended in an *i*.

I find a table with no one, which suits me just fine. But before I can even salt my scrambled eggs, there's someone across from me. It's Sean.

He looks at me and then down at his tray immediately, like he's ashamed, or like he thinks I'm mad at him. And in my present mood it's hard to appreciate how gorgeous he is, so I'm sure I'm scowling. What's he doing here, anyway?

He says grace and immediately puts more jam on his toast than I think I've consumed in the last year, and then he doesn't even take a bite before he says, "Taylor, I'm real sorry about yesterday. Really. I was just going toward you guys to quiet things down. But I didn't get there soon enough."

He drinks his juice almost in one gulp. Then, "If only so many people hadn't heard you. Y'know? But everybody did. So I had no choice." He takes a huge mouthful of jam. I mean toast.

"I'm in a tough spot. It's kind of like I'm one of you guys, but I'm not. D'you see?"

What can I say? And I'm not sure I do see. I shrug.

He looks down at his plate and I don't see the whites of his eyes again until he's nearly done eating. Which actually doesn't take long.

Then he says, "I have to get to the laundry room. Get things set up. But—look, you gotta understand my position. I can't slide. I can't give them any reason to think I'm not toeing the line."

He looks at me, and there's this intensity in his eyes that pulls at me across the table. It makes me want to hold him, to tell him it's okay. Which is weird, 'cause I'm the one who's in SafeZone. I'm the one who's got to make the Public Apology about something I don't even think was wrong. But he looks—I don't know, fragile. And again I get that sense that even though he's probably a sweetheart, I wouldn't want to depend on him if my back were up against it.

I sort of nod and shrug at the same time, hoping he'll get that I understand and he can now stop pleading, or whatever he's doing. And he finally throws the last bits of his breakfast into his mouth, washes it down with the dregs of his coffee, and gets up. He holds the tray in one broad, powerful hand, and with the other he squeezes my shoulder.

"You're a stand-up guy, Taylor." And he leaves.

A stand-up guy? I wonder how many other impressions I could leave people with by not speaking, by allowing them to draw whatever conclusions they want to about me with nothing more to go on than what they want to see in me.

When I show up at the laundry room, Sean puts me to work on towels again. That's good; I don't have the focus to learn anything new, and if I had to work with someone else—like Sheldon yesterday—well, let's just say it's better not to. When break time comes I sit on a bench as far away from everyone else as possible, under the green overhang, which is a little noisy today with drizzle falling onto it. Then back to towels.

No sign of Charles at lunchtime. That's weird. I go to an

empty table in a corner and get out my pen and that piece of paper, the one I'd stashed in case anyone asked where Charles was instead of at breakfast. Between bites of ham sandwich, I write down everything the Saint told me to include: I did wrong; I blame only me; I pray I didn't tempt others. I'm just starting to write ideas about what's wrong with what I did when I'm interrupted.

"Hello, Taylor."

I look up. Shit; it's Marie and Jessica. I wave hello, goodbye, whatever, and bend back over my paper again. Maybe they'll go away.

They don't. They sit. Marie on my right, Jessica across from me.

"Where's Charles?" Marie wants to know. Like I can tell her anything.

Shrug, shake my head. Back to the paper.

"We didn't see him at breakfast either. Very mysterious. I do hope he's all right."

I want to glare at her, but even more, I want to ignore her. I ignore her.

But she doesn't give up. "What's that you're writing?"

Just in time I catch a flash of motion as she reaches out to take it, and I snatch it away. I scowl at her, fold it up, and struggle to get it and the pen back into my pocket.

"Taylor, brother, you seem to need some coaching. We have rules here, as you know very well, about consideration for each other. Especially around how boys should treat girls. And even more, about secrecy."

Head down, I'm still tucking things away, wondering how I can get away from her before I do something she *really* won't like, when a now-familiar voice speaks.

"And, sister, perhaps you could use some coaching as well. Especially around how residents treat brothers who are in Safe-Zone."

It's Shorty. Nate. And he sits in the empty chair next to me. Guess he's not ignoring me today. Or really, what he's doing is rescuing me from Marie. I could be anybody—Charles, Leland, it doesn't matter—but I'm grateful nonetheless.

Marie's face turns sour, but what can she say? He's right. Again. She says something anyway. "There are no secrets here. There are not *supposed* to be any secrets here. If Taylor is hiding something, it needs to see the light."

Nate turns to me. "Taylor, are you hiding something?"

As it happens, what I'm working on will be public soon enough, and that's not secrecy. So I shake my head.

"There; you see?"

"He is! He snatched it away when I asked to see it. That's hiding."

Quietly, Nate says, "Taylor, as you know, residents in Safe-Zone are supposed to write comments to other residents only when there is a pressing need. Now, here's where I see things at the moment. You were writing something that Marie tried and failed to see, so you weren't writing to her. So that rule wasn't broken. However, she's now accusing you of being secretive. That is serious and could constitute a pressing need. So I offer you two alternatives. If you would like to offer an explanation, tear off part of your paper and write what it is. If you don't feel an explanation is necessary, just shake your head, and I'll support you. Which is it?"

On the one hand, I don't want to give Marie the satisfaction of an explanation. But on the other, if Nate is going to stand up for me, he has a right to know why. I pull out my paper, and on one corner I write, "I'm preparing something I'll read aloud tonight." I tear that off and give it to Nate.

And he laughs. Then he pockets my scrap of paper, looks right at Marie, and says, "I will bear witness that what brother Taylor is doing is not secret, and that in truth he's not hiding anything. Sister Marie, if you still feel there has been a serious transgression, then we should all petition Mrs. Harnett and request her advice."

"I want to see what he gave you."

"There's no need. I've borne witness, and I'll maintain it. If you persist, and we go to Mrs. Harnett, part of what she learns will be the nature of your conversation before I was fortunate enough to join you here."

Wow. Now, this is useful. I take a close look at Nate, closer than ever before, and I realize he's probably at least a year older than me. I hadn't thought that because he's short and his voice is a little high, but he must be older. And Harnett had said this was his third summer here.

I refold my paper and stow it away again.

"Now," Nate goes on, "perhaps we'd benefit more by talking together about last night's meeting. It was very moving, sister Marie, when you approached Leland toward the end. What was in your heart?"

Marie blinks a couple of times, clears her throat, and finally says, "There was so much in my heart, I'm not sure I could tell you the half of it."

"Understandable. So just share one thing."

This guy is *so good!* Understandable, indeed; it sure is, but not in the way she wants us to understand.

"Well, I felt love."

"Love?"

"Of course. For Leland. We're commanded to love each other, after all."

"Yes, and I'm sure you do. And you made it so obvious, going over to him like that. I wonder if you felt, too, any remorse."

"Remorse? For what?"

"Terrible things happened after you reported Leland kissing Ray."

WTF?

Her back goes very straight. "Why should I feel remorse?"

"Why not?"

"Why not? Well—why *not?* Because they shouldn't have been doing that! They were endangering each others' souls. I had no choice!"

"Oh, sister, I'm sorry. I wasn't clear. I didn't mean remorse for watching those two brothers for days until they finally exposed their true intentions to you. Though, of course, they didn't know you were following them. No, I meant remorse in a more general way, for the pain Leland must be feeling. Perhaps sympathy would have been a better word. Were you feeling that?"

I'm not sure whether it would have been more fun to watch Nate's face or Marie's. I'm glad I opted for Marie's, because over the course of Nate's last reply her expression changed about five times, from indignation to self-righteousness to anger to fear to something like faked dignity. And maybe a few more in there that I can't quite name.

"Don't be absurd, brother. Of course I felt sympathetic for his pain. But you can't say he shouldn't be feeling it. After all, if he hadn't tempted Ray, Ray would be alive today."

"Now, that's an interesting connection you're drawing there. In essence, you're saying that something one person does or does not do can have a direct influence over another person committing a sin, breaking a rule—that sort of thing. Yes?"

"Well, couldn't it?"

"I suppose it could. Just like the way you were addressing Taylor a few minutes ago could have influenced him to break Safe-Zone. I know exactly what you're talking about. Begetting one sin with another. And I would have felt sympathy for Taylor in that case."

He bites a huge hunk out of his sandwich and watches her as he chews. He's describing something not very unlike what he'd done to me yesterday. Though I doubt he'd meant to tempt me, as Marie certainly had. Is he aware? If so, he gives me no indication. He just keeps looking at Marie, who finally seems at a loss for words.

Eventually she sputters something like, "I do hope you're not accusing me of deliberately tempting Taylor to break Safe-Zone."

Nate swallows, smiles broadly, and says, "I hope not, too." And he takes another bite.

I haven't been paying any attention to Jessica through all of this, but now that Nate is done dissecting Marie's motives—or, at least, it appears she's going to do her best to avoid giving him any more opportunities—it occurs to me that Jessica's been entirely silent. And she's barely moved, looking mostly down at her plate. Why hasn't she been more interested in what was happening to her friend? Maybe because she couldn't help her?

God knows I wouldn't want to take Nate on as a verbal adversary. But—not even to react? She must sense me looking at her, 'cause she raises her eyes, sees mine, and lowers hers again very quickly.

I'm not getting any writing done, or even any thinking about what I'm going to write, but I think this is the most fun I've had since I got here. And I owe it to the guy whose fault it is that I have to stand up tonight and read a Public Apology.

Wild. This place is wild. And Nate came back voluntarily? *Twice?*

I hide in a corner again at afternoon break, trying to think. It isn't drizzling as much as this morning, but the grass is damp, and I've come down from that little high Nate had given me at lunch. I still have to do this thing tonight, and I still don't know how I'm going to carry it off.

Break is almost over when I notice Nate. I haven't been paying much attention to who was out on the grass, but he must have been working his way around the edge of the courtyard very slowly or I think I would have noticed him before he got to the fence. He's moving in a casual kind of way, plucking at something in one hand—grass blades, maybe—with his fingers. When he gets to the place where the chain-link fence meets the concrete wall of the building, he stands there staring out for a minute, for all I can tell at nothing in particular. But then he drops the grass bits, puts his hand on the fence, fingers curled around the wires, and then—how could this be?—there's something in his hand. There must be somebody around the wall, someone I can't see from where I'm sitting.

Well, well. I don't have a clue how I might use this, and I know the chances are good that if I try to use it against Nate, he'll still manage to best me somehow. But I file it away for the future, in case of need. He may have come to my rescue at lunch, and maybe I'll stop referring to him in my mind as Shorty, but he's hardly on the short list for Ty's Best Friend in this place. And John McAndrews doesn't seem to like him very much, for whatever that's worth.

Back inside, thinking of the task before me that I'll have to do once I'm in my room, I'm anxious for Contemplation time to arrive and yet wishing I could delay it indefinitely. Of course, this means time passes quickly and seems to take forever. But when Sean calls to the SafeZone kids that it's time to leave, I want to hold on to something and not let them drag me away. I'm the last to leave, and Sean seems like he's not sure whether he's allowed to look at me or not. I look at him, though. And I actually feel sorry for him.

So, no MI today. Just this other thing. This thing that doesn't have to be long. But—Christ. Where to start?

"Well, Ty," I can almost hear Will say, "start by sitting at your desk." So I do. The only things on it are a box of tissues, a lamp, a pad of paper, a couple of pens, and my Bible. I turn on the lamp. I don't need to blow my nose, and I'm not planning to think of Will in a way that'll cause me to need tissues, not at this moment. I'm not ready to pick up the pen or write on the paper. So I pick up the Bible.

At first I play drop the finger, which is just opening the Book at random, closing your eyes, and reading from wherever your finger lands. I do one or two of these, knowing I'm wasting time. But I do one more anyway. I land on the word *forgive*, in the middle of a verse that seems to have no relevance to me at the moment. But then, on impulse—or maybe just to waste more time—I look the word up in the concordance, along with other forms of it, like *forgiveness*. One reference reads, "For if indeed I have *f*— anything." After recovering from what else *f*— might have stood for (the concordance uses only the first letter of the word you're looking up, for some reason), I open up to the reference in Paul's second letter to the Corinthians and read.

Ha! Jackpot. It's perfect.

I can do this. I'll use the concordance to help me find verses that fit my need. People do this all the time. As long as I don't try to twist the meaning of the scripture, there's nothing wrong with it.

By the time I'm done, I have quite the little speech ready. I almost can't wait to read it.

Almost.

It's time for dinner already, and I haven't spent my half hour thinking of Will. But he's been with me the whole time, and I promise him I'll think of him tonight, in bed. Okay, that might be a little dangerous, but I'll risk it.

Charles shows up just as I'm tucking my speech into the front of my Bible. He looks like shit, and I wish I could ask him what's wrong. He grabs his own Bible, and we go in to dinner together. I'm dying to ask where he's been, to tell him how Marie had been so concerned about him, but—maybe tomorrow, when I'm out of SafeZone.

Yes!

My mood is so good, relatively speaking anyway—and for the first time since I got here—that on the way to the dining hall I have to keep stopping myself from turning to Charles to talk to him, to tell him something funny, to get him to laugh or at least chuckle. To get him to respond to me, really. It's frustrating. But probably since it's the first time I've *wanted* to talk to him, it's the first time it hits me how quiet he is. How little he says. Now, I suppose this could be a kind of consideration; I can't reply, so he won't tempt me. But today I think there's more to it than that. It's like he's holding his breath. Holding something vital in. Maybe something he's afraid of, or ashamed of, or can't control. Or all of the above. And if he says something real, something that's got too much of himself in it, the dam will break.

All of a sudden I feel sorry for Charles.

It gets more intense during dinner. He sits with me, and I'm not sure why, because he doesn't eat anything. Okay, he has a glass of water. But that's it. It makes me feel weird, eating while he sips at his water, looking like death warmed over. I keep hoping someone will sit with us, someone like Dawn, who might make him account for himself. I mean, I can't very well ask him what he thinks he's doing.

But it's Hank who sits with us, with Sheldon in tow again. After a couple of ritualized greetings, Hank seems to take in that Charles isn't eating, but all he says is, "No dinner, Charles?"

"No."

"Stomach upset?"

"Just don't feel like it, that's all."

And that ends it. The talk from there goes into what job as-signment Charles has this week, which is Library. Hank's doing Yard and Garden Detail, which he likes 'cause it's outside, but he's wondering if he might like Library. I'm trying to take in things that might be useful for my own future assignments, and Sheldon looks like he's not taking in anything but food. That, and whatever he sees with the furtive looks he keeps shooting around the room. Ye gods; how would the guy survive if he had to do what I have to do tonight? But I guess Leland survived it. At least, I haven't heard anything about him following Ray.

During Fellowship I decide to make Leland my mission. I want to see how he is in this environment. I leave Charles lis-tening patiently to someone yammering on about some differ-ence between one Gospel and another, and wander around the room a little. I see Monica—she's hard to miss—looking her usual surly self over in one corner. The other corners also hold kids looking like they want to avoid discussion, though only one other is wearing a yellow sticker. But no Leland.

I'd have expected him to seek the shelter of a corner, but since he isn't in one, I follow the walls instead; next best thing. Working my way around one clump of Fellowshippers I see a three-quarter shot of Marie from the back, and I nearly duck in my effort to avoid having her see me. I have to go further into the crowd to get around her and whoever she's talking to, and once I've done that I steal a glance back.

Christ. It's Leland. She's got him trapped. And he looks awful. And why not? She's the one who spied on him and Ray, who ratted on them. *She,* not Leland, is the one who killed Ray. Almost instinctively I look around for Nate; where is he when Leland needs him? Barring that, is there anyone else who could swoop in there and rescue him? Anyone who would even know to do that? Dawn! Whether she knows what's going on or not, she'd be a perfect buffer. Where is she?

I stand on tiptoes and scour the crowd, but to no avail. Turning back toward Leland I see he's turned his face away from Marie, and he's pressed against the wall. Walk away, man! I want to shout at him. And he sort of tries. He moves a few feet along the wall, hanging on to it for support, but she follows with him. He's out of SafeZone, so he could reply to her, but if he feels as bad as he looks, he probably doesn't have the emotional strength to keep up with her passive-aggressive banter. Or leave her in the dust, which is what I would do.

What I would do. . . . And what I *have* done, in fact, on one or two occasions.

Well, I guess it's up to me, then. I'll rescue him.

I ease my way through the crowd until I'm right behind her. Leland sees me, and it's like he's seen a life raft from his precarious hold on a piece of rough timber. Marie, seeing his attention focus elsewhere, turns. I smile at her. So sweetly. So charmingly. So falsely.

She blinks a few times before she says, "If it isn't brother Taylor. Where's your friend Nate? I thought you two traveled together."

Now, this is the sort of thing I can imagine hearing from someone like her in a typical high school setting. Maybe middle school. But my point is, it isn't exactly Program dialogue. Everything we say to each other in here is supposed to be supportive, or constructive. Spiritually uplifting or spiritually coaching. But the sarcasm is still dripping from her comment. And she knows it.

I'm standing so close to her that I can see her eyes cloud with the realization that she's let one of her true colors show. And I see the nanosecond of panic as she does a mental grasp at something—anything—to recover from it.

"You seem like such good friends." It's lame, and she knows it, but it's probably the best she can do. She's just lucky I can't speak.

I move over next to Leland and put my hand on his shoulder. We're allowed to do that, as long as others are around; it says so in the Booklet. He closes his eyes and takes a deep breath. Marie is looking at me like she expects me to say something, but I just smile.

Finally Leland says, "Taylor, is it? I'm sorry, I've been a little out of it. Wait—you're Charles's roommate, aren't you?"

Unfortunately, Marie's found her voice again. "Yes. Now that poor Ray is gone. Taylor's the one who forgave Charles for interrupting his first Contemplation."

Now, that's not exactly what I was forgiving him for. It went much deeper than that. She may or may not understand that, but if she does, then she's tempting me to retort. If not, her comment was shallow. And in either case, she's just twisted the knife she'd already planted in Leland's heart. So I throw her this look that I hope registers as "You are so pathetic." I turn back to Leland, squeeze his shoulder once, and jerk my head in the direction of the exit door.

"Sure," he says. "Let's get there a little early. See you later, Marie."

And we're off. We don't even look back. In my head I hear Will say, "Good move, Ty."

Once we're in the hall, Leland half-collapses again, but he manages to say, "Thank you, Taylor. Thank you so much. Was it that obvious that I was, you know, desperate?"

I grin at him and nod. And I really would like to get to the meeting room a little early to go over my minispeech one more time, so I keep walking, and he stays with me. He's quiet, but that's okay with me.

By the time the others start to arrive, I've gone through my motions a few times. Leland is puzzled, but he knows I can't tell him what I'm doing. I figure at least I'm giving him something to think about other than what's going to haunt him the rest of his life.

I choose a seat with easy access to the front of the room, wondering if I shouldn't be taking one near the exit instead, and then wait patiently while the girls stand around chattering. Charles stands next to me, as usual. I turn to him and smile. He looks kind of out of it. And suddenly I wonder if he's gone all day without eating. Wasn't at breakfast; wasn't at lunch; didn't eat dinner. What's he doing, going on some spiritually inspired fast? Does Harnett know? Is this condoned? Should I be worried about him? Well, starting as soon as I've delivered my little speech, I'll be out of SafeZone; Harnett said that would be my release from it. So I can grill him afterward.

After her prepared/ad-lib prayer for the group, Harnett reads a few verses that are apropos of my transgression by way of intro, like she did for Leland last night. Then she closes her Bible and, again like another edition of last night, she says, "Brother Taylor, please come to the front."

Unlike Leland, I don't sit there glued to my chair. I stand, even though my stomach is shaking itself and me into a frenzy, my breathing is shallow and useless, and my pulse is making crashing noises in my brain. Harnett is waiting for me, and she reaches out and pulls the yellow sticker from my shirt. Then she chooses a chair for herself where she can watch the show. With my hands shaking just a little, I raise my Bible.

I close my eyes, take one very deep breath, and then look around the room. There are confused expressions everywhere. They may have recognized the signs of someone being called front and center for a Public Apology, but most likely those are carried out much as Leland had done last night. Which is to say, somebody just carries a piece of paper and reads from it and then cries. But I raise my Bible. And I read.

"Paul's Second Letter to the Corinthians, chapter two, verse ten: 'Now I also forgive whomever you forgive anything. For if indeed I have forgiven anything, I have forgiven that one for your sakes in the presence of Christ, that no advantage may be gained over us by Satan; for we are not ignorant of his schemes.'"

I take my paper out of the Bible cover, lower the Book, and—shaking just a little—I read, "Brothers and sisters, I have transgressed. Yesterday in the laundry room a brother chastised me for something I believed wasn't my fault. And I spoke." I pause a minute to let this sink in. "That was wrong of me. I understand that SafeZone means I may not speak, and yet I spoke. I broke a Program Rule. I could say I was provoked, but I could also say I allowed Satan to outwit me, for I spoke. I could say there is nothing for which I need forgiveness, but I see Satan's schemes called to life all around me every day, and I see others fall prey to them. I don't want to be one of those victims." I'm dying to look right at victim Marie here, but—no.

Bible up. No more shaking. "Psalm fifteen, verse two: 'He who walks blamelessly does what is right, and speaks truth in his heart; he who doesn't slander with his tongue, nor does evil to his friend, nor casts slurs against his fellow man . . . He who keeps an oath even when it hurts, and doesn't change . . . He who does these things shall never be shaken.' Psalm eighteen, verse twenty-five: 'With the merciful you will show yourself merciful. With the perfect man, you will show yourself perfect. With the pure, you will show yourself pure. With the crooked you will show yourself shrewd. For you will save the afflicted people, but the haughty eyes you will bring down. For you will light my lamp, Yahweh. My God will light up my darkness. For by you, I advance through a troop. By my God, I leap over a wall.' "

Bible down, paper up. "I am not blameless. I don't know anyone who is. But I believe that blaming others for my own sins will heap more blame upon me and make darkness return. I have enough blame of my own and don't need to go looking for more by throwing it around. With the help of God, I want to leap over walls. I cast no blame for my transgression on anyone else, or in the darkness I won't even be able to see that wall." I like that one a lot.

I really want to know what Harnett's face looks like. Is she impressed? Furious? Struggling to hold herself back from shouting me down? But no one says anything, so I go on.

"The Letter from James, chapter one, verse thirteen: 'Let no man say when he is tempted, *I am tempted by God,* for God can't be tempted by evil, and he himself tempts no one. But each one is tempted, when he is drawn away by his own lust, and enticed. Then the lust, when it has conceived, bears sin; and the sin, when it is full grown, brings forth death.' "

I take a chance here and glance up. All eyes are on me, that's for sure.

"God does not tempt. If Jesus is God made into man, Jesus does not tempt. Our task on earth is to follow in the footsteps of Jesus. Therefore, I must not tempt. And if by my transgression yesterday I tempted other brothers and sisters to break their SafeZone, or to break any rule, then I am deeply sorry. For I will not be the cause of anyone's spiritual death. I pray I do not even cause another to stumble. I must not tempt."

Paper folded back into Bible. Head bowed. "I ask forgiveness."

This was the point last night when Marie stood and pointed her condemning finger at Leland and shouted scripture at him. Tonight, though, from the corner of my eye, I can see she's as still as glass. As well she might be; half of this was for her.

Nothing happens for long enough that I finally raise my head again. Harnett is standing, looking around the room. But all is quiet. So Harnett turns toward me and says, "Brother Taylor, do you repent?"

Now, I've carefully avoided using that word, even though I had a feeling she'd say this. But she didn't say repent what. Repent means choose a different path, vow not to repeat something. And I'd mentioned quite a few things in my monologue. So, really, the way she said it, I can select for myself. I select tempt; I really don't want to do that. In as humble a voice as I can manage, I say, "I repent."

"Brothers and sisters?" she says to the room. "Do we forgive brother Taylor?"

Leland stands. "I forgive you."

Charles stands. "I forgive you."

One by one, and sometimes two by three, they all stand and say the same thing. Or almost all. By the time the room is quiet, the only person sitting is Nate. At first Harnett doesn't seem to notice, but as she's flashing a beaming smile around the room, her eyes land on him at last.

"Brother Nate? You withhold forgiveness?"

Now he stands, and he weaves through the chairs and people until he's right in front of me. And then he kneels. "I'm not worthy of forgiving brother Taylor for this transgression. Not as long as the sin of temptation is on me. For whether I meant to or not, I tempted him, and he fell. Brother Taylor, will *you* forgive *me*?"

I'm standing there struggling not to let this go to my head. This was supposed to be *my* little theatrical demonstration, my part in a play. One I could in good conscience portray, to be sure. But if I forgive him now, there's a very weird juxtaposition going on. On the one hand, it will be even more like theater. But on the other, it will be even more real for me. And I don't want to get sucked into it. I don't want to lose control. I don't want to take this too seriously.

Not that I have much choice about what to do here. So I nod. And then I remember I'm allowed to speak again, so I say, "Yes."

Two things happen at once. Nate gets me in this bear hug, and Harnett starts shouting, "Satan loses again! Rejoice, children of God, rejoice!"

Then, as everyone is shouting the usual *Halleluiahs* and *Praise the Lords*, a third thing happens, and I feel Nate's hand behind me digging into my hip pocket. WTF? I didn't *think* he was gay, but—in this place, who knows? His fingers move like they're jamming something between the fabric layers, and then in my ear I barely hear him say, "Don't read this until you're sure you're alone." Then he presses his hand against my ass, takes my shoulders in his hands, and beams at me before he walks away.

Anxious for this whole weirdness to end, I go back to my chair and stand there, head down and hands crossed over my groin (which has swollen a little, I confess, from brother Nate's ministrations), and wait. At least, my body waits. My brain waits for nothing; it's racing like a panicked rabbit, bolting and dodging in no particular pattern to try and confuse whatever is chasing it. Whatever that is. And I haven't a clue.

So I miss most of the confessions of Earl, a kid who looks like the alcoholic he says he used to be. He's made an attempt to clean up, but his hair obviously doesn't want to look combed, and his clothes don't seem to fit right. He's skinny—scrawny, really— and even though he's probably only about a year older than me, his skin looks faded. Kind of gray. I try to follow his story, but— I mean, holy shit . . . what *is* this thing in my pocket?

It's all I can do to flip through my Bible in some attempt to look like I'm following along as the meeting goes on from here, trying not to think about Nate's deposit. Something I can't touch, something I must pretend isn't there. Whatever it is, Nate has taken a huge chance. All I have to do is take it out now and start reading it, and someone will see and ask what is it and where did I get it, and . . . and it will be all over for brother Nate. Whatever it is. No matter how innocent. Because it was given in secret. But since he did it in secret, how innocent can it be? *What* can it be?

And by *not* taking it out now and letting all that happen, I'm by default in collusion with Nate. Breaking another rule, right on the heels of having been forgiven for another.

Then it occurs to me that Nate never did say he forgave me. Was that intentional?

Jesus Fucking Christ, but I'm confused. This gets worse every day. Thirty-nine more now? May as well be lashes. At least that would be quicker.

Chapter 7

Watch! Stand firm in the faith! Be courageous! Be strong! Let all that you do be done in love.

—Corinthians 16:13

So the meeting ends, and I'm torn between rushing to get someplace alone so I can read this thing—though where that might be, I haven't figured out—and asking Charles what's going on with him.

Truth be told, I'm a little afraid of this thing in my pocket. I turn to Charles. "Are you going back to the room?" It feels weird to speak to him, but I'm sure I'll get over that.

He shakes his head, touches my shoulder with one hand, and turns away.

"Whoa! Wait. Where are you going?"

He looks exhausted, and stopping to answer my questions is a strain. "The chapel."

"You on some kind of fast or something?"

He opens his mouth once or twice, finally says, "I'll see you in the room later," and leaves. I suppose I could tackle him, but I'm not sure I want to focus Harnett's attention on him. Not until I know what's going on. So all I can do is watch.

And as I watch, I feel a slight touch on my upper arm. It's Nate. He says nothing, just nods, walks past me, and follows Charles. Quietly. From a distance.

To the rescue again. I guess I'll have to trust him.

I'm standing there considering my options in terms of being alone to read when Harnett's voice sounds in one ear.

"Taylor, that was quite an example you set tonight."

I can't read her face. I'm sure she banks on that with everyone. "I wasn't trying to set an example. What kind of example did I set?"

She doesn't answer my question. "How long did you work on that?"

I blink. Who cares? "I dunno, most of Contemplation, I'd guess." I want to ask why she wants to know, but I'm not anxious to continue the conversation. She may start to smell the burning fabric of my hip pocket, which feels hotter by the second.

"And the idea? Where did that come from?"

"The idea? For what?"

"For using scripture like that to make your points."

What's she looking for? All I can give her is the truth. "It's not my idea. You do it all the time. My minister does it. Everyone does it."

"We've never had a resident do it during an Apology."

"Oh. I'm sorry; I didn't know I wasn't supposed to."

She just nods. "We'll talk tomorrow morning. See you in my office at ten." And she turns to speak with someone else.

Leland is standing by the door, eyes on me. I head his way, but Hank is in front of me suddenly.

"I, uh, that was really great. The way you did that. It was great."

A man of few words, Hank, so he needs to repeat some of them. He holds out his hand for me to shake it, so I do. Then Silent Sheldon's replaces his, and he just smiles and nods. He's not out of SafeZone yet; probably tomorrow.

Before I can move toward Leland again, Dawn is upon me.

"You do not hide your flame under any bushel, do you, brother? Come here." She wraps me in this big hug and sways side to side a few times. I can't help grinning, though in the back of my head something is saying, "You don't really know what she means. Which flame? Be careful." She lets go, slaps my back, and leaves.

There are a few more hands to shake, sometimes accompanied by someone saying, "Welcome home from SafeZone" or something along those lines. I don't hear from Marie, which suits me just fine.

By the time I can escape, Leland isn't there any more. I go out into the hallway and look up and down, but I don't see his head among the others.

I sort of want to go to the chapel and see how Nate and Charles are getting along, but that seems like an intrusion. Plus there won't be any good light, and I want to read this thing.

Wait! There's no one in my room!

Trying not to be too obvious, I head that way, nearly limping from the burning weight on one side of my ass. When I get there I practically throw the Bible onto my desk and start to shut the door before I remember I'm not supposed to do that. And doing it would not only break a rule, but it would also mean someone would be very likely to open it and coach me. I've had quite enough coaching for a while.

First I step behind the open door, where no one can see me, and I reach into my pocket. It seems to be a folded piece of paper, standard white eight-by-eleven or whatever. I open it to see that it's a photocopy of a newspaper page with one article title circled in green. My eyes go quickly to the other green marks at the bottom of the page, where it says,

> *Ty—*
> *The world will catch on. You'll be okay, boy. And I'll be here. KOTL*
> *—W*

I have to grab the back of Charles's chair for support. Will! This is from Will! My Will! Holy mother of God, how—where— and then I remember Nate walking over to the fence at break and ending up with something in his hand.

I'm nearly screaming in frustration. Was Will *right there?* Fifty fucking feet from me, and I didn't see him?

Christ!

I pull the chair out and sit, panting, close to weeping. I've crumpled the paper in my hand without knowing it, and as I sit there gasping I flatten it out on the desktop. I stare again at the green. Will's signature color. I smile, but it wobbles, and just for a minute there I do cry. A tear falls onto the paper and just misses where Will wrote my name. I blot it quickly; I don't want any smudges on this.

But—what can I do with it? Where can I keep it?

Well, first I need to read it. There's no telling how quickly Nate might talk Charles into coming back to the room, so I can't stay at this desk. It occurs to me to take my Bible to the library, this paper folded inside, but I don't know what this thing is yet, so I don't know what my reaction will be. I could go to the bathroom, but there will be guys there showering and talking and wandering around.

I decide the best thing is to sit at my own desk, as far from the door as possible to keep my face from being in full view of anyone walking by, fold the paper in half the way the article falls on the page, tuck it into my Bible, and pretend to be reading that.

It works pretty well. The light's not great this way, but it works. And here's what the article, from the *Springfield Crier* says.

Local Boy Takes Own Life
By Alek Baxter

In an apparent suicide, Ray Johnston, son of Spencer and Jeanette Johnston of Springfield, was found a week ago hanging from a balcony in the chapel of a Christian program designed to address troubled youth located in Warren.

The program, called Straight to God, uses scripture, prayer, and peer encouragement to help modify the behavior of teens who have been on drugs, who have abused alcohol, who have exhibited entrenched delinquency, or who are homosexual.

Residents in the program are strictly monitored in terms of bathroom time, clothing and appearance, and interaction with other residents. Their time is allocated among assigned activities such as meals, work assignments, and prayer meetings.

Like other residents, Ray, who asserted that he was

homosexual, was allowed to write home to his parents once a week. According to Spencer Johnston, the first two letters were encouraging.

"Ray seemed like he was really into it," said Mr. Johnston. "He said he was beginning to understand why he was there. He thanked us.

"But he didn't write again," continued Mr. Johnston. "And we got worried."

Toward the end of Ray's fourth week in the program, the Johnstons received the news that their son had hanged himself. According to Straight to God's director, Dr. Emmett Strickland, Ray had been caught kissing another boy and had been put into a disciplinary status known as SafeZone, during which Ray was not allowed to speak, and he was forbidden to sit or stand near the other boy.

Strickland told the Johnstons that two days after Ray was put into SafeZone, he hanged himself.

The Straight to God center is affiliated with the First Century Christian Church, organized under its own nonprofit charter. According to its founder, Reverend Mathew Mattingly, the center was established by the church specifically to "provide Christian teens with clear direction regarding behavior that the First Century Christian Church believes is essential in order to be worthy of God's grace."

During a brief interview, Dr. Strickland explained how important it is in the philosophy of Straight to God for program residents to "learn a new way of being" and to "allow the purity offered by the program to give them a new definition of themselves."

When asked whether the measures might be too intense, for Ray is not the first resident to commit suicide, Strickland said, "Better a boy like Ray should take his own life than return to his gay lifestyle. Homosexuality leads to death of the spirit. If he dies before he commits himself to that pit, God may still take his soul. I pray for Ray's soul every day."

Since Straight to God opened its doors twelve years
ago, eleven residents have committed suicide while in the
program, and eight known others have done so within
six months of leaving. Most of these children were struggling with homosexuality.

When asked if Straight to God had ever been investi-
gated, given the seemingly high incidence of suicides,
Strickland said, "There have been questions, but no
charges have ever been brought against us.

"Teenagers have the highest suicide rate of any demo-
graphic in the nation. As you can imagine, homosexual
teenagers are even more unstable. Straight to God can't
be held accountable for a fact of life," Strickland added.

Insane. The man is insane. He must be. Where in God's own
Bible does it say that suicide is a good way to save yourself from
anything? It doesn't! I don't even have to browse through the
concordance to know that!

Hatred. I struggle with hatred. It's harder when you have
specific objects for it. Like Strickland. Like Marie. Thank God
my folks would be unlikely to see this newspaper. But how had
Will found it? I fold the paper into the middle of my Bible and
set the Book on my desk. Then I fold my arms over it and put
my head down.

I can't say how long I've sat like that before I hear footsteps
coming into the room. I look up; it's Charles. His eyes are puffy
and red, his face blotchy. Just like me on my first night here.
Just like me after spending time in that chapel. What is it about
the chapel?

He sort of nods at me and falls onto his bed.

"Taylor." I jump at the voice from the door. It's Nate. "Why
don't you come with me and we can give Charles some privacy?"

It seems unlikely that I'll get anything out of Charles tonight
about what's going on with him, so Nate's idea is a good one on
two counts—privacy for Charles, and I can also ask about Will.
I stand quickly and nearly push my Bible onto the floor, grabbing it just in time. The article is in there! I stare at it. Should I

leave it here? Why would Charles or anyone look in my Bible? Nate solves this problem, too.

"Why don't you bring that? Perhaps we can do some scripture study."

Not exactly what I have I mind, but it'll do for an excuse. I pick up the Book. "Where are we going?"

"Someplace we can talk."

We take the most circuitous route, and I'm trying to guess our destination. Library? Nope. Prayer Meeting rooms? Nope. Someone's room?

Sort of. We stop by Sean's room. He's at his desk, and as I gaze around it's obvious this is his room. Alone. I want to ask why there's no roommate, but Nate doesn't give me time.

"Hey, brother," he says to Sean. "Less than an hour?"

Sean digs in a drawer, coming up with a key. "That's about all you've got till lights-out, anyway." He looks at me and nods, almost like he'd expected to see me.

The key opens the door to the laundry room. Makes sense Sean would have it; but why do we? Nate locks the door again behind us, and something about the way he's going about things gives me the feeling we need to be quiet. The room is fairly dark, but a couple of overhead lights are on. We work our way to the far corner, behind a bank of washing machines. Then he sits on the floor, so I do, too.

"Do you know why I've brought you here?" he asks.

"To talk?"

He grins. "To talk very quietly about things we wouldn't want just anyone to overhear. Do you trust me?"

"Do you trust *me*?"

He laughs, and has to clamp a hand over his mouth. "I like you, Taylor. Yes, or I wouldn't have given you that paper, and I certainly wouldn't have brought you here. Now. Do you trust me?"

"I guess I could get you into a lot more trouble right now than you could get me into, so I suppose I do."

"As you say, right now. That's key. If we go on much longer with our conversation, we'll both be in the thick of it. I'm already there, of course, but you probably have more to lose."

This seems odd. So I ask, "Why do I have more to lose?"

"I'm here voluntarily, and I'm on my way to college next year. I'm eighteen. My guess is that you don't have the same kind of flexibility."

I shrug; I don't have a clue where all this is going, so I want to tread carefully.

He says, "You read the article?" Nod; I may be out of Safe-Zone, but nodding is quieter. "Got any questions?"

"Who gave it to you?"

"Will."

I close my eyes. Fuck, fuck, fuck. He was *right there*. Eyes back on Nate, scouring his face for any sign of anything, I ask, "This afternoon?"

"Yes."

I'm amazed to feel anger, but that's what it is. "How the f— How the heck do you know him?"

"Will started hanging around the place several days before you got here. I was on yard detail one day—they needed an extra for something. I usually work in the laundry room. Anyway, I saw him that day, but he didn't talk to anyone. The next day I was back in the laundry room, and I was at the fence on break when I saw him. He was looking right at me, but he wasn't close enough to talk. We sort of nodded at each other.

"But the next day I saw him again, and the day after that he was waiting for me. He said he needed to get a note to someone."

"Who did he know—"

"No one yet. He was feeling me out. He convinced me it was just to encourage someone he cared for, and I did my best to convince him he could trust me. We couldn't talk much, obviously. He came back the next two days but didn't speak to me. Then the next day he gave me your name and said you weren't here yet."

"Why did he do all that?" I'm really asking myself, but Nate answers.

"I'm guessing he figured that if I thought he was interested in someone who was here already, and if I couldn't be trusted, then within a couple of days there'd be someone waiting to confront him. That didn't happen."

"Why not?" In other words, Nate, convince *me* that Will and I can both trust you.

Nate takes a deep breath and thinks for a few seconds. "Let's finish this part first. The day he gave me your name, I asked if he was gay. He said yes and so were you, and I told him I'd look out for you. I told him it would be better if you didn't know we'd talked. For your sake. He said he wasn't allowed to talk to you anyway, because you were grounded. Then I suggested he look in that newspaper from Springfield for the article, and I told him I'm the one who contacted the reporter. To help him understand I'm on his side. And yours."

Okay, now I'm speechless. *Nate* gave them that story? All I can think of to say is, "Are you gay?"

He shakes his head. "No. I came here my first time because of drugs and petty theft."

"So, why . . ."

"It's wrong. What they're doing here is wrong. Guys like you and Ray and Leland and a few others I could mention—"

"Charles?"

"I never out someone. Ask him, if you want to know. Anyway, you and a few others I could mention should not be here. This Program helped me in so many ways, I don't know how to tell you. And it's helped lots of others, too. But you shouldn't be here. Ray would probably still be alive if he hadn't been sent here, and so would lots of others. Do you think you can pray away this part of who you are?"

"I don't think I can, and I don't think I should. God made me this way, and he didn't do it to fuel programs like this one."

Nate laughs again. "Okay, now let me finish about Will. He wants you to know that if you have any doubts, any trouble, any real grief, while you're in here, you should just think of him and remember that he'll be there for you. Whatever happens in here, he's out there waiting."

My turn to grin. "I know. He's already been talking to me. In my head, anyway." I decide to take a risk. "Wanna know one thing he said?"

"Sure." He looks like he thinks I'm gonna say something sugary. He's wrong. I tell him who Jesus's favorite is. And after I've told him, he has to stuff his shirttail into his mouth this time, he's laughing so hard. After a minute he starts to recover, and I can't resist saying, "Shall I find you a sheet to roll around on?"

He sobers up pretty quickly. "Do you know why I did that?"

"No."

"Same reason I ratted on you your first day. For humming that tune."

"What?" Too loud.

"Shh! Listen, I have a cover to maintain, and you need to know what will get you the wrong kind of attention. So I killed two birds with one stone."

I nearly hiss at him, "But I got punished for the sheet thing!"

"And that was extremely useful to me. The way you responded? What you did tonight? It convinced me that I could give you Will's note. That article, I mean. That I could let you know what's going on here besides what you see. That I could invite you to join us."

I rub my face. I don't know how much more confusion I can take. "Join who?"

"Taylor, you don't buy into this stuff the way Reverend Bartle and Dr. Strickland do. You don't even buy into it the way Charles does. But you get Jesus. You understand his message the way I do. You know he wants us to love each other and accept each other. Right?"

I nod, wondering what I'm getting myself into. I say, "Connection."

"Exactly! There are others here who feel the same way. There are others every year. Which is part of why I keep coming back. It's not that the Bible is wrong. It's that it's being *used* wrong. It's not a weapon for people like Marie to hurl at people. It's not an arsenal of weapons to use on each other. If there are swords in the Bible, they're for God to use on the reader, not for the readers to use on each other."

"And what do you think you can do about that?"

"If I could have gotten to Ray, I might have helped him hang on till he got out of here safely. I'm helping Leland hold on. And I'm trying to help Charles hold on. And then there's the kids in the circle, and we help each other understand and then spread the word. And I think you could be one of us."

"Circle."

"It's just how we refer to the group. I got invited about half way through my first visit, and the next summer I was asked to lead it. And I'm leading it again this year."

"And you want me in it?"

"Yes."

"What would I have to do?"

"For one thing, keep your mouth shut about it. No one but the leader is supposed to tell any other resident. If there's someone you think should be invited, then you'd tell the group. We'd talk about it and figure out a way to be sure it was the right move and make the decision together."

"And you've already decided about me?"

"Sean suggested you right away. I had my eye on you anyway because of what I'd told Will."

Had his eye on me. And ratted on me immediately. Suddenly I have to know something. "Remember at that break when I hummed "Battle Hymn" to you? Were you, like, thinking of any lyrics in particular?"

He chuckles. "I think you have a pretty good idea. They can get pretty raunchy. But there is one alternative line I've always liked: 'We've broken all the rules; our truth is marching on.' "

We sit there a couple of minutes, him kind of waiting to see what I say next, me trying to think which of the fifty million things I want to start with. My first priority wins. "Is Will coming back?"

"Yes, but I'm not sure when. And if you start hanging out at that end of the break yard, I'll have to tell him to stay away for your own good. What's your threat, by the way?"

"Threat?"

"What will happen to you if you get kicked out of here, what-ever?"

"Military school."

Nate shakes his head. "I almost wish they'd think of some-thing original. It's the most common one. But it's not the worst. I know of a kid who got literally thrown out on the streets. Had to go into foster care for a year. And then there are those who wait until they've left here to really get out. The way Ray got out, I mean. Taylor?" He waits until I look at him. "You aren't likely to do that, are you?"

"Hell, no. I want out of here alive so I can be with Will again. So I can have my life back. I won't give it to them."

"You know, they aren't actually evil here." I open my mouth and he holds a hand up. "I know, I read that article. I know what Dr. Strickland said. But you need to remember that he re-ally, really thinks he's doing what God wants. He *wants* to love you. It's just that he wants to do it in a very limited way. But he doesn't see it like that. Do you know about Mrs. Harnett's older son?"

I shake my head, wondering how many other stories Nate can tell me.

"Her gay son was in the program, but when he got out he told her he hated her and left to go live in San Francisco. She hasn't heard from him since."

"And this makes her feel how, exactly?"

"She doesn't talk about it a lot. But Taylor," and again he waits to make sure he's got my attention, "there is sin here. Around the gay thing. But it isn't yours. Sin is doing something, or not doing something, that causes love to stop. Whether it's your love or someone else's. So in the case here, the sin is with people who try to condemn you for being what you are. Dr. Strickland saying that about suicide, that's totally sin. What he's doing to kids like Ray is causing them to hate themselves. Look at Charles. Poor fellow is desperate to find something to love about him-self, and no matter how good he manages to be, he can't be someone he isn't. And as long as he believes people like Dr. Strickland, he can't love who he is. The ironic thing, if you think about it, is we're actually commanded to love ourselves. Indirectly."

He waits until I bite. "What do you mean?"

"In Matthew, chapter twenty-two, verse thirty-nine, Jesus says that the second greatest commandment, after loving God, is 'Love your neighbor as yourself.' Well, you can't do that unless you already love yourself. Jesus commands us to love each other, and he compares it to loving ourselves. So, Taylor, love yourself. Jesus commands it. And Dr. Strickland's approach stops that, because he's trying to convince boys like Ray and Charles that God can't love them as they are, and if God can't love you, how can you love yourself? So what Dr. Strickland is doing goes against the commandment, and that's sin."

He's got my attention all right, and I wonder if he realizes he's just outed Charles. "Look, Nate, I know Charles is gay. You don't have to out him to me. But—why would they give him Ray, or me, for a roommate? Why do they put two gay guys in a room together and then say, 'Don't do it'?"

Nate chuckles. "I guess that might seem a little odd if you don't know the rationale. They would put a guy like you in with Charles for a couple of reasons. One is that Charles is so, so determined that prayer can change him that he'd never allow anything to happen between you, and he's seen as nearly ex-gay by the directorship here. Plus you're supposed to see, through his example, that you can do it, too. And if they gave kids private rooms, how long do you think it would be before there was some illicit entertainment going on? So they have the new gay kids room with guys like Charles whenever they can, and he can keep an eye on you and provide an example at the same time. They don't always put new gay residents in with other gay kids, but when they've identified someone they think can help, they do it. And if you need another reason, didn't they already tell you that which sin you've committed isn't important? That what matters is that it was sin? If they want to maintain that position, they can't on principle avoid putting gays with gays."

That makes a certain amount of sense. But in one way, Charles isn't a very good example. He sure as hell doesn't love himself. My mind goes back to Nate's comment about that "second greatest commandment." I've heard of things that have a gay subtext, but the idea of a subtext of any kind in scripture was totally new to me. I said, "I've never heard anyone talk about loving ourselves, like what you said a minute ago. Or about that commandment like that."

"If you join us, you'll hear lots more of this kind of approach. This is what we do. We reassess the Bible in terms of who we are, not in terms of who some small group of people think we should be. We apply it to who we really are. You can't fake who you really are. And you can't fake love."

"This circle. Is it all gays?"

"Most of the members are gay, because they're the ones who really don't belong in here. Like I said, the program can help kids like me. The members who aren't gay come to circle because they're interested in a deeper understanding of the scriptures."

"How many of you are there?"

"Depends on the week and who leaves the program. And not everyone comes every time we meet. It would look suspicious if the same kids were missing frequently. Usually we have about five in any meeting. We try to meet at least twice a week, different nights. I don't always come; that would definitely arouse suspicion. There was going to be a meeting tonight, but we decided to invite you. And this way, if you decide to rat—well, I'm the only one you know about."

"I'm not ratting."

He reaches over and squeezes my shoulder. "I knew you wouldn't."

We sit there for a minute, him watching me and me poking into my shoe with a finger. I know he's waiting for an answer, but I don't know if I'm ready. I stall for time. "Why couldn't you get to Ray?"

"Charles. Ray was Charles's roommate before you, remember? He kept a pretty tight leash on Ray, especially after Marie reported Ray and Leland. Charles stuck to him like glue, determined not to let him slip."

"So how did Ray get away from him?"

"After Prayer Meeting on the second night of his SafeZone assignment, he begged Charles to let him go to the chapel alone. Charles undoubtedly knew that John would be watching Leland . . ."

"John?"

"John McAndrews. He's Leland's roommate."

"Not Rick Caruso's?"

"No. Rick's just a hanger-on. He's kind of a McAndrews groupie."

"How did Leland and John get into different Prayer Meetings?"

"Bit of a long story having to do with John's status here. He's like me—keeps coming back. But for different reasons. For now, I'll just tell you that he's definitely not in our circle. Enough said?"

"For now."

"Fair enough. Anyway, Charles insisted on walking Ray to the chapel, but he agreed to leave him alone in there. Ray must have sneaked back to the nearest bedroom that had no one in it at the moment, took a sheet from the bed, tore it into strips, and tied them together. Then he hung himself from the balcony in the chapel."

Holy shit, for real. This explains a lot about Charles's behavior, especially since Leland's Apology. "Wait—you said Ray begged Charles. But Ray was in SafeZone."

"He wrote."

Something about Nate's tone makes me remember one of my burning questions. "What happens to the pieces of paper that SafeZone kids write on?"

Nate looks at me out of the corner of his eyes for a second. "Why do you ask?"

"Someone collects them, don't they?"

"Have you ever looked at the bottom of the wastebasket in your room?"

"No. Why would I?"

"It identifies your room. So it identifies you. And your handwriting."

"And they go through the trash," I finish for him. "I thought so."

It's Nate's turn to be curious. "What made you think that?"

"Harnett told me I was abusing the writing option. That I wasn't using it only for emergencies. So if she knows what I write, then either Charles and Sean deliberately turned them in to her—they're who I wrote to—or someone goes through the trash. But they know, don't they? Charles and Sean? They know someone goes through the trash. I wrote to Sean to ask who the heck you were, and he crumpled it up and stuffed it into his pocket."

Nate looks worried all of a sudden. "What made you ask him about me?"

"You seemed like contradiction after contradiction. One minute you're giggling at lyrics you know are obscene even though I'm only humming, and the next you're spouting scripture like everyone else here. Then you give Leland a quiet shoulder squeeze when he needs it, but you yell at Sheldon and me for nothing. So, yeah. I knew there was something wacko going on. But if it's any comfort to you, I would never have guessed about the circle."

He's nodding. "Okay, I guess that makes sense. I just need to be really careful how I balance those two sides. And I'm guessing you had a better chance than most to notice it, 'cause I was focused on you." He shifts his leg position and says, "So. What do you think? Will you meet with us?"

"Sean's in the group?"

Nate looks a little uncomfortable. "No. Sean . . . well, Sean supports us, but he's in a tough position. He works for the church most of the year. This has been his summer assignment for a few years now, and he needs it. He avoided prison on condition that he work here—Reverend Bartle spoke for him—and he can't afford to be caught in a group like this. Plus I think he's still too confused about the gay issue. So. Will you meet with us?"

What would Will do?

"Yes."

Nate extends a hand to me, and I take it. He says, "Be here

tomorrow night after Prayer Meeting. Follow me inconspicuously so you'll know how to get in. And Taylor, I think you should know that this is the first time I know of that someone's been asked to join so soon after they got here."

I nod, not sure whether this is a good thing or a bad thing. "Who else is in the group?"

He just grins at me. "You'll meet them all, I promise. And now I have a suggestion I think you'll like. Would you like to write a couple of lines for me to give to Will next time he shows up?"

Would I! "Now?"

"I have a pen and I have a piece of paper. Here you go. And Taylor, no names. But if you can think of some symbol or something that would help him be sure it's from you, include that."

I think for a minute, imagining Will coming all the way out here all those times just to exchange notes with Nate. Which is a risk for everyone. Much as I want to think of him as close by, it's almost worse knowing I can't see him except through Nate. So I write, "You'll be there; I trust that. And soon I'll be with you. So no need to do this again. GLYASDI." I fold it up and hand it to Nate. He opens it.

"Hey!"

"Sorry, kiddo. It's my reputation on the line here, and the safety of several others depends on us doing everything right." He reads. "Um, what's *GLYASDI?*"

"It's IM lingo. God Loves You And So Do I. He'll know it's from me."

"Cool. I like it. You're telling him not to come again?"

I take a shaky breath. "It seems best."

Nate looks at me hard for a few seconds. "I knew we were doing the right thing with you. And now, my friend, we need to get back. I'm hoping Charles is asleep, but if he isn't he'll be watching the clock on account of you. Plus someone will be prowling the halls looking for reprobates and curfew breakers."

"Wait—how are you helping him?" Suddenly it's important.

"I'm trying to give him some balance. Working with scripture to help him let go of the guilt. Otherwise he'll make himself crazy in no time."

"Does Harnett know?"

"Let's just say she knows I have a way with some of the residents."

"Did I do something wrong tonight? Using scripture to make my points?"

Nate thinks for a minute. "No, not wrong, exactly. It was like you were taking on a role that's traditionally used by program leaders, though. Kind of a teaching role. You're new, so you couldn't have known that. But it shows a certain initiative that most kids who come here don't have, at least in the beginning, and later they don't show it the way you did. If new kids show initiative, it's in other areas. Like rebellion. Now, we need to get outta here, brother!"

It feels great to have him call me that, and I'm grinning as I grab my Bible and get onto my feet. On the way to the door I ask, "What do you think I should do with the article? I've been trying to come up with a good hiding place."

"Taylor, if you so much as pick your nose in this place, they'll know. Tear it up in little shreds and flush it down a toilet."

"I can't do that!"

"You have to. If you can't promise me you will, I'll have to take it back and destroy it myself. You gotta understand, if someone finds it, you won't be the only one taken down."

"I told you, I wouldn't rat."

Just before opening the door to leave the laundry room, Nate stands still and looks at me. "Did Reverend Bartle take you to the chapel your first day here?"

"Yeah." It's a scene I'd rather not remember.

"Do you even remember what you said? And do you want to do that again?"

"But . . . God, I can't destroy this! It's all I have of Will."

"Are you kidding?" Nate hits me on the shoulder. "He talks to you in your head, doesn't he?"

So I promise. But it hurts.

Back at the room, Charles has gone to bed and left my desk light on for me, like I'd done for him yesterday. Was it yesterday? All I know is that it's Wednesday night, I'm out of SafeZone, Will is waiting for me and I'll be with him again in five and a half weeks, and—the most amazing thing of all—this place is either nowhere near as crazy as I'd been thinking or it's even crazier.

I sit for a little while at my desk, Bible open to Will's note. I don't read the article again; it would only make me angry. And I don't want to feel anything negative right now. So I focus on the green ink at the bottom. "I'll be here." And "KOTL"—Kiss On The Lips. I close my eyes for a minute and imagine that. Of course, body parts other than lips get involved in my fantasy, and I'm going to be in trouble if I don't stop.

A glance at my watch tells me it's too late to be up without breaking a rule. I fold the note again and decide the safest thing for now is to put it inside my pillowcase. In the morning I'll figure out what to do. I haven't brushed my teeth or anything, but it's too late for that. I can get away with having to take a leak in the middle of the night, but if I'm caught brushing my teeth it'll be suspicious.

Lying in bed trying to fall asleep, listening to the sound of Charles's even breathing, my mind keeps going to the conversation with Nate. To what he's asked me to do. Jesus, to what I've agreed to do. What was I thinking? But how could I not? Nate was right; I do get Jesus the same way he does. And it is what Will would do.

Will. I decide I haven't thought about him nearly enough today and that it's time now. Especially considering all those trips up here he made. He must have come up here the day after I gave his sister that note.

That's so like him, you know? The green ink. The "I'll do it my way" attitude. He sees what's right, and he just does it.

I've thought of Will as brave ever since that day in World History, when he stood up to Ted Tanner. Here's Will, the new kid, and he knows he's gay even if Ted doesn't. He could have pretended he didn't know that interesting fact about King Richard. Or he could have just let Ted cackle like the idiot he is without responding to him. But that's not Will.

The day I called him brave to his face was a couple of months ago. He'd turned seventeen and gotten his license, and we drove together for a while—our first road trip—and ended up at this park area. It was a gorgeous spring day. You know, where all kinds of sap starts moving, like the kind that makes me want Will and vice versa.

We found a remote spot where it looked like kids probably came at night and left their crap behind. Empty beer cans, used condoms, the occasional shoe. It was away from everyone else, which was its most appealing quality for us at the time. We took advantage of it.

I think I like kissing in springtime more than in any other season. The air was just cool enough to make me acutely aware of the warmth of Will's body, of his breath, of his lips everywhere they touched me. And they touched me everywhere. So I knew he was feeling that warmth when I returned the favor.

We like taking turns going down on each other. That day, I went down on him first. I felt like some old pro. And I did it all perfectly, if his response was any indication.

Because we were sort of in public, we hadn't actually undressed, and he fastened himself back up and then did for me what I'd done for him. After we kissed, he got up saying he had to take a leak, and I decided to lie there just as he left me, all exposed, until he came back. My soft dick lay there, too, sort of flopped over like a flag after the breeze dies, and I concentrated on the temperature difference—warm inside, cool outside, the sun overhead just beginning to make promises of heat.

"Well, well. Mike, what have we got here?"

I sat up so quickly I nearly hurt my exposed tender parts, and the sight of two tough-looking guys staring down at me caused me to shove myself back into my pants so fast it's a wonder I didn't castrate myself with the zipper.

Mike, I guess, said, "Some tender young morsel by the look of it. Hey, cutie. What's with the indecent exposure? Can I get in on the action?" He grabbed at his crotch with one hand, holding what looked like a bag with a six-pack in it with the other, while the guy who'd spoken first moved toward me.

I scrambled to my feet as fast as I could, but Mike's cohort pushed at me and I fell backward.

Suddenly Will was standing beside me.

"Hello, boys," he said. "Here for a tryst?"

I could tell by the looks on their faces they weren't quite sure what that meant, but Mike decided to treat it as rhetorical. "So this tender meat isn't here alone, eh?" He looked down at me, still prone on the ground like some lame child. "Hey, Stu, they're fags."

As I was scrambling up again I was thinking, Where's King Richard when we need him?

Then I heard Will say, "And what are you boys doing here? Together?"

Stu didn't much like that. I suppose neither of them much liked it. But it made Stu boil. He pulled an arm back like he was getting ready to strike, saying, "Why, you little . . ."

Will put his arms out to his sides, bent at the elbows, one of them in front of me and pushing me back a little. "Whoa there, guys. You sure you wanna go there? Could be dangerous."

Stu's arm paused, and Mike barked a laugh and said, "You think you're dangerous?"

"Deadly."

"Really. You gonna pretend you're some kind of karate expert or something?"

"Don't need to." Will's voice was so calm. I didn't understand how he could do it. "All I have to do is spit on you and you're dead."

Stu's arm was completely down now. The guys looked like they were trying to make sense out of this. So was I, actually.

"What the fuck are you talking about?"

"AIDS."

The four of us stood there regarding each other for maybe six seconds, and then Mike slapped Stu's arm. "Let's get outta here. They aren't worth it." They turned and left. Rather more quickly than they needed to, I thought.

I felt Will's arm wrap around my neck and pull me down toward the ground again. I resisted.

"C'mon, Ty. They won't be back. Let's not waste the day."

"Wait. Just wait." I ran a hand through my hair. "What you told them . . ."

"Ty, be serious. If I had AIDS, don't you think I'd have told you before we did anything?"

"But . . . All right, fine. But you can't get it from somebody spitting on you."

He shrugged. "Obviously, those idiots don't know that." He sat down and held a hand up to me.

Feeling dazed, I sat down beside him, but I wasn't ready to just dive into springtime pleasures again just yet. "That was . . . Shit, Will! That was beyond brave. More than courageous. You were so calm."

"It's essential. The last thing you want a bully to know is that you're afraid of him."

I shook my head. "You hide it well."

"What?"

"Fear."

"Oh, that's not it. Courage is something you need to overcome fear. I wasn't courageous. I don't feel fear from things like that."

"Again, *what?*"

"They're just idiots, Ty. They didn't worry me."

"What if they hadn't been stupid as well as idiots? What if they'd known better than to think they could get AIDS from spit?"

Another shrug. "Then maybe there would have been reason for a little fear. And I would have had to think of something else. But, Ty, you can't go around the world as a gay guy and advertise that you're afraid. And really, if they know you're gay, they expect you to be afraid. So when you're not, it throws them. In a very different way from how I'm gonna throw you right now."

He wrapped himself around me and we rolled on the ground for a minute, testing each other's strength. Finally I pinned his arms on the grass, or maybe he let me pin his arms on the grass, and I kissed him. Deeply. Warmly.

I dropped down beside him and snuggled till our bodies

touched all down our sides, and we lay there like that in the teasing sunshine until I nearly spoiled it. I brought up something I'd been trying not to think of ever since that first time we'd been together, in my room last fall.

"Whenever somebody acts like that, says things like that—"

"You mean those assholes?"

"Yeah. I start hearing voices in my head. They're quoting verses from the Bible. About us. About what we are."

"You mean like the ones that were written thousands of years ago when it was okay to sell your daughter into slavery? But not your son because sons are really people whereas daughters are not? Those verses?" I shrugged, and Will raised himself up on an elbow to look at me. "You're afraid those voices in your head mean that those idiots who thought they could get AIDS if a fag spit on them are right?"

"Look, you're making it sound all one-sided. Maybe those guys are idiots, but it *is* what it says in the Bible."

"Ty, even those assholes can read. But they aren't that great at thinking. They're barely this side of Cro-Magnon man. It's up to people with brains, people like you and me, to understand that God is not about calling names and trying to make other people feel like shit. God is about love. Jesus said so." He lay back again and, his voice teasing, added, "And Jesus is my hero. Who's yours?"

That's Will. Mixing all the things that life is made of into one glorious package. I answered, "You." And to prove it, I went down on him again.

Lying here now, thinking of making love with Will, and despite my roommate sleeping a mere six feet or so away, I pull until I come.

As I'm starting to drift off into sleep, it's hard to distinguish whether the warm glow I feel is coming more from thinking about Will or from being asked to join the circle. They start to blend together, the way stuff does when you're falling asleep, and it hits me again that joining the circle is exactly what Will would do. Nate had given me this chance, and—this hits me so hard I wake up a little—I hadn't felt fear. I hadn't needed courage to say yes to Nate.

And then it occurs to me that the circle is actually my prayer being answered. You know? The one I'd prayed Monday night about finding other kids who feel like I do? And the answer to the question, to my prayer, is yes.

Chapter 8

One who trusts in himself is a fool; but one who walks in wisdom, he is kept safe.

—Proverbs 28:26

That stupid shrieking bell wakes me up. I hate it, but in a way it's good, because as soon as my brain is in gear I remember what happened last night. Will got through to me because of Nate, who wants me in the circle. This place has an underground. Who knew? And I'm in it.

Suddenly I sit bolt upright: I'd nearly forgotten I have to see Harnett at ten o'clock! I'll have to keep my euphoria in check.

Charles hasn't gotten out of bed yet, which surprises me considering his past behavior. So I call over to him, "Charles? You awake?"

"Yes." But he doesn't move. Just lies there, face to the wall.

Fine. I get up and grab my shower kit and towel, and then I remember what's in my pillowcase. And what I have to do with it. I stand there a good thirty seconds or so, trying desperately to think of a way I can keep it and not jeopardize the circle. But I can't. Not really. Not in this place. So I go back and get it, fold it smaller, and tuck it into my pajama top pocket. Charles is still lying there; hasn't moved. I'm wondering if he's sick. He hasn't eaten since Tuesday.

"Hey, are you okay? Do you want me to get someone?"

"No. I'll be up. Don't worry about me. See you in the bathroom."

In the shower stall it occurs to me that this would be the best place to shred the paper. If I get it wet, it won't make any noise. Standing against the closed door so no one on the other side can see, I take it out of my pocket and unfold it, and just once more I read the green ink. "I'll be here." Funny thing about love notes. You can lose the note and still keep the love.

I kiss it once, fold it up again, and as I'm showering I get it just wet enough to make it quietly and easily shreddable. Somehow I manage to keep it in my hand as I make my way, wrapped in my towel, to a toilet booth, nearly giggling when it occurs to me I could have hidden it up my ass for this part of the journey. I sit on the toilet long enough to do what I have to do, which also gives me time to shred the note. The first tear rips part of me as well, but it's necessary. And then it's gone.

But it isn't. Because I remember it. And because Will is there.

Charles is just getting to the bathroom as I'm leaving. We nod. And he doesn't get back to the room until it's time to leave for breakfast.

"I'll wait for you while you dress," I tell him.

"No, don't do that. I'll see you in there."

"I don't trust you."

"What?"

"I don't trust you not to fast again. I'm waiting."

He gives me a look that's got something frantic in it, but I'm sitting at my desk by then. What can he do?

He's still behind the curtain dressing when there's a knock at the door. It's Nate.

He looks at me and says, "You're going to be late, brother Taylor."

"I'm waiting for Charles."

"You go ahead. I'll wait for Charles." And he sits in Charles's chair. So I leave.

Full tray in hand, I survey the dining hall on this, my first breakfast out of SafeZone. I can sit anywhere, talk to anyone. Off to my right I hear my name called.

"Taylor! Please, join us."

It's John McAndrews, with Tonto. I mean Rick, of course. I

stall for a second; Nate gave me the distinct impression this guy is on the bad list. Or at least not on the good one. But—what the heck, may as well get to know the enemy. And the last thing I dare do is give John the impression that I'm avoiding him.

He waits for me to bow my head for grace, but then he doesn't waste time. "I heard about your Public Apology last night, brother Taylor. Very impressive."

"I wasn't aiming for that. And I'm not sure it was such a good idea."

"Oh? Why not?"

"I've been thinking about it, and now it seems a little presumptuous of me." This is cool, actually; I'm practicing for my meeting with Harnett.

"Presumptuous. An interesting word to choose." I pack my mouth full of toast so that I don't have to respond. He tries again. "I'd love to talk with you sometime about your approach."

I swallow. "Approach? To what?"

"To putting something like that together. What your thinking was as you selected your scriptural references. Why one and not another. I assume you used a concordance?"

Now, this is interesting. I'm surprised he's asked that; few kids wouldn't need to use one. True, he's posing it as an assumption, but what he really doesn't want me to say is that I just came up with those references based on my in-depth knowledge. Unable to resist the temptation, I dissemble. "Why do you assume that?"

He blinks. As I take a forkful of scrambled eggs he says, "Well, unless you are extremely well acquainted with scripture, you'd need one. And I assume that the reason you're here means you're not."

I finish chewing, swallow, and say, "Really. Do you know why I'm here?"

He actually seems a little uncomfortable. Slow down, Taylor, I warn myself. You don't want to make this guy think you're anything other than wowed by him. It's what he expects from everyone. He says, "I have a unique position at Straight to God. Perhaps no one has described it to you."

"Nope." Hey, Dawn, that one's for you.

"Let's just say I'm here on a different basis from most other residents. So yes, I know why you're here."

"And what is there about why I'm here that makes you think I wouldn't know scripture really well?" I'm not good at slowing down, am I?

He leans forward, like he's about to tell me some secret. "Brother Taylor, if you did, you wouldn't have been doing what you were doing. You'd know better, because you'd know how God feels about that."

The things that come into my head first would almost certainly have gotten me into trouble. I do my best to temper my response. "We're all sinners, brother John. And some of us know the Bible very well indeed."

The way he's looking at me is starting to worry me. So I decide to toss him a bone. "But as a matter of fact, I did use a concordance. Don't you?"

He takes a sip of coffee. "Sometimes. Sometimes not. I prefer to match my own understanding of the scriptures with my memory of what's in them."

I decide to change the subject so I can avoid having to tell him I have no intention of having him pick my brain about how I made my choices. "I'm really looking forward to the barbeque tomorrow night."

It's a curveball, and it takes him a second to recover. "Oh. Sure. Me, too. Rick and I are planning to be there a little early to help set up. Do you want to meet us here at around five thirty?"

A thunderbolt strikes suddenly. An idea out of nowhere. "Well, actually, I need to talk with you about that. I know I said I'd go with you guys, and if you really need me, then I will. But I don't think anyone has asked Marie Downs to accompany them. So I was hoping it wouldn't be out of place for me to do that. What do you think?"

For the first time since I sat down, I have Rick's attention. Then he looks at John, who says, "Oh. Well. I mean, it's a little unusual for a new resident to ask someone to an Activity. I, uh,

I don't know that there's any rule against it, it's just that it doesn't happen."

"Kind of like what I did last night doesn't happen? Okay, enough said. Then I won't. I just hated to think of her not being asked, that's all." And I take a bite of bacon.

"Tell you what, I'll talk to your staff leader and let you know what our advice would be."

"Our" advice, is it, John? Pulleez. "Oh, that's a good idea. Actually, I'm meeting with Mrs. Harnett this morning, so I'll ask her then. I'll let her know we talked about it." And while he's trying to decide how to reply to that, I drain my glass of juice. Then I say, "Listen, thanks so much for asking me to sit with you. I'd like to get to my work assignment as early as possible, since I have to take time out for my meeting. I'll let you know what Mrs. Harnett says. God bless you, brother." And I'm off.

Making my way through the breakfast crowd, I look around until I see Charles and Nate. There's food in front of both of them, and it looks like Charles is actually eating. I feel relieved. And a little possessive.

All the way to the laundry room I'm chuckling over my conversation with John. If Harnett says it's too early for me to invite a companion to an Activity, then I get credit for asking permission. And if she says it's okay, then going with Marie could serve to throw off anyone—like John—who might be suspicious of me. Of course, it will be a sacrifice going with Marie. But she might say no. And if she doesn't, and I have to go with her, at least I can talk now. And other than violating SafeZone, I'll bet there ain't much she could tempt me to do.

Sean is almost abrupt with me when I ask for my assignment for the day, but I don't take it personally. I understand he can't afford to have anyone suspect anything, and that means there can't be any obvious special understanding between us. So I play along.

He says, "Do you suppose you and Sheldon could work on sheets today without getting into any trouble?"

"Sure. Oh, I have to see Harnett at ten."

"Mrs. Harnett."

"Sorry. Mrs. Harnett. Do I need anything special by way of a hall pass or anything?" I don't really expect he'll say yes; I'm teasing him a little.

"You do. I'll have one ready for you."

Oh. Well. Wonder if it's time to pick my nose now. . . . "Thanks."

Sheldon isn't here yet, so I start without him. I've almost gotten the fitted-sheet-folding technique figured out when he shows up. I'm happy to see him; we'll actually be able to talk to each other for the first time. I've never heard his voice, other than when he's laughing. As he's walking toward me, I hold up my hand for a high-five, but he stops short.

"Taylor, no. We can't do that."

"Why not?"

"It's FI."

"That's bogus. Who told you that?"

"John McAndrews."

Careful, Taylor; don't give anything away. I try to keep the sarcasm out of my voice. "Oh well, then. I guess we shouldn't, if he says so. Is it okay to shake hands?"

Sheldon looks a little sheepish. "I guess so." And we do.

"I have to see Mrs. Harnett at ten o'clock. We can work together until then."

"You'll have to get a pass."

"Yeah. Sean knows." Maybe Sheldon isn't going to be any fun after all. He seems like a bit of a wuss at the moment.

We work silently—just like old times—while I try to think of something to say. At one point I see Nate come in, but I'm careful not to take any special notice of him. Finally I ask Sheldon, "So, why were you sent here?"

Sheldon cringes like he's been caught doing something he shouldn't. Or like he's about to be. "Taylor, jeez."

"Jeez what? Is it something you don't want to talk about? I'll tell you why I'm here, if you want to know."

"Look, I don't want any trouble. I've left all that behind me, okay? I've wiped my slate clean. Dr. Strickland said so."

"And Reverend Bartle prayed it out of you?"

Sheldon looks over his shoulder like he's afraid people are listening. "I've repented. I'm not revisiting any of that. So please stop asking me."

"Okay, okay. What do you wanna talk about?"

"I dunno. Something that won't get me into trouble."

Won't get him into trouble. I wonder if he knows what trouble is. "How long will you be here?"

"Six weeks."

"Me, too. What's the first thing you'll do when you get out?"

He's quiet so long, I'm not sure he heard me. We finish a sheet and he sets it on the pile and leans on it. He doesn't look at me, but he says, "Do you mind if we don't talk so much?"

I'm *so* tempted to ask what he's afraid of. But I know he won't tell me, and he's already freaked out. So I just say, "Whatever," and pick up another sheet.

We're still folding away, as silently as on Tuesday, when Sean signals me from the office door. Pretending I'm still in Safe-Zone, I gesture to Sheldon that I have to go. I think the point is lost on him.

Sean hands me a slip of paper that has Mrs. Harnett's name and his on it. "Here. She'll give you another one to get back."

"Thanks." Being out of SafeZone isn't nearly as much fun as I'd hoped.

Harnett is waiting for me, sitting behind her desk, hands folded in front of her. "Good morning, Taylor. Please close the door behind you and then have a seat."

As I sit, I notice my MIs are under her hands. I say, "Good morning," and wait for her to start.

"You're a very interesting resident, Taylor. And honest, thanks be to God. The tone of these two documents varies one from the other according to the moods you were most likely in when you wrote them. Do you accept Jesus Christ as your savior, Taylor?"

Was that a non sequitur, or did I miss something? "Yes, ma'am."

"You wrote on Monday that bad words had occurred to you multiple times. Are you finding the frequency to be lessening?"

Just last night I'd changed *fuck* to *heck* when I was talking to Nate. That should count for something. So I say, "No, but I'm finding it easier to change them to something less offensive."

She blinks at me. "You make it sound as though you've been speaking them."

"In my head, I have. But on Monday and Tuesday, I didn't change them to something else."

"So you can see how SafeZone can help you. And now that you're speaking out loud, you change them?"

"I guess that's it."

"Why are you changing them?"

Okay, I know what kind of an answer she wants here. I decide to give her as much as I can without lying. "They're wrong here. I'm trying to leave them outside."

She looks at me for a second and then says, "They're wrong outside, too, Taylor. Do you understand that?"

"Yes, ma'am. But I have to take it one step at a time. I've been saying them for years."

I think she's trying not to chuckle. "Very well. Now, you mentioned you were reported to be humming an inappropriate song. You also mentioned you changed the song to something else when you hummed later. Tell me about that."

Tell her about it? That's what I did in the MI. "I'm not sure . . . What do you want to know?"

"Were you surprised that someone reported you?"

"Yes."

"When you were humming the first time, did you sing the lyrics in your head?"

"Some of them. The ones I could remember."

"Didn't you recognize them as FI?"

"No. Not until Sean pointed it out. Then I started humming something else."

"But did you understand, after Sean spoke to you, that it was wrong?"

I shrug. "That song doesn't have anything bad in it. So if it's just a question of reminding me of how I was before I came here, then I understand. But the song itself seemed fine to me."

"Do you understand, Taylor, that you're being born anew in the time you spend with us?"

I want to say I was born okay the first time. But I just tell her, "Yes, ma'am."

"When you leave here you'll be a new person. It's a chance few people get in their lifetimes, and I hope you will cherish it in the way it deserves. Only God can give you this chance, Taylor. God and the people who love you."

I bow my head, hoping that will do the trick. It seems to.

"Now, your MI goes on to say that you were chafing in SafeZone. You said it made you want to lie about what had happened because you didn't feel you'd done anything wrong, and yet you couldn't explain yourself." She looks at me. I wait her out, and she goes on. "Tell me now what you think about Safe-Zone."

Brainstorm. "I think it's like a double-edged sword. It cuts both ways."

She sits forward just a squidge. I have her. "Go on."

"Well, it can still be extremely frustrating, at times when I feel strongly that I need to communicate something. When I think I'm being misunderstood or misjudged. Like with the sheets in the laundry room, when Nate chastised us. But at other times it's good. Like, being new, I don't know all the ways we're supposed to behave. How we're supposed to respond to things. So it's good to be able to watch without being expected to speak. And, like I said earlier, maybe it kept me from saying some things I shouldn't. Things I'm used to just blurting out."

She's nodding; good. But then she says, "So, what if I told you I was going to put you back into SafeZone?"

A number of those "wrong" words occur to me at once, and it's everything I can do not to react. As quietly as I can, I say, "I guess I'd hope you'd tell me why."

"I mentioned that you are a very interesting person, Taylor. Many times, interesting people are also presumptuous. Many times, they rebel against authority. Many times, they find humility an almost unbearable challenge. I think you are one of those people."

Don't speak, Taylor. Don't speak. Say nothing. Presumptuous; that's what I'd said to John. . . .

"Are you one of those people?"

"Do you think that because of what I did last night? Because if you do, I didn't mean to do anything wrong."

"No, I don't think you did mean to do anything wrong. And strictly speaking, you didn't. But you revealed many things about yourself nevertheless. Initiative is not necessarily a bad thing, Taylor. In fact, once it's harnessed, it's a very good thing. Yours has, I think, yet to be harnessed. Partly that's because you're young. And partly it's because you are a leader. But because you are a leader, it's that much more important for you to learn to curb your impulses, to manage them, to shepherd them in ways that lead others to the glory of God rather than in ways that break down discipline. Do you understand what I'm saying?"

Okay, this is a trap. If I say no, I get SafeZone as punishment. If I say yes, I get it because I asked for it. I try a distraction. "Are we going to talk about my second MI?"

I hate the look I see on her face right now. It's like she's not falling for it, but she knows I've tried.

"Your second MI isn't nearly as interesting as your first. It's more a laundry list of transgressions, and the one that preyed most heavily on your mind was forgiven last night. And I think you understand now about the writing." Oh, I understand, all right. I understand you'll see anything I don't flush down the toilet. "So, no, I don't think we need to dwell on the second one. But we do need to figure out how to address the situation that has arisen around your leadership. Were you aware of the effect your Public Apology had on your brothers and sisters?"

Effect? No; what effect? "Some of them spoke to me afterward, that's all I know." I'm trying not to sound sulky, and not succeeding. I know where this is going, and I can't see a way out.

"They were very impressed. Some of them who typically speak out when the Apology is finished were silent. And as for speaking to you afterward, I don't think I've ever seen residents praise a brother or sister after an Apology. If they express anything, it's sympathy or understanding. Support. But they praised you."

Thanks, Dawn. Thanks for nothing. I'll have to learn to hide my light under a bushel from now on. "I wasn't looking for praise. I just wanted to be understood."

"I believe you. If I thought you had deliberately set yourself forward in pride, your punishment would have been severe. As it is, I think one more day of SafeZone will help you understand how you must modify your—let's call it zeal. Redirect it."

She sits back and folds her hands on the edge of the desk. "You are bold, brother Taylor. This is a good thing. But your boldness, your energy, must be harnessed and directed toward the glory of God. Perhaps you didn't intend to direct it toward self-glorification, but it would be far too easy, and extremely dangerous, for others to glorify you because of it. And that can lead to delusion, to glory of self. Do you understand?"

Am I in SafeZone yet, I want to ask? Foolish. That would be beyond foolish. So I tell her the truth. "I'm not sure how to answer that."

"Very well. Because you're in SafeZone again until noon tomorrow, you will be released from your work assignment at four o'clock today for Contemplation. I suggest you spend that time to come to the understanding you don't yet have. And don't forget to do your third MI. I'll see you here tomorrow at noon precisely." She picks up a pen and writes something on a paper. "Keep this note with you until I see you again, in case anyone stops you in transit." She hands it to me and then reaches into a drawer. In her hand is a sheet of yellow stickers. "Do you have any questions before you enter SafeZone?"

It's an effort to breathe normally. I'm sure my face is beet red, and fury is making my stomach boil up whatever it was I had for breakfast. I struggle to keep my voice even. "Yes. I was planning to ask you whether I could invite Marie Downs to accompany me to tomorrow night's barbeque. But if that would be putting myself forward inappropriately, I won't."

"I'm glad you understand, Taylor. It would, in fact, be putting yourself forward inappropriately. Not only because this is your first week, but also because I suspect your reasons are not altogether admirable. Why Marie?"

Think fast, Taylor. "Well, she seems to be kind of desperate. Like she's struggling for something she can't quite see. And it can make her seem abrasive. No one had asked her, so I thought it might make her feel better if someone did. That's all."

Harnett gives me a long look, like she's trying to see into my brain. "Well, maybe for some future Activity you could ask her. But for now, I think you should go with John."

Ha! So he *is* in on this with her. Otherwise, how would she know there had been any plan to go with him? It's so tempting to say something here. Like, "Did he tell you he wants to understand my scriptural-research methods?" But I just sit there, trying hard not to look angry. Hell, trying not to look like the wrath of God. Plus if I say anything else, she might make me do a Public Apology for my Public Apology.

She asks, "Anything else?"

But I've said all I'm going to say. I was trying to be honest in here, at least as honest as I could be. But this isn't the first time being honest has gotten me into something shitty. If I'm forced, and I'm beginning to think I am, I can give her only what she wants to hear. I can play her game. I can fake humble and harnessed and curbed. Because now I'm in the circle. And because Will is waiting for me. "No."

"Stand, then, brother Taylor, and accept your mark."

The mark of Satan? The mark of something evil, that's for certain. She hands me a sticker, I take it, and I slap it onto my shoulder. It's an effort not to extend my arm into the air. Heil, Hitler.

"You have the note I gave you?" Nod. "Go with God, Taylor."

I turn on my heel and leave, shutting the door behind me as quietly as I can manage.

Chapter 9

The disciples told him, "Rabbi, the Jews were just trying to stone you, and are you going there again?"
—John 11:8

I head for the nearest boys' room. How could she do this to me? I was trying so hard! Inside a booth, I stand so no one can see my face. Christ, but I hate this place. How can Nate stand it? And how could he willingly have sacrificed two fucking summers for it *after* having suffered through one?

It's a misery just thinking of what the rest of my day will be like. Everyone who knows me will see this mark of disgrace—and that's what it is now, not an indication of new arrival any longer—and imagine all kinds of things I've done wrong to deserve it.

I did nothing wrong! At least, not as far as Harnett knows. Unless Nate isn't what he pretends to be. Unless he's really some kind of mole, tempting kids like me and trapping them. Is that what's going on?

No. It can't be. For one thing, I refuse to allow myself to fall back into the state of confusion I was in before he conscripted me. For another, it just feels wrong. He's good at this game, but he can't be *that* good.

Shit. He'll see this sticker, too. He'll think I've done something wrong. Something that might disqualify me from the circle, and he won't be able to ask me what. At the very least, it will alert him that Harnett's got her eye on me.

Will I still be able to go to the meeting tonight? And if I do, can I talk?

I want to hit something so badly! My eye falls on the toilet paper roll. If I attack it where it is, I'll catch hell for destruction of property. It takes me a frustrating ninety seconds to figure out how to release the thing from its holder. Then I pound it.

I don't even put it back on the holder when I leave the booth.

What a rebel. (Sarcasm alert.) I used to be pretty gutsy. What the hell's happening to me?

I'll have to go back to the laundry room now, where pissy little Sheldon will see this and be glad he's such a coward. Well, if I'm yellow on the outside, he's yellow on the inside. I will not be humbled. And even more, I will not be humiliated. I stand in front of the mirror and square my shoulders. Chin up, Taylor! Look 'em in the eye, and smirk!

Back at the laundry room, I show Sean my note. He starts to take it, but Harnett had said to keep it, so I pull my hand back. Sean looks up at me.

"What's going on? Oh . . ." And he sees the sticker. He closes his eyes and works his jaw for a second. "You need to keep this note?"

Nod.

"I, uh, I'm sorry, Taylor. I dunno what to say." He looks around like he also doesn't know what to do next. Then he says, "I put someone else on with Sheldon, so why don't you portion out detergent again. Do you remember where everything is?"

Nod. This could be worse; at least I don't have to watch Sheldon avoid my eyes as we fold sheets together.

I'm hard at work, if this can be said to be work, when I sense someone near me. I turn. It's Nate. He opens his mouth like he's going to say something, but then he sees the sticker. The tiniest gasp escapes him. He pretends he needs to get something on a shelf over my head, and under his breath he says, "Do you still want to come tonight? Nod or shake."

Nod.

He busies himself with something, not looking at me. Still very quiet, he says, "Please remember that if anything has happened that jeopardizes the circle, you shouldn't come. Has it?" I shake my head. "Okay, then. But you won't be able to speak. If anyone asks you tomorrow if you spoke at any time, you need to be able to say no and not lie. Do you understand?"

I'm getting a little tired of people asking me if I understand things I don't like. But there's nothing for it. So I nod again. And he leaves.

At least I'm not forbidden access to the circle. And maybe he'll let me write out for him what happened. There's hope. Meanwhile, though, my meeting with Harnett made me miss break period for the laundry room. Did Will come back? Did Nate give him my message? Did I miss a chance to know that he was near me? I can't even ask! I'm angrier than ever now.

Charles is not waiting for me for lunch. He doesn't know yet about the SafeZone. But I miss him. I'm standing alone, tray in hand and looking for the least conspicuous landing spot, when Nate appears next to me. "Come on," he says, and I follow him.

We sit at a table where Dawn and some kid I don't know are already settled. Nate says, "Dave Ivy, this is Taylor Adams. Taylor, Dave is in the same prayer group as John McAndrews."

This puts me on my guard immediately, but one look at his face—the wry grin and the tiny nod—makes me like Dave. He's saying, silently, "Yeah. Lucky me."

Dawn sees my sticker. She nearly whispers, "Holy moly, Taylor! What's going on? Sorry; I know you can't tell me. But— Nate, what happened?"

"Don't know yet." He looks around casually, but I know he's making sure he won't be overheard. "We'll give him a chance to explain tonight."

I look quickly at Dave and he winks at me. And suddenly I'm breathing easier. These are my people. The people Jesus sent me to. It'll be all right.

Or so I thought. Suddenly John McAndrews is hovering over us. The first thought I have is that he's suspected there was something going on between all of us at the table. Maybe he even suspects about the circle? Did I do something to give it away? I'll never forgive myself if I've . . .

"Taylor, here you are. Listen, I need an extra pair of hands in the kitchen this afternoon, and Mrs. Harnett and I thought you might enjoy a change of scenery."

What's he saying? Is he pulling me out of the laundry room? Away from Nate? Away from where I can watch for Will at break?

The panic must show on my face. He laughs and says, "Don't look so alarmed! You might actually enjoy it. Just come to the kitchen whenever you've finished your lunch. It'll be a nice break for you." He smiles, nods at the others and then at Nate, says, "Brother Nate," and walks off.

I throw a pleading look at Nate, but he just gives me this wobbly smile. "He's right, actually. You might enjoy it. And it's just for the afternoon." I'm thinking how to ask, without speaking and without letting on even to Dave and Dawn about Will, how I'll be able to stand not seeing Will if he shows up. Maybe Nate gets it. He adds, "Don't worry; if you miss anything monumental, I'll be sure to fill you in."

It's not enough, but it will have to do. Needless to say, I'm in a foul mood when I darken the doorway to the kitchen.

Actually, kitchen detail is kind of fun. It's true I was worried, and I had my doubts, with John McAndrews as supervisor. But he does nothing the whole time I'm there that makes me feel like he's suspicious, or like he's watching me in any particular way. And I have to admit, the place wouldn't have been the same without him. He teases everyone he thinks can handle it and is gentle with kids who seem more fragile.

I get teased. My first time in here and he's got me peeling onions. The paid staff take care of all the cooking, but there are kids doing the prep work. Now, I never had to peel onions before, and I gotta tell ya, I don't like it. The onion juice makes my eyes ache and sting and water like crazy, and when John sees this, it looks like he might be about to laugh—though I can barely see him through the watery fountains of my eyes. But he gets all solemn, takes the knife away from me and sets it down, and then drapes an arm around my shoulders.

"Brother Taylor, I am troubled in my heart to see you in so much distress! Now, I know you can't talk today. Let's see if the others can help." And he steers me out into the middle of the floor. I'm thinking, What now? Then he says, "Brothers and sisters, as you can see, brother Taylor is deeply troubled. But because he's in SafeZone, he can't tell me what the problem is. Can anyone help?"

Someone calls out, "He really wanted to do garlic, but he's too loving to take it away from me!"

A girl's voice says, "He asked me to accompany him to the luau next Friday, but I turned him down." Everyone laughs at that one, and I don't know whether to giggle or not.

A guy says, "He just had a visit with Reverend Bartle!"

By now, the room is in hysterics. Even John is fighting laughter. I can imagine why they all think the Bartle comment is so funny, but I don't. I really don't. And evidently, someone near me doesn't either. I can't see very well, but I hear some boy's voice say, "Reverend Bartle gives me the creeps. He's so gross, always touching me." I know what he means; the guy gives me the creeps, too.

I start to wipe the water off my face, but John grabs my hands, trying to speak, but he's laughing for real now. Finally he almost squeaks out, "Taylor, no! If you wipe your eyes with oniony hands it'll only get worse!"

The girl who mentioned the luau comes over, still giggling, and takes my hand in hers. "Maybe I won't go to the luau with you, but I'll take you to the sink." And she leads me over there, turns on the cold water, and washes my face with a wet paper towel. Then she rubs my fingers against the stainless steel sink and takes some detergent and squirts it on my hands.

"Here," she says, "wash your hands off. Be sure you get under the nails."

"Okay, everybody," John calls out, a chuckle still in his voice, "I think that's done it for brother Taylor. Let's all get back to our chores, or dinner won't be ready on time." Then he comes over to me. "All set?" I nod. "Great. 'Cause you've still got several more onions to do!" He laughs again as he walks away, and I guess I have no choice but to go back to them.

But before I leave the sink, my rescuer says, "I'm Reva. And if you take care not to dig too deeply into the onion while you're peeling it, you might be able to keep from getting so much of the juice into the air. And onto your face. Rubbing your fingers on the steel sink helps, too. By the way," she lowers her voice, "I would go to the luau with you if you decide to ask me."

I do a double take. Her smile says she's not kidding.

Somehow it feels different being in SafeZone this time. I can't figure out if it's because I know I can handle it if I have to, or if it's that I'm in the circle now and the Harnetts of the world can do only so much to me as long as I don't actually mutiny.

But I do feel weird leaving at four o'clock with the few who are in SafeZone; most of the new kids got here over the weekend and they're in laundry room, anyway. Only the kids who are in SafeZone again for some reason (whether they understand it or not!) are still wearing yellow. So I'm feeling almost jaded as I make my way back to my room to write my third MI— an opus I haven't a clue about in terms of what I can put into it. Oh, and I'm anxious, because I don't know whether Will showed up today.

Jaded leaves real fast. Anxious doesn't. As soon as I'm in the room, all bets are off. The place has been tossed.

Okay, *tossed* is a little dramatic. But it's obvious a search has taken place here. All my clothes, and all of Charles's as well, are stacked in piles on the bureau tops. We didn't have much in our desks—not allowed to, really—but what we had on the surfaces is now stacked neatly in identical piles: Bible just so; ruled pad just so; pen just so; tissues, lamp, and so on. I pull open my top drawer, where I'd kept my diminishing pile of those folders I'm to put my MIs into. Since I've submitted two, there were two left; Harnett had given me enough for one week. Now there are six folders. I slam the drawer shut and look frantically around the room, feeling watched.

The beds have been remade. At least, mine has; it's too neat.

They must have gone through the bedclothes, under the mattress—maybe even inside the pillowcase, which I would have thought would be safe. Charles's bed, of course, is always neat, so it's harder to tell, but everything else of his was looked-through.

Holy shit. Nate had been right! Thank you, Jesus, for making me take his warning seriously! OMG, if they'd ever found that article from Will, and his note . . . Even my Bible wouldn't have been safe. Is nothing sacred?

It doesn't take long for me to go from a mood of thanksgiving to one of outrage. How dare they do this? I mean, are body-cavity searches next? Just you wait until I see you again, Harnett. Just you wait until I can talk.

I sit down at my desk and turn to look around the room once more. I wonder if Charles knows, and if this has happened to him before. Or if it's happened to Nate. Wait—is there any chance someone knew there might be something to look *for*? Could Nate have done this to test me, to see if I did what he said?

Stop it, Taylor. Don't get paranoid. Then a voice in my head says, Just because you're paranoid doesn't mean they're not out to get you.

Stop it! I rub my face and try to calm down. What would Will do?

I close my eyes and picture him. He's laughing. And he tells me, "They really can't look inside your head, you know, Ty. And by the way, the trash has been taken, and they won't come for it again until tomorrow. In case there might be anything you'd want to throw away that might be, I don't know, damp?"

I'm smiling before I even know it. Grabbing a handful of tissues, I step behind the door, where I really can't be seen from the hall. I lean my hands against the wall and pretend Will is imprisoned there. We kiss. And kiss. And pretty soon I need those tissues.

So, head cleared (as it were), I sit at my desk to do my MI. First, the damp tissues go into one of my drawers this time until I can take them to the bathroom. I sit there quietly for a few minutes, eyes closed, picturing the green-ink message I'd been forced to destroy, the one that still exists in my mind. I can call it up whenever I want. And I want it now.

When Charles appears at the door to our room before dinner, I'm at my desk. At first, from where he's standing, all he sees is the sticker on my shirt. He leans on the doorjamb. "Taylor, what happened? No—sorry. No, don't write, Taylor!"

I tear a sheet off the pad so that only the hard desktop is under it and no one could see an impression of what I write: "It's okay. I know they take these pages. I'll destroy this one." I hold that up for him to read and then write again. "Evidently I was too full of myself last night. I'm being humbled. My boldness is being harnessed. Some such sh—."

The look on his face tells me he understands what's happened, and maybe also that he doesn't like it.

Feeling boldly unharnessed, I add, "I'm not feeling very humbled. And look at the room."

He's been so intent on my altered state that he hasn't taken in the state of the room. His eyes go from the piles on my bureau to the ones on his, and then he wheels toward his desk. I'm watching to see if maybe they were after something of his, but it's hard to tell. He puts a hand to his forehead for a second, like he's trying to remember something, and then he sits down hard on his desk chair. He's relaxed again, so I have to assume there was nothing.

"Wow. You know, I've heard about this happening to some of the residents, but it's never been done to my room before."

I write, "It must be me." And suddenly I *know* it must be me. And it must have something to do with John McAndrews. He's the one who'd pulled me out of Laundry and into Kitchen where he could keep an eye on me!

Charles says, "Was there, um, do you think they found anything you didn't want them to?" I shake my head; I don't know where to begin about John. Charles's voice is thoughtful as he adds, "It's interesting that there was no attempt made to leave things the way they were. They want us to know they were here."

In the kaleidoscope of moods I've had since seeing this, that thought hasn't occurred to me. We contemplate the room silently for a few seconds. The message I see is that they're not afraid of us, but we'd better be afraid of them. And if that's it, they've picked on the wrong impenitent.

Just before we leave the room, I grab my used tissues and stuff them into a pocket, and I crumple in one hand the page I've been writing on. Charles follows me to the bathroom but stays outside, I guess so he won't witness what I'm doing with the paper, and I manage to wet the page while pretending to wash my hands, and then I flush the tatters of it, and the tissues, down the toilet. And I wash my hands again, just in case.

Dinner feels weird. We sit alone off to the side to avoid having to explain to anyone. At Fellowship, Charles sticks with me. He barely talks to anyone else, and together we spend a lot of time watching the room from the corner, moving away if it looks like someone might be headed toward us. His loyalty to me is really something. I'd never have expected it.

Nate finds us at some point. "Hope you enjoyed Kitchen, Taylor. Believe me, you missed nothing in the laundry room today!" He claps Charles on the shoulder and wanders off again.

Whew. No Will today. Otherwise I'd have had to murder John.

Prayer Meeting is surreal. Charles and I select chairs in as inconspicuous a place as we can find. He doesn't volunteer anything the whole time, so we just watch the show. Tonight it's Monica, who's falling apart about how ungodly her life has been, what with her tendency to steal things. All kinds of things, evidently. At first I think how weird it is that she'd do this, confess to the group so willingly and make a scene, but then it occurs to me that stealing is probably a way to get attention that she has some control over. Note to self: be aware of your pockets if she's anywhere nearby. As she finishes, there's one of those group hugs. Charles and I stand so we won't be the only kids who don't, but we don't get into the hug, we don't cry, we don't even smile. I just want this stupid thing to be over so I can find a quiet way to follow Nate to the laundry room for the circle meeting.

But Harnett keeps looking at me, and I do my best to look humbled rather than outraged; not sure how well I do.

Not well enough, it seems. Because toward the end of the meeting, even though we've already had our participatory drama for the night, she stands up and calls my name.

"Taylor Adams. Please stand."

Charles is trying not to look at me, I can tell. I can also tell that he's worried.

"Brothers and sisters, as you can see, brother Taylor is in SafeZone once again. I bring your attention to him not to embarrass him, but to enlighten all of you about the reason." I hold my chin up and look right at her. "Brother Taylor has a great deal of potential. One day he will be capable of bringing great glory to God. But first he is learning humility." She pauses, and looks around the room. "Does anyone have any advice for him on this score?"

There's a bit of a lull as we wait to see who will cast the first stone. Last year in school we read a story called "The Lottery" by Shirley Jackson about this community of people who select one member to die every so often, and everyone else hurls stones at them until they're dead.

I'm going to disappoint them. I'm not going to die.

Maybe it's too bold of me, considering what I'm supposed to be learning, but I look around the room, offering myself as a target. I settle my gaze on Marie. And sure enough, resistance is beyond her. Saints above, forgive me; I've tempted her. She stands. Take your best shot, sister.

"Jesus warns us against assuming that the place of honor should be ours. We should take the lowest place."

I'm thinking, Is that the worst you can do? when, true to form, Nate goes next, not quite but almost coming to my rescue. "Brother Taylor, humility is always advised. Jesus is our best example. If you're humble, you couldn't ask for better company."

Well, I think to myself as I bow my head, I'm not sure I'm up to the example of Jesus—after all, he was humbled to death, and didn't I just refuse to die?—but I could learn a thing or two from Nate. He always manages to walk that line between caving in to the Harnetts of this world and remaining true to God.

Then the room is quiet. I glance up at Harnett, who's looking around at everyone. When there are no volunteers, she tries prodding. "Anyone else? This is an important lesson for all of us to learn. Is there no other advice for brother Taylor?"

Silence. As I look around the room again, I see a variety of expressions. Some eyes fall rather than meet mine, but other faces have tiny smiles, almost secret ones. *For* me, not against me. Dawn isn't smiling, but she looks defiant. It's almost like she's saying, "I'll be damned if I'll humiliate brother Taylor."

I'm just starting to get high on the idea that no one wants to drag me through the mud. And then, to my horror, Charles stands.

"The book of James tells us humility can come from wisdom. When brother Taylor begins to use his wisdom in humility, he will be a formidable soldier for God."

I'm still blinking at him as he sits down again. This may not be having quite the effect Harnett wanted. It's praising with faint damnation. Then something occurs to me, and I turn to face her.

She's not doing this just to humiliate me. She's doing this to test the others, too. Who will stand? Who will say what? Who understands the lesson *I'm* supposed to be learning? Her eyes and mine lock, and there's this electric shock of recognition. She knows I get it. She knows that I know what she's doing.

She smiles, and it's a real smile. I almost want to smile back. But I don't quite do it.

Chapter 10

This is my commandment, that you love one another, even as I have loved you. Greater love has no one than this, that someone lay down his life for his friends.

—John 15:12

Charles is hard to shake when Prayer Meeting ends. I think he's expecting me to feel vulnerable, or weepy, or something. But I don't. I feel an odd mixture of happiness, wonder, and—yes—humility. Charles starts in the direction of our room, expecting me to go with him, I guess, because when I hang back he looks at me.

"You aren't ready to go back?" I shake my head. "Shall we go to the chapel and pray together?" I smile and shake my head. "Do you want to go to the library?"

Hmm . . . that might work. But before I can decide he asks, "Do you want to be alone?" That's it. Nod. "Okay. Are you going to the room?" I shake my head; I don't want him going someplace like the library and come back to the empty room before my circle meeting is over to find that I'm not there.

He reaches out and squeezes my shoulder. "I understand. I'll see you later, then." He starts to turn away, but then, almost panicky, he looks at me again. "You're not going to the chapel alone, are you?"

Is he worried I'll pull a Ray on him? I smile and shake my head. I feel almost guilty; he's trying to be so accommodating, and I'm trying to escape to a secret meeting I can't tell him about. I hug my Bible to my chest, lower my head like I'm deep in thought, and walk slowly along the hall, doing my best to look contemplative but not inviting. Nate walks by without acknowledging me in any way, and I follow, doing my best not to attract attention.

This seems to work, because by the time I start down the hallway that leads to the laundry room, there's no one in sight. Except Nate, who's waiting for me at the door. We go in, and like last time, he takes the key and locks the door from the inside, then goes with me to the corner where there are five kids sitting on the floor.

He says, "Anyone else coming that we know of?"

Jessica—Jessica!—says no. I look around the semicircle, which is how they're arranged on the floor, to see who else is here. Jessica is on my left, and next to her is Dawn, and then Dave. There's another girl and one other guy I don't recognize. The girl is holding a pad of paper and a pen out to me, so I take them. She smiles. Nate stands between me and Jessica.

His tones hushed, he says, "Taylor, you know Jessica, Dawn, and Dave already. This is Danielle, and this is Jamie. There are only two other members. I'm sure you'll meet them soon."

I start scrawling immediately. "Are you Charles's Danielle?" I hold it toward the girl who'd given me the pad and pen.

She smiles. "In a way, I guess. I know what you mean."

Nate sits on my left and pulls me to the floor with him, so Jamie is on my right. "Taylor, is there anything you want to write about why you're in SafeZone again?"

I think for a minute. Then I write, "Is there anything you need to know that you don't?"

Nate turns to the group. "For those of you who aren't in our prayer group, Taylor made a public apology last night, introducing his points with scriptural references. And, it seems, we are not the only ones to have recognized his leadership potential." He looks at me. "Taylor, am I right in assuming Mrs. Harnett thought you'd overextended yourself?"

I nod and write, "Too bold. Need to be harnessed."

A few kids chuckle. Dawn looks disgusted, and I love her for it. I smile at her, and then I notice she's holding hands with Jes-

sica. Ah. So. Who else is gay, I wonder? Or, who isn't? Before I can
dwell on this question, Nate opens the meeting.

"Welcome to the circle, Taylor. You've accepted a sacred
trust in joining. It means you must maintain total secrecy about
the group and who its members are. Do you understand this?"
Nod. "Do you agree to undertake this trust?" Nod twice. "Does
anyone here have any questions for Taylor, or want to express
any concerns?"

To Nate, Dave says, "What about Charles?"

"What about him?"

"He watched Ray like a hawk. What if Taylor can't manage
him?"

Nate turns to me. "Taylor, we all know lying is a sin. But if you
had to, could you lie to Charles to maintain the circle's secrecy?"

Nod. I write, "I had to do that already. I hated doing it, but it
was necessary."

"What do you think Charles would do if he found out about
us?"

I write, "Not sure. Our room was tossed this afternoon, and I
wrote to him so we could talk about it. He let me destroy the
paper, as long as I did it out of his sight."

There's a silence so big I almost fall into it. Then Nate says,
"Your room was searched?" Nod. "Do you think they found anything?"

Shake. I write, "Nothing to find." I hold it up and look right
at Nate's face.

Nate asks, "Do you think they expected to find anything?"

Well, if he needed to ask that, then no; he would have been
their source of information. I shake my head and write, "I think
it was supposed to be a humbling experience."

A few kids are nodding; I'm glad this makes sense to them,
too.

"Okay," Nate says, "so Charles is willing to bend a little. But
do you think knowing about this group would be too much for
him?"

I think for a second and then nod.

Nate looks around the circle. "Let all of us be alert. If Taylor needs help with Charles, we'll do what we can." And to me, "Taylor, we'll need to rely on you for good judgment. If you're planning to come to a meeting and it will make him too suspicious, you may need to sacrifice attending for the good of the group. Are you willing to do that?"

I nod, and then I write, "I understand how serious it is."

Nate looks at Dave. "Any other concerns?" Dave shakes his head. "Anyone else?" No stones are cast. "Very well. Then let's begin the meeting."

There's quiet while everyone seems to focus. Finally Nate speaks again.

"What must not fail?"

In unison, they say, "Understanding that the path to God is love."

Nate asks, "Where must we start?"

In unison again, "From where we are and from who we are."

"What must we do?"

In unison: "Establish and maintain loving connection in everything we do."

Then Nate says, "This must seem like a church service to you, Taylor. In fact, it is a church service. After Jesus died, people would meet in small groups, in secret places, to talk about what he'd said and what it meant to their lives. That's what we're doing."

He looks at the group. "Does anyone have a struggle they want to bring to the circle?"

"Yeah, I do," Dawn says. "I don't like that Taylor was put into SafeZone again. He was a terrific example last night of exactly what we should be doing, and he gets slapped down because he was brave enough to do it. I'm struggling to feel love through that. I'm angry."

I smile at her; thanks.

Nate says, "Taylor, are you angry?"

I blink. Am I? I write, "I was."

"And now?"

I write, "I guess it's changed. The way everyone acted tonight, I felt love there. Anger faded."

"So what do you feel now?"

I look at Nate, and I look at Dawn. I write, "Humble." It surprises me.

"Do you feel love?" Nod. "Giving, or getting?"

I write, "Both."

Nate looks at Dawn. "Does that help you at all?"

"It will. I need to let it set a while."

Nate says, "Anyone else?" Silence. Then, "I have a topic tonight that Taylor will be able to get his teeth into. Is everyone okay with that, or does anyone have something they really need to suggest?" No one says anything, so he goes on. "Great. Here it is. Lots of times we hear someone say that because Jesus never said anything about homosexual love, it's not the sin that Moses and St. Paul would have us believe. Let's look at it from the other viewpoint: Why *didn't* Jesus say anything about it? If he knew everything God knows, why didn't he mention it in some other way either?"

Well, this is heavy stuff. No one speaks for a minute, and then Jamie says, "Well, first of all, I believe God is in all of us, really. Jesus was enlightened, and maybe he knew everything God knows and I don't, but God is in all of us."

Nate responds, "Great job pinpointing that assumption. What other assumptions are in what I just said?"

Assumptions?

Jessica goes next. "You're assuming that everything Jesus said is in the New Testament. But there were lots of other writings."

Dave: "You're assuming that what's in the New Testament is correct and complete, when we know lots of stuff has been changed since the originals were written down."

I write, "You're assuming it's not a sin."

Nate grabs my pad and holds it up. "Do you see what Taylor has written? You're all right. Those are all assumptions. But look at this one." He turns the pad slowly so they can all see it. "Is it a sin?"

"No," from Jamie and Dawn simultaneously.

Dave asks, "What is sin?"

Jessica: "It's the opposite of loving connection. Anything that stops love or makes it difficult to love."

Nate gives me the pad back and says, "It means missing the mark, literally. And what's our mark?"

Two or three voices at once say, "That which must not fail."

"So," Nate continues, "sin is anything that prevents us from getting to God, and we believe that path is love. Or sin could be something we do that prevents someone else from loving, which really prevents both parties. And do we always know what that is?" Silence. "Did Mrs. Harnett sin when she put Taylor back into SafeZone? She made him angry, which made him and others like Dawn struggle with love, but then he found even more. Did she know that would happen? If she did, was it not sin? And if she didn't, was it sin?"

Danielle has been very quiet, but here she says, "She thought she was doing it out of love."

Nate looks around the group. "It can be pretty difficult to tell sin, can't it? We know that Leviticus declares it would be sin for us to wear clothing with mixed fibers or to plant different kinds of plants together. And we eat things the ancient laws say we shouldn't, and Danielle's father could have sold her as a slave to someone from Canada because she's a girl and Canada is a different nation from ours. Today, we'd think that was sin, wouldn't we?"

Everyone agrees with that, of course. Jamie is persistent. "Homosexuality is not a sin."

Nate: "If you had lived two thousand years ago and you'd refused to marry a woman and have kids because you're gay, Danielle's children would have to take care of you when you got old. No pension plans. No social security. No retirement homes. Would she love you for that? Would her kids? Or would you be endangering the community by setting that example? If seven percent or more of the people in a community deliberately didn't have kids, what then?"

Dawn says, "Then why didn't Jesus say anything about it?"

Jamie: "Because it isn't a sin."

Nate: "What could Jesus say? Even if God loves gays, and even if Jesus knew that, if he'd said it to people two thousand years ago they would have thought he was crazy, because it would have made no sense given where they were. Given what their

lives were like. Jamie said a minute ago that he's not enlightened. Not many people are. Not many people were when Jesus
was here, either. So he might tell them things that cut into their
hearts about love, but he couldn't say things that made no
sense at all. Who were his original disciples? What did most of
them do before they became disciples?"

Danielle: "They were fishermen."

Nate: "And how many times does Jesus talk to them using
fishing examples?"

I'm trying to follow this, but they're going round and round.
It's hard to take it all in. Plus I'm not used to this kind of freedom,
of being in a group where you can just say "Homosexuality is
not a sin" and not have someone jump down your throat. To try
and clarify things for myself, I write, "Homosexuality *was* a sin."

Almost as soon as I've lifted my pen, Nate grabs the pad
again. "Look!" he says in a hoarse whisper. "Look! This is key."
And again he holds it out and turns so everyone can read it.
"Where must we start?"

Danielle says, "From where we are and from who we are."

"Where are we, in terms of time?"

"The twenty-first century."

"Where were we when Jesus was crucified?"

"The first century."

Nate lowers his arms and says, "A lot of things have changed
in two thousand years. Do we have retirement funds today? Will
it make any difference to Danielle's children if Taylor and
Jamie live right next door to her and don't have kids? And is
that different from how things were when St. Paul was writing?"

Dave says, "That was then. This is now."

Nate: "Exactly! Is it possible that homosexuality could rea-
sonably have been considered sinful then because of what it
would have meant to the rest of the community, whereas today
things are different?"

Jessica: "It's possible . . . Like the shellfish and the mixed
fibers . . . And the slavery!"

Nate turns to me. "Taylor, did you want to come to this program?"

I shake my head vigorously.

He hands me my pad. "Why were you sent?"

I write, "Because I'm gay. They want me to change."

To the group Nate says, "We've changed our minds about a lot of things that were once sacred laws because they don't apply in our time. If people could see that homosexuality was a sin but isn't any longer, would Taylor have been sent here?"

A few voices say, "No."

"Would Ray have died like that?"

"No."

"Would there be less hate in the world, and more love?"

"Yes!"

"What must we do?"

"Establish and maintain loving connection in everything we do."

"Why? What must not fail?"

"Understanding that the path to God is love."

Nate takes my pad and pen and sets them down, and then he takes my hand and Jessica's. All around the circle, kids take each other's hands, and they bow their heads. So I do, too.

There's no sound. No words.

I've never felt anything like this in my life. There's something like an electric current passing around the circle through our hands, and we are one. All one person. Some gay, some not; some boys, some girls; some forceful like Dawn, and some gentle like Danielle; some obstinate like Jamie, and some brilliant like Nate; all one. And that great feeling I'd had on Monday night after Charles had begged forgiveness? That was real, but it was only a shadow of this.

We can't stay any longer and still get back to our rooms in time, but what a high to leave on. They decide the next meeting isn't until Sunday night, and it makes me sad to think that maybe not all these same kids will be there. Maybe I won't even be there.

Nate walks with me to the door, his arm around my shoulders. "Taylor, I can't promise that every meeting will be like this one. I've been saving that topic for a special occasion, and you were it. Mostly we get high on the chance to be open about God, like they did in the first century. In secret meetings. Outside the rule book, outside the program. And that's a great high, too." He slaps my back. "I'll, uh, deal with the paper you used tonight, by the way."

I smile and nod; thanks.

Everyone is leaving one at a time, silently. Nate hangs back, I suppose to lock the door, and I head back alone toward my room. As I round a corner I see Danielle not far ahead of me, so I slow down; it would be better not to overtake her. She turns to look around her, sees me, waves, and moves on.

And I see that she's pregnant.

Charles is at his desk, hunched over a pad of paper. Writing a letter, it looks like. And for the first time I remember that I'm allowed to write home once a week. Maybe this weekend; I haven't been here quite a week yet, after all, impossible though that seems.

He can't ask me where I've been—or, he can't expect an answer—so we just nod at each other. It looks as though he's trying to shield whatever he's writing so I won't see what it is. What do I care? I practically throw myself on my bed and lean against the wall, hands behind my head, and watch my roommate. Charles the honest. Charles the true. Charles the tender. Imagine him always asking Danielle to accompany him, and she's pregnant. And not by him.

This has been one of the two most amazing evenings of my life, and I can't talk about it. The other, of course, was the first time I was with Will. Come to think of it, I didn't do much talking about that one, either.

I can't talk, but I can feel. And the thing that makes both that evening and this one so wonderful is love.

Chapter 11

Are all apostles? Are all prophets? Are all teachers?
Are all miracle workers? Do all have gifts of heal-
ings? Do all speak with various languages? Do all
interpret? But earnestly desire the best gifts. More-
over, I show a most excellent way to you.

—Corinthians 12:29

The next time I get a chance to talk is during my noon meeting with Harnett. She's got my third MI, which has almost
nothing in it. Just that I was angry about being in SafeZone and
about having my room searched. I have no idea whether she's
planning to take the sticker off or make me do more time, and
I'm in a strange mood 'cause it looked like there might just
maybe have been someone Nate talked to at break today, but I
couldn't be sure.

I shut the door and sit when she says to. Then she says, "Have
you spoken since our meeting yesterday?" I shake my head.
"Were you tempted?"

Was I? Sure, I was angry when I realized I couldn't speak at
the circle, but that's different. Finally I shrug; it's a compromise.

"And have you had time to think about the things you wrote
in here?" And she holds up the MI. I nod. "You may take the sticker
off now." I do, and she takes it away from me. "Where have those
thoughts led you?"

One thing I'd been thinking about a lot since my circle
meeting is that discussion we had about sin, and I was wondering if Harnett did something that felt like sin to me but that led
to something good, was it sin? And how much credit or blame
does she deserve?

I tell her, "You're in a weird spot. I mean, your role. It's like you have to teach, but you can't teach anything important just by telling. So I don't even know how much of what I've thought about is what you intended, or if any of it's coming to me the way you expected it to."

She sits back in her chair, nods slowly two or three times, and closes her eyes. I almost get the feeling she's about to cry. Finally she opens her eyes again and says, "What has come into your heart?"

"Love. I felt lots of love last night when no one wanted to say anything to make me feel bad. Well, almost no one."

Her smile is so personal, I don't think she knows she's doing it. "And what's the lesson? Can you articulate it?"

"I can't be humble just by deciding to be humble. And I can't love just by deciding to do that, either. And I can't do any of it alone."

"You need God?"

Well, what I was thinking was, I needed the other kids, but she isn't wrong. So I say yes.

She digs in her desk for a minute and comes up with a digital camera. And before I can believe she's going to, she takes my picture. I'd forgotten about that; Strickland had done that last Sunday before he'd turned me over to Charles. It takes a minute for her to upload the image to her computer, and while she's working on it, she tells me that there may be other photos as well. It's to show us residents how even our facial expressions change when we let the Program help us. When she turns the screen so I can see it, both shots of me are there.

"Take a good look at these two faces," she says. Then, "What do you see? How are they different?"

The first one looks pretty much like I'd expect. "Fuck you" was what I'd wanted to communicate, and I had. The second one—well, it's much harder to describe. But I try. "It's like I've gone from hating the world to being puzzled by it."

"Would it be fair to say that the puzzled one also looks open?"

I look again. "Yeah. I mean, yes, ma'am. It does." I kind of hate to admit it to her. But it does.

She turns the screen back and closes the program. "Taylor, you are at a crucial point right now. Before, you were stuck. But now you're in motion. At the moment you're moving in the right direction for you; and as a result, you're moving toward God."

She waits to see if I have anything to say, but I don't. Not yet. So she says, "I told you yesterday that you'd impressed your brothers and sisters. And I think you believed I was talking about the way you delivered your Public Apology. Yes?"

Funny; when Nate had used that phrase last night, it hadn't sounded like it had capital letters. "Yes."

"There's another way you've impressed those who have been here a while and those who have returned. The expression in the image I just took of you is one we don't usually see in residents until well into their stay, if at all. I tell you this because there are people who will say something about this rapid progress. Some of them will say it in honest respect, and some will say it with a derogatory tone. And you must listen to none of them. If you do, you run the danger of getting stuck again. It wouldn't be in the same place, but our lives must be a constant movement toward God. We can't afford to let pride or anger or anything hold on to us, pin us down. Do you understand what I'm saying?"

I do, actually. "Yes, ma'am."

"If you feel you're getting stuck, don't limit your struggles to your own prayers. God works through others to help us. Talk to me, talk to Charles, talk to John, talk to Nate. We all love you, Taylor. And we're all here to help each other." We sit there and breathe for a few seconds. "Would you like to say anything at this point?"

"I'm wondering why my room was searched."

The look on her face is not what I expect. Smug, righteous, maybe even saccharin, I would have understood. Instead what I see is something like apprehension, or fear. Just for a second. Just for a split second. Then she says, "Why do you think?"

"Nothing was missing, so I'm thinking it was to leave something."

"Like what?" Her back is up a little; maybe she thinks I mean they bugged the room?

"Like a message. Like, be afraid. Be very afraid."

"Are you afraid, Taylor?"

"I don't think so."

"Do you know what a metaphor is?"

"It's like an example, something that represents something else."

"That's right. And it isn't only a room that could be searched."

"So . . . you mean, like, searching my heart?"

"Anyone's. Doesn't Charles have a heart, too?"

"Charles's heart doesn't need searching."

"Taylor, everyone's heart needs searching. Including yours."

"But *you* can't do that."

"But we can help you, or Charles, to do it for yourself. And none of us can predict when it's going to happen to us next."

"So you're not going to tell me."

"I think I already have."

I look hard at her. I don't think she knows why it was searched, or whether it was me or Charles who was supposed to get the message, and I don't think she knew it had even happened until I put it in my MI. I think she invented a reason that might maybe just possibly make sense—that comparison between searching rooms and searching hearts. All things considered, this last response of hers seems pretty lame. But if she doesn't know, then it won't do any good to try and worm any more out of her. Plus it wouldn't help to . . . um . . . get stuck on that, would it?

Again, no sign of Will during afternoon break, and I manage to get Nate alone to ask about this morning; no Will then, either. He's been carrying my note around, and I get the sense it's beginning to weigh on him; what if it's found?

After the break Sean pulls me into the office and asks me to work with a guy I haven't even spoken to yet. I've noticed him a few times, mostly in the break yard and in some corner of the Fellowship room. He's wiry, angry looking, a tough kid. Quite a few tattoos.

Sean says, "His name is Terry. Terrence. He may tell you to call him T, but don't do it. We're trying to get him to leave that FI behind him."

A gang handle, I wonder? "Sean, I'm not sure I'm the best person to deal with this guy."

"Nate says you are." Like that puts an end to it. "He's out of SafeZone, but he's struggling."

"What's he in here for?"

"That's not supposed to matter."

"Maybe not, but most times it does anyway."

He ignores me. "I need you to show him how to clean the dryers."

Oh boy. My favorite. "Why me?"

"I've got to work with a new kid. Even more of a problem—I mean, someone who's struggling even more than Terry. You'll need to stay with him to make sure it's done right."

"Why does it need to be done at all? I just did it earlier this week. And nobody stayed with me."

"Taylor, cut it out, will you? Just do it? Besides, you didn't do all of them, and you know where you stopped."

I sigh. "Where's the doohickus?"

Somehow Sean knows exactly what this is and fetches it from a cabinet, and I take it out onto the floor and look around for Terry. He's slouching, hands in his pockets, as he leans against a dryer about as far away from everyone else as he can get. If I think the clothing we have to wear here isn't the real me, it's even less the real him. It seems like he's willing the prescribed stuff to fall right off his body.

"Wish me luck," I throw over my shoulder at Sean, and head toward Terry. He sees me coming but looks away like I'm of absolutely no consequence to him.

"Hi," I say, holding my hand out. "I'm Taylor." He looks at me but totally ignores my outstretched hand. "Fine," I say, and shrug. "I didn't ask for you, either, y'know. But we're stuck with each other."

He scowls at me a second and then looks away again. I try another tack. Sarcasm, though I have to hide it in here. "'See how good and how pleasant it is for brothers to live together in unity!' Psalm one thirty-three."

He moves his jaw like he's chewing on gum or maybe tobacco, glances at the clock on the wall, and says, "Leave me the 'eff' alone. T two fifty-three."

At first I don't get it. But when I do, I laugh. It looks like he's trying not to.

"Okay," I tell him when I think I have his attention, even though he's still not looking at me. "I'm a T too, y'know. For *Taylor*. But some people don't call me Taylor. Some people call me Ty." I can see Will's face looking at me over Terry's shoulder, tongue nearly protruding through his cheek. "So what if they don't want you to call yourself T in here? Do them one better. How about if I call you Rye?"

He looks at me like he's trying to pretend he's not interested. "Rye?"

"Sure. R-y-e. Covers a few bases. *R* and *y* are the last two letters of the name *Terry*. Put an *e* on the end, and either you've got a kind of bread or a grain they make liquor out of. Make them wonder. Plus it sounds like w-r-y, which strikes me as something along the lines of how you'd like people to see you."

"Rye." I can't tell whether he's making fun of me or giving the idea serious consideration.

"Look, why don't you mull that over while I show you how to use the magic wand?" I wave the doohickus in the air toward the dryers.

He gets in a few more gnaws on his nonexistent gum and then says, "Fine. So show me."

He catches on to the routine right away. I even manage to get a few grumbled phrases out of him about how he's helped his black-sheep uncle work on car engines, making it clear that cleaning out dryers isn't much of a challenge for him.

We get to one dryer that has an OUT OF ORDER sign on it. He unplugs it anyway, which he should, but after he's cleaned it he opens the door to the tumbling chamber and plays with it a little. Then he walks around behind the machine, lifts off a panel, and pokes around.

"I could fix this."

"Why don't you?"

He looks at me and then over at Sean across the room. "Captain Bligh there would have a friggin' cow."

I'm amazed he has that literary reference at his command, but I try not to show it. "Why don't you start on the next machine and I'll ask." Rye shrugs (see how I've incorporated his new name already?) and moves on, and I head over to Sean.

I say, "Terry thinks he can fix that broken dryer. Is it okay if he has a try?"

"The repairman will be here next Tuesday."

"So what have we got to lose?"

"If he makes a mess of it, the repairman will know. The center will be in trouble with its maintenance contract."

"Sean, it's the one thing the guy has that he thinks we value, and he volunteered. I think it's worth the risk."

He stands there looking torn; he knows it's a good idea, but he's afraid, I can tell. I know him now. So I say, "If he screws it up, you can blame me." And I walk away like it's a done deal.

Someone, maybe Machiavelli, maybe the Little Prince, once said something about not giving an order you know will be disobeyed. Rye is already up to his elbows in dryer parts by the time I get back to him.

"Find the problem?" I ask, like I have any idea what he's doing.

Teeth gritted in effort, arm deep into the dryer innards, he grunts and then says, "Get me a long screwdriver. Phillips head."

I look in Sean's direction again to see that he's come closer. "Toolbox in the office?" I ask.

"In the cabinet to the left of the door. Lower drawer."

By the time Rye is finished, the dryer is working. Sean comes up, holding a note toward me. "Here. Go with Terry to the bathroom so he can wash his hands."

"Rye," Rye says to him.

"What?"

"The name is Rye. Don't call me Terry." And he heads for the door, me in his wake.

Well, well, I'm thinking as I stand there watching him scrub grease from his hands. So he took it. My name for him. And if I so much as say one word about it, it'll be gone. My eyes travel up to the tattoo on his neck—a spiderweb, extending down his shoulder past where I can see, with a black spider below his ear. The tattoo is black, but the spider's eyes are red.

I ask, "What're you in for?"

He shrugs. "The usual. Theft. Drugs."

"What'd you steal?"

"Cars." Cars. Plural. He adds, "You?"

"Gay."

He grabs a paper towel and wipes up to his elbows with it. "That's bullshit." He throws the towel into the trash and walks away, leaving me wondering whether he meant that he doesn't believe I'm gay or that gay kids shouldn't be sent here. I decide to believe the second. I also decide not to report him for swearing.

Sean's watching the door, and as soon as we're back he comes over to us. Rye starts to go around him, but Sean steps in front of him and extends a hand.

"Thanks, Rye."

Rye looks at his face, finally nods, and gives Sean's hand one shake.

At five thirty I show up at the appointed spot to meet John and Rick for barbeque-setup detail. They're there waiting for me, along with another guy. I haven't seen him before. He's stunning—nice build, grey-green eyes, and very dark hair; I'd have remembered him.

John says, "Taylor Adams, this is Peter Connors. He's going to help us, too."

We move a lot of stuff out onto the grounds. There's a tent already set up, and we have to move the tables and some chairs, and the paper plates and stuff, and get them ready for the big event. There's a few other kids helping, too. I guess they have a different drill sergeant, and we have brother John. But it beats just hanging around and waiting for this thing to start. Peter doesn't talk a lot, but he does his share of work and more.

He pulls me over at one point and asks, "Do you know any-thing about setting up a sound system?"

"For what? What do you mean?"

"There's a Christian band coming tonight. We need to set up. Wanna help with that?"

Well, of course I do. So he tells John we're headed that way, and off we go. I don't know much about it, but Peter sure does.

"I used to do a lot of this," he tells me. "My brother has a band, and I've helped them set up. I can't do anything musical to save my soul, but I love the electronics."

I can't say I learn a lot—mostly I run cables and connect things Peter tells me to connect—but he does his best to ex-plain it. And one thing I really like is that he laughs. Not many people around here laugh, and that absence is something you notice more when it does happen than when it doesn't.

Before long, kids are starting to arrive, and it gets crowded quickly. The band is still warming up and testing things when Peter and I head for the food tables. It's an interesting arrange-ment: boys go along one side of the tables and girls on the other. We're most of the way along our side, food piling up, when I ask him about this.

"You know how we're supposed to be courteous, especially around women? Well, this is a bit of a reprieve. Rather than making all the guys wait for all the girls to get their dinner, we just get our own side. Works out much better this way!" He grins and holds up his plate, which is about to overflow. And in fact, it does. We're watching stuff tumble off—a roll, a piece of corn-on-the-cob—and there's no good place for us to set down our plates and do something about it. We're laughing like id-iots when I finally manage to find a spot on the table beside me where I can set my own plate down. I bend over to retrieve Peter's fallen food, laughing still, and when I stand up again I'm looking across the table and staring right into the face of Marie Downs. She lowers her eyes, which puzzles me, because I would have expected her to spout scripture at me about un-seemly behavior or wasting resources.

And then I see the yellow sticker on her blouse.

You know, maybe a few days ago that would have made me feel like gloating. I would have been delighted to see her in disgrace. But that's not how I feel. She looks up again, and what I do feel must show in my eyes, because she turns away. What I feel now is sympathy. And from the way she reacts, it probably makes her feel worse than if I looked gloating. When someone gloats, it's like they give you something you can rebel against. You can deny the disgrace. But when someone feels sorry for you, there's no way to deny the reality of how you feel about yourself.

"You okay?" Peter asks. He's holding out a napkin for the dropped bits.

I snap out of it. "Yeah. Here you go."

We decide to sit on the lawn. It leaves more chairs for the girls, and we can get closer to the band. We don't talk much, and I spend lots of time wondering if Peter is gay. There's no way I can do a real test here; so many people would see if I so much as sit too close to him. I've just about worked up the guts to ask why he's here when John plunks himself down on the ground on the other side of me. He seems to have lost Rick someplace.

"They have a great sound, don't they?" he asks. Like anyone needs to say so. He goes on about nothing in particular, and I swear mostly what he's doing is trying to keep me from being able to focus on Peter.

I decide to take advantage of his special position. I ask, "I saw Marie Downs at the table. She's in SafeZone. Do you know why?"

"Brother Taylor, if that's for you to know, you will be told."

Well, this seems unfair; I'm sure people talked about me. They must have.

By the time the evening ends, Peter has gone off somewhere, and I've tried and failed to figure out what it means to "accompany" someone to this kind of Activity. Charles and Danielle sit together, but as far as I can tell, they're just hanging out. Other kids come and talk to them like there's nothing along the lines of a date going on. But the truth is, there's not likely to be anything, really, going on between Charles and Danielle.

I find myself thinking how frustrating it must be for Jessica, and for Dawn, not to be able to hang together—to have Jessica tied to Marie like it's some kind of penance. Or some kind of sacrifice. Like it was for Will and me at school. Only maybe even worse.

Saturday, although I had expected something different, is essentially the same as any other day of the week. So I spend my day in the laundry room, and I spend my break time with my eyes glued to the chain-link fence. And today, it pays off. I don't get to see much, but I'm watching Nate as he saunters that way during afternoon break. I've positioned myself so I'm at an extreme angle to the spot where Will must have been the time I saw Nate take something through the chain links and as close to that fence as I dare; if I see Will, I'm not sure I'd be able to pretend I wasn't looking at something worth more than gold to me.

Nate's progress is slow and casual, and he walks past the spot at first. He leans against the fence, facing the inner yard, gazing at nothing for a minute, before he turns and heads back.

And that's when I see it. Will's hand, with the leather thong on his wrist. Nate is dragging his hand along the fence, and I imagine it must have my note in it. And sure enough, when he gets close enough to that hand, there's an exchange. Just for a second I see Will's fingers snatch the scrap of paper, and then they're gone. My hands grip the outsides of my thighs in a superhuman effort to force myself not to call out, not to run to the fence and scramble over it, not to go after Will and wrap him up in myself so tight he'd nearly strangle.

Finally Nate moves away from the fence, his gaze grazing everyone in the yard including me. And, just barely, he winks at me. I close my eyes and struggle to calm my breathing.

I've sent him away. I've told Will not to come again. What was I thinking? Was I crazy?

But I know this is the only way we can win. We just have to wait them out.

* * *

Saturday night there's a movie. Some Disney thing. They've set up folding chairs all over the Fellowship room. We all go, or most kids do, because the only other thing to do is read or pray. Plus there's popcorn and soda.

Marie is at the movie, and her sticker is gone; guess Harnett just wanted to make a point. The barbeque eclipsed the Prayer Meeting Friday, and the movie takes over tonight, so there's no opportunity for me to spout scripture at her. Not that I know enough of it to do that, anyway.

After the movie there's a few announcements, like about the luau that's happening this coming Friday night. Then I go to the library to see what's there, and I sit looking through some book about the differences among various translations of the Bible, not reading it, but instead trying to come up with cool topics for tomorrow night's circle meeting. I'm not even sure I'll be allowed to suggest anything, being the newest member— don't want to appear presumptuous, do I? But I want to be ready.

I really liked what Nate had done—stated something with an interesting twist to it and had us reduce it to assumptions. I wish I could scribble a few notes down, but it's such a hassle to destroy stuff. Besides, this place is watched over by at least two librarians at all times, one of them wandering around and checking out what everyone is doing. So I just think, trying to make a list of some of my own assumptions. What assumptions had I made before my folks dropped me off? What assumptions had I made about the leaders? About the other kids? About why I was here?

I do remember wondering, that very first night, if being here was a Job test for me. And because of that warm gush that happened, I assumed that was God's answer: "Yeah, kid; you're Job, and this is a test." But was I right?

So let's review. All these horrible things happen to this dude who's always been devout and God-fearing, or whatever a good Jew of the day was supposed to be. And yet God allowed Satan to destroy the guy. He loses his livestock and his family members, he gets hideous plagues, and people reading that story have always seen it as a test of Job's faith.

But would God kill one person just to test another? It's never made any sense to me to hear someone moan about losing a child or a loved one and wonder if God is punishing *them*, not the loved one. I mean, who the hell do they think they are?

So if I'm in here as a test, then why is everyone else in here? Would God put all of them in here, through all this, just to test me? Isn't it pretty stupid of me to think a place like this exists just to test me? If killing everyone else to get at Job is stupid, then what was it Job was supposed to learn? Maybe that it wasn't all about him?

Whoa. Where did that come from? Was it *not* all about Job? And if it isn't all about me, then this place doesn't exist to test me.

So what everyone assumes first is that whatever "it" is, it's all about them. Is that wrong? If it's wrong, who's it all about?

God.

And what is God?

Love.

Bingo. It wasn't just a test of Job's faith. It was a test of his understanding. If Nate's right and Strickland isn't evil, if Strickland thinks he's acting out of love but in a very limited way, then Strickland is really trying to make this all about him. Strickland wants me to be like him.

But this isn't about him. It's about God.

I slam the Book shut and several people, including both librarians, glare at me.

Strickland and everyone else need to learn to love me for who I am, for who God made me, not to try and make this all about them. Which means they have to question their own assumptions about homosexuality. They assume that God is just as uncomfortable with it as they are. So it's as much a test for them as for me. And *that's* why everyone is in here together.

Gotcha.

And I've got a heck of a topic for a circle meeting.

There's still a good forty-five minutes before lights-out. I want to find Nate and ask if this can be our subject tomorrow. Where would he be? I try his room, which I have to look up on the library roster. His roommate is there, but he doesn't know where Nate is. I try the dining hall to see if he's raiding the kitchen; nope. It isn't until I start roaming the halls where the Prayer Meeting rooms are that I find him. He's in Isaiah, with Leland, and they're reading scripture together. Or, at least from my peek in, I can see they have Bibles open.

It's tempting to listen, but that's rude.

Okay, so I stand there for only a few seconds. Nate is saying, "So how bad is it?"

"It kind of hurts, but not too bad. There's some spotty red specks, kind of like a rash. You know?"

"I think you should stop, Leland. I don't think you should be doing that."

"I know! That's what Reverend Bartle says. That's why he's making me do it with a washcloth. He says if I—you know, play with myself often enough in a way that hurts, I won't want to do it anymore."

"Uh, Leland, that's not what I mean. I'm saying you shouldn't be rubbing yourself raw with *anything*."

"But he's gonna ask me about it! And what will I tell him?"

"Here's what you say. You don't even have to tell him you're going to stop. Just tell him you recognize what a sin it is, and you're going to put it in your next MI."

"He already told me not to do that."

Nate's voice sounds like he's trying to control himself. "Leland, the people in Leadership are supposed to care about the things you don't put in your MI that you should. But there's no rule that says you can't put in anything you want, as long as it's true. And if you feel weird about this, then you're breaking a rule if you *don't* put it in. Tell him that."

I've heard more than enough. I know what I'd say to anyone who tried to make me rub my dick raw with a washcloth, and it wouldn't be pretty. I'm getting a more complete picture of just what Nate is doing to help Leland. He's protecting him from the assholes who run this place, because Leland is too timid and probably too vulnerable to defend himself. Awful as some of the "leadership" in this place can be, it seems beyond their usual level of horrendous to tell Leland to do that to himself. God have mercy on their souls.

I make my way slowly back to my room, which is empty; don't know where Charles is. Maybe I can get started on a letter home, which they'll probably let me send tomorrow or Monday. So I brush my teeth, get into my pajamas, and settle in at my desk.

First, I think about Will. I go over all his features—not just the ones on his face—and imagine kissing every inch. This has a predictable effect, but I'm quick with my tissues, and I know what I have to do with them afterward. I won't put Charles in an awkward spot.

Charles. What's his story, really? I know only the obvious things: gay, praying to be straight; desperate to love and be loved; taking on bad things that happen as if they were his fault; being loyal to me in ways I would never have predicted; anxious always—always—to do the right thing. And most of all, to be what's expected of him, even if that's not what he is.

Suddenly I get it. The android impression. The one I'd had when I'd first met him? It's because he's trying so hard to be something he isn't that he's all wooden outside. Or metallic. Something stiff, anyway. I want to shake him up. I want to get inside him, into his heart of hearts. I want him to burst out of that artificial shell and be real for himself.

Yeah, right. And just who the fuck do I think I am? This isn't about me. It isn't about what I want. It's about Charles. But maybe both "abouts" can exist together—my want, Charles's need. And maybe that's the true test—to figure out a way to help each other. That first night, when Charles had made me kneel with him and he'd prayed out loud, thanking God for me, I'd thought it was way over the top. I'd thought he was this big hypocrite. But now I think it was real. He was thanking God for giving him another gay roommate to watch over, like God had said, "Okay, kid, but don't lose this one, got it?"

And I'd prayed my own prayer, and I'd decided so smugly that I would show Charles another path. What an infant I'd been. I didn't understand a fucking thing then.

But there is another path, and I'm on it now. And I want him to see it.

I'm still sitting at my desk, pen tapping on the pad, chin in my hand, when the object of my ponderings walks in. He says a quick "Hi" and grabs his bathroom kit. He's beat lights-out by only about fifteen minutes, which is cutting it close for him. When he gets back he pulls the curtain and puts his night-clothes on, pushes the curtain back again, kneels for a few minutes, and climbs into bed. Not a word to me. I turn in my chair and look at him. Can't see more than a lumpy pile of cloth; he's turned to face the wall.

I throw my pen down and flip off my desk light, the only one still on. From where I sit on the edge of my bed, I can hear Charles breathing. A couple of times he snuffles.

That does it.

"Charles?"

Silence. Then, "Can't talk. It's lights-out."

"Got five minutes yet. Besides, the lights are out. Are you crying?"

More silence. "Go to sleep, Taylor."

"No."

That gets him. He sits up. "What?"

"I said no. I won't go to sleep. Y'know, my first breakfast here, Jessica—or Marie, I forget which—accused you of being secretive. Of harboring things that need to see the light. I'm beginning to think she may have been right."

He throws himself back down again. "I don't know what you're talking about."

"You do so. Look, I know you couldn't say a lot to me the first few days because of SafeZone, and then there was more of it, but we should be able to talk to each other now. You've been pretty great to me all around, but you don't talk."

"Now's not the time to start." But I get up and sit on the edge of his bed. Suddenly he's frantic. "Taylor, what do you think you're doing? Go back!"

"Hush. You'll bring the German shepherds in on us. I want you to talk to me. I'm not leaving this spot until you do."

"All right, all right! Now go over there." I go back to my own bed, and he sits upright, facing me. "What do you want to talk about?"

"What's with all the fasting?"

"I—I'm not going to talk about that. Choose something else."

"Are you gay?"

"No!"

"You are, too."

"I'm not. I was."

"When?"

"Before coming here. Before being reborn."

"And what are you now?"

A few heartbeats go by. "Don't be absurd."

"When you sit next to Danielle, are you even tempted to take her hand? Do you wish you could kiss her? Do you want her to like you in that special way?"

"Taylor, you don't know anything about it."

"Now *you're* being absurd. Of course I do. Did you have a boyfriend?"

There's a shaky breath from the other side of the dark room, and then he says, "Why do you want to talk about this?"

"First, tell me this. Will you be reporting me to anyone?"

"If you break a rule, I'll have to."

"No, I mean, is Mrs. Harnett or anyone going to come to you and ask for your opinion about how well I'm doing?"

"That's not how it works. She'll make her own determination. And so will Dr. Strickland, when he talks to you. And you'll see, um"—there's just the slightest hesitation here, like he doesn't want to say the name—"Reverend Bartle again, probably tomorrow."

"Joy."

"Taylor, that's FI. Sarcasm."

"Charles, my f . . . my gosh-darn *name* is Former Image. I had it before, I still have it. What makes you think you're not gay anymore?"

"You'll see. If you really want him to, Jesus can work miracles through your prayer. But you have to really want it, Taylor. Do you?"

"Why would I?"

I can almost see him blink in the dark. "Why . . . why would you? Why *wouldn't* you?"

"Do you think God makes mistakes?"

"You've got to stop thinking like that. It's a trap the non-Christians use to get us to forsake God's word."

"So words written by men about God are more important than God? Y'know, the nine-eleven hijackers flew planes into buildings and killed thousands of people in the name of God. Calling out 'In the name of God' doesn't make it right."

His voice is a hoarse whisper, desperate. "Taylor, if you don't stop I *will* have to report you! Don't you know you're talking heresy? Honestly, you sound like a Roman Catholic! We live by scripture. You know that."

"What happened to Ray?"

My eyes are getting used to the lack of light, and I can see Charles rub his face with both hands. "I don't want to talk about Ray."

"Why not? Did God fail with him?"

"God doesn't fail."

"So God feels the same way Strickland does?"

"Dr. Strickland? What do you mean?"

"He says he'd rather lose one of us to suicide than homosexuality. So why do you feel so bad about Ray?" Nothing I'm saying is particularly connected to anything else I'm saying, really. Truth be told, I'm doing my damnedest to confuse Charles and get him to blurt something out.

"Taylor, he died! He killed himself! That's mortal sin."

"Now *you* sound Catholic. So is killing yourself worse than being gay? Because he must not have thought so. He must have thought death was preferable. But maybe it wasn't that death was preferable to being gay. Maybe it was preferable to being hated."

"I didn't hate him!"

I debate for a few seconds and then decide to say, "But this isn't about you, Charles." There's an odd noise from his side of the room, and I realize he's trying not to cry. I ask, "Do you hate me?"

His voice strangled, he says, "No, of course not."

"Because I'm gay, Charles. God made me gay, and I don't believe he wants me to do anything to change that. I believe he wants me to learn how to love even the people who hate me because of it. And he wants them to learn to love me just as I am. Just as he made me."

"No! We have to deserve God's love."

"That's bullshit, Charles."

"Taylor! I have to report that!"

"You do not. And you're not going to. Because I know that you're still gay. Your prayers haven't made you something you're not, because God doesn't want you to be different from how he made you. His answer is no, you'll never want Danielle's body the way you want a boy's, or a man's. Give it up."

He throws himself down and pulls the pillow over his head. I can barely make out his words. "You're tempting me! You're deliberately tempting me!" And then, "Get behind me, Satan!"

He's sobbing by now. I get up again, sit on his bed, and pull him up. At first he fights me, but it's feeble. I hold him, and his arms go around me. I tell him, "I love you, Charles. I really love you. I don't *want* you, not that—I love you. And God loves you. You don't have to do anything but be who you are for God to love you."

"But I do. I do have to change."

"Why? So Harnett and Strickland and Bartle can love you in their limited way? God is not so limited. He can love you whether you're gay or straight."

He pushes me away and wipes the back of his hand across his face. "We're not supposed to do this. We can't hold each other. We can't touch except in the presence of the brotherhood."

I let go, but I don't get up. "Fine, but you can't stop me loving you. And you can't stop God either. Do you know how many kids there are like Ray? Do you know how many of us have killed ourselves because we couldn't stand the hate? Eleven kids in twelve years, while right here in this place, have taken their own lives because they were so desperate to do something they couldn't do. And others have killed themselves after they left."

"That doesn't change what the Bible says. . . ."

I ignore him. "I don't want you to be one of those kids, Charles. I'm going to watch you like a hawk." He might not be able to see, but I'm grinning at him. The tables have turned, brother Charles. You're the one in danger now.

And I think he knows it. After a brief silence he says, "You'll go to hell, Taylor. You know that."

"Is that were Ray is? Did God fail Ray?"

"I told you. God doesn't fail."

"So God wanted Ray to go to hell and was going to get him there one way or another? Either he's gay or he kills himself. . . ."

"Stop!" He slams his hand down on the bed beside him. "If you don't go back to your bed right now and be quiet, I will report you immediately. Do you know what they'll do to you?"

"It can't be any worse than what you're doing to yourself." I get up and fetch a tissue. A clean one. "But I'm no martyr. And they can't fool me. And if Strickland wants my suicide, he's got a long wait. And Charles? I'll never be straight. And if you say you are, you're lying."

"One more word . . ."

I hand him the tissue. "Amen."

Chapter 12

*For am I now seeking the favor of men, or of God?
Or am I striving to please men? For if I were still
pleasing men, I wouldn't be a servant of Christ.*

—Galatians 1:10

When the bell screams in the morning and I sit up, Charles is fully dressed. He's sitting on the edge of his bed, watching me.

"Praying for my soul?" I ask. He nods. "That's great; I can use all the help I can get." I throw the covers back and face him. "How are you?"

He sort of shrugs. I'm about to stand up when he says, "How do you do it?"

"Do what?"

"How can you be so confident?"

I want to ask how he can be so desperate, but he looks kind of fragile. "Jesus is all about love, Charles. And think about this. He says we must love each other as we love ourselves. Which means we must love ourselves. He *assumes* we love ourselves. He doesn't say, 'Love each other as you love yourselves once you've mortified and mutilated and fixed yourselves.' So—I guess I love myself. And that's the place I love you from." This is pretty good, I'm thinking, for first thing in the morning.

"Who told you that?"

I can't really say Nate did. "A very wise person." Let him think it was my boyfriend.

"Do you think you'll still be gay when you leave here?"

"I'll be gay all my life. I have been gay all my life, though I didn't know it until a year or so ago, and I will always be gay. It's who I am. It's not a choice, and it's not a mistake."

"But . . ." His voice trails off, like it's tired of repeating the litany.

"It's like Harnett said last week—Monday? Yeah; the night you confessed. Her opening prayer said that God gives us all things. Not just joy, and pleasure, and beauty. He gives us everything. So it would be a mistake to try and change the way he made me just to get a pat on the head from Reverend Bartle. It would be like denying part of what God gave me. Which is not to say that being gay is bad. But as long as people like Strickland would rather see us dead, there's going to be pain involved."

I can tell this isn't stuff he's ever heard before. Some of it's stuff *I've* never heard before. Charles doesn't quite know what to do with it. So he says, "Go shower or we'll be late for breakfast. Then there's church."

Even though it's not true, I say, "I showered last night."

He looks sharply at me and I wink. He turns away, trying not to grin. And failing.

Charles is right about Reverend Bartle. I don't know why I haven't taken to referring to him as Bartle all the time. Mrs. Harnett is Harnett, and Dr. Strickland is Strickland. Anyway, there's a note in my box at the office. I've been forgetting all week to look there, but Charles suggests we walk by—probably because he's expecting me to have an appointment. And I do. It's for two o'clock. I'm to go to the chapel and wait outside until he comes for me. I'll try to find Nate before that and ask about tonight's topic.

Finding Nate alone isn't easy; everyone is together for everything today, so there's not much chance for a private talk. First breakfast, then church, then Fellowship. And that's when I manage to corner him. I tell him my idea—what Job's assumption was and what we should learn from it. And he likes it, especially the bit that had occurred to me later about the test being how to help each other.

I'm trying to spend most of my time with Charles, to make sure he's okay, but after I talk to Nate I see Charles and Danielle are standing together, quietly, not even talking. I leave them alone.

So at one fifty-nine I'm standing outside the chapel door, practically at attention, waiting for Bartle—there, I did it; no *Reverend*—to come for me. Sounds like the grim reaper, doesn't it? That's about what I expect to happen.

The door opens and a girl whose name I don't know comes out, sniffling and wiping her eyes. Bartle looks at me, says he'll be with me in a minute, and goes back in. Cool trick, I'm thinking; trying to make it worse for me by seeing someone else come out in pieces and then making me wait some more. I'm determined not to fall for it. I think of Will.

Will, who's broken the rules of Straight to God a few times now. Will, who helps me keep what's going on here in perspective. Will, who actually tried to rescue me before I was incarcerated.

After I'd seen him read that note I'd given to his sister, based on what my dad had said and on my being grounded in every way imaginable, I expected I wouldn't have a chance even to talk to Will before I was carted off. But I underestimated him.

The Saturday night before I came here—hell, just a week and a day ago now!—I was in my room, door shut tight (I'd read the pamphlet from Reverend Douglas, and I knew shut doors would soon be a luxury I wouldn't be allowed), staring at luggage full of clothes I hated stacked on one side of the room, sitting on my bed and feeling so frustrated and so sorry for myself that I was nearly crying. I could barely hear the TV from the living room, where my parents were watching something. Beside me was some book my mom had bought, full of the testimonies of people who call themselves ex-gay and the stories of how they got there.

Ex-gay? What the fuck is that? Taken literally, it means no longer happy. That would be me. I had no intentions of ex-ing anything out of myself, and if I was praying around this issue it was to beg for support to live through it and come back to myself again. Back to Will.

Suddenly over the drone of the TV I heard a sharp sound. My head snapped toward the window. It happened again. It was a pebble bouncing off the screen. In about point-ten seconds I was there, hands on the sill, straining to see into the dark of the backyard.

"Ty!"

OMG! I left the window only long enough to snap my light off so I could see him better. But when I got back, he was gone. Then I heard rustling in the maple tree that grows near the house. Will was climbing up to me! God, how much more romantic could he be? As quietly as possible, I pulled on the spring posts that held the screen in place and lifted the whole thing out, setting it against the wall beside me. I sat on the windowsill and watched as Will got closer and closer, and finally he reached out a hand and I grasped it. I tried to pull, to help him in, but he resisted.

"Ty, I'm not coming in. You're coming out."

"What?"

"We're blowing this joint. I won't let them put you in this place. Grab a couple of things and throw them into your schoolbag. I've got my mom's car. We'll head for Mexico or something."

I was shaking my head, even as my heart was trying to get me to obey him. "Will, no. We can't. You can't. You'll lose too much."

"Yeah? Like what?"

"You have to go to college and then grad school. You have a mission, remember? Those books you're going to write about us, showing how what we are is something that has always been and always will be. Forever and ever amen. You have to do that."

His whisper was harsh. "Fuck that shit, Ty! This is your *life*! Don't you know what happens to kids in there? Some of them come out a wreck, and some don't come out at all."

"I'm not like those kids, Will. I know exactly who I am, and they can't take that away. It's only six weeks, and I'm not risking your future to avoid it."

"But—"

"Listen. If I go through this and Dad still arranges for mili-

tary school, we'll reconsider. Now please, go away before someone finds you here."

"Move."

"What?"

"Move aside. Get into the room."

Puzzled, I did as he asked, and the next thing I knew he'd
swung from a branch and was perched precariously on the sill.
Frantic, I reached out and helped him in.

"Will, what are you doing? We'll be in so much trouble!"

He took my face in his hands and kissed me. "How much
trouble can you get into beyond what you're in already?"

"You will!"

"Only if they find me." He started taking off his clothes. "It's
only, what, nine thirty? Your folks will be in front of the boob
tube another half-hour at least." He leaned on my shoulder
and pulled his shoes off. "We can be quiet by then, and when
they come upstairs I'll go into the closet or something." He almost giggled. "Don't worry, I'll come out again!" His jeans and
underwear were on the floor now and he was standing there
stark naked and so fucking gorgeous. I didn't need much light
to see that. "And then we can make love again. If you're determined to go, I'm going to send you off with as much gay sex
under your proverbial belt as I can get there in the next several
hours. Consider it psychological armor."

He started on my clothes next, kissing me between buttons
and zippers and shoes. Then he pushed me onto the bed. "Still
got your secret stash of lube and condoms?" I nodded. I'd contemplated throwing them away, but the way my folks were
watching me I couldn't do more than put them in a wastebasket,
and how stupid would that be? Quickly Will went to the bookcase
and pulled out the VHS cover for *Die Hard* that Nina had given
me. He stood at the closed door for a few seconds, listening.

"I can hear them talking, so they're both there watching."
He moved over to where I was on the bed, propped up on my
elbows and watching him. "We'll have time for sweet nothings
and tender kisses in the afterglow, you beautiful, sexy homosexual. Now get ready to fuck."

I pulled out the towel I usually had stashed inside my pillow-case and complied.

After my folks went to bed, Will and I lay in each other's arms for a long time. We did lots of kissing, but the talk was bittersweet.

"You were coming to rescue me," I said, nuzzling under his chin.

"I still would, if you'd come with me."

"Very romantic, Will, and a little stupid."

He sighed. "I know. I just couldn't think what else to do, Ty. I hate the idea of you in that place, with them doing their damnedest to prove that Jesus doesn't love you until you change, that you can't get into heaven the way God himself made you. I told Nina, and she's ripshit, too. And I'm serious about what happens in that place. Or places like it, anyway. It scares the shit out of me to think that something might happen to you." He teased my hair with his fingers as he spoke. It was hypnotic, or mesmerizing, or something, and I almost missed the words "I love you, Ty."

It was the first time he'd said it. I guess I'd known for a long time that he felt that way. For sure, I'd known that I did. And I'd never said it either. I positioned myself over him, stroked that crazy hair away from his forehead, and kissed him lightly. "I love you, too. And I will love you just as much in six weeks." I dropped another kiss. "*And* in the same way." The next kiss was far from light.

He left sometime around four. We'd had sex maybe five times by then, in one way or another. Neither of us had more than dozed a little. Or been in any position where we weren't touching somewhere. It was tricky for him to get out: he had to jump from the window and grab a branch. Then he climbed back up so our fingertips could touch. He kissed his, I kissed mine, and we reached them toward each other. He dropped to the ground and was gone.

As I sit here now, waiting for Bartle and picturing Will drop away from me that morning, I'm near tears. Quickly I sit up and swipe at my eyes to get rid of any moisture that might have sneaked out. To help myself, I picture Bartle. Tall, white mop of hair, sharp nose. And Will's voice says, "He reminds me of a scarecrow." I giggle. And just then Bartle opens the door.

I don't think he heard me chuckling, but it puts me on edge that he might have. He gives me this beatific smile and holds the door open for me. "Brother Taylor."

"Reverend Bartle." We're all so very polite, aren't we?

I walk in and stand, waiting for him to indicate what he wants next. He leads the way to the front, but instead of kneeling at the altar this time, he sits in a pew and gestures for me to sit beside him. There's about two minutes of silence, and ordinarily I would have been nervous every second waiting for him to say something. But not this time. When I figure out that he's doing this deliberately, I start to pray silently.

Jesus, thank you for loving me. Thank you for helping me love Charles. Help me get him to see that he's worthy of your love just as he is. That he doesn't need to change into anything he's not. Help me to—

"Brother Taylor, what are you thinking?"

"I was praying."

"Tell me."

"I was thanking Jesus for helping me to love my roommate."

"Why did you need help?"

"Do you know Charles Courtney?"

Bartle evidently has no sense of humor; not even a chuckle escapes him. "Brother Charles is a wonderful young man. Have you had trouble loving him?"

"Of course."

"Why?"

"Because he's a wonderful young man. It's easier to love people who are less wonderful."

I'm not sure how he's going to take this, and obviously he's not sure how he wants to take it because he moves on. "I've read your MIs." He waits. So do I. Finally he says, "You're slacking."

Okay, Taylor, don't take the bait. Calm. Patience. "I don't think I know what you mean."

"The first two were very real. They were different from each other, but they were real. The second two show a certain reluctance to be open."

"Why do you think that?" I'm not going to assume I know what he means. No assumptions. And I'm not on this earth to please him.

He turns toward me. "You have changed a good deal in the past week. Are you aware?"

"Aware of change?" And I wait.

"Aware of *how* you've changed."

"I don't think it's wise for me to assume I know what you're seeing. I know how I feel, but I don't know what you're seeing."

"And how do you feel?"

This is how the interview goes, at least for a while. I feed him as many questions as answers, and always I toe the line between honesty and lying very closely. I tell him I feel closer to God, which is true; that I know myself better, which is true; that I'm learning more scripture, which is true (I carefully avoid talking about interpreting said scripture). I tell him some of the things that have impressed me, like Harnett's little speech about God giving us all things, not just the good ones. I have to be very careful; this man could have a lot to do with whether I get out in six weeks or eight. And maybe whether I still have to go to military school.

"What have you learned?"

"More than we have time to talk about." What I'm praying I've learned is how to survive a session with someone like him without breaking down.

"And what have you repented?"

Careful, Taylor. "Arrogance. Pride. Anger. Stubbornness." I stop.

"What else?"

"Hatred. Rebellion. Judging people too harshly." Again I stop.

He sighs. "We have only an hour today. But we have much time in the coming weeks if we need it. What else?"

"What is it you want me to say?"

His voice is louder. "Have you repented your sinful lust?"

I think for just a second. If he hadn't qualified it, if he hadn't called it sinful, I'd have been in trouble. But he did. And he didn't say anything about sex. "I have repented sinful lust." You see, what I feel for Will isn't sinful, not in this century, and it's only partly lust. I'm not sure I've ever really committed sinful lust, but that makes it that much easier to repent it.

He picks up a Bible from the pew seat. With one hand he holds it in my direction but doesn't release it. "Place your hand here."

I oblige him. He puts his other hand on top of mine, which feels weird, and not just because his is a little too warm. It's like that kid said that day in the kitchen. Creepy.

"Repeat what you said."

I do, looking as humble as possible, trying not to see Will raising his eyebrows comically at me over Bartle's shoulder.

He withdraws his hand and then the Bible, but he doesn't set it down. "Tell me what it means to repent."

I tell him, evidently to his satisfaction, because he doesn't correct me. Instead he opens the Bible and tells me to read certain passages. Of course, they have to do mostly with sex and sin and men lying with men. Each time I finish one, he makes me talk about it. And each time, I manage to say something that satisfies him without saying something that will add lying to the list of things I must repent. I didn't realize there were so many places in the Bible where sex of one kind or another is mentioned. He must have found them all. But I also didn't realize how few there are that refer specifically to me. To gays.

It's an effort to remain seemingly humble without looking false. I'm really not a humble person, but I know I've got to carry it off or regret it. When it starts to feel too artificial, I think about Charles standing up at Prayer Meeting the night Harnett let everyone throw stones at me. He'd called me wise. And he'd said the wisdom must be tempered with humility and then I'd be a formidable soldier for God. And that's what I want to be. Just not quite the same kind of soldier as Bartle.

Without warning, Bartle closes the Book and says, "You were laughing when I opened the door earlier. At what?"

At what? I barely remember. But I do remember it wasn't something I'd want him to know, so I come up with something else. "This morning I got Charles to chuckle. Well, at least grin. That's rare."

"How did you do that?"

I actually chuckle a little myself as I tell him. And because the story really begins when I was still in SafeZone, the morning I'd tried to avoid showering, I manage to work in some of the sins I've repented. I'm thinking I've done pretty well when Bartle stands up to face me. I stand, too, but he pushes me back onto the pew.

"I am concerned, brother Taylor. I'm worried that your feelings for Charles are not pure."

A sharp puff of air escapes me; is he kidding me with this? Ah, but hold on, Taylor; maybe he is. Or testing. I take a breath and try to remain calm. "If you're thinking I love him, you're right. If you're worried I lust after him, you needn't. I don't. I feel grateful to him. He's been patient and spiritual and kind, and I'm very glad I got him for my roommate. And that's it."

"Come with me."

Christ, now what? He kneels to face the altar, and I kneel as far away as I can without drawing attention to it. Or so I think. He looks at me and points to indicate I should move closer. But I'm willing to get only so close to the guy.

"Now," he says, "I want you to pray for Charles. For what he needs most. Aloud."

I breathe a few times, bow my head, close my eyes, and do my best to pretend that man is not beside me. "Holy Father, sweet Jesus, I ask for your guidance. Not for me, though I know I need it, but for my brother Charles. Help him to understand how much you love him. To know that even when he thinks his efforts are not enough, that your strength is always there. Calm his anxiety and take away his desperation. Help him to put his trust in you, to know that you guide him in everything, whether he can always see it or not. And make him know that I love him, and that you can help him through others. Even through me. Amen."

Bartle waits a discreet moment or two and then says, "What is Charles desperate about?"

This feels odd. Wrong, even. Charles has told me that he won't be pumped for information about me, but I feel like Bartle is pumping me about him. But I don't think I'm telling Bartle anything he and Harnett don't know already. "To be right. Righteous, really. It's not that there's error in that, but he's so desperate for it that he's not convinced it's there. And he seems desperate for God's love, too. Which could mean he doesn't quite believe in it yet."

Without meaning to, I've actually given Bartle what he wants. I've given him honesty, at least about Charles. I've been open.

There's a long silence, and I'm not sure what to make of it. I'm a little uncomfortable here; Bartle is looking at me the whole time. Finally he says, "Charles may be leaving us soon."

He's watching me, so I do my best not to react in any particular way. "Really? He hasn't said anything to me."

"This is the end of his sixth week with us." I nod, but I don't really know what that means to Charles. When I don't say anything, Bartle asks, "Do you know whether he's anxious to leave?"

"No, sir. I don't. He hasn't talked about that either."

"What would you say if I told you we were putting you back into SafeZone?"

I can't help a look of resignation. "I guess I'd say I'm getting used to it."

"Would you know why?"

"No."

He looks at me another minute and then says, "I think we're done here for today, Taylor."

I can't quite believe it; if it's true, I've gotten off really, really easy today. He walks me to the door, and I'm wondering whether I'm in SafeZone or not, whether he's waiting until the last possible second to hit me with something in his arsenal. But he doesn't hit me at all.

It hasn't been an hour yet, so there's no one else waiting

their turn in the pit. We say "Go with God" or some such thing that maybe neither of us means, and as I'm walking back to my room—mostly because I can't think where else to go at the moment—it occurs to me that maybe he'd just wanted to see how I'd react to a threat. And maybe to repeat the subtext—be afraid—I got from the room search, which I'm sure he was in on because it seems like just his style.

But I won't. I won't fear him. I'll placate him if necessary, but I won't fear him.

Charles is in the room when I get there, finishing his weekly letter home by the look of it. Though he shields it again. Who the hell cares what he puts in his letter? I sit at my desk and watch him for a minute, and finally I say, "How much longer will you be in this place?"

He looks up, and something about him makes me think of a rabbit that's trying to figure out which way to run. "I'm not sure. I thought I might be going home this weekend, but Mrs. Harnett told me at least one more week."

"What difference will that make?"

He looks off into space. "I'm not sure."

"Do you trust me?"

"Trust you to what?"

"And should I trust you?"

"Taylor, what are you talking about?"

"Just now, Reverend Bartle was pumping me about you. He asked me to pray aloud for you about what you need most."

Charles swallows hard. "What did you pray?"

"I asked Jesus to help you feel less desperate. To help you see how much love there is for you."

His eyes hang on mine, and if I thought he was desperate before, that was nothing. And suddenly I get it. He loves me. And not quite the way I love him. He wants me. It comes as an unbelievable shock. And he's been fighting this for—how long now? Maybe he said something to Harnett, or enough to make her suspect, and she told Bartle, and he was trying to find out how I feel about Charles. And maybe to find out how dreadful it might be to me if I was in SafeZone right before Charles leaves.

Charles covers his face with his hands.

I ask quietly, "Do you want a different roommate?"

Without looking at me he shakes his head. "I can't heal myself by avoiding things that make me sick."

So many things occur to me, so many things I want to say to him, shout at him, that I can't stay in the room with him.

We're allowed onto the grounds more or less unsupervised on Sundays, and it's a hazy, nasty, hot day, but I go outside anyway. There's a volleyball game going on, and softball out in the back field, but I find a tree and sit under it, leaning against the strong, firm trunk for support. I'm feeling really shitty, and I don't know why. Should I be doing something to help Charles, or is he just determined to make himself miserable beyond anyone's help? And if I try and fail, will I feel about him the way he feels about Ray? Not that I think Charles is about to do himself in.

I'd asked him if he wanted a different roommate. Maybe I should consider that option for myself. I love Charles, sure; but I don't want him. I hadn't lied to him when I'd told him that. Even if it weren't for Will . . .

Will. I close my eyes and paint his face. It seems fainter than just a couple of days ago, and when I realize that, I nearly cry out. I won't forget him! I won't! I press my palms against my eyes like it will hold his image inside my brain, but the clearest thing is the leather thong on his wrist—the one I'd seen when Nate gave him that note yesterday. And when I finally let my hands fall, I see stars. To clear my vision, I look out across the yard to the street, and then down the side of the building away from the sun. And I can see there's someone standing at the far corner. Near where the chain-link fence begins.

It looks like Will.

Hell, it *is* Will! Did he think he could contact Nate today? I look around, desperate to look casual—contradictory though that sounds. Anyway, I need to get to him. I have to. He draws me like a magnet. I do my best to saunter toward the near corner, lean against it a minute, hands in my pockets, and look all around me. When I look in Will's direction, he's looking right at me.

Holy shit. My breathing is odd, but there's not much I can do about it. He's *so* obviously not a resident; his clothes are his own—not of this place. And that hair! Christ, but I want to grab a fistful of it! I look back toward the yard again to see if anyone is looking my way. Don't think so. I make my way slowly along the side of the building, avoiding windows. Across the street is a huge utility and storage shed, but I don't think there's likely to be anyone in there today, and I can't afford to worry about everything. So I keep going. And Will is moving slowly toward me, like he's aware that quick movements are more likely to draw attention.

We're three feet away from each other and I'm about ready to scream when he reaches for me. His tongue is in my mouth in a nanosecond, and we collapse onto the ground, hands everywhere, panting. Finally he pulls away and takes my face in his hands.

What to say? Nothing is right. Nothing touches what I'm feeling. He kisses me again and then reaches into a pocket. He pulls out some paper that's folded small and hands it to me.

"Ty, you've got to read this. It's fucking amazing. Are you okay?"

I nod, grinning like an idiot as I tuck the paper away into my khakis. It's so good to hear the word *fucking* spoken aloud. It's so good to hear his voice at all. "Yeah. Christ, I miss you."

"Me, too." Another kiss. "But seriously, read this. It will help. It'll help you, and it might help some of the others as well. That kid Nate said he wasn't gay. Is he?"

"No. Why?"

He gives me his gorgeous lopsided grin. "Good. I was feeling a little jealous. He looks like a great guy, and if you liked him . . ."

I start to laugh but have to smother it. "He is a great guy. But no worries. You're it for me."

Another invasive kiss, and I say, "You've got to leave. You weren't supposed to come back at all."

"I had to get this to you. Shit, but I'm glad I got to give it to you and not Nate."

"Go. Please. If we're caught I'll be in here much longer."

One more kiss. "Hang in there, Ty. I'll be here."

From my spot on the ground I watch him walk away. He turns a few times and grins at me, and then he rounds a corner, and then he's gone. I whip my head around to see if anyone is watching.

Someone is. Someone else who, like me, must have wanted to be left alone, had found a spot under a tree a little farther away than the one I'd chosen. It's Rye, and he's watching me.

Shit. Well, there's nothing for it now. We'll see what he's made of. I hadn't reported him for anything; maybe he'll return the favor.

I let my head fall back against the building and close my eyes against the sun. And on the insides of my eyelids, I see Will's face. It's clear again.

Thank you, Jesus.

When I feel like I can stand again, I turn back toward where I'd come from, and now, between me and Rye, is none other than John McAndrews. He's at the corner where I'd leaned so nonchalantly earlier, looking at me. I do my best to smile at him as I walk in his direction.

"Brother Taylor? What do you think you're doing?"

Maybe if I ever get out of here I'll consider a career in acting. The look I give him is puzzled but not concerned, I'm sure of it. "Just getting some sun away from the crowds."

"Don't you know you aren't supposed to leave the yard?"

"I'm sorry, brother. I wasn't thinking of this space"—and I gesture along the building where I was sitting—"as not in the yard. I'll come back, since you think it's important."

He looks at me like he can't quite figure out whether I'm having him on or not. Maybe I'm not such a great actor after all. But what can he do? He can't have seen Will or he'd be confronting me with that. And I wasn't doing anything like trying to escape, or masturbating in the open air, and I'm doing as he says. I glance at Rye, wondering where his head's at. He half-smiles and nods once. I decide to take this to mean that he'll keep his mouth shut about Will.

John says, "I was looking for you. I wanted to thank you for helping out Friday night."

"No problem. I loved the band. And Peter taught me a few things about PA systems."

"Also, I wanted to talk to you about something. Someone, really. Walk with me."

We saunter along the edge of the yard, and it seems John is carefully avoiding getting too close to anyone else. I'm almost aware of a crinkling sound coming from Will's folded paper in my pocket. After a minute or so, John says, "It's about Charles. I'm wondering if we should suggest a change in rooms for him."

What is he, like, clairvoyant? And does he think I'm in love with Charles, like Bartle did? I do my best at a casual shrug. "I don't know what purpose that would serve. How much longer will he be here, anyway?" Maybe he knows, and can tell me, what Bartle wouldn't.

"Might be a week, might be two."

"Who decides?"

He looks at me from the corners of his eyes. "No one person. Will you miss him?"

"Of course. He's a terrific guy. Honest, kind, full of God's love." You know, I never used to talk like this before I got to this place. . . .

"Something's troubling him. Do you know what it is?"

I look right at him. Is he kidding? And is he really the second person today to ask me something like that? "I'm not sure what you want me to say. We're all troubled in one way or another." That seems safe enough.

"True, but there's something particular on his mind. Something's eating at him."

I have to be careful not to say anything that lets John know how much I differ from him on what I see as the problem. "Couldn't it be that he's struggling so hard to change himself?"

"I suppose." He sounds unconvinced. "But I feel in my heart there's more to it. I've seen lots of boys struggling with issues around Inappropriate Love, and his struggle seems to have some other source. I just can't put my finger on it, and I was hoping you might be able to shed some light."

Much as we might disagree on one important point, I have to say I believe John at this moment. I believe he's worried, I believe he believes what he's saying. And he just might be right. But if I say too much, it might screw up Charles's departure schedule, and I think he needs to get out of this place. So all I feel safe saying is, "I wish I could."

We've come to where some kids are sitting in the shade, watching the volleyball game. John stops, turns to me, and says, "Well, thanks, Taylor. If you can think of any way you and I can help, please come talk to me."

"I will. Sure." Wouldn't do to make an enemy of this guy; he's in too good with the establishment. And if he hadn't been involved in my room search, I might actually like him.

Chapter 13

He lies in wait near the villages. From ambushes, he murders the innocent. His eyes are secretly set against the helpless. He lurks in secret as a lion in his ambush. He lies in wait to catch the helpless. He catches the helpless, when he draws him in his net.

—Psalms 10:8

If it hadn't been for that illicit, marvelous meeting with Will, I might be more focused on what John has said about Charles. As it is, what's driving me crazy is that I can't seem to get alone long enough to read what Will gave me. It's still in my pocket, crinkling quietly whenever I sit or stand or walk, or maybe I'm imagining it, but I'm aware of it all the time. I try going to my room for some privacy, but Charles is writing at his desk again. He can't be writing home still, can he? How long are these letters supposed to be? Or maybe he's stocking up on MIs for the week? But Charles wouldn't do that. I'll never know for sure, 'cause he keeps leaning over whatever it is and I never get a chance to see it.

I'm on my way to hunt for an empty Prayer Meeting room, just starting in that direction, when I see Leland coming toward me nearly at a trot.

"Taylor!" His voice is a hoarse whisper.

I imitate his tone. "What?"

He's shaking his head and looking around him like he's scared of something. When he gets close enough he says in a low voice, "I've been looking for you. I have to talk to you."

First John, now this? Who else is scheming to keep me from Will's message? "Fine. Talk." But then I really look at him. "Are you okay?"

"No," he says, nearly sobbing. "No. Please. Can we go some-place?"

Now, the last thing this place is set up for is to let two gay guys go anyplace together and be alone. Finally I say, "Will there be anyone in the dining hall right now?"

"Good idea. Not many, for sure, and we'd see them before they could overhear us."

"We need a cover. Got your Bible?" He didn't, and neither did I, but there's always spares in the meeting rooms. So we head that way and grab a couple. I debate whether to stay in here and let Leland dump whatever it is he's dying to say, but someone could sneak up to the door and listen from the hall-way and we'd never know.

In the dining hall I suggest we get soft drinks to add to our cover. Besides, I'm thirsty. We find a remote table, open our Bibles to Psalms, and try to look scripturally earnest. At least, I do; Leland is getting more frantic by the second.

"Okay, Leland. Spill. What's up? You look—"

"Here." He lays his palm on the table and nearly shoots it to-ward me. There's a tiny corner of paper visible, and I hold it down with one finger while he withdraws his hand. I hold my Bible up, my back to the wall, and unfold the paper over Psalms 77:1: "My cry goes to God! Indeed, I cry to God for help, and for him to listen to me."

Here's what the paper says.

L—
If you find this and something's happened to me, it's Reverend Bartle. I couldn't tell you before because he said he'd hurt you too if I told anyone. But if this is still here and I'm not, look out for him.
—R

Suddenly this is even more important than what's crinkling in my pocket. I mean, Holy Fucking Shit.

"Leland, what do you think this means?"

"He didn't kill himself!" I can barely hear him, his voice is catching so badly. His eyes are streaming. "Reverend Bartle killed him! Don't you see?"

I look down at the note again. I've come to the same conclusion, but—I mean, I'm no fan of the guy, but could that *possibly* be true? And why? I ask, "Where did you find this?"

Leland rubs his face and gains a little control. "I was sitting on my bed, writing a letter home, and the mattress slid a little. When I got up to move it back I saw a corner of this sticking out from underneath."

I guess they haven't tossed that room. Of course not; John is Leland's roommate. "So you believe he meant to come and fetch it again if all was well, or for you to find it if all wasn't?"

"Taylor, what should we do?"

I have to ask. "Why did you come to me with this? Why not John or Mrs. Harnett?"

"Nate told me that if I ever needed to talk to someone and I couldn't find him, I should go to you. I couldn't find him."

Well, this floors me. Nate could have told a person, for one thing. But why me? Whatever; the deed is done. And now I'm the one who needs to find Nate. But first I have another question. "What do you think Ray meant by hurting you? What's *hurt* mean, d'you think?"

Leland swallows and kind of shudders at the same time. "I think he was raping Ray."

"What?" I have to slap a hand over my own mouth, that comes out so loud. "Why would Ray let him do that?"

"You didn't know him. He was . . . well, he was small and kind of pretty. And his uncle used to, you know, hurt him—when he was younger. He was all mixed up about it. He *really* wanted not to be gay, I think partly because he thought that might make him safe. And maybe he thought Reverend Bartle could help him. But I don't know why Ray would let him do that."

Christ. He must have been *very* mixed up. "But why would Bartle kill him?"

"Ray must have wanted to stop. He must have said he'd tell or something, don't you think?"

It makes sense, if you can picture the thing in the first place. "What makes you think Bartle was doing that?"

"Ray was always being called to the chapel, and he wouldn't tell me why. But every time he got one of those notes, he'd clam up and wouldn't talk to me until the next day. I got curious once and followed, thinking if I overheard what they were talking about, maybe I'd understand. But I couldn't hear anything, so I barely cracked the door, and I still couldn't hear anything. I opened it. And Taylor, there was no one in there! He'd gone in. I'm sure of that."

"Are you sure the notes were from Bartle?"

"Yeah. I saw a couple of them before Ray started being secretive about them."

This is too much. What the hell am I going to do with this? Some of the smarmy feelings I'd had earlier today—Bartle's hand on mine, going over all that sex stuff, when he asked about my relationship with Charles—come back to me and it's my turn to shudder. If it's true, then it could be happening to someone else right now.

Jesus Fucking Christ. Is he doing something to *Charles?* All that time in the chapel . . .

I slam my Bible shut. "Leland, are you a little calmer now?"

"Sort of."

"Do you think you could act casual and try again to find Nate while I go ask Charles something?"

"Okay. I'll try. What should I do if I find him?"

I check my watch; an hour and a half to dinner. "Tell him to meet me in Isaiah. I'll get there as soon as I can. If we don't hook up before dinner, then tell Nate what you told me. Do you want the note back, or do you want me to hang on to it?"

He takes a shaky breath. "I'll take it."

I know how he feels. "We can't lose it, do you understand?" He nods. I pass it back to him and give his hand a gentle squeeze as he takes it. "Okay. See you soon."

It is *so* hard to walk back to my room as though I wouldn't fly there if I could. I'm hoping Charles is still at his desk.

But no. Shit. I check his desk to see if maybe he's gone to the bathroom and will be back, but everything's packed neatly away. I nearly run to the library, but almost no one is in there, including Charles. So I head for Isaiah, where I wait for maybe twenty minutes, pacing back and forth, picking things up and putting them down, restacking Bibles, anything I can think of. Finally Nate and Leland arrive, and I can tell Leland's already told him enough.

I say, "Leland, did you happen to see Charles as you were looking for Nate?"

He shakes his head, and Nate says, "Why?"

I take a deep breath. "Let's just say I'm worried."

Nate understands immediately. His face goes from very intense to very calm rather quickly and he says, "Tell you what, brothers. Shall we avail ourselves of the cool of our beautiful little chapel this hot summer afternoon? Shall we go and pray?"

I get it. "Why, yes, brother Nate. Let's just do that."

Leland looks perplexed, but he comes with us. Quietly, Nate tells him, "We're going to see if there's anyone in the chapel. If there isn't, we'll go in and sit quietly as long as we can until dinnertime. We'll just see what happens. And then we'll decide what to do. Remember: quiet."

At the chapel, we listen carefully at the door. Can't hear a thing. Nate cracks it open a teeny bit, and still no sound. So we go in. There's no one anywhere in sight, and it's silent. So we hunch down side by side in the back pew far to one end, open some Bibles, and wait.

And wait. And wait, until dinnertime is within about half an hour. Then the door in the front to the side of the altar opens, and we hunker down even further. And who should come through that door but Charles. He doesn't see us. He walks down the far side of the chapel, head down. His face is all crumpled, he's breathing oddly, and he's holding his rib cage with his arms like he's in agony.

When he's gone, Nate whispers, "Let's get out of here. We don't want the good reverend to see us."

Nate leads us to his room, which is empty, thank God. He's getting a new roommate tomorrow, he says, but right now the room is his. We huddle behind the door, listening carefully for sounds from the hallway, and talk.

I start. "Well, this burns it. I've got to talk to Charles. This has got to stop! I can't fucking . . ."

"Stop!" Nate says. "You won't. *I'll* talk to him tonight. I'll come to your room well before lights-out, you'll make yourself scarce for as long as you dare without breaking curfew, and I'll see what I can find out."

"You? Why you?"

"Taylor, brother, I love you. And I love your directness. But what Charles needs is gentleness. He's going to clam up if there's a frontal assault. Obviously, he has some reason to think this is what needs to happen. Maybe he's punishing himself. Maybe any number of things. But he hasn't said anything about it to anyone so far, so it's not going to be easy to get it out of him now. So. Agreed?"

It's grudging, but I say, "All right."

I find Charles at dinner. He's sitting with a kid who's in Safe-Zone. Interesting; that concept works two ways sometimes, doesn't it? Charles doesn't have to talk.

"Can I join you?"

He won't look at me. He says, "Please don't take offense. I just want to sit quietly. Please, can you sit someplace else?"

I struggle with my directness. Gentle, Taylor. Be gentle. "You want the room tonight? I can go to the library."

He does look at me now. He looks—God, he looks awful. It makes me feel shaky. Then he closes his eyes and nods. So I find Nate and sit with him. Sheldon is with him, as well as Leland, so I can't say anything. But we wait Sheldon out, and after he's gone I tell Nate, "Charles wants to be alone. I told him he could have the room and I'd go to the library. He looked grateful. So he's all yours."

Nate smiles at me. "Thanks, Taylor."

"See? I can be gentle." I grin back at him.

Nate turns to Leland. "Hey, kid, do you mind giving Taylor and me a couple of minutes?"

"Yeah, okay. Taylor, can I hang out in the library with you?"

Nate speaks first. "Just be careful. The three of us have been together for a while this afternoon. It would be better if you don't sit together."

Leland sighs and leaves.

Nate watches him a few seconds and then turns to me. "You

may need to be even more gentle later. Tell you what. I'll come find you in the library if it doesn't get too close to lights-out and let both of you know how it went. You may not be able to say much of anything to Charles if he's in a lot of pain. If it's really bad, I might just take him to . . . Um, actually, Taylor, I'm gonna have to trust you with something really huge. Are you okay with that, or don't you want this burden? It's big."

"If it has anything to do with helping Charles, I can carry whatever I need to." Even as I say this, I'm thinking how only a week ago I couldn't stand the sight of Charles. He was an android. A suck-up. A brownnoser. A loser.

Nate sits back casually and takes a few seconds to look around. Most people have left by now, except Charles is still at his lonely table. The SafeZone kid is gone. There are maybe five kids left in the dining hall. Nate leans forward again and talks in really quiet tones.

"You know the circle?"

"Holy sh . . . I almost forgot! There's a meeting tonight."

"There is. And I won't be there. I want you to lead it. I'll go to the library and find Leland. I'll tell him I've got you working on something and you won't be there until later. Okay?"

"Wait, wait. Back up. You want me to do what?"

"I want you to lead. Have Peter lead the litany unless you're sure you remember it, and then ask if anyone has any struggles. If so, encourage the whole group to talk about it. Then tell them I've asked you to introduce the Job lesson you told me about. Keep an eye on the time, and about half an hour before lights-out—not later—wrap it up and have the group hold hands in unity. We'll try to meet again Tuesday, but tell them it's tentative. If they don't hear, there's no meeting. Got it?"

"You want me to do what?"

"Taylor, knock it off. You know very well you can do this. In fact, you want to do this. So just do it. Tell them I got tied up and asked you to."

"Who's Peter?"

"Now, Taylor, I'm sure you remember Peter. I saw the two of you working on the cables for the band setup. Why do you think John went over to distract you?" I just blink at him. "Don't play coy. There was more electricity coming from you than the band used for their whole show. By the way, just so you know, Peter's not gay." He grins at me. "Now. Can we go to the confidential part?"

I take a deep breath and nod. Jeez; leading the circle. But he's right; I can do it.

"Okay. If things get bad with Charles, which is to say that if he, like, you know, goes to pieces, I may have to call Mrs. Harnett."

"Huh?"

"Hush. Here's the confidential part. She's my mother."

"But . . . but her son moved away! And you're not gay! You told me. . . ."

"Will you be quiet and let me finish?" He waits. I make a face. He says, "That was my older brother. I'm trying to work on him. He doesn't believe how much she's changed. But that's another story. The important part is that she's with us. She's completely bought into how much good this place can do. Like I told you, kids like me. But now she understands about the gay thing. She hates Dr. Strickland's position, and she knows about the circle. She supports it. And, by the way, she had nothing to do with your room getting searched; that shocked her."

I interrupt. "Do you think John knew?"

"No, John's not like that. I know he's a bit narrow in his approach, and he couldn't tolerate the circle, but he'd never terrorize someone. He's in on a lot that goes on around here—he's being groomed for Leadership—but he doesn't know about me. People like Dr. Strickland and—I can't call him Reverend—Bartle know about Mom and me, but no more than that."

"But . . ." There has to be something wrong with this picture. All I can think of is, "Your name's different. You're not Nate Harnett."

"My father left us not long after I was born. She married my stepfather about five years ago."

I have a test for him. "What's her first name?"

"Caroline."

I don't even remember if that's true. He sounds convincing, but . . . It's not that I can't see the picture. It's just that the disconnect is so huge. Have I been *imagining* that Nate's been as critical about her as I have? Have I been assuming that he's bought into my position about the leadership of this place? I guess I have. He did tell me, the night he asked me to join the circle, that they aren't all evil here. I'm gonna have to give this some more thought later. Right now, I do my best to get with the program. Nate's program. I say, "Okay. So if it gets to be too close to lights-out, I'll go to my room. If no one's there, I'll assume you've taken him to . . . um, Mrs. Harnett. Is that it?"

"That's it."

Like that's all there is to it. Like this hasn't been an even crazier day for me than last Sunday was. Sunday. Half a year ago, now. But— "Why can't we get to her now?"

"She's not here. My grandmother is very sick, and Mom spends as much time as she can with her lately. She can come back if it's an emergency, and I can get to a car if I have to, but she's almost an hour away." We just look at each other for a minute, and then he says, "I wouldn't have burdened you with this except for this thing with Charles. You may need to create some cover. Leland's not going to sit quietly by and wait for the truth to make itself known in the fullness of time. He's going to want resolution. And he can't know about the circle. You, um, you may need to lie."

"I'm prepared for that." Now that I think of it, Mrs. Harnett wasn't here last Sunday either. "But there was a Prayer Meeting last Sunday. Who led it?"

"John."

"John? McAndrews?" Being groomed, all right.

"The same." He waits, but I don't know what to say to that. So he says, "Taylor, I'm really glad you're here. I know I can count on you."

I have to look down at the table. One of those Aw-shucks moments.

He says, "We need to get going. You've got circle soon. Get the key from Sean and be at the laundry room before seven thirty. It's earlier tonight because of no Prayer Meeting. Let me leave here ahead of you." He looks around and so do I. Charles is still sitting there, so Nate says, "I'll go help the kitchen-cleanup crew for a bit." And I know he'll watch for when Charles leaves.

It's a little early, but I decide to pick up my Bible and head for Sean's room to get the key. On the way I carelessly shove the hand not holding my Bible into my pocket. Guess what's there.

I want to smack myself in the head. How could I have forgotten that? But then, considering everything else that's going on, I suppose I could be forgiven. It's not like I've forgotten Will. I smile, thinking of his kisses.

Bless Sean's gorgeous black head, he's in his room. "Hey," I greet him. He responds in kind. I say, "Nate told me to get the key from you. He can't come tonight, so he asked me to open the room and get things started."

He looks at me a little suspiciously. "Where's Peter?"

I guess Peter must usually do this when Nate can't. I shrug. "Nate was pressed for time and I was at dinner with him."

"I guess it's okay." He digs in his desk and hands me the key.

And then I get an inspiration. "Listen, I have a favor to ask." He looks at me like he's afraid of what I'm going to say. I peek into the room just to make sure no one else is there, and although he doesn't have a roommate, there's a desk behind the door. Great. "I need a place to sit quietly and read something."

"Read something. Not your Bible, I take it."

"Uh, no. But I can hold it inside my Bible for cover if that helps. Can I sit at the other desk?"

He gets up and peers into the hall. No one is around. "Okay. But be quiet. And do put it in the Bible, will you?"

I turn the chair so the back is to the wall and pull the wad of paper out. It's a printer-friendly version of a newspaper article. It's all I can do not to start reading before I have it positioned, but I'd promised Sean. I do cheat a little and look first for green ink, which is right there at the top: "ESO!" And a little farther down: "YAIMP." Equipment Smarter than Operator? What does he mean by that? Have I been in here so long I can't remember IM lingo anymore? I get *You're Always In My Prayers,* but *ESO?*

Puzzled, I lay it out flat, fold it into quarters, open the Bible to the Gospel of John, and tuck it in before I settle down to read. And you won't believe what I read.

It's kind of long, so I have to unfold and flip a lot, but here's the gist: In this scientific study, gay men responded to the pheromones of other gay men more than they responded to the pheromones of straight men. And they didn't respond to female pheromones at all! So help me God. That's what it says. Something to do with an interaction between the hypothalamus and the pituitary. The report from the study came out in 2005.

Holy Mary, mother of God.

I read it so quickly the first time that when I'm done I have a hard time believing I didn't just make stuff up. So I read it again. And it says the same thing the second time. I look up at Sean, and he's watching me. He says, "You okay? You're making some odd noises over there."

"Sorry. I was trying to be quiet. I—Sean, are you gay?" He blinks at me a couple of times but doesn't answer. So I say, "You gotta read this."

"Not readin' nothin' that's gonna get me in trouble."

I get up and check outside the room; silence. I stand in the doorway so I'll know if the scene changes, and I keep my voice low. I'm shaking with excitement as I tell him what I've read. He's scowling at me, and then he glances at my Bible on the other desk, the article still in it. He goes over to it and picks up the article to read it for himself. First he gets hung up on the green ink, but I tell him that's not important, so he reads the rest. Then he looks up at me with a pained expression on his face.

I say, "Do you know what this means, Sean? When was the last time you were aware of your hypothalamus sending a sex wake-up call to your pituitary? You don't know anything until the pituitary has already gotten you feeling aroused. Get it? This proves what we've been trying to tell them all along. This is not a choice. And God made us this way."

"This is awful."

"What?"

"All of us who've been trying so hard to change? Do you know what this means to us?" His hand goes to the top of his head and clutches. "It's different for you. You never had any intention of changing, did you? But I really believed I could. And I was almost there. I—I've put so much into this! I've suffered so much. But you, you haven't. . . ."

"You mean you had almost convinced yourself. Now you don't have to."

"But, Taylor, the Bible says it's a sin!"

I check the hall once more and move over to stand close to him. "It *was* a sin. It was a sin when Moses was alive and when St. Paul was alive. But not anymore."

"That makes no sense." He's worrying me; sounds like he's almost going to cry.

"Sure it does. Times have changed. Christians eat shellfish; the Bible says it's a sin. We wear clothes with mixed fibers; the Bible says *that's* a sin. We change how we interpret some of these rules depending on our situation. Why can't we reinterpret this one? Especially when believing it literally causes so much hate, and pain, and when it's a natural way to be anyway. Look, you've spent a lot more time here than I have. How many kids have you known who killed themselves on account of this? And as for that bastard, Bartle . . ." I've gone too far.

He draws to his full height, and there's this immense dignity about him. Slowly he goes back to his own chair. "Taylor, I think you should leave now. And I don't want you to mention this to me again."

"But Sean . . ."

"I mean it. I gotta think about this, and I don't wanna hear your fancy ideas about interpreting scripture till I'm done."

I draw a shaky breath. "Okay. And thanks. You know. For letting me read this here." I fetch my Bible and fold the papers back into my pocket. I offer one more "Thanks" as I leave.

Chapter 14

Multitudes, multitudes in the valley of decision! For the day of Yahweh is near, in the valley of decision.

—Joel 3:14

Somehow I'm left with the same problem I had before. I need a place where I can be alone to think about what I've just read, to digest it. And, if I can be really creative, a place to keep it.

I duck into the nearest boys' bathroom and go into a booth. Leaning against the closed door I shut my eyes and take several deep breaths. Sean hadn't reacted anything like I'd have thought a gay kid would. For me, it had felt like—oh, I don't know, monumental? But in a good way. In a fucking fantastic way. So why had the monumental part for Sean been the bad kind? It's like science is finally agreeing with us that it's not a choice. But even more than that, it's a natural process. Biology in action.

And suddenly I get the *ESO*. We do what we're supposed to do whether we understand it—hell, whether we even know it or not. Take that, Reverend Douglas! I *knew* you were wrong.

Obviously, I'll have to bring this up tonight in the circle. I really wish I could talk to Nate about it first, but that can't happen.

In a moment of inspiration I take off my right shoe, lift the inner sole out, and fit the article into the bottom of the shoe. Thank God it's a tie shoe, not a loafer or something that might come off. I make sure the laces are snug. Walking back out of the bathroom I listen carefully, but I don't hear any crinkling.

Even so, I think about it all the way to the laundry room. I want to segue into it from the Job discussion somehow. But what's the hook? Just as I'm turning the key in the laundry room door it comes to me. It's all about assumptions, and assuming everything is all about you.

Peter sits right across from me, which is a little distracting 'cause he's so gorgeous, gay or not. Once we're sure everyone's here who's coming, I go lock the door. Then I take my place in the circle.

"Nate asked me to let you know he can't be here tonight. He asked to have Peter start us off, and then I'm to introduce a topic. Is that okay with everyone?"

There's no objection, and Peter leads the litany. It's great to be able to say the responses with them this time.

"What must not fail?"

"Understanding that the path to God is love."

"Where must we start?"

"From where we are and from who we are."

"What must we do?"

"Establish and maintain loving connection in everything we do."

Peter looks at me and I say, "Next meeting is Tuesday, but it's tentative. If you don't hear for sure, it's not on." And then I open the discussion.

It's such a rush, presenting this idea. Nate had opened with a combination statement and question. So I do the same.

"When we read the story of Job, it can seem like a test of his faith in God. His love for God. This interpretation would mean that it's all about Job. But when we look more closely at all that happened—dead livestock, dead people—we have to ask ourselves: Is it all about Job? And if not, then what?"

At first, it's like a graveyard. No one says a thing. Some of them look at each other, and I'm thinking this is going to be a total bust. I'm just about to take it back, try something else, when suddenly kids start firing assumptions at me. I try to respond to them the way Nate had. The discussion goes round and round, and I have to focus really hard to follow it, to try and remember who says what so I can refer back to some of their comments. And some of them are really good. Danielle even thinks of something really great that I hadn't. She says it's like people who think everything is all about them are trying to create God in their own image rather than the other way around. Just like the conclusion I'd come to about my own folks.

So I guess I'm doing something right, because they come to the same conclusion I had. That it's all about God. And that when we think it's all about us, it's like we think we're the center of the universe. And we're not, except when we're fully with God. At which point it's still all about God.

So I restate a comment from Dave, that we assume it's about Job because we identify with him, and we assume everything is about us. And when we do that, we can fall into a trap where we assume that everyone is *like* us, or should be. And that's when I hit them with the findings of this report.

Because, really, heteros don't know any more about what their hypothalamus is doing than I do. So they assume that my response should be the same as that of a straight guy, and they don't rub two gray cells together in any effort to think about it. But this report should make them do that. Will it? That's what I ask the group, with Sean's panicked reaction still fresh in my mind.

Jessica says, "They'll say if you pray hard enough, God can accomplish miracles."

Danielle, quietly, says, "They need to believe. They want something absolute."

"Structure," says Jamie. "They need structure. They need to have their morality and ethics spelled out for them. Spoon-fed."

Peter: "But we know that no one's situation is absolute. Not ours, not St. Paul's. It keeps changing. So the things we do to keep from failing—which must always begin from where we are— may not be absolute, either."

Nobody says anything for a few seconds, so I ask, "So what can we do for the gay kids who think they need that structure? Kids who don't want to hear about the science, who won't believe it matters?"

Jamie says, "None are so blind as those who will not see."

"But they're in pain," Danielle says, "so they don't *dare* look. They think they know what to do, and they're in pain."

Jamie, it seems, has little patience for pain. "Then they're cowards."

I picture Sean. Is he a coward? Possibly. And then Charles. I don't think Charles would want to look at this evidence, either. But I don't think he's a coward. "I don't think we can judge them so hard. We can't tell what kind of pain they're in, or what pressures they're under. So is there anything we can do to help someone who doesn't dare look at this?"

Dawn says, "Love them."

I haven't looked at my watch, but this seems like a good place to stop for tonight. I say, "What must we do?" And everyone chants the response. I take the hands of the kids next to me, and everyone else does the same. At least we can start here. At least we can love here.

Kids are leaving one by one and I'm standing there watching them when suddenly I remember that I'd forgotten to ask if there were any struggles anyone wanted to talk about. I strike a fist against my thigh. Danielle sees this and comes over to me.

"What is it?"

I tell her, but she just smiles, and then she gives me a hug and kisses my cheek. I hold her close and feel the swelling of her baby. She will be such a good mother. We need people like Danielle to be mothers.

As everyone is leaving, Danielle holds me back to talk about Charles, and we follow the others from a distance.

"He's been an angel to me," she says. "And I'm so worried about him. Taylor, there's so much love in him, and he gives and gives and won't accept any in return."

Little does she know how much *I'm* worried about him. Or why. But I can't talk about that, so I say, "He doesn't seem happy, does he?"

"No. He's trying so hard to change, and he really believes it's the right thing to do. But—can you talk to him about that study?"

"Danielle, I—I think Charles is one of those people who won't want to see it."

"But can't you try?"

I look at her. Her face is so earnest, and she's so worried. I say, "I'll see. I'll look for a good opportunity. But I think, with him, it would have to be just the right time."

And I can't quite imagine what that right time would be.

It's too early to go to my room; Nate might still be in there hammering at Charles to get him to fess up. But no; Nate's going to be gentle, right? I'm the one who hammers. In any case, I go to the library to see if Leland is there, as he's supposed to be.

He is. I approach where he's sitting at a table, a pile of books beside him and one open in front of him. Observing library rules I speak softly. "Hey. Fancy meeting you here."

He looks up, an expression somewhere between surprise and sulk on his face. He looks back down at his book. "Where've you been?"

I decide not to answer. "No sign of Nate yet?"

He shakes his head, and I can tell he's all the way into sulk now. At first I'm irritated, but then I think what this must be like for him. I mean, he must have felt that at least some part of what happened to Ray was his fault, and now he finds out the guy was probably murdered. Absentmindedly I reach for one of the books in Leland's pile and open it so it looks like I'm reading. But I'm not. I'm thinking that this whole thing seems so immensely unlikely. Really. Bartle murdering people? I can sort of see him abusing kids, but—murder?

I stare down at the printed page, but instead of seeing it my mind is focused on the sight of Charles hugging the far wall on his way out of the chapel earlier. The way he was holding himself made me hurt just to see it. Head down, face all crumpled, arms around his ribs so tight it's a wonder he could breathe. What had the man done to him, really?

The front corner of the chapel is where Charles had come from. I guess there must be an office or a storeroom, some place where things could happen unobserved. And they must happen quietly, too. Without protest. But why in God's name would Charles let that happen? What could Bartle have said to him to get him to put up with—well, with being raped?

I catch a movement out of the corner of my eye. It's Nate. He beckons for me to follow and to bring Leland, and he leads us to his room.

"I couldn't get anything out of him. But I'll tell you this. Something's going on. But I don't think there's anything we can do tonight."

Leland is pacing, but he stops long enough to ask, "So what are we supposed to do? Just sit back and let this happen? Just let that . . . that creep get away with what he did to Ray?"

Nate says, "No way. But for tonight, we can't take any more steps." He's sitting at his desk, and he reaches for his Bible. I can't tell at first what word he's looking up, but he lets the concordance lead him, and he reads. Finally I figure out that the word is *patience*. I like one verse in particular from Romans that goes like this: "For we were saved in hope, but hope that is seen is not hope. For who hopes for that which he sees? But if we hope for that which we don't see, we wait for it with patience."

It looks like he's about to start on another series of references when I get up from where I've been sitting on the floor. "I think I'll go be with Charles now." Nate looks up at me, and I add, "Don't worry, brother Nate. I'll be gentle."

"I'll walk with you a ways. Oh, Leland, may I borrow Ray's note?"

Leland seems reluctant, but finally he hands it over. Then the three of us walk Leland to his room, and once Nate and I are away from his door Nate says, "I think we need to see my mom tomorrow. Maybe I couldn't get much out of Charles, but there's definitely something to get. Do you want to come with me?"

"Heck, yeah. I'm with Leland. Patience is great, but the longer we wait, the more damage gets done."

"I'll phone her tonight, and let's plan to meet in her office before breakfast. Can you shake free of Charles in the morning, do you think?"

A kind of snort escapes me. "I think he's likely to be avoiding me. I'll be there, in any case. But wait . . . how can you phone anyone? And what was that about getting a car?"

Nate grins at me. "Nepotism has its advantages." He veers off without saying more, and I go on alone to see if Charles is still alive.

He's in bed, actually, and only my desk light is on. Guess he doesn't want to risk talking tonight. I grab my bathroom kit and get the brushing of teeth and the taking of leaks over with. It's nearly lights-out anyway.

Once I'm in bed and quiet, I can just make out the sound of Charles sobbing nearly silently. I go and sit on the edge of his bed. His back is to me, so I just stroke his arm gently for a while. I want so much to tell him that I know, that we're going to do something about it. But I can't.

He never says a word, and neither do I.

In the morning I get up quickly and rush through my shower so Charles will still be in the bathroom when I leave and I won't have to tell him where I'm going so early.

Mrs. Harnett (now that I know she's Nate's mom and that she's with us, she gets her title back) is waiting for us. I'm ahead of Nate, but only by about ten seconds, so the lady and I don't get much chance to acknowledge her change of status in my eyes. She gets right to business.

"Nate, please close the door. Boys? Sit, please. Now, what's this all about?"

Nate hands her Ray's note. "Leland found this under his mattress yesterday afternoon."

She reads it, and despite what I believe are her best intentions to look calm, it's obvious she's upset. She doesn't say anything right away, just pulls out a couple of files, opens them, and studies something in each. She puts them away.

"It isn't Leland's handwriting, as far as I can tell. It might be Ray's, and it might not."

Nate says, "There's more. We waited in the chapel yesterday to see if Charles came out of Reverend Bartle's office."

"Why?"

"Well—he did come out. And he was obviously in emotional agony. Maybe physical pain as well. He didn't see us. I tried to talk to him last night, but he dug his heels in."

"Charles? You think . . . *Charles?*"

Nate and I look at each other, I look at his mom, and I nod. She puts her head in her hands.

Nate says, "What are we going to do about this?"

She takes a few seconds and then looks up at him. "I can't talk about that. It wouldn't be appropriate."

Not *appropriate?* I say, "Look, Mrs. Harnett, if this is really happening, then he's raping Charles Courtney in the name of God."

She's on her feet. "Taylor, I know this is very difficult for you. It's hard for me, too. Please understand that I will do everything I can to investigate this and take whatever steps are called for. But I cannot, at this time, talk to you about it."

"But, Mom—"

"Nate, please. Don't press me. I assure you I am not taking this lightly. In fact, I am taking it very personally. But I cannot share with you the nature of my discussions with the center's board of directors or with the other staff leaders. You will just have to trust me."

So we stand as well, though I'm gritting my teeth. Nate leans over and retrieves the note.

"Leave that here, Nate."

"I can't. Leland wants it back. So unless you want him to know you're involved, I have to return it."

She thinks for a second and then says, "I'll walk out with you and make a photocopy, then. By the way, Taylor, it doesn't look as though you've picked up your messages. You'll find one from John letting you know that you're assigned to kitchen detail this week. Breakfast is done by paid staff, so your hours are the same as they were for the laundry room."

Kitchen? I throw a glance at Nate, who gets my drift and tells me, "I have special dispensation to stay in the laundry room. I keep an eye on the new kids."

Well, this sucks. Not much I can do about it, though. Maybe I'll get a chance to test John's leadership potential.

At the copy machine outside her office, she keeps the copy she makes and hands Nate back the original. Then she turns to me. "See you at ten, Taylor."

Crap. I'd nearly forgotten our appointment.

I grab the message from my mailbox, and Nate and I walk toward the dining hall. He keeps his voice low as he says, "I know that seemed rather less than satisfying. But believe me, she is really upset. She won't just sit back. She'll do something; I just don't know what."

"Look, Nate, I don't doubt you, or her, or your intentions, but what will she be able to do other than confront the guy? We need to get rid of him, get him away from—"

"I know. Listen, you know how I've been coming back year after year?"

"I do. I think you're nuts."

"When I get to college, I'm going to study psychology. And what I've been doing here, with my mom's support, is stuff like leading the circle, like talking one-on-one with kids like Ray and Leland and Charles, because both Mom and I want to understand what's driving kids to kill themselves. Especially gay kids, so we can stop adding to that by what goes on here. So we've collected a lot of information, including things Bartle has been saying in his own one-on-one meetings. We've been building a case against him. We just never knew he'd go as far as rape. Or murder."

"So she'll put all this together?"

"Exactly. And go after him. And she'll take some steps to protect Charles."

"But in the meantime . . ."

"In the meantime, Taylor, you stay the hell away from Bartle."

"I was gonna collect a whole bunch of us villagers and hand out torches and clubs . . ."

"Hush." He's trying not to laugh. But he knows it isn't funny.

We step into the dining hall and I do a quick scan. No roommate in sight. I say, "I'm going back to the room to get Charles."

"Okay. If I hear anything, I'll let you know."

Charles is not expecting me to walk into the room. He's at his desk, writing again, and when he sees me he jumps nearly out of his chair and frantically reaches for whatever he was writing to turn it over. When I've seen him do this in the past, I've just assumed he was writing home. He's always hidden his writing immediately. But he's never been so frightened. I just look at him, wracking my brains for some way this could be connected with Bartle.

I guess my silence disconcerts him even more. He has to clear his throat before he speaks, and then his voice is kind of squeaky and odd. "Taylor! I, uh, I thought you'd gone to breakfast."

I watch his face for a few seconds. Then, "You didn't show up. I'm here to escort you."

"That's not necessary. I'll just finish this up and be right there." He gives me this big, fake smile.

"I'll wait." I pull out my chair, sit, and watch him. I'd warned him already. I'm the hawk now.

He does not—I mean, *does not*—want to go back to whatever he was writing with me sitting there. "Taylor, you know, this is . . . well, it's kind of private."

"Fine. I can't see it from over here."

He makes a few attempts to write, but I can see his hand shaking. He sets the pen down. "Taylor, you're going to be late for breakfast."

"I won't if you come with me now. If not, then we'll both miss it, won't we?"

His hands flutter in the air for a few seconds as he tries to decide what to do with them, and finally he gives up on whatever his writing project is. "All right, all right. Could you just wait outside the door for a second, please?"

I give him a heavy look. "Secrecy, brother? Do you need coaching?"

This makes him kind of shake all over. "Taylor, please. I really need you to do this for me."

It's got to have something to do with Bartle. From just outside the door I hear drawers opening and closing, things shuffling around, and it sounds like Charles is moving around the room. I imagine he's looking for a good hiding place. Try the inner sole of your shoe, I want to tell him. That's where I'm still hiding the article Will brought me.

Danielle had begged me to tell Charles about it. But I don't think he can stand any more stress right now. It will have to wait.

Between breakfast and my ten o'clock meeting with Mrs. Harnett, I decide to take the time to write a scanty letter home, still not very pleased with my folks for forcing me to come here. Maybe they couldn't know there'd be someone like Bartle here, and I have to believe they never knew the whole truth about Strickland's attitude, but they still want me to be someone I'm not. Someone I can't be.

The letter doesn't take very long, so when I've finished I devote a little bandwidth to something that's been kind of nudging at me from the back of my brain since yesterday afternoon. It had gotten kind of smothered with all the stuff about Bartle, but it deserves some thought. And it concerns the person I'm to see at ten.

Mrs. Harnett is Nate Devlin's mother.

I struggle to recall some specifics of our past conversations. Times when I was sure she was just another mouthpiece for Straight to God's philosophy. Sure, I remember how angry I was that she'd put me back into SafeZone, but the only other unpleasantness I can come up with is in the conclusions I'd made about her. Conclusions based on the false assumption that she was on the other side of the gay issue from me.

So if she's on the same side of that can of worms, which is what it is around here, why haven't I been able to tell? Maybe because she couldn't afford to let me know?

What stands out the most in my memory are times like the day I'd told her how tough I thought her role was. How she couldn't teach something just by saying it, that she had to find a way to get me to learn it for myself. She had seemed—well, gratified. Hugely gratified. And she'd tried not to show that, either. She had seemed like a real person.

But now she's refusing to let on what steps she's taking about Bartle. The question is, should I trust her, as she's insisting? She hasn't proven herself to be untrustworthy, exactly, but can

I just sit back and do nothing? Even God doesn't want us to do that.

By the time I show up at her office, she's recovered from her earlier distress and is her old calm self again. It's like nothing happened earlier this morning in this very room.

"Do you have any impressions you'd care to talk about, Taylor?"

I guess I'll have to play along. "Well, I've survived my first week; only five more to go. I suppose it's a good thing I'm not counting in days anymore."

"Were you counting days?"

"I was counting minutes."

"And now it's weeks?"

I consider this. "Actually, now it's minutes again. Because I'm worried about Charles in every one of them."

"I appreciate that, Taylor, but I need to ask that for now we don't refer to that situation. I assure you I'm doing everything in my power to address it."

The rest of the meeting is pretty meaningless. I ask if I can stay in the laundry room, and she says no, that I need to learn the other aspects of service. Fine. Whatever. By the time I leave, I don't know any more than before what she's going to do about Bartle. All I know is, I can't sit back and do nothing. I just have to decide what to do.

Every chance I get all day, I look for Charles. I even stop by the mailboxes as often as possible to see if he's got a summons from Bartle, but there's never anything in there. I see him at lunch, but he's already at a full table, so I can't sit with him. I'm so focused on him that it's hard to appreciate the fact that I'm eating lunch I helped make.

In the afternoon John has me breaking apart lettuce heads, which is about as mindless as filling detergent containers in the laundry room. You know where my mind goes. What the hell am I going to do about Charles? How the fuck can I help him? And what, if anything, is Mrs. Harnett going to do?

I can't help thinking about Bartle, about the smarmy things

he did. I think back to last Sunday, the day I got here, and try to remember: had he done anything like that then? The comment from that kid in Kitchen last week comes to me, and then I'm nearly stunned by a mental image of poor Leland's dick rubbed raw. But as for me, I guess it's been just the neck squeeze when Charles turned me over to him, and of course that hug he gave me after tearing me apart.

What a bastard. Who would do such a thing?

And then I realize that I've done it myself. I did the exact same thing to Charles Saturday night. I hammered at him, just like Nate said, until he cried. And then I held him.

If I'm going to prove myself better than Bartle, I have to help Charles. I just *have* to.

One thing I can do is watch. After Prayer Meeting Charles goes to the library, not the chapel. It makes me wonder if Mrs. Harnett has said anything. I sit there for a while at another table, until I'm sure he's not leaving to go meet his tormentor.

Tuesday at lunch Dave finds me. He says, "Looking forward to seeing you later this evening, brother." Which I know means there's a circle meeting. Then he adds, "By the way, there's something in your mailbox."

"Thanks, brother. See you later, for sure."

After lunch I head toward the offices, and the message is a summons from the famous Dr. Strickland to see him at three o'clock today. I haven't seen him in over a week, and he'd promised an audience when I was out of SafeZone. But I guess he didn't say how long out of it. Maybe John will give me onions to work on and I'll be really smelly by the time Strickland and I have our little consult.

No onions; too bad. As it turns out the whole thing with Strickland is pretty much a formality. All through it I get the sense he's just doing it so he can say he did. I'm sure he's had tales from Mrs. Harnett and Bartle about me, and he's probably trusting them to provide the necessary carrots and sticks to ensure my purification and humiliation. There's no mention of Charles. Or Bartle.

I distract myself every few minutes by wriggling my right foot and imagining I hear crinkling. And I need the distraction; without it I wouldn't be able to stop thinking that this is the man who'd rather see me kill myself than be gay. I'm struggling not to feel hatred, for him and for Bartle.

Strickland seems his usual self. Or as much himself as I can assess, given my limited exposure to the man. He seems just as cool, just as sure of himself, as before. Why doesn't he seem as insane as his comments in that article? I wriggle my toes again and think of Will. And I remember the conversation we'd had—our first one, really—when we'd talked about self-confidence. Will had said that people who are truly self-confident are most comfortable around other self-confident people. I wonder if that's true for Strickland, or if his seeming self-confidence comes more from the need to feel superior. A kind of righteous arrogance. If the latter, then it might be kind of fun to try and puncture it—though probably not worth it.

And out of nowhere it comes to me. I realize what I have to do about Charles. For Charles. As soon as I'm out of there I start laying plans.

Chapter 15

Whoever causes the upright to go astray in an evil way, he will fall into his own trap; but the blameless will inherit good.

—Proverbs 29:10

As soon as I'm released from kitchen detail so I can get ready to eat the dinner I've been helping to prepare all afternoon, I dash to my room, fling myself into my desk chair, and grab a pad and pen. I've been thinking about what should go into this note ever since I left Strickland's office, but I still need to work on it a little. I decide to start writing and see how it looks. But when I'm done, I realize it's a little over the top. Especially the quote about lust from James that I've recycled from my Public Apology. So I scratch some stuff out, tone some down, and this is what I end up with:

> Reverend Bartle,
> I have lied to you. Worse, I feel lust for another brother. You were right on Sunday. My thoughts and feelings about Charles are not pure. He is blameless and has done nothing to tempt me. He probably doesn't even know how I feel. But my feelings are beginning to overwhelm me. The more I pray, the more I'm sure that I'm hateful to God. The more I know I'm unworthy of grace. Help me, please.

That will have to do if I'm going to get it into his mailbox before dinner without Charles seeing me. As I'm standing in front of

the mailboxes, eyes glued to where the label that says J. BARTLE—
he has a first name?—is taped, I ask myself if I'm really, really,
really sure I want to do this. I take a deep breath, pop the note
in, and then push myself away.

The first part of the evening is kind of a blur. The only thing
I remember is that I'd hoped to sit beside Charles in Isaiah, but
he's managed to sandwich himself between Hank and a new
kid named Ronald.

Before I head toward the laundry room for circle, I go to
check the mailboxes. I want to know if Bartle has picked up my
note. I know which box is his now, so my eyes lock onto it from
a little distance away. And it's empty.

I stand there and take several breaths. I'm just about to turn
away when I notice something in my own box. Can't be another
summons from Strickland. Could it be a message from Mrs.
Harnett about our little situation? But it seems unlikely she'd
communicate with me about it like this. I pull it out and open
it.

It's from Bartle.

All it says is,

> *Pray with me tonight in the chapel after your meeting.*
> *J. B.*

Pray with him. Oh God.

But—there's a circle meeting. I'm sure that's not the one
Bartle meant. Nate had said, though, that there would be times
I'd need to decide when I shouldn't go, and that not everyone
always comes.

Now I'm really torn. Torn nearly to pieces. I could forget the
whole thing and go to circle. But Bartle has taken the bait, or so
it would seem, and the only way to follow through is to show up.
But it's going to be hell dealing with him. I don't know what
he'll do, what he'll say, or how much trouble I'm going to get
into. What I want, of course, is for him to come on to me, to
think he can treat me like he treats Charles. But I won't let him,
and then I'll have proof that he's a monster. Though it's also

possible he won't do anything at all. I mean, I'm not actually sure that he's mistreating Charles physically. He's certainly capable of reducing kids to tears just by talking to them.

Circle? Or Bartle? Retreat to the safety of loving friends, or take this guy out for Charles and Ray and anyone else he's hurt?

Okay, Taylor, you set this trap, and you know what you have to do.

I start walking, my knees shaking, my arms wrapped around me not unlike the way Charles's arms had been wrapped around him. When I get to the chapel, the doors are closed. I sit on a bench along the wall for a couple of minutes. Collapse on the bench is more like it.

Deep breaths, Taylor. Focus. What would Will do?

Will would probably just charge in there and accuse the guy and see how he reacts. But I don't think that will work; Bartle's been at this far too long and I'm just another kid. If he's really doing this, then I need to catch him, not accuse him. I need proof.

Sorry, Will. This time I'm doing what *I* have to do.

I stand, feeling a little more secure now, and open the door.

There's no one in sight. I start down the center aisle, hearing nothing but my heart pounding in my ears. Is it possible he wants me to go to that corner room?

"Close the door please, Taylor."

A sound escapes me, and I smell a sharp odor—my own fear. I wheel around. Bartle is sitting in the far corner, just about where Nate and Leland and I had lain in wait for Charles on Sunday. If I'd thought my heart was pounding before, well, let's just say I didn't know what that meant. But I manage to go back and close the door. Then I turn to face Bartle, who's now walking slowly toward me. He stands there a minute, scouring my face with his eyes, and I know he can tell I'm terrified. But this might be a good thing; if I'd meant every word of my note, wouldn't I be afraid?

He turns suddenly toward the altar. "Come."

Oh God. Is he leading the way to that room? But no, he stops at the front and kneels. I sort of assume I'm to do the same, so I do. He doesn't look at me, but he speaks.

"Taylor, my son, thank you. Thank you for your honesty, for your sincere desire to turn away from sin. You say you are praying, but I'm sure that there are ways to make it more meaningful." About a hundred of my heartbeats go by, and then he says, "Does Charles know you're here?"

I swallow. "No."

"Who does know?"

My belly is quivering. "No one." Too late, I realize it might have been a good idea to let somebody know.

"What have you been praying? What have you asked God for?"

Now, I've actually given this a little thought. It occurred to me during my brain-wracking in the kitchen this afternoon that I was going to have to say something that sounded convincing. So what I decided to do is give him Will, like I hadn't done that first Sunday, but not Will the person. I'm going to pretend that I feel for Charles what I feel for Will. That's not only convincing, it's also very real for me. I won't have to make anything up—remember how complicated that can get?—and it will reel Bartle all the way in.

But I have to lie a little to get things started. "I've prayed that he won't be in the room when I get back after Prayer Meeting, so maybe I could go to sleep before seeing him. I've prayed not to dream about him. I've prayed that he'd be sent home. I've prayed—"

"And what have you done?"

"What?"

"Your note said you feel lust. What have you done about that?"

"Well . . . I've masturbated. I put that in my MI."

"In one of them. Have there been other times?"

"Yes."

"Tell me about them."

I close my eyes. "Once I pretended I was pinning him against the wall near his desk. Behind the door, where no one walking by could see. I had his wrists in my hands, against the wall above his head, and I kissed him." I wait.

"And then what?"

"I, uh, I sucked on his neck, and then I pulled his hands together over his head so I could hold them both with one of mine. He struggled, but not very hard. And I ripped his shirt open."

Bartle clears his throat. "And then?"

"I sucked his tits while I undid his belt and then his fly." I stop again. I'm going to make him work for this.

"Did he cry out?"

"What? No. I mean, he wasn't really there, you know?"

"Of course. Go on."

"Well, you know."

He takes a breath. "Taylor, if we're going to purge these feelings from you, you'll need to be specific about what they are. Pretend I don't know."

But I know he does. I *know* he does. "Okay. Well, like I said, his fly. And I pulled him out—"

"You pulled what out?"

"His dick. I pulled his dick out." I risk a sideways glance, and I can see Bartle is really getting into this. "It was hard. Really hard. He wanted me really badly. In my imagination. And by now he was pretty helpless, so I could let go of his hands and he stayed where he was, and I knelt in front of him. I took him—I mean, his dick—in my mouth." Time to test again; how much detail is he hoping for?

He swallows. "Is that all?"

"Well, no. I mean, I've done this before, so I know what to do." I close my eyes again. "I ran my tongue in circles around him, and covered my teeth and sucked, and then I poked into his balls with the tip of my tongue." I can hear him breathing next to me. "His hips started spazing a little, and his ass clenched. And he was making these quiet little grunting noises, and—"

"Stop!"

I look over at him. His head is hanging forward, his jaw is clenched, and his eyes are tight shut. Then he breathes loudly once or twice and says, "Almighty Father, be with us here. Come into Taylor's heart and purify it. Help him to understand that these desires are beyond sinful, that they are devouring his very soul. Tell him what he must do in order to drive Satan out, to make room for our Lord Jesus. Please. Please, speak to Taylor."

Maybe thirty seconds of silence later, he lifts his head, but he still doesn't look at me. He says, "Taylor, did you hear God's words?"

"Um, no. I didn't hear anything."

"Father above, I pray that you will help Taylor understand that it is you he longs for, not Charles. Not a boy, not a man. Only you." More silence. "Listen hard, Taylor. Can't you hear? Can't you open your heart and your mind, and understand what God is asking? What God is requiring?"

Okay, so I listen again. I could fake something, but that's too dangerous. "I'm sorry. I can't."

"Father, tell me what I can do to make Taylor hear you. To make him understand." Silence. Then, "Is that the only way?" Silence again. It's like listening to one side of a telephone conversation. Then he bows his head. "The Lord's will be done."

Slowly he gets to his feet, and I'm thinking, okay, what did The Man say? Bartle holds out a hand to me, but I don't want to touch it. I say, "You want me to get up?"

"Come, Taylor. Come and learn how you will shed this sin." His hand is still out, but I don't take it. I'm wondering at what point, exactly, I'll have the proof I need. The look on Bartle's face is weirding me out—kind of wide-eyed, like he's focusing on something in the distance, and no expression to speak of. Like he's been taken over by something.

I get up without help and stand a little away from him, but he moves toward me. This is too creepy. Without really meaning to, I say, "Look, you're scaring me." Damn! I shouldn't discourage him.

He stops, closes his eyes, and lowers the hand he's holding out toward me. "It's a powerful thing, Taylor. I don't mean to frighten you." He opens his eyes, and he looks sort of normal again. "Feel the love, Taylor. Feel God's love. It's all around us. And it's in me, too. God's love for you is coming through me." He smiles. It's almost convincing.

"What did God say to do?"

He stops smiling and just looks at me. "Perhaps you're not ready for this. Perhaps you need to lose more of your soul first."

This sounds good to me; it means I can leave. But if I do that, I won't have my proof, and he'll be back at Charles again in no time. And maybe other kids, too.

"What do I have to do?"

"Receive love, Taylor. That's all. Let God's love take the place of Satan's urgings."

"But . . . how do I do that?" This is so fucking hard. I don't *want* to lose those urgings, and I don't believe they come from Satan.

"Are you sure you're ready?"

"Ready for what?"

"I think maybe we need to give you some more time. You obviously don't trust God yet, and without that—I'm afraid I can't do anything to help."

"I trust God."

"If you trusted God, you wouldn't keep asking for details. You wouldn't keep asking why, what, where, on and on."

This is bullshit, and I know it, but if I don't give in, I won't get my proof. "Okay, I'll stop asking."

He looks at me for what seems like a really long time. I'm actually starting to get a little dizzy. Finally he says, "Do you want purity?"

He waits until I say, "Yes."

"Do you want love?"

"Yes."

"Do you forsake Satan?"

"Yes."

"Then come." And he turns away and walks toward that corner room. He doesn't look around to see if I'm following, he just keeps walking. Slowly, but he keeps walking.

I'm rooted. How the fuck can I go in there with him? But how can I not? And what can he do to me, anyway? I mean, he's tall, but so am I, and he's kind of scrawny and I'm no weakling. Plus I can scream really loud.

But, who would hear me?

Do I have a choice?

Of course. I could leave right now. I could turn this whole thing over to Mrs. Harnett and just not let Charles out of my sight.

Bartle disappears into the room.

This isn't about me now. Not really. And suddenly I remember what Will was ready to do for me. How he was ready to sacrifice his college plans to keep me safe from this very place.

I lift one foot off the floor, and I come so close to setting it down in the direction of the hall outside. But I don't. I go toward the room.

I stand in the doorway. Bartle is sitting in a chair to my left, its back to the wall beside the doorway, and there's another chair facing him, sort of facing the door. He's looking at the chair, not at me. So I sit in the chair. At least he doesn't close the door.

"Have you ever eaten too much sugar, Taylor?"

"What?"

"It wouldn't have to be sugar. Have you ever eaten so much of anything you wanted that it made you sick?"

"Once when my mom was making chocolate chip cookies, the phone rang, and I made off with the bowl of batter. I ate most of it."

"Did you get sick?"

"I didn't throw up or anything, but I felt really sh—really crappy."

"I'll bet you didn't do that again, did you?"

"No."

He nods. "You are a very special person, Taylor. I've felt this since the first time I met you. I was even more convinced on that Sunday when we brought you into the Program. Many would have been discouraged by how you acted at our last meeting. You were pushing me aside. You were denying my help, denying me, denying God. But you are very special. And God has put you in my care. God has commanded me to help you."

Mrs. Harnett had told me to beware of people who said things like this to me, about how special I am. I wonder if she suspected anything like this.

He stands, and I start to get up but he shakes his head. He moves to my left, goes behind the door, and opens the drawer of a filing cabinet, but he doesn't reach into it, which seems weird. But this whole encounter is so frigging weird; what's one more thing? And now that he's back there, he pushes the door closed. My eyes follow the slow swing all the way to the door jamb. The handle clicks into place. It looks like an ordinary handle; I'm sure I could open it in a hurry if I needed to.

"What we're going to do, my special boy, is teach you not to eat cookie batter. It's interesting, you know? You can't get too much of God's love, but you can get too much of Satan's lustful sin. And just like the cookie batter, when you've finally had too much, you won't want any more."

WTF? What's he going on about?

And now he's between me and the door. "Stand, Taylor."

Okay, that's better anyway. Easier to make a run for it from my feet.

"Now, I want you to use your mind. Use your imagination. Pretend to yourself that I am Charles."

"I—uh, I don't think . . ."

"It might help if you close your eyes."

"No. No, I don't think that would help."

"You told me you've been praying that God will send Charles home. But you can't heal yourself by avoiding things that make you sick. That's only a very temporary solution. You need to be purified. Do you want to be purified, Taylor?"

Holy shit. That's exactly what Charles had said, about avoiding things that make you sick. Christ, how many boys have bought this line? This whole mess? But I'm so close now; and I don't think I could go through this charade again, so I need to get my proof and get out of here.

Jesus, help me. Be with me. Protect me. And I close my eyes. Now, *this* is trust in God.

"I'm Charles," he says. I can smell him, his soap, his breath. One hand is on my hip. "Remember that I'm doing God's bidding. What happens next gives me no pleasure. No pleasure at all. If it weren't for God's instructions, I'd be risking my own soul to save yours. But God has commanded me." The other hand is behind my neck.

Before I can even think, he yanks on my waistband, pulling my groin against his, and I sure as hell know what it feels like when a guy's hard dick is pressing against me. Bartle's is hard. Then he kisses me. Right on the mouth. Hell, right *in* the mouth. He's stronger than I'd thought, and it's really hard to push him away. But I do. His back hits the door, though, so I can't get out quickly.

We stand there staring at each other for a minute, then I wipe my mouth off, and his face softens. His voice is silky. "Trust! You must trust. This is what Almighty God has commanded me to do. I hate it; please know that. I hate doing it. I hate what it is and everything about it, just as you will. I promise you that. It will save you, Taylor. This is the only way. You must have too much of what Satan wants you to have, and I am God's tool. Now, close your eyes and submit to God's will."

Not a chance, fucker. "I've got what I came for."

He blinks stupidly at me. "What did you say?"

You know all those movies you see where the hero has caught the bad guy, the perp, gun in hand and about to do the bad deed? And instead of getting help or doing anything sensible, he tells the perp "Gotcha" and the perp shoots the hero? And you always say to yourself or whoever's watching with you, "Why the hell is that idiot telling the perp what he's going to do?" Well, I have a better understanding about that now. It's like you can't help yourself.

"You're doing this to Charles, aren't you? And you were doing it to Ray. He didn't kill himself. I know that, and you know that. You murdered him. And how many others?"

He stares at me, nostrils flaring. "No! No, you have to understand. The boys who died were too far gone. Some of them died by their own hands, and some died because God commanded me to end their sinning before it consumed them. This isn't true for Charles, and it doesn't have to be true for you. Pray with me, Taylor. Pray hard, and God will let you see through me, his humble tool, how truly evil this is! Please, for the sake of your very soul!"

It occurs to me to wonder if maybe he really believes this shit he's spouting. Could it be that he doesn't consider it murder because he has some sick voice in his head he's mistaken for God Almighty?

Whether he believes it or not, I'm getting out of here. "My soul is doing just fine, you sicko pervert. I pray, but not for this. Not for your services!"

His face kind of sags, sad, pathetic. He says, "What are you going to do?"

"What d'you think? I'm gonna spill my guts. You're done here."

For a second he looks like he's about to cry, like he's ashamed. And then he lowers his head and steps to the left and away from the door. But it's a fake. Just as I'm reaching for the handle, he shoves me hard and I go flying to the right. I fall over something on the floor, barely aware that he's turned to that open file drawer and back toward me, and by the time I can get to my feet again he's got a rope around my chest, arms pinned to my sides.

He's lassoed me!

I struggle to get a hand up high enough to grab onto his arm, the rope, anything, but he's too quick. He wraps more rope around me, the coarse fibers digging into the skin below my short sleeves. It hurts to struggle, but I don't care. I have to break out of this!

I try kicking, but he just pushes me over; you can't keep your balance very well when you can't use your arms. So now I'm helpless *and* I'm on the floor. I guess this is the time to scream. So I do.

He just stands there, watching me. Then, "Really, Taylor, who's going to hear you?"

I fill my lungs and scream again. He sits down in a chair to watch. Shit. Fuck! How the hell did this happen? I'm trying so hard not to cry. I absolutely *refuse* to cry. But I'm scared shitless.

"I made a mistake with you. I took more time with the others, prepared them better. I see now that Satan has had a hand in this. He got me to move too fast, and I've failed you. The only chance for you now is for God to take you before you can sin any more."

"What the fuck are you talking about?" My voice sounds like someone else's.

"See? See?" He shakes his head almost sadly. "You know, I didn't kill all those other boys. Well, maybe one or two. But mostly they just couldn't go on living, knowing what God thought of them. So they killed themselves."

"Are you like Strickland?" I'm nearly spitting at him. "Do you think death is better—"

"Than living a life of abomination? Absolutely. I'll be God's tool, one way or the other, to do his will regarding you. You've rejected the way that would have saved your soul while you lived. It will be up to God what happens to it when you're dead."

"No! No. You can't do that. You have to let me go. What choice do you have?"

"Oh, I have lots of choices. I may not have lots of time, but I have lots of choices. My only decision at this moment is whether to teach you a lesson before you kill yourself. Of course, I'm talking about the cookie batter here. If you leave the world hating it, Satan may lose his chance to claim your soul." And he starts undoing his belt.

Okay, I'm hyperventilating now. He's going to rape me and then kill me? I have to raise my head off the floor to look him in the eye, but I do it. "You can't exactly leave a violated corpse. They'll never believe suicide."

"You poor, desperate boy. You know, Taylor, I've done this before. You haven't." Why does this sound familiar? In what previous lifetime have I heard those words? "And besides, I have God on my side. He won't risk losing his instrument. So he'll help everyone believe that you tied yourself up, you see? With that noose as a start, it's not inconceivable. You tied one end of the rope to the kneeling bench in the balcony, then you put the noose around your arms and turned round and round until it circled your neck a few times, and then you jumped. You'd been tying yourself up in an effort to keep yourself from sticking whatever you could find up that hungry ass of yours, but it hadn't helped, so you asked God and this is what he said to do. It will all come out when I tell them about your confessions to me. God will dictate to me what I should say. I'll blame myself, of course. I should have taken action when you told me some of the things you've put up there. As long as they don't find semen, it will all fall into place. A condom will suffice for that." He stands and pushes his slacks and underwear down to the floor. His dick is pointing at me, red and angry. "And it's my fault, too, for not preparing you well enough. But God will forgive me. You've been such a challenge."

My last-ditch effort is to try and roll away from him. And one final prayer: "Almighty God, help me! Please!"

The door behind Bartle crashes open. I wrench my body so I can see in that direction, and there's a very impressive black figure standing there.

It's Sean.

Bartle wheels around. For several tense seconds nothing happens except for Bartle pulling up his pants, and then Sean says, "Let him go."

"Sean, my son, he has denied sanctification. He has denied—"

"Let him go. Now." No one moves. Sean raises his voice. "Now!"

Bartle takes a step toward Sean, who pulls his fist back, ready to strike. They're frozen like that for four, maybe five seconds. Then Bartle starts shouting scripture.

"Blessed are those who have been persecuted for righteousness' sake, for theirs is the kingdom of heaven! Blessed are you when people reproach you, persecute you, and say all kinds of evil against you falsely, for my sake." His arms shoot up over his head and his voice rises so he's almost screaming. "Rejoice and be exceedingly glad for great is your reward in heaven! For that is how they persecuted the prophets who were before you."

Bam. Sean's fist shoots straight out from his body like a pile driver and Bartle goes flying. Actually, he lands on top of me, or part of him does. I kick like the devil, aiming for his shins, and I hear him cry out. I'd aim for his groin if I thought I could reach it, but I do what I can.

Sean, however, hasn't finished. He leans over and drives that weapon of a fist right into Bartle's nose, and from where I am I can see the blood splatter. Bartle rolls completely off of me, half crying, begging Sean to stop. Sean leans over to me and grabs a handful of rope, hauls me to my feet, and throws me onto his shoulder.

He carries me out of the room, shuts the door behind him, and then sets me gently on my feet. As he's loosening the ropes I ask, "How did you know? Why did you come?"

He's breathing hard, and I don't think it's just with effort. It's like he's trying to contain a monumental fury. Once I'm free he sits hard on the pew nearest the door he's just shut. I sit next to him.

"Sean?"

He leans back and closes his eyes, his breath rasping through his nose. Then he shakes his head hard, like he's flinging water off himself. He says, "You didn't come to circle. Nate got worried and sent Peter to find me and help him look for you. I don't know where Peter is; we split up. And I remembered what you called Reverend Bartle. So I put it all together."

"But . . . I don't quite get it. Why did you come here?" His eyes close again. And suddenly I know. "He was 'purifying' you, wasn't he?"

Just then the door opens. Sean is on his feet in a flash, and when Bartle sees him he tries to run. But Sean tackles him neatly, banging Bartle's head against the wall in the process.

"Get the rope, Taylor."

It feels so good being able to return the favor, tying Bartle up. When we've got him sufficiently trussed, he starts muttering scripture. I can't really tell what he's saying, but he sounds demented or something.

Sean says, "I'll stay here and watch him. You go get help. Get John. He'll know what to do. Then get to the laundry room as quick as you can and get them out of there."

"John? You want me to get John McAndrews?"

"He'll know what to do."

Well, what we've got to do is call the police. But I'm not gonna argue with the guy who just saved my life. I hightail it out of the chapel, wondering where I should start, but before I get too far into the main building I see Peter.

"Hey, Taylor! Did Sean find you?"

"Yeah. Do you know where John is?"

"His room. I just walked by."

"Get everyone out of the laundry room *now*. They can't be in there. The shit's gonna hit the fan."

"What? Why?"

I'm shouting now. "Just do it!" And I dash off.

I squeak around the corner to the boys' wing and head for John's room. He's there, just like Peter said, and no Leland in sight. I stand there panting, not knowing how to start.

"Taylor?"

"Sean said to come get you. It's Bartle. He attacked me. Sean has him tied up in the chapel."

He's on his feet before I even finish, fishing a cell phone out of his pocket. I walk—trot—beside him, listening to his side of the conversation.

"He attacked Taylor. . . . Yes, ma'am. . . . No, he's okay, he's with me. He says Sean has the reverend in the chapel. Tied up." He looks at me for confirmation and I nod. "I'm on my way there now. . . . I don't think there's any choice, but I'll call you as soon as I get there. . . . Okay. See you soon."

I ask, "Was that Mrs. Harnett?" John sure sounded like he already knew something about this thing and I want to know if she's told him. If she really trusts him.

"Yes. Taylor, quickly, can you tell me what happened?"

This might get a little tricky. "Bartle and I were in the chapel, praying together. Then he started talking about how I could be purified if I could get too much of what Satan wanted me to have. So he took me into the corner office and he came on to me. He pulled his pants down. . . ."

John stops dead in his tracks. I screech to a halt, and he looks hard at me. "Taylor, this is very important. Are you absolutely positive? What did he do?"

"He kissed me. On the mouth. And with his tongue. He pulled our hips together and said to pretend he was someone I wanted."

John's in motion again. "Maybe you should go back to your room."

"I really need to see this through."

Sean and Bartle are pretty much as I'd left them. John says, "You hit him?"

"He had Taylor tied up. He was gonna kill him."

John punches on his cell again and moves off a little. I look at Sean's face. He's calmed down quite a bit. Maybe too much. He seems out of it. I ask, "You okay?"

He nods. "Did he hurt you?"

"No, thanks to you. He was going to. He was going to rape me and then kill me. He said so." There's an awkward silence, and then I add, "Thank you."

He looks at me, tears in his eyes, and then he hugs me. When he lets go I have to sit down. It's just starting to hit me what nearly happened in there, and I'm feeling pretty shaky.

John comes over. "Mrs. Harnett is on her way. She's phoning the police and Dr. Strickland. They're going to want to talk with both of you. I'll wait here. Sean, if you like, you can wait with me. Taylor, I think maybe Charles should be told what's happened, don't you?"

So he did know the whole thing. But still, probably not about the circle. I nod. "I need to sit here for just a minute." John paces around, but Sean stands over Bartle like some saintly version of Cerberus, guarding the domain of Hades, making sure no demons escape. I watch Sean watching Bartle, and I wonder what will happen to their arrangement now. Nate had said something about Bartle speaking for Sean so he could stay out of prison. And Sean's paid quite a price, though I'll bet no one but the three of us know about that. So far.

The thought of Charles pulls on me. I get up and tell Sean, "I'll go talk to Charles now." He just nods.

John calls to me, "Taylor, please stay in your room so we can find you when the police are ready to talk to you." I wave an acknowledgment.

I keep thinking I'm going to meet up with someone, maybe one of the circle kids as they head back to their rooms in ones and twos, but the halls are empty. I'm glad; I'm not really sure what I'd say to them. It's all I can do to put one foot in front of the other while single-frame images of my ordeal flash onto my mental view screen, out of sequence. The sight of that open door waiting for me. Bartle's jaw grinding while he makes me talk dirty to him. Blood spurting from Bartle's nose. Bartle raising his arms to the heavens as he shouts scripture at Sean. Sean's fist launching from his body. Bartle trussed up on the floor, mumbling in tongues. Bartle looking possessed as he describes what he'll do to me.

Something hits me from the side and I realize I've stumbled against the wall. I lean there for a minute, eyes closed, breathing shallow. I try to calm myself by thinking only about being rescued. Sean punching Bartle's lights out. Sean carrying me out on his shoulder—hey, under other circumstances, that might have been fun.

I allow myself a moment of near-hysterical giggling, and when I manage to push off again my head seems clearer.

The door to my room is open and the lights are on. In fact, there's someone seated at my desk. It's Nate.

I stand there in the doorway staring at him like an idiot. Why's he here? He just looks at me. Finally I say, "Where's Charles?"

Nate looks toward the other desk. I peek around the door, and there's my roommate, head on his arms, leaning on his desk. He doesn't look up.

Nate gets up and says, "You look like the wrath of Satan, Taylor. Here, sit." I do, and he hands me some papers he's holding that I hadn't even noticed. He shuts the door and stands there watching me.

I look down at the papers and try to focus, but the letters just swim. I clench my eyes shut, open them, and try again. I give up. "What is this?"

Nate scowls a little. "Charles was working on this when I got here, looking for you. Um, are you okay? Where were you?" He can't exactly ask why I sent Peter to scatter the members of our little house church. Not with Charles right there.

I look over at Charles, still bent over his arms, and say, "I was with Reverend Bartle."

That gets him. He sits up and looks at me. "What did you say?"

"Charles, I know what he was doing to you. He was doing it to Ray. He probably killed Ray. He tried to kill me. When did he start hurting you?"

He's flustered, but he manages to say, "After Leland's Apology."

Looking back, this makes sense; it's about when Charles started getting really weird. And if he'd known what Bartle did in there before Ray died, he'd never have let Ray go to the chapel alone the night he died. I turn to Nate. "You told Charles about Leland's note, right?"

"I—yes. Taylor, what did you do? What d'you mean, he tried to kill you?"

I set the papers on my desk and take a shaky breath. "I tempted him. I told him I was unable to stop lusting after boys and I needed his help. He took me into his office"—here Charles covers his face with his hands—"and told me he was going to give me too much of what Satan wanted me to have to make me not want it anymore. Then he tried to have sex with me. When I refused and tried to get away, he tied me up with a rope and told me he was going to kill me, after he—you know. Sean found us, and he hit Bartle. He saved my life."

The silence in the room is a testament to the impact of my story. But it doesn't last long. Pretty soon Charles's sobbing breaks it.

Nate takes my shoulder and gets me to my feet, and we both get Charles up. We stand there together, holding Charles while he cries. Then somehow we're all sitting on the floor, a box of tissues beside Charles.

Charles speaks first. "You did that for me, didn't you?"

"Mostly. But also for Ray." And for Sean, though I didn't know it then.

Charles says, "You didn't even know Ray."

"He was a brother, just the same. And he was gay. And he shouldn't have been here, any more than you or I should." There's quiet, and then I ask Nate, "What are those papers, anyway?"

Nate looks at Charles. "Do you want to tell him?"

Charles exhales and says, "Reverend Bartle made me write down all my feelings, my impressions, of what happened when—when I was in his office. He said it would help reinforce the lesson I was supposed to be learning. Nate . . . well, he found me writing them."

So this is what Charles had been hiding all those times. I laugh, more of a bark. "Lesson? He was just getting off on it. He made you give these impressions to him, didn't he?" Charles, looking absolutely miserable, nods. I go on. "He wanted me to tell him all the details of my imagined encounters with the love of my life. He couldn't get enough. Every time I would stop, he'd say, 'Go on,' and his voice was getting all hoarse. He was lapping it up. He's a pedophile, Charles. A rapist. The worst kind, 'cause he used God as a weapon."

"And you exposed him."

Nate chimes in here. "And nearly lost your life in the process. Taylor, what were you thinking? I told you to—"

"Look, don't go on at me. You know very well we needed evidence. I just didn't know how bad it would get. I didn't mean to nearly get myself offed, you know."

"Well, I'm sure Mrs. Harnett will not be so easily put off. She'll take you to task, risking your life like that. What's happening now?"

"The police are on their way. They may be here by now. John's in the chapel with Sean, and your . . . I mean, Mrs. Harnett is probably there by now, too. John called her, and she was going to call the police. They'll be coming in here when they're ready to talk to me."

"They'll want those," and Nate nods toward the papers on my desk.

Paper. I untie my right shoe, pull out the inner sole and then the article, and hand the paper to Charles. "Here. You're already weepy, and it's possible this might make it worse, but it's something you need to know."

He takes it kind of gingerly, like it might bite him. It just might. But he needs it. Nate looks at me, a question on his face. "Let him read it first. Then you," I tell him. "I talked about it in . . . um, to Peter already."

Charles looks up at me once about halfway through, a pained expression on his face, but he goes back to reading. Then he hands it to Nate in utter silence. His eyes aren't focusing on anything. I'm dying to ask what he's thinking, but I want Nate on board first, so I keep quiet, hoping he'll read fast.

When Nate finally looks up, Charles looks at me and says, "It's all lies."

"Charles, it's science. They—"

"No, I mean what they've been telling us here. All lies."

"Not lies," says Nate. "They're just misguided about this. If our situation were the same as it was two thousand years ago, it would still be a sin. It would jeopardize our whole community if all the homosexuals didn't have kids. But things have changed. It's just that people really want to know exactly what they should and shouldn't do, and for most people it's easy to go on calling what you are a sin. But they're wrong."

"Some things haven't changed," I add. "It must still be a sin to murder or rape. But not to be gay."

"Rape," Charles echoes. "I knew it had to be wrong. I knew it. Why did I believe him? Why did I let him do that to me?" His eyes close, and he strains his head back, obviously fighting a new deluge from his private vale of tears. Nate and I sort of look away and wait until Charles seems to recover. He takes a shaky breath and asks, "What's *ESO?*"

I laugh, and it sounds high and weird. Guess it's the tension. "Equipment Smarter than Operator. It's IM. It means that even when we don't know what biology is doing inside us, and even when we fight it, it knows what's right for us."

"That's why I was fasting, you know."

"What?" He's confused me, coming up with that out of nowhere.

"I wasn't making any progress. And I wanted you. So I tried fasting. It didn't help."

"Christ, Charles . . ." I don't know what to say to that.

Nate hands the article back to me. "Do I want to know where you got this?" Which I take to mean, can you tell me in front of Charles?

I grin at him. "Nope." I hand it to Charles. "Do you want to keep this? If you do, find a good hiding place. Like under the inner sole of your shoe."

Bless his heart, he takes a shoe off and does just that. He's redoing his laces when we hear noises in the hall. I say, "They're coming to talk to me."

And I'm right. But when they open the door and ask for me, I suggest we go someplace else so Charles can rest. Mrs. Harnett is with them, and she says they want to talk with him, too. So I guess the word is really out. But they don't want us both together.

"Can you talk to him first, so then he can rest?"

Mrs. Harnett smiles and sort of shakes her head. "Taylor, shouldn't you be the one to rest?"

"No. I'm okay. Sean came in before anything could happen."

So they go off with Charles, and Nate and I have a little time to talk. I'm telling him about Will appearing on Sunday afternoon to give me kisses and paper (the article, of course) when we hear someone else approaching. It's past lights-out by now; who can that be?

It's Strickland. Nate and I are on our feet in a flash. Now, I can't see my own face, so I don't really know how bad I look, but Strickland looks worse. I'm sure of it.

"Brother Taylor, I'm here to apologize to you. I'll apologize to Charles as well. I've already spoken to Sean."

"Will he be okay? Can he stay here?"

"Yes. He has no worries on that score. But I've let all of you down. I've put someone in charge of your spiritual guidance who is a scion of the devil."

He stops, like he's waiting for me to say something. So I do. "I accept that apology. Maybe you couldn't have known about him. But you owe me another one. One that's just as important."

Nate looks at me like I'm crazy, but I just stand there waiting. I'm not afraid of Strickland. Finally he says, "What apology is that?"

"I know you'd rather see me kill myself than be who God made me. I want an apology for that. I want repentance for that. And then maybe I'll forgive you."

He sways a little and grabs hold of the door frame. He's scowling at me, and I can tell he's trying to be impressive. He says, "Better your body die than your spirit!"

"You're limiting God."

"What?"

"Even if God wants me to be straight, he's not going to give up on my spirit. My will to be who I am is not stronger than God's love for me." There's so much more to say, but most of it would just wash off this guy's back. But I can't resist just a little more. "You want us dead? Well, that's what happened to Ray. Let's say he did kill himself. Is that what God wanted? Was God so determined to see Ray in hell that he made him gay just to see which sin would get him there faster?"

Strickland is kind of sputtering at this point. I'm feeling bolder by the second. So I go on. "Do you repent, Dr. Strickland? Or do you persist in trying to second-guess God Almighty?"

I'm not sure whether he can't think of anything to say or doesn't think it's worth wasting his breath on a soul as lost as mine. Whichever, he turns and leaves.

Nate is looking at me, his expression somewhere between amused and amazed. I shrug and say, "You know, I never used to talk like this. Not before I came here."

Nate smiles and shakes his head. "You sure told him."

"It's funny, you know? Nearly dying does a lot to put things into perspective for you. Dr. Strickland is just another sinner to me now. Just another person on earth. Just as easily misled as anyone else." And then I realize I've tested him. Strickland. The arrogance versus self-confidence thing? He's arrogant. I've proven it.

I heave a huge sigh, walk to my bed, and fall onto it, shoes and all. I'm completely exhausted and oddly exhilarated. Nate falls onto Charles's bed, and we just lie there like that until Mrs. Harnett and the police bring Charles back and say they're ready for me. Nate says he'll stay with Charles until I get back and then he'll go talk to Leland. I don't even know what time it is. I don't care. This is one night I'll never, ever forget, and in a funny kind of way I want to experience every minute of it.

Chapter 16

We love him, because he first loved us.

—John 4:19

In the morning there's a lot of scurrying around by people like John and Nate and Jeffrey to make sure everyone is in the dining hall at breakfast time for an announcement. I'm sitting with Leland and Dave and Charles, practically falling onto my plate with exhaustion, when Mrs. Harnett comes in and claps her hands for attention. She gets it pretty quickly.

"Many of you have already heard that Reverend Bartle has been arrested. You will not see him on our campus again. Dr. Strickland is accepting personal responsibility for Reverend Bartle's crimes, and he has resigned his position. Before he leaves, he will be assisting in the task, which is already underway, of notifying your families of what has happened." She takes a breath and looks around, taking all of us in. Then she continues.

"I have been asked to assume the director's position that Dr. Strickland is vacating. Because this will take so much of my time, and because this current situation is so delicate, I will not be able to lead my assigned group any longer. This position, with its honor and its responsibility, is hereby assigned to John McAndrews."

There's a bit of a rumble. Most kids really like him. I like him, myself, or I would if he'd just get his act together on the gay issue.

"Each of you should check your mailbox after ten o'clock this morning. Your assignment leaders will release you in pairs to do this. You will find a notice about an individual meeting time with your own group leader to answer any questions you may have about these developments. Those of you who are in SafeZone are hereby relieved of that restriction until further notice, given the unusual circumstances.

"I'm sure you have many questions. I would if I were in your position. However, I ask that you hold them until your individual meetings, where you can be sure to receive complete information that is pertinent to you specifically. For now, I ask that when you leave this room, you go to your assignments as quietly as possible and with as little speculation as possible. We will make every effort to respond to your questions during your meeting. Until then, anything is gossip. Let us bow our heads."

Everyone does.

"Almighty God, we ask that you have mercy on Reverend Bartle, that you reach into his soul and help him understand that what he has done is not worthy of him. Help him cast away the darkness of Satan and return to your light. We ask that you comfort Dr. Strickland and help him see that his role of supporting Reverend Bartle's errors was unintentional, that it was done in ignorance. Help him to gain insight so that he cannot again be complicit in Satan's schemes.

"I ask that you be with each of the children here, that you help them to trust in the triumph of your love, in the protection you offer from evil. And I ask that you guide me in every step I take, in every word I utter. Help me to lead in ways that increase understanding and acceptance, that bring everyone entrusted to my care closer to you.

"Amen."

The kitchen is nearly silent. John isn't there; he must be off working with Mrs. Harnett to make all the arrangements for meetings, maybe calling parents. There's a girl in charge—young woman, I guess—I haven't met before. Her name is Dorothy, and she must have been in charge of kitchen detail in the past 'cause she takes over smoothly. I'm just managing to stand up and get my carrots chopped. No sleep for me last night, that's for sure.

At lunch I look for Charles and don't see him, so I wait until he gets there. We sit with Leland and Rick, John's old groupie, who seems a little lost. Conversation all around the room is nonstop but quiet. Charles and I know too much, and so does Leland, so we can't really talk with Rick there. Maybe we wouldn't have anyway; what's left to say?

Nate's nowhere to be seen. John, same thing. They're either going without food, or they're having it brought to them. I suppose it's possible Nate's helping to make phone calls. I wonder who's calling my folks. I wonder what they'll be told. "Your son was nearly raped and murdered last night. He's got four and a half more weeks here. . . ."

I'm expecting my private meeting to be with John, since he's my new group leader. And my note says to see him at four fifteen. But before that, I'm to see Mrs. Harnett at four. Charles, too, has a meeting with Mrs. Harnett. His is at two forty-five. He doesn't have a note about meeting with John, and we look at each other, wondering what that means. We agree to meet in the room before dinner to compare notes.

I'm nearly comatose by four o'clock, but I make my way to Mrs. Harnett's office. The door's closed, and the secretary tells me I have to wait for the kid before me to leave. When the door opens, Sean comes out.

"You okay?" he asks.

"Yeah. You?"

He nods, smiles, and then hugs me. I hug him back, hard.

I close the door and help myself to a chair. Mrs. Harnett looks at least as exhausted as I feel. She's probably been up all night, too.

"Taylor, I hope you know how sorry I am about what happened to you. But I also hope you know how much of it you brought on yourself, given what you knew."

"Yes, ma'am. I just felt I had no choice."

"Praise the Lord, it has worked out for the best, considering everything. You're safe, and this evil influence has been removed. Now, I need to tell you that Charles's parents will be here this evening to take him home. They'll be here just after dinner, so you'll have a little time to bid him farewell. I understand from him that the two of you have developed a very special relationship."

It surprises me how sad this news makes me feel. I try not to show it. "He's pretty terrific."

"He thinks the same of you." She sits back and gathers her thoughts before she goes on. "I've personally spoken with your mother about this situation. I've let her know of your bravery and loyalty, and I've told her you're unharmed. She was inclined to come and get you tonight and take you home. I've convinced her to consider her decision a little longer, to give you at least another overnight to see how you feel. If you stay, you'll be assigned a new roommate Friday afternoon. A new boy whose parents have decided to have him come to us despite what's happened here. He'll be a bit of a challenge, but I happen to think you're up to that. I can't think of anyone I'd rather assign him to."

"Why's he being sent here? Is he gay?"

She smiles. "You know we don't reveal that kind of information. He'll tell you why if he wants to. Do you think you might be willing to stay?"

"I haven't given it much thought. What if my folks really want to come and get me?"

"If you want to stay, I'll try and convince them. But the decision is theirs, of course. I suggest you call home this evening to assure them you're all right and that you're willing to give this some thought. How does that sound?"

"Fine, I guess. I'm so tired I'm not thinking straight."

She starts to laugh. And she laughs for several seconds before I get it. Of course I'm not thinking straight. How can I do that? I'm gay!

It takes a minute or so for both of us to recover from the laughing fit, but then it makes me wonder about something. "You do know that John isn't very accepting, don't you?"

She doesn't pretend she doesn't understand me. "I'm going to tell you something I don't want repeated, at least for now. Will you bear that responsibility?"

Hell, I'm keeping so many secrets already. What's one more? I nod.

"I've been designing a training program for all the group leaders. It stresses that a resident's sexual orientation is not an issue that we will address. Gradually, we'll also expand this position to our intake policies. It does not mean that no other homosexual children will come to us. What it means is that for those who are here, the issue that will be addressed is Inappropriate Love." I start to protest, but she holds a hand up. "That may not mean quite what you think. It doesn't mean that you'd be reprimanded for having feelings for another boy. It means that you'll be reprimanded if you engage in inappropriate activity with him. Whether someone is gay or straight, sex outside of marriage is inappropriate."

Yes. Well. We'll just have to agree to disagree on that one. And anyway, I still have a bone to pick. "Excuse me, but the church won't let me marry my boyfriend."

She smiles at me again. "I know. But I'll tell you what. If you decide one day to commit yourself to someone you love deeply, spiritually, whether that person is a man or a woman, I'd be honored if you invite me to the ceremony. And I'd be delighted to be there."

I grin. "And you promise not to reprimand us?"

"I promise." She looks at her watch. "Do you have any questions?"

"There's something I want to ask about Leland. About what happened with him and Ray. Marie Downs caught them kissing and reported them, and they were both punished, and Leland had to do a Public Apology."

"That's right."

"Why?"

"Why the Apology, you mean? If Ray had lived, he'd have had to do one as well. I understand why you're asking, and I wish I could give you a different answer from the one I have. But once

Marie reported this incident, given the policy of Straight to God under Dr. Strickland, that kiss between them was much worse than if one of them had been a girl. Mind you, if one of them had, they would still have been punished, because that behavior is strictly forbidden here. I'm sure you'll remember that from your Booklet. What I want, what will be the case under my directorship, is for that kiss not to have been any worse between Ray and Leland than it would have been between Nate and, say, Andrea."

"Who did Marie tell?"

"I'm not obliged to tell you, but it's no secret that it was John, who came to me. He had no more choice than I did. But as I've said, I intend to make some changes." She takes a breath. "Any other questions?"

Lots. Next, I go with this one: "You said you've been designing this new program I'm not to tell anyone about. That means you've been working on it for some time, and Nate says you knew about the circle, so you must have felt differently from Strickland . . . from Dr. Strickland for a long time. Meanwhile, you've just been holding the corporate line? How could you do that?"

"Now, Taylor, I think if you're honest with yourself, you'll acknowledge that there were a number of times when you and I managed to communicate without words. Times when each of us knew that there wasn't such a huge gulf between us after all."

She had me there. The first one was during my very first Prayer Meeting, when she didn't try to find out whether Charles had some reason he thought it might be necessary to surprise me during Contemplation—or ask him what he'd seen when he did. Then there was the night she'd practically invited the other kids in Prayer Meeting to throw stones at me, when I was back in SafeZone for another day, when we had that shock of understanding between us, when I got that what she was doing wasn't really about me. And Marie had stepped right into the trap, and for all I knew, that's why she ended up in SafeZone for the barbeque dinner.

The third time was the very next day, after I'd realized how hard it is for her to get us to see things that it wouldn't do much good to just come out and say. She could have told me till I was blue in the face that I needed to feel humble. But until she offered stones to the other kids and most of them threw love at me instead, I couldn't have understood what she meant. In our meeting the next day, when I'd sympathized with her position, she'd nearly cried. Plus Nate had told me I was right about her being surprised when she heard my room had been searched.

I hate to admit it, but I tell her, "I guess so."

"Besides, you may not know this, but Nate and I talked about you and I encouraged him to recruit you into the circle."

I shrug and change the subject, if only slightly. "And how will you get away with this change in plans? I mean, won't the church leaders defrock you or whatever?"

"It's an interesting point you raise. And one I intend to exploit. As I'm sure you know, nowhere in the four Gospels of the New Testament does Jesus make any references whatsoever to same-sex love. Now personally, I believe—as Nate does, and as I believe you do—that it would have been an impossible way of life in the first century, even if we think things have changed since then. And I think that if we could go back and ask Jesus, he would tell us it couldn't be supported. Not then. St. Paul does mention it a few times, but he can't be said to be quoting Jesus, only interpreting his message for that time, that place, and those people. So our church, in its charter doctrine, does not actually take a stand on this issue. It's been assumed by almost everyone in the Leadership, and in the congregations, that we condemn it. But it's not stated anywhere."

She does something I've never seen her do, something I never expected to see her do. She shrugs. "I'm going to do my best. I'll be praying and working with the leaders at Straight to God so that we present a united front if the church resists this position. If I get ousted, I get ousted. But I have to try. And with God's help, and Nate's, and maybe yours, anything is possible."

She's right. We're both risk takers. The gulf between us is pretty small after all.

"I'm afraid we're almost out of time, Taylor. Do you have any more questions?"

"Just one. For now. The police last night said I might have to testify."

"Would you rather not do that?"

I shrug. "I guess I'd be willing. I mean, wouldn't I be, like, a main witness?"

"Yes. But you're a minor, and your parents may not allow it."

"Then he might go free!"

"Sean will be testifying to what he saw. And Charles may testify; he'll probably be over eighteen by the time the trial occurs."

"I want to testify."

"That's good. I'll keep that in mind as the case progresses, and in any event I'm sure you'll be contacted. It could take some time, though; these things move slowly. So. Any other questions?"

God, so many! But for now . . . "I guess not."

"Then you'd better get out of here for your meeting with John. Which you're going to be late for if you don't leave now." She smiles at me one more time.

At the door I turn toward her. I say, "Thank you."

John, it seems, has taken up temporary residence in Dr. Strickland's office. He says, "There wasn't time to move Mrs. Harnett in here yet. We have to hold these meetings first."

I nod and take a chair. "I've just come from Mrs. Harnett." I'm not sure what he can tell me that she hasn't.

"Yes, I know. Did you decide whether you want to stay?"

"I'm thinking about it." And, in truth, I haven't decided.

On the one hand, if I leave here I can go back to my life and be with Will again. A little piece of heaven as a reward for my persecution here. But if I leave here early, my folks may try to keep me on a tight leash. There shouldn't be any question about military school, since it isn't like I would have flunked out of here, but my dad can be very stubborn. Letter of the law, that kind of thing. I can just hear his voice: "It doesn't matter why you didn't finish. Fact is, you didn't finish. So off you go."

And then there's the new kid. I tell John, "I understand Mrs. Harnett already has a new roommate picked out for me."

He looks at me like he's trying to figure out how seriously to take my tone of voice. "That's right. Kent Finnigan. What did she tell you about him?"

"That he'll be a challenge."

"She thinks you can handle it."

"You don't?"

"Let's say I'd be willing to give you a chance. But let's be honest, Taylor. What you did, nearly sacrificing yourself on the altar of Satan like that, shows that maybe your powers of judgment need a few checks and balances. And it's also risking another soul."

Okay, I don't like the implication I'm getting here. "And that means what, exactly?"

He smiles and shakes his head. "Don't take it as criticism, exactly. All I mean is that having a new roommate is a big responsibility. And the more challenging, the more room for mistakes. If you take this assignment, I'll need to work closely with you. I wouldn't expect you to tell me everything he does, but I would want to be sure he was getting the guidance he needs. Do you remember how Charles was with you at first?"

"I do. And I don't think I'd be quite the same."

"No. I expect you wouldn't. I don't think Charles's style would be good for this boy. But it was good for you. It chafed you in all the right ways, just enough, and you found your own way into the residence. Your style would be better for this boy. But because you're still Step One, it would be my responsibility to monitor how things are going. Do you understand why that would be necessary? For the good of the boy and of the Program?"

"I guess so."

"Are you going to call your folks tonight?"

"Yes. Probably after Charles leaves. I want to see him off."

He nods. "Okay, then. Please let me know if you make a decision tonight, and what it is. Any other questions for me?"

I decide to give him a little bit of a test. "When Reverend Bartle had me tied up in his little cell last night, he said he didn't kill all eleven of the kids who've died in here. Just one or two. But is that the truth? And how many did he rape?"

I don't think I imagine the cringe John can't quite suppress. But he takes a breath and gives me at least something by way of an answer. "There will be a thorough investigation, Taylor. I can't tell you for sure whether he killed anyone at all. I realize it looks like he killed Ray, and maybe he did. And you say he threatened to kill you. If he told you something right before he expected you to die, then from a psychological point of view, it might be safe to believe it. As for how many he raped?" He shakes his head and looks away from me. "Who can say? All we can do is pray the truth comes out in the trial." He looks back at me again.

I can tell he's about to bring the interview to a close, but I have one more question for him. "Do you agree with Dr. Strickland's view about gay kids?"

He blinks. I think he's hoping that I'm talking about something other than what I'm talking about. "What do you mean?"

"That we'd be better off dead?"

He's got a hold of himself; no sign of a cringe this time. "I don't agree with that, no. I don't like to disagree openly with him, even though he's not our director any longer. But I will tell you that it doesn't make much sense to me that God would want anyone to die before they understood the nature of any kind of sin. As long as someone's still alive, they can continue to examine their own actions and thoughts, and God can work through Jesus and through other people to help."

Any kind of sin? I'm just about to ask him if he thinks homosexuality is a sin when he holds up a hand. "Taylor, I know what's on your mind. And someday soon I hope you and I will have more time to talk about it, because I think we both have much to learn from each other. But I'm not prepared to do that now, and we don't have time for that discussion." He half-smiles and sits back in the chair. "So. Do you have any other questions, or would you just as soon leave a few minutes early?"

I guess that will have to do for now. "I'll head out." I stand and so does he. And he holds his hand out for me to shake.

"I hope you'll stay, Taylor."

"Thanks."

Leaving John's temporary digs, I make an executive decision. Or maybe it's a test. I decide I'm not going back to kitchen detail. Dorothy has everything under control, she doesn't need me very badly, and I want to go and talk with Charles. Plus, as I haven't tired of pointing out, I'm tired. When I get to the room, Charles is kneeling on the floor beside his bed, head on his hands. His bags are already packed and waiting. I stand in the doorway, not sure whether to let him know I'm here or not, but either he's finished his prayer or he senses someone there. He looks up.

"You're leaving," I say, stating the obvious.

He sits on the side of his bed. "I'm going to miss you."

"I'm going to miss you, too." I sit on the side of my own bed, facing him. "Still have that article?"

"Do you want it back?"

"No. There's more where that came from."

He takes this in and then asks, "And where is that?"

"Promise you won't tell?"

He nods, smiles, and says, "I promise."

"My boyfriend brought it. He's brought a couple of things to me. He sneaked the first one in through someone else, but he brought that article to me himself. We had just a few seconds, so we made the most of them, and he left that with me."

He's shaking his head. "Taylor, you are so amazing. I can't tell whether you're brave or crazy or both, but you're just about the best guy I've ever known."

We give that statement a bit of space, and then I say, "They want me to take on a new challenge. A new roommate."

"Are you going to do it?"

"Not sure. I kind of want to go home to Will, y'know?"

"Is Will your boyfriend?"

"Yeah." I can't help but grin just thinking about him. "He's there, waiting for me. He's made that clear. And what's there to stay for?"

"God. You could stay for God. And for everyone else here."

There is that. It's not all about me, is it? I shrug. "But I want to be with Will."

"He'll be there. He said so, right? Maybe you could get a letter out to him."

I blink. Is this Charles? My Charles, suggesting insubordination? "I'm not even sure how I'd do that."

He laughs. It's the first time I've heard it. "Silly. You could give the letter to me. I can mail it once I'm out of here."

I nearly fall off the bed. "Are you shittin' me? I mean—Jesus!—I mean . . . Charles, are you sure?"

He's still grinning at me. "I'm going to have to report that language, you know."

"Like hell you are. Would you really take my letter out?"

"Yes. It's the least I can do after what you did for me. Why don't you write it now so I can stow it away as safely as possible?"

I don't need any urging. But first I pull Charles to his feet and give him a fierce hug. And then—horror of horrors!—I kiss him. And he kisses me back. It's so sweet, and so loving, and it's the only time we'll ever do it. But it's great.

My folks are both on the line while I talk to them. Mom's in the kitchen, of course, and Dad's in the living room. His voice booms over the line.

"Your mother wants to fetch you home, son. Now, I know this has been a horrible experience for you, but I want to know what you think. How tough is it for you?"

Now, I've gotten pretty good at reading between the lines with my dad. What he's not saying, but he's really saying, is that if I can prove to him that I have the guts to stay, then I'm man enough that I won't need to be sent to military school to learn how to be a man. But—shit, I really want to see Will! And I'd love to have a home-cooked meal, and sit and chat with Mom over iced tea in the kitchen, and I'd even like to see my dad. So I tread carefully and don't commit myself too deeply.

"I'm made of pretty tough stuff, Dad. I risked my life, remember? And I'd do it again. The thing is, it's kind of weird here. My roommate, the one who was being hurt? He left after dinner tonight. He's a really great kid, which is one reason I did what I did. And they're talking about giving me a new roommate. I don't know what he's in for, so it could be drugs or something." I hear a tiny "Oh!" escape Mom. "So, how about this? He's getting here Friday afternoon. Why don't we give it the weekend, and if you call and insist on speaking to me Sunday night, they'll let you. I mean, given everything that's happened."

I can see my dad nodding. "Taylor, I like that plan. Give it a chance. See how things go."

There's half a minute or so when no one knows what to say and we can hear each other breathing over the line. Then Dad says, "They, uh, they tell me you're doing really well there, son. Said you're proving yourself to be a real leader."

Wow. "They said that?"

"I just want you to know, I'm, uh . . . I'm proud of you."

"Thanks, Dad." More breathing. "So, should I expect to hear from you Sunday evening?"

"Yes. Say seven thirty. I'll call the after-hours number they gave me and ask for you. If we decide it's time for you to come home, your mom can drive out on Monday. How does that sound?"

"Like a plan, Dad. Sounds great. So, I'll talk to you then."

Mom chimes in finally. "Oh, Taylor! I miss you so much. I want you to come home, but I know it might not be best."

"I'm okay, Mom. Honest. I miss you, too."

Dad can't quite bring himself to say that. But he's already shocked me enough with the "proud of you" line. So I just say, "So long, then." And I hang up.

Things seem really weird, just like I'd told Dad. Several kids I knew are gone now; their parents came and fetched them away as soon as they could get out here. I miss Leland a lot. Sheldon is gone, and Hank, too, though his time was almost up. Monica Moon is gone, but I don't think she was doing very well, anyway. Rye is still here. I notice him more, now that there are fewer kids, and now that I know who he is. You feel a certain kinship with someone you've named. Reva's gone, so I won't get to take her to the luau. They're gonna hold it anyway, though

I'll probably miss at least some of it with my new roomie's arrival.

I don't get a lot of face time with Nate; he's obviously still in the thick of things. But we do steal a few minutes during Fellowship one night. We sneak into a corner, and I tell him about my conversation with John, that official meeting where I'd questioned him about Strickland's position.

"Wow. You didn't give him even a day to catch his breath, did you?"

"Why should I?"

"Well, remember that everything happened real fast. One minute he's got to do things Strickland's way, and even if he doesn't agree you're better off dead, he still thinks of it as sin. The next minute he's got a new boss who wants to reverse that particular philosophy, and he hasn't had more than an hour of her time to talk about it when you smack him upside the head with that hot potato. Sorry for the mixed metaphors or whatever, but you see what I mean?"

I shrug. "I guess."

"Seems to me he handled himself pretty well under your third degree. You wanna cut him some slack? He'll get there. After all, I'm working on him, too, y'know." He smacks my shoulder.

And I have to admit, John's pretty good at leading Prayer Meetings. He's got a lot of charisma, and he sure does know his scripture. I'd been thinking Nate might have to help him out a little, but that's not the case at all. Nate tells me John is twenty-three. I wouldn't have guessed before, but now I see it.

Circle's not the same without Jamie, whose folks absconded with him. And this is Peter's last week anyway. I'll sure miss his beautiful eyes. But there's a bonus. Sean joins the circle. And of course Nate isn't going anywhere as long as his mom's still around. But there's a really sober moment on Thursday night as we're all sitting on the laundry room floor.

Nate says, "Brothers and sisters, I can't tell you what being in the circle has meant to me. And I know you all feel the same, or you wouldn't still be taking risks to be here." He smiles and looks around at everyone. "So it's kind of wonderful and kind of sad that I'm not sure how much longer we'll have a mission. Now that we have new leadership, there's a change in philosophy. Pretty soon, I'm hoping that the official Prayer Meetings will be as accepting as we are. They'll be the sort of place where we'll be able to speak more freely, to express ourselves more honestly. If that happens, the circle will have accomplished its goal."

He waits to see what everyone will say. Dawn speaks first.

"But Nate, we can't stop! It's the only place people like Jessica and me can be open!"

"I think that's going to change, is what I'm saying. Until it does, there's still a need for this. But wouldn't it be better if everyone could be open, not just the kids in the circle?"

No one can argue with that. Okay, maybe it's good news in a way, but it sure puts a damper on the meeting.

But . . . yes . . . wouldn't it be terrific?

That night I have trouble falling asleep. It's been pretty weird in the room ever since Charles left; I got used to hearing someone else breathing. Plus I miss him. But that's not the problem tonight. Tonight I'm thinking about Kent, about what he'll be like, about why he's coming here. I mean, Mrs. Harnett is the director now, right? And she'd told me outright that she won't be taking kids just because they're gay. So either she can't put that new rule into effect just yet or Kent isn't gay. Or he's gay, but he's got some other problems, too.

Bottom line here is, I'm gonna have a new roommate. I might hate him. He might hate me. He might be some miserable lowlife, or he might be a stuck-up self-righteous bastard, like I thought Charles was, until I got to know him. Whatever he is, both Mrs. Harnett and John said he'd be a challenge. One that John isn't quite convinced I'm up to.

So. Do I stay and accept the challenge, or do I bail, go home, and see what happens? Knowing my dad, he'll be a lot more impressed if I stick it out. Sure, I get credit for being willing to wait and see, but if I whimper on Sunday and beg them to take me home, that credit might get wiped out. And it still might mean Dad points a stern finger at military school.

Let's say I stick it out here, do the full sentence, and don't screw up too badly with Kent. In four more weeks, I'll go home having seen it through. See, the thing is, Dad didn't say to me, "Son, you're going to have to come out the other end of this summer a real man. You're going to have to be straight, not gay anymore, or else it's military school." He just said I had to go through the program that's *designed* to straighten me out. His assumption—ha, another one—that of course it would work is so hidden from him that he didn't think to add that qualification.

So what's he gonna do when he finds out it didn't take? That I'm still gay? I gotta have a plan for that. It won't be enough to say, "Gee, Dad, you never said I had to change." It won't even be enough to say, "I did my best! I did everything you asked!" Though I will say that if I have to. I did everything he asked and more.

It's the "more" that's got me worried, actually. I *really* don't think there's any way I can get him to see this new vision of Christianity, the one the circle got me to see. It will never be enough for him that it used to be a sin; I don't think he'll ever buy that it isn't anymore. He's too hung up on his own idea of what it is to be a man. That is, a man is like him. It's Strickland's problem all over again.

Could I get Dad to see it anyway? Am I up to that battle? Even if I am, if I'm in military school I won't be able to carry it out. So now I have two reasons to avoid being sent away: being able to see Will, and convincing my dad—and my mom—that I'm not a sinner simply because I'm gay. It's like I have a mission now. Something beyond my own need to be who I am. I want other people to get it, too.

And suddenly I realize that's my plan. If my dad wants to know whether I'm still gay, the answer is yes. But if he tries to send me away, I'll offer him a compromise: I'll come back here next summer. It would actually be tolerable by then, under Mrs. Harnett's new philosophy. Hey—maybe Will would come, too. . . .

Somewhere between teaching my dad a new way to think of

Jesus's message and making eyes at Will across Isaiah next summer, I fall asleep.

There's a message in my mailbox on Friday after lunch saying that Kent Finnigan will be arriving at four. I'm to make myself available starting at four thirty by waiting in my room until I'm called to come and meet him. John sees me reading it.

"Pretty clear, Taylor? You know what you need to do, right?"

There's a sheet of yellow labels and a map for Kent here, too, and I'm looking down at the map. "I think so. Give him an orientation tour, like Charles did for me."

"And then bring him to the chapel."

My head snaps toward him.

"The church has found a replacement for Reverend Bartle. He's going to pray with Kent, and Mrs. Harnett will be there. She was involved in the selection, too."

That's okay, then. "How will I know when I should look for him again?"

"You should go to dinner and go back to your room to wait. I'm sorry there has to be all this waiting, but the process is changing. You okay with this?"

"Sure." What can I say?

So I'm in my room at five fifteen when Jeffrey, who's still with us, comes to get me. And just like Charles had done, I knock on the frame of the open door that used to be Strickland's.

Mrs. Harnett, who has moved in by now, says, "Taylor. Please come in. Taylor Adams, this is your new roommate, Kent Finnigan. Taylor will show you around, Kent. Make sure you're oriented and understand what's expected. I'll see you again in the chapel shortly."

I extend my hand, and for a second there, it almost looks like Kent's going to bite it. But I just hold it out: I'm not goin' anyplace, Kent. Eventually he stands, and we shake. He's not a very big kid. Scrawny. Looks to be maybe fifteen. There's a piercing hole in his left earlobe; nothing in it, and there won't be while he's here, that's for sure. Dirty blond hair, buzz cut.

They'll make him grow it out a little. For some reason he's wearing a long-sleeved shirt despite the summer heat.

I lead him on the tour. Laundry room, dining hall, Fellowship room, Isaiah and the other prophets. He's silent through the whole trip. Just like I had been. Then we go into the bathroom. He's just as reluctant to do anything in there with me hanging around as I'd been with Charles. I don't really have a clue whether he'll be as long in the chapel as I was, but with his attitude it seems likely. So I give him the same warning Charles gave me.

He nearly growls, but he goes into a booth. I don't know whether he's trying to cover the sounds of his own pissing or if he's decided it's time to take some kind of stand, but he starts talking to me. Maybe it's finally dawned on him that this will be his last chance to talk for a while. SafeZone is still alive and well.

"This is a fucking screwed-up place. I hope you don't fucking expect me to be toeing any fucking line. You guys can't teach me shit here."

I'm leaning against the wall opposite the stall, arms crossed over my chest. It's kind of refreshing to hear this stream of obscenities, more or less paralleling the stream of piss. But there's an edge to his voice. He's afraid. Plus he's overdoing it.

He's not going to admit that, even to himself. So I chuckle loud enough for him to hear. "I hope you don't think I haven't heard those words before. In fact, I hope you don't think I haven't used them."

Kent throws the door open and glares at me. "You here because you're a fairy?"

Now why would he ask that question? Even when I'm at home, there's nothing femme about my appearance, my voice— no giveaways. And in here, where every guy dresses in almost exactly the same boring khaki crap, there's really no way to tell a gay guy unless he's outright swishing.

Mrs. Harnett had refused to say why this kid was coming here. That he'd tell me why if he wanted me to know. I'm thinking he's telling me why. I'm thinking that between the heavy hand with the obscenities, the belligerent attitude, and the fear so close to the surface, I know why he's here. I think he's gay.

Several retorts occur to me. I choose the simplest for Kent. "Yeah. What are you here for?"

"Huh! Not that, and you'd better keep the fuck away from me." He heads for the door.

I think, "Liar." But I say, "We always wash our hands here, Kent." Charles's words coming out of my mouth. Who knew?

In Kent's face I see myself. I see what I must have looked like to Charles less than two weeks ago now. Only I had opted not to flip my middle finger at Charles. Kent shows no such scruples. I ignore it, standing there like patience incarnate. And he goes to the sinks.

He doesn't bother with soap, but as long as he uses water and a paper towel I'm not pushing for more. I watch as he extends his arms. And as he does, I see something showing from under the long sleeves. Something white.

Bandages. On both wrists.

Gotcha. Gay. Gay and suicidal.

I know what I'm going to say to my folks on Sunday night.

And I know that Will, my sexy, marvelous boyfriend, even after four more weeks, will be waiting for me. I have faith in that. It's because of love.

THINKING STRAIGHT

Robin Reardon

ABOUT THIS GUIDE

The suggested questions are intended to
enchance your group's reading of
Robin Reardon's *Thinking Straight*.

Discussion Questions

1. Angela, the girl Taylor's parents try to fix him up with, says that if you don't have to make sense, you can say anything at all. She's talking about religion. Could what she said apply equally as well to politics? To race issues? To homosexuality? Do you think it's always the case that what someone says makes sense to him or her? Or do you think people know when they're expressing absurdities, or when they haven't given the topic any thought at all? How often is this something you do?

2. Taylor observes that his father's version of God acts like his father, and his mother's is more like her. It seems that for some people, it's easier to believe in a God who agrees with their own view of the world. Others seem to modify their view of the world to match that of the God they worship. Are there observations that can be made about each of these approaches that pertain to the people you meet at Straight to God?

3. A few times over the course of his stay at Straight to God, Taylor sees characteristics in Sean that he takes for cowardice, or at least a lack of assertiveness. And yet Sean proves himself to be a powerful ally when Taylor most needs him. What do you think contributed to Sean's apparently cowardly behavior before that crucial event?

4. People like Dr. Strickland are known to point to specific verses in the Bible to support their condemnation of homosexuality. Yet they almost always ignore the many other sacred laws that exist side-by-side with anti-homosexual scripture. *Leviticus 20:9* says children who curse their parents are to be put to death. Leviticus also forbids wearing clothing of mixed fibers, or planting different kinds of plants in the same field. A Jewish man

of that time could not marry a divorced woman. These supposedly sacred laws are generally ignored or explained away. People tend to cherry-pick certain scriptures they think should be followed; one person will decide to follow certain scriptures, while another will select different ones. How do you think people who follow a religion should decide which scripture to observe and which to ignore?

5. When Will climbs into Taylor's bedroom the night before Taylor is to leave for Straight to God, Will has already seen the article in which Dr. Strickland expressed his belief that suicide is better for teenagers than living a homosexual life. Will is trying to convince Taylor to run away with him rather than go into the program. Why do you think he doesn't mention this article to Taylor?

6. Taylor changes his opinions over time about many of the people he encounters at Straight to God. How many times were his first impressions close to correct, and how many times were they far off base? To what degree do you think Taylor's expectations of what the program would be like colored his initial assumptions about the people he met?

7. At one point, Taylor tells Mrs. Harnett that he sees how difficult her role is, that she has to find a way to communicate very important messages without saying them directly. She nearly cries. What do you think is going through her mind? What moved her so much?

8. John and Nate seem to have different ways of offering leadership. John tells Taylor that Nate "takes an awful lot onto himself." Nate tells Taylor that John is "definitely not in our circle." Taylor and Nate become good friends, and over time Taylor leans to respect John and, eventually, to trust him. Can you describe their differ-

ent leadership styles? Do you think they will find more common ground with the changes Mrs. Harnett plans to make at Straight to God, or will their different approaches to leadership and to scripture tend to keep them apart?

9. Nate sets Taylor up to work with Rye. Later, John explains to Taylor that although Charles was a good mentor for Taylor, Taylor's personal style will be better for Kent than Charles's would have been. What do Kent and Rye have in common that makes Taylor a good mentor for both of them? What is it about Taylor that made both Nate and John point him toward similar boys for mentoring?

10. We often hear the phrase, "Love the sinner; hate the sin." What if that "sin" were that you had been born in the month of March? What if it were that you had blue eyes? If you had to interact every day with people who wanted you to believe they're following God's wishes when they express hatred for your birthday, or for your blue eyes, would you feel loved?

11. When Taylor is waiting for Kent in the boys' room, he comes to the conclusion that Kent is gay. Do you agree?

12. Taylor's father sent him to Straight to God because he wanted his son to change in a very specific way. Taylor didn't make that change, but did he change in other ways? How do you think his father will react when Taylor comes home still gay?

CPSIA information can be obtained at www.ICGtesting.com
Printed in the USA
BVOW08s0339100516

447442BV00001B/3/P